John Mor

Diderot and the Encyclopædists
Volume 2

John Morley

Diderot and the Encyclopædists
Volume 2

1st Edition | ISBN: 978-3-75241-140-9

Place of Publication: Frankfurt am Main, Germany

Year of Publication: 2020

Outlook Verlag GmbH, Germany.

Reproduction of the original.

DIDEROT

AND

THE ENCYCLOPÆDISTS

BY

JOHN MORLEY

VOL. II.

CHAPTER I.
OTHER DIALOGUES.

We may now pass to performances that are nearer to the accepted surface of things. A short but charming example of Diderot's taste for putting questions of morals in an interesting way, is found in the *Conversation of a Father with his Children* (published in 1773). This little dialogue is perfect in the simple realism of its form. Its subject is the peril of setting one's own judgment of some special set of circumstances above the law of the land. Diderot's venerable and well-loved father is sitting in his arm-chair before the fire. He begins the discussion by telling his two sons and his daughter, who are tending him with pious care, how very near he had once been to destroying their inheritance. An old priest had died leaving a considerable fortune. There was believed to be no will, and the next of kin were a number of poor people whom the inheritance would have rescued from indigence for the rest of their days. They appointed the elder Diderot to guard their interests and divide the property. He finds at the bottom of a disused box of ancient letters, receipts, and other waste-paper, a will made long years ago, and bequeathing all the fortune to a very rich bookseller in Paris. There was every reason to suppose that the old priest had forgotten the existence of the will, and it involved a revolting injustice. Would not Diderot be fulfilling the dead man's real wishes by throwing the unwelcome document into the flames?

At this point in the dialogue the doctor enters the room and interrupts the tale. It appears that he is fresh from the bedside of a criminal who is destined to the gallows. Diderot the younger reproaches him for labouring to keep in the world an offender whom it were best to send out of it with all despatch. The duty of the physician is to say to so execrable a patient—"I will not busy myself in restoring to life a creature whom it is enjoined upon me by natural equity, the good of society, the well-being of my fellow-creatures, to give up. Die, and let it never be said that through my skill there exists a monster the more on earth!" The doctor parries these energetic declamations with sufficient skill. "My business is to cure, not to judge; I shall cure him, because that is my trade; then the judge will have him hung, because that is his trade." This episodic discussion ended, the story of the will is resumed. The father, when on the point of destroying it, was seized with a scruple of conscience, and hastened to a curé well versed in casuistry. As in England the agents of the law itself not seldom play the part of arbitrary benevolence, which the old Diderot would fain have played against the law, the scene may perhaps be worth transcribing:

> "'Nothing is more praiseworthy, sir, than the sentiment of compassion that touches you for these unfortunate people. Suppress the testament and succour them —good; but on condition of restoring to the rightful legatee the exact sum of which you deprive him, neither more nor less. Who authorised you to give a sanction to documents, or to take it away? Who authorised you to interpret the intentions of the dead?'
>
> 'But then, father Bouin, the old box?'
>
> 'Who authorised you to decide whether the will was thrown away on purpose, or mislaid by accident? Has it never happened to you to do such a thing, and to find at the bottom of a chest some valuable paper that you had tossed there inadvertently?'
>
> 'But, father Bouin, the far-off date of the paper, and its injustice?'
>
> 'Who authorised you to pronounce on the justice or injustice of the document, and to regard the bequest as an unlawful gift, rather than as a restitution or any other lawful act which you may choose to imagine?'
>
> 'But, these poor kinsfolk here on the spot, and that mere collateral, distant and wealthy?'
>
> 'Who authorised you to weigh in your balance what the dead man owed to his distant relations, whom you don't know?'
>
> 'But, father Bouin, that pile of letters from the legatee, which the departed never even took the trouble to open?'
>
> 'There is neither old box, nor date, nor letters, nor father Bouin, nor if, nor but, in the case. No one has any right to infringe the laws, to enter into the intention of the dead, or to dispose of other people's property. If providence has resolved to chastise either the heir or the legatee or the testator—we cannot tell which—by the accidental preservation of the will, the will must remain.'"[1]

Diderot the younger declaims against all this with his usual vehemence, while his brother, the abbé, defends the supremacy of the law on the proper ground, that to evade or defy it in any given case is to open the door to the sophistries of all the knaves in the universe. At this point a journeyman of the neighbourhood comes in with a new case of conscience. His wife has died after twenty years of sickness; in these twenty years the cost of her illness has consumed all that he would otherwise have saved for the end of his days. But, as it happens, the marriage portion that she brought him has lain untouched. By law this ought to go to her family. Equity, however, seems to justify him in keeping what he might have spent if he had chosen. He consults the party round the fire. One bids him keep the money; another forbids him; a third thinks it fair for him to repay himself the cost of his wife's illness. Diderot's father cries out, that since on his own confession the detention of the inheritance has brought him no comfort, he had better surrender it as speedily as possible, and eat, drink, sleep, work, and make himself happy so.

"'Not I,' cried the journeyman abruptly, 'I shall be off to Geneva.'

'And dost thou think to leave remorse behind?'

'I can't tell, but to Geneva I go.'

'Go where thou wilt, there wilt thou find thy conscience.'

The hatter went away; his odd answer became the subject of our talk. We agreed that perhaps distance of place and time had the effect of weakening all the feelings more or less, and stifling the voice of conscience even in cases of downright crime. The assassin transported to the shores of China is too far off to perceive the corpse that he has left bleeding on the banks of the Seine.

Remorse springs perhaps less from horror of self than from fear of others; less from shame for the deed, than from the blame and punishment that would attend its discovery. And what clandestine criminal is tranquil enough in his obscurity not to dread the treachery of some unforeseen circumstance, or the indiscretion of some thoughtless word? What certainty can he have that he will not disclose his secret in the delirium of fever, or in dreams? People will understand him if they are on the scene of the action, but those about him in China will have no key to his words."[2]

Two other cases come up. Does the husband or wife who is the first to break the marriage vow, restore liberty to the other? Diderot answered affirmatively. The second case arose from a story that the abbé had been reading. A certain honest cobbler of Messina saw his country overrun by lawlessness. Each day was marked by a crime. Notorious assassins braved the public exasperation. Parents saw their daughters violated; the industrious saw the fruits of their toil ravished from them by the monopolist or the fraudulent tax-gatherer. The judges were bribed, the innocent were afflicted, the guilty escaped unharmed. The cobbler meditating on these enormities devised a plan of vengeance. He established a secret court of justice in his shop; he heard the evidence, gave a verdict, pronounced sentence, and went out into the street with his gun under his cloak to execute it. Justice done, he regained his stall, rejoicing as though he had slain a rabid dog. When some fifty criminals had thus met their doom, the viceroy offered a reward of two thousand crowns for information of the slayer, and swore on the altar that he should have full pardon if he gave himself up. The cobbler presented himself, and spoke thus: "I have done what was your duty. 'Tis I who condemned and put to death the miscreants that you ought to have punished. Behold the proofs of their crimes. There you will see the judicial process which I observed. I was tempted to begin with yourself; but I respected in your person the august master whom you represent. My life is in your hands: dispose of it as you think right." Well, cried the abbé, the cobbler, in spite of all his fine zeal for justice, was simply a murderer. Diderot protested. His father decided that the abbé was right, and that the cobbler was an assassin.

Nothing short of a transcript of the whole would convey a right idea of the dramatic ease of this delightful dialogue—its variety of illustration with unity of topic, the naturalness of movement, the pleasant lightness of touch. At its close the old man calls for his nightcap; Diderot embraces him, and in bidding him good-night whispers in his ear, "Strictly speaking, father, there are no laws for the sage. All being open to exception, 'tis for him to judge the cases in which we ought to submit to them, or to throw them over." "I should not be sorry," his father answers, "if there were in the town one or two citizens like thee; but nothing would induce me to live there, if they all thought in that way." The conclusion is just, and Diderot might have verified it by the state of the higher society of his country at that very moment. One cause of the moral corruption of France in the closing years of the old *régime* was undoubtedly the lax and shifting interpretations, by which the Jesuit directors had softened the rigour of general moral principles. Many generations must necessarily elapse before a habit of loosely superseding principles in individual cases produces widespread demoralisation, but the result is inevitable, sooner or later; and this, just in proportion as the principles are sound. The casuists practically constructed a system for making the observance alike of the positive law, and of the accepted ethical maxims, flexible and conditional. The Diderot of the present dialogue takes the same attitude, but has the grace to leave the demonstration of its impropriety to his wise and benevolent sire.

II. We shall presently see that Diderot did not shrink from applying a vigorous doubt to some of the most solidly established principles of modern society. Let us meanwhile in passing notice that short piece of plangent irony, which did not appear until many years after his death (1798), and which he or some one else entitled, *On the inconsistency of the Public Judgment on our Private Actions.* This too is in the form of dialogue, but the argument of the story is in its pith as follows. Desroches, first an abbé, then a lawyer, lastly a soldier, persuades a rich and handsome widow to marry him. She is aware of his previous gallantries, and warns him in very dramatic style before a solemn gathering of friends, that if he once wounds her by an infidelity, she will shut herself up and speedily die of grief. He makes such vows as most men would make under such circumstances; he presses her hands ardently to his lips, bedews them with his tears, and moves the whole company to sympathy with his own agitation. The scene is absurd enough, or seems so to us dull people of phlegmatic habit. Yet Diderot, even for us, redeems it by the fine remark: "'Tis the effect of what is good and virtuous to leave a large assembly with only one thought and one soul. How all respect one another, love one another in such moments! For instance, how beautiful humanity is at the play! Ah, why must we part so quickly? Men are so good, so happy, when what is worthy unites all their suffrages, melts them, makes them one."[3] For some time all went well, and our pair were the happiest of men and women. Then various assaults were made on the faithfulness of Desroches. He resisted them, until in endeavouring to serve a friend he was forced to sue for the goodwill of a lady with whom in his unregenerate days he had had passages of gallantry. The old intrigue was renewed. Letters of damning proof fell by ill hazard into his wife's hands. She reassembled her friends, denounced the culprit, and forthwith carried away her child to seek shelter with her aged mother. Desroches's fervent remorse was unheeded, his letters were sent back unopened, he was denied the door. Presently, the aged mother died. Then the infant. Lastly, the wife herself. Now, says Diderot to his interlocutor, I pray you to turn your eyes to the public—that imbecile crowd that pronounces judgment on us, that disposes of our honour, that lifts us to the clouds or trails us through the mud. Opinion passed through every phase about Desroches. The shifting event is ever their one measure of praise and blame. A fault which nobody thought more than venial became gradually aggravated in their eyes by a succession of incidents which it was impossible for Desroches either to foresee or to prevent. At first opinion was on his side, and his wife was thought to have carried things with too high a hand. Then, after she had fallen ill, and her child had died, and her aged mother had passed away in the fulness of years, he began to be held answerable for all this sea of troubles. Why had not Desroches written to his wife, beset her doors, waylaid her as she went to church? He had, as matter of fact, done all these things, but the public did not know it. The important thing is, not to know, but to talk. Then, as it befell, his wife's brother took Desroches's place in his regiment; there he was killed. More exclamations as to the misfortune of being connected with such a man. How was Desroches responsible for the death of his mother-in-law, already well stricken in years? How could he foresee that a hostile ball would pierce his brother-in-law in his first campaign? But his wife? He must be a barbarian, a monster, who had gradually pressed a poniard into the bosom of a divine woman, his wife, his benefactress, and then left her to die, without showing the least sign of interest or feeling. And all this, cries Diderot, for not knowing what was concealed from him, and what was unknown and unsuspected even by those who were daily about her? What presumption, what bad logic, what incoherence, what unjustified veering and vacillation in all these public verdicts from beginning to end!

Yet we feel that Diderot's impetuous taunts fail to press to the root of the matter. Diderot excels in opening a subject; he places it in a new light; he furnishes telling concrete illustrations; he thoroughly disturbs and unsettles the medium of conventional association in which it has become fixed. But he does not leave the question readjusted. His mind was not of that quality which is slow to complain where it cannot explain; which does not quit a discussion without a calm and orderly review of the conditions that underlie the latest exhibition of human folly, shortsightedness, or injustice. The public condemnation of Desroches for consequences that were entirely strange to his one offence, was indefensible on grounds of strict logic. But then men have imagination as well as reason. Imagination is stronger than reason with most of them. Their imagination was touched by the series of disasters that followed Madame Desroches's abandonment of her husband. They admit no plea of remoteness of damage, such as law courts allow. In a way that was loose and unreasonable, but still easily intelligible, the husband became associated with a sequel for which he was not really answerable. If the world's conduct in such cases were accurately expressed, it would perhaps be found that people have really no intention to pronounce a judicial sentence; they only mean that an individual's associations have become disagreeable and doubtful to them. They may think proper to justify the grievously meagre definition of *homo* as *animal rationale*, by varnishing their distaste with reasons; the true reason is that the presence of a Desroches disturbs their comfort, by recalling questionable and disorderly circumstances. That this selfish and rough method many a time inflicts horrible cruelty is too certain, and those to whom the idea of conduct is serious and deep-reaching will not fall into it. A sensible man is aware of the difficulty of pronouncing wisely upon the conduct of others, especially where it turns upon the intricate and unknowable relations between a man and a woman. He will not, however, on that account break down the permanent safeguards, for the sake of leniency in a given case. *A great enemy to indifference, a great friend to indulgence*, said Turgot of himself; and perhaps it is what we should all do well to be able to say of ourselves.

Again, though these ironical exposures of the fatuity and recklessness and inconsistency of popular verdicts are wholesome enough in their degree in all societies, yet it has been, and still remains, a defect of some of the greatest French writers to expect a fruit from such performances which they can never bear. In the long run a great body of men and women is improved less by general outcry against its collective characteristics than by the inculcation of broader views, higher motives, and sounder habits of judgment, in such a form as touches each man and woman individually. It is better to awaken in the individual a sense of responsibility for his own character than to do anything, either by magnificent dithyrambs or penetrating satire, to dispose him to lay the blame on Society. Society is after all only a name for other people. An instructive contrast might be drawn between the method of French writers of genius, from Diderot down to that mighty master of our own day, Victor Hugo, in pouring fulminant denunciations upon Society, and the other method of our best English writers, from Milton down to Mill, in impressing new ideas on the Individual, and exacting a vigorous personal answer to the moral or spiritual call.

One other remark may be worth making. It is characteristic of the immense sociability of the eighteenth century, that when he saw Desroches sitting alone in the public room, receiving no answers to his questions, never addressed by any of those around him, avoided, coldly eyed, and morally proscribed, Diderot never thought of applying the artificial consolation of the Stoic. He never dreamed of urging that expulsion from the society of friends was not a hardship, a true punishment, and a genuine evil. No one knew better than Diderot that a man should train himself to face the disapprobation of the world with steadfast brow and unflinching gaze; but he knew also that this is only done at great cost, and is only worth doing for clear and far-reaching objects. Life was real to Diderot, not in the modern canting sense of earnestness and making a hundred thousand pounds; but in the sense of being an agitated scene of living passion, interest, sympathy, struggle, delight, and woe, in which the graceful ascetic commonplaces of the writer and the preacher barely touch the actual conditions of human experience, or go near to softening the smart of chagrin, failure, mistake, and sense of wrong, any more than the sweet music of the birds poised in air over a field of battle can still the rage and horror of the plain beneath. As was said by a good man, who certainly did not fail to try the experiment,—"Speciosa quidem ista sunt, oblitaque rhetoricæ et musicæ melle dulcedinis; tum tantum cum audiuntur oblectant. Sed miseris malorum altior sensus est. Itaque quum hæc auribus insonare desierint, insitus animum mœror prægravat."[4]

III. We may close this chapter with a short account of the *Supplement to Bougainville's Travels*, which was composed in 1772, and published twenty-four years later. The second title is, *A dialogue on the disadvantage of attaching moral ideas to certain physical actions which do not really comport with them.* Those who believe that the ruling system of notions about marriage represents the last word that is to be said as to the relations between men and women, will turn away from Diderot's dialogue with some impatience. Those, on the contrary, who hold that the present system is no more immovably fixed in ultimate laws of human nature, no more final, no more unimprovable, no more sacred, and no more indisputably successful, than any other set of social arrangements and the corresponding moral ideas, will find something to interest them, though, as it seems to the present writer, very little to instruct. Bougainville was the first Frenchman who sailed round the world. He did in 1766-69 what Captain Cook did about the same time. The narrative of his expedition appeared in 1771, and the picture of life among the primitive people of the Southern Seas touched Diderot almost as deeply as if he had been Rousseau. As one says so often in this history of the intellectual preparation for the Revolution, the corruption and artificiality of

Parisian society had the effect of colouring the world of primitive society with the very hues of paradise. Diderot was more free from this besetting weakness than any of his contemporaries. He never fell into Voltaire's fancy that China is a land of philosophers.[5] But he did not look very critically into the real conditions of life in the more rudimentary stages of development, and for the moment he committed the sociological anachronism of making the poor people of Otaheite into wise and benevolent patriots and sound reasoners. The literary merit of the dialogue is at least as striking as in any of the pieces of which we have already spoken. The realism of the scenes between the ship-chaplain and his friendly savage, with too kindly wife, and daughters as kindly as either, is full of sweetness, simplicity, and a sort of pathos. A subject which easily takes on an air of grossness, and which Diderot sometimes handled very grossly indeed, is introduced with an idyllic grace that to the pure will hardly be other than pure. We have of course always to remember that Diderot is an author for grown-up people, as are the authors of the Bible or any other book that deals with more than the surface of human experience. Our English practice of excluding from literature subjects and references that are unfit for boys and girls, has something to recommend it, but it undeniably leads to a certain narrowness and thinness, and to some most nauseous hypocrisy. All subjects are evidently not to be discussed by all; and one result in our case is that some of the most important subjects in the world receive no discussion whatever.

The position which Diderot takes up in the present dialogue may be inferred from the following extract. The ship-chaplain has been explaining to the astonished Otaheitan the European usage of strict monogamy, as the arrangement enjoined upon man by the Creator of the universe, and vigilantly guarded by the priest and the magistrate. To which, Orou thus:

> "These singular precepts I find opposed to nature and contrary to reason. They are contrary to nature because they suppose that a being who thinks, feels, and is free, can be the property of a creature like itself. Dost thou not see that in thy land they have confounded the thing that has neither sensibility, nor thought, nor desire, nor will; that one leaves, one takes, one keeps, one exchanges, without its suffering or complaining—with a thing that is neither exchanged nor acquired, that has freedom, will, desire, that may give or may refuse itself for the moment; that complains and suffers; and that cannot become a mere article of commerce, unless you forget its character and do violence to nature? And they are contrary to the general law of things. Can anything seem more senseless to thee than a precept which proscribes the law of change that is within us, and which commands a constancy that is impossible, and that violates the liberty of the male and the female, by chaining them together in perpetuity;—anything more senseless than are oaths of immutability, taken by two creatures of flesh, in the face of a sky that is not an instant the same, under vaults that threaten ruin, at the base of a rock crumbling to dust, at the foot of a tree that is splitting asunder?... You may command what is opposed to nature, but you will not be obeyed. You will multiply evil-doers and the unhappy by fear, by punishment, and by remorse; you will deprave men's consciences; you will corrupt their minds; they will have lost the

polar star of their pathway." (225.)

After this declamation he proceeds to put some practical questions to the embarrassed chaplain. Are young men in France always continent, and wives always true, and husbands never libertines? The chaplain's answers disclose the truth to the keen-eyed Orou:

> "What a monstrous tissue is this that thou art unfolding to me! And even now thou dost not tell me all; for as soon as men allow themselves to dispose at their own will of the ideas of what is just and unjust, to take away, or to impose an arbitrary character on things; to unite to actions or to separate from them the good and the evil, with no counsellor save caprice—then come blame, accusation, suspicion, tyranny, envy, jealousy, deception, chagrin, concealment, dissimulation, espionage, surprise, lies; daughters deceive their parents, wives their husbands, husbands their wives; young women, I don't doubt, will smother their children; suspicious fathers will despise and neglect their children; mothers will leave them to the mercy of accident; and crime and debauchery will show themselves in every guise. I know all that, as if I had lived among you. It is so, because it must be so; and that society of thine, in spite of thy chief who vaunts its fine order, is nothing but a collection of hypocrites who secretly trample the laws under foot; or of unfortunate wretches who make themselves the instrument of their own punishment, by submitting to these laws; or of imbeciles, in whom prejudice has absolutely stifled the voice of nature." (227.)

The chaplain has the presence of mind to fall back upon the radical difficulty of all such solutions of the problem of family union as were practised in Otaheite, or were urged by philosophers in Paris, or are timidly suggested in our own times in the droll-sounding form of marriages for terms of years with option of renewal. That difficulty is the disposal of the children which are the fruit of such unions. Orou rejoins to this argument by a very eloquent account how valuable, how sought after, how prized, is the woman who has her quiver full of them. His contempt for the condition of Europe grows more intense, as he learns that the birth of a child among the bulk of the people of the west is rather a sorrow, a perplexity, a hardship, than a delight and ground of congratulation.

The reader sees by this time that in the present dialogue Diderot is really criticising the most fundamental and complex arrangement of our actual western society, from the point of view of an arbitrary and entirely fanciful naturalism. Rousseau never wrote anything more picturesque, nor anything more dangerous, nor more anarchic and superficially considered. It is true that Diderot at the close of the discussion is careful to assert that while we denounce senseless laws, it is our duty to obey them until we have procured their reform. "He who of his own private authority infringes a bad law, authorises every one else to infringe good laws. There are fewer inconveniences in being mad with the mad, than in being wise by oneself. Let us say to ourselves, let us never cease to cry aloud, that people attach shame, chastisement, and infamy to acts that in themselves are innocent; but let us abstain from committing them, because shame, punishment, and infamy are the greatest of evils." And we hear Diderot's sincerest accents when he says, "Above all, one must be honest, and true to a scruple, with the fragile beings who cannot yield to our pleasures without renouncing the most precious advantages of society."[6]

This, however, does not make the philosophical quality of the discussion any more satisfactory. Whatever changes may ultimately come about in the relations between men and women, we may at least be sure that such changes will be in a direction even still further away than the present conditions of marriage, from anything like the naturalism of Diderot and the eighteenth-century school. Even if—what does not at present seem at all likely to happen—the idea of the family and the associated idea of private property should eventually be replaced by that form of communism which is to be seen at Oneida Creek, still the discipline of the appetites and affections of sex will necessarily on such a system be not less, but far more rigorous to nature than it is under prevailing western institutions.[7] Orou would have been a thousand times more unhappy among the Perfectionists under Mr. Noyes than in Paris or London. We cannot pretend here to discuss the large group of momentous questions involved, but we may make a short remark or two. One reason why the movement, if progressive, must be in the direction of greater subordination of appetite, is that all experience proves the position and moral worth of women, taking society as a whole, to be in proportion to the self-control of their male companions. Nobody doubts that man is instinctively polygamous. But the dignity and self-respect, and consequently the whole moral cultivation of women, depends on the suppression of this vagrant instinct. And there is no more important chapter in the history of civilisation than the record of the steps by which its violence has been gradually reduced.

There is another side, we admit. The home, of which sentimental philosophers love to talk, is too often a ghastly failure. The conjugal union, so tender and elevating in its ideal, is in more cases than we usually care to recognise, the cruellest of bonds to the woman, the most harassing, deadening, spirit-breaking of all possible influences to the man. The purity of the family, so lovely and dear as it is, has still only been secured hitherto by retaining a vast and dolorous host of female outcasts. When Catholicism is praised for the additions which it has made to the dignity of womanhood and the family, we have to set against that gain the frightful growth of this caste of poor creatures, upon whose heads, as upon the scapegoat of the Hebrew ordinance, we put all the iniquities of the children of the house, and all their transgressions in all their sins, and then banish them with maledictions into the foul outer wilderness and the land not inhabited.

On this side there is much wholesome truth to be told, in the midst of the complacent social cant with which we are flooded. But Diderot does not help us. Nothing can possibly be gained by reducing the attraction of the sexes to its purely physical elements, and stripping it of all the moral associations which have gradually clustered round it, and acquired such force as in many cases among the highest types of mankind to reduce the physical factor to a secondary place. Such a return to the nakedness of the brute must be retrograde. And Diderot, as it happened, was the writer who, before all others, habitually exalted the delightful and consolatory sentiment of the family. Nobody felt more strongly the worth of domestic ties, when faithfully cherished. It can only have been in a moment of elated paradox that he made one of the interlocutors in the dialogue on Bougainville pronounce Constancy, "The poor vanity of two children who do not know themselves, and who are blinded by the intoxication of a moment to the instability of all that surrounds them:" and Fidelity, "The obstinacy and the punishment of a good man and a good woman:" and Jealousy, "The passion of a miser; the unjust sentiment of man; the consequence of our false manners, and of a right of property extending over a feeling, willing, thinking, free creature."[8]

It is a curious example of the blindness which reaction against excess of ascetic doctrine bred in the eighteenth century, that Diderot should have failed to see that such sophisms as these are wholly destructive of that order and domestic piety, to whose beauty he was always so keenly alive. It is curious, too, that he should have failed to recognise that the erection of constancy into a virtue would have been impossible, if it had not answered first, to some inner want of human character at its best, and second, to some condition of fitness in society at its best.

How is it, says one of the interlocutors, that the strongest, the sweetest, the most innocent of pleasures is become the most fruitful source of depravation and misfortune? This is indeed a question well worth asking. And it is comforting after the anarchy of the earlier part of the dialogue to find so comparatively sensible a line of argument taken in answer as the following. This evil result has been brought about, he says, by the tyranny of man, who has converted the possession of woman into a property; by manners and usages that have overburdened the conjugal union with superfluous conditions; by the civil laws that have subjected marriage to an infinity of formalities; by religious institutions that have attached the name of vices and virtues to actions that are not susceptible of morality. If this means that human happiness will be increased by making the condition of the wife more independent in respect of property; by treating in public opinion separation between husband and wife as a transaction in itself perfectly natural and blameless, and often not only laudable, but a duty; and by abolishing that barbarous iniquity and abomination called restitution of conjugal rights, then the speaker points to what has been justly described as the next great step in the improvement of society. If it means that we do wrong to invest with the most marked, serious, and unmistakable formality an act that brings human beings into existence, with uncounted results both to such beings themselves and to others who are equally irresponsible for their appearance in the world, then the position is recklessly immoral, and it is, moreover, wholly repugnant to Diderot's own better mind.

CHAPTER II
ROMANCE.

The President de Brosses on a visit to Paris, in 1754, was anxious to make the acquaintance of that "furious metaphysical head," as he styled Diderot. Buffon introduced him. "He is a good fellow," said the President, "very pleasant, very amiable, a great philosopher, a strong reasoner, but given to perpetual digressions. He made twenty-five digressions yesterday in my room, between nine o'clock and one o'clock." And so it is that a critic who has undertaken to give an account of Diderot, finds himself advancing from digression to digression, through a chain of all the subjects that are under the sun. The same Diderot, however, is present amid them all, and behind each of them; the same fresh enthusiasm, the same expansive sympathy, the same large hospitality of spirit. Always, too, the same habitual reference of ideas, systems, artistic forms, to the complex realities of life, and to these realities as they figured to sympathetic emotions.

It was inevitable that Diderot should make an idol of the author of *Clarissa Harlowe*. The spirit of reaction against the artificiality of the pseudo-classic drama, which drove him to feel the way to a drama of real life in the middle class, made him exult in the romance of ordinary private life which was invented by Richardson. It was no mere accident that the modern novel had its origin in England, but the result of general social causes. The modern novel essentially depends on the interest of the private life of ordinary men and women. But this interest was only possible on condition that the feudal and aristocratic spirit had received its deathblow, and it was only in England that such a revolution had taken place even partially. It was only in England as yet that the middle class had conquered a position of consideration, equality, and independence. Only in England, as has been said, had every man the power of making the best of his own personality, and arranging his own destiny according to his private goodwill and pleasure.[9] The greatest of Richardson's successors in the history of English fiction adds to this explanation. "Those," says Sir Walter Scott, "who with patience had studied rant and bombast in the folios of Scuderi, could not readily tire of nature, sense, and genius in the octavos of Richardson." The old French romances in which Europe had found a dreary amusement, were stories of princes and princesses. It was to be expected that the first country where princes and princesses were shorn of divinity and made creatures of an Act of Parliament, would also be the country where imagination would be most likely to seek for serious passion, realistic interest, and all the material for pathos and tragedy in the private lives of common individuals. It is true that Marivaux, the author of *Marianne*, was of the school of Richardson before Richardson wrote a word. But this was an almost isolated appearance, and not the beginning of a movement. Richardson's popularity stamped the opening of a new epoch. It was the landmark of a great social, no less than a great literary transition, when all England went mad with enthusiasm over the trials, the virtue, the triumph of a rustic ladies'-maid.

In the literary circles of France the enthusiasm for Richardson was quite as great as it was in England. There it was one of the signs of the certain approach of that transformation which had already taken place in England; the transformation from feudalism to industrial democracy. It may sound a paradox to say that a passion for Richardson was a symbol that a man was truly possessed by the spirit of political revolution. Yet it is true. Voltaire was a revolter against superstition and the tyranny of the church, but he never threw off the monarchic traditions of his younger days; he was always a friend of great nobles; he had no eye and no inclination for social overthrow. And this is what Voltaire said of *Clarissa Harlowe*: "It is cruel for a man like me to read nine whole volumes in which you find nothing at all. I said—Even if all these people were my relations and friends, I could take no interest in them. I can see nothing in the writer but a clever man who knows the curiosity of the human race, and is always promising something from volume to volume, in order to go on selling them." In the same way, and for exactly the same reasons, he could never understand the enthusiasm for the _New Heloïsa_, the greatest of the romances that were directly modelled on Richardson. He had no vision for the strange social aspirations that were silently haunting the inner mind of his contemporaries. Of these aspirations, in all their depth and significance, Diderot was the half-conscious oracle and unaccepted prophet. It was not deliberate philosophical calculation that made him so, but the spontaneous impulse of his own genius and temperament. He was no conscious political destroyer, but his soul was open to all those voices of sentiment, to all those ideals of domestic life, to those primary forces of natural affection, which were so urgently pressing asunder the old feudal bonds, and so swiftly ripening a vast social crisis. Thus his enthusiasm for Richardson was, at its root, another side of that love of the life of peaceful industry, which gave one of its noblest characteristics to the Encyclopædia.

To this enthusiasm Diderot gave voice in half a dozen pages which are counted among his masterpieces. Richardson died in 1761, and Diderot flung off a commemorative piece, which is without any order and connection; but this makes it more an echo, as he called it, of the tumult of his own heart. Here, indeed, he merits Gautier's laudatory phrase, and is as "flamboyant" as one could desire. To understand the march of feeling in French literature, and to measure the growth and expansion in criticism, we need only compare Diderot's *eloge* on Richardson with Fontenelle's *éloge* on Dangeau or Leibnitz. The exaggerations of phrase, the violences of feeling, the broken apostrophes, give to Diderot's *éloge* an unpleasant tone of declamation. Some of us may still prefer the moderation, the subtlety, the nice discrimination, of the critics of another school. Still it would be a sign of narrowness and short-sight not to discern the sincerity, the movement, the real meaning underneath all that profusion of glaring colour.

> "O Richardson, Richardson, unique among men in my eyes, thou shalt be my favourite all my life long! If I am hard driven by pressing need, if my friend is overtaken by want, if the mediocrity of my fortune is not enough to give my children what is necessary for their education, I will sell my books; but thou shalt remain to me, thou shalt remain on the same shelf with Moses, Homer, Euripides, Sophocles!

> "O Richardson, I make bold to say that the truest history is full of falsehoods, and that your romance is full of truths. History paints a few individuals; you paint the human race. History sets down to its few individuals what they have neither said nor done; whatever you set down to man, he has both said and done.... No; I say that history is often a bad novel; and the novel, as you have handled it, is good history. O painter of nature, 'tis you who are never false!

> "You accuse Richardson of being long! You must have forgotten how much trouble, pains, busy movement, it costs to bring the smallest undertaking to a good issue,—to end a suit, to settle a marriage, to bring about a reconciliation. Think of these details what you please, but for me they will be full of interest if they are only true, if they bring out the passions, if they display character. They are common, you say; it is all what one sees every day. You are mistaken; 'tis what passes every day before your eyes, and what you never see."

In Richardson's work, he says, as in the world, men are divided into two classes, those who enjoy and those who suffer, and it is always to the latter that he draws the mind of the reader. It is due to Richardson, he cries, "if I have loved my fellow-creatures better, and loved my duties better; if I have never felt anything but pity for the bad; if I have conceived a deeper compassion for the unfortunate, more veneration for the good, more circumspection in the use of present things, more indifference about future things, more contempt for life, more love for virtue." The works of Richardson are his touch-stone; those who do not love them, stand judged and condemned in his eyes. Yet in the midst of this tumult of admiration Diderot admits that the number of readers who will feel all their value can never be great; it requires too severe a taste, and then the variety of events is such, relations are so multiplied, the management of them is so complicated, there are so many things arranged, so many personages! "O Richardson; if thou hast not enjoyed in thy lifetime all the reputation of thy deserts, how great wilt thou be to our grandchildren when they see thee from the distance at which we now view Homer! Then who will there be with daring enough to strike out a line of thy sublime work?"[10] Yet of the very moderate number of living persons who have ever read *Clarissa Harlowe*, it would be safe to say that the large majority have read it in a certain abridgment in three volumes which appeared some years ago.

Doctor Johnson made the answer of true criticism to some one who complained to him that Richardson is tedious. "Why, sir," he said, "if you were to read Richardson for the story, your impatience would be so much frighted that you would hang yourself. But you must read him for the sentiment, and consider the story only as giving occasion to the sentiment." And this is just what Diderot and the Paris of the middle of the eighteenth century were eager to do. It was the sentiment that touched and delighted them in *Clarissa*, just as it was the sentiment that made the fortune of the great romance in their own tongue, which was inspired by *Clarissa*, and yet was so different from *Clarissa*. Rousseau threw into the *New Heloïsa* a glow of passion of which the London printer was incapable, and he added a beauty of external landscape and a strong feeling for the objects and movement of wild natural scenery that are very different indeed from the atmosphere of the cedar-parlour and the Flask Walk at Hampstead. But the sentiment, the adoration of the *belle âme*, is the same, and it was the *belle âme* that fascinated that curious society, where rude logic and a stern anti-religious dialectic went hand-in-hand with the most tender and exalted sensibility.[11] It is singular that Diderot says nothing about Rousseau's famous romance, and we can only suppose that his silence arose from his contempt for the private perversity and seeming insincerity of the author.

Diderot made one attempt of his own, in which we may notice the influence of the minute realism and the tearful pathos of Richardson. *The Nun* was not given to the world until 1796, when its author had been twelve years in his grave. Since then it has been reproduced in countless editions in France and Belgium, and has been translated into English, Spanish, and German. It fell in with certain passionate movements of the popular mind against some anti-social practices of the Catholic Church. Perhaps it is not unjust to suppose that the horrible picture of the depraved abbess has had some share in attracting a public.

It is thoroughly characteristic of Diderot's dreamy, heedless humour, and of the sincerity both of his interest in his work for its own sake, and of his indifference to the popular voice, that he should have allowed this, like so many other pieces, to lie in his drawer, or at most to circulate clandestinely among three or four of his more intimate friends. It was written about 1760, and ingenious historians have made of it a signal for the great crusade against the Church. In truth, as we have seen, it was a strictly private performance, and could be no signal for a public movement. *La Religieuse* was undoubtedly an expression of the strong feeling of the Encyclopædic school about celibacy, renunciation of the world, and the burial of men and women alive in the cloister.

The circumstances under which the story was written are worthy of a word or two. Among the friends of Madame d'Epinay, Grimm, and Diderot was a certain Marquis de Croismare. He had deserted the circle, and retired to his estates in Normandy. It occurred to one of them that it would be a pleasant stratagem for recalling him to Paris, to invent a personage who should be shut up in a convent against her will, and then to make this personage appeal to the well-known courage and generosity of the Marquis de Croismare to rescue her. A previous adventure of the Marquis suggested the fiction, and made its success the more probable. Diderot composed the letters of the imaginary nun, and the conspirators had the satisfaction of making merry at supper over the letters which the loyal and unsuspecting Marquis sent in reply. At length the Marquis's interest became so eager that they resolved that the best way of ending his torment was to make the nun die. When the Marquis de Croismare returned to Paris, the plot was confessed, the victim of the mystification laughed at the joke, and the friendship of the party seemed to be strengthened by their common sorrow for the woes of the dead sister. But Diderot had been taken in his own trap. His imagination, which he had set to work in jest, was caught by the figure and the situation. One day while he was busy about the tale, a friend paid him a visit, and found him plunged in grief and his face bathed in tears. "What in the world can be the matter with you?" cried the friend. "What the matter?" answered Diderot in a broken voice; "I am filled with misery by a story that I am writing!" This capacity of thinking of imaginary personages as if they were friends living in the next street, had been stirred by Richardson. His acquaintances would sometimes notice anxiety and consternation on his countenance, and would ask him if anything had befallen his health, his friends, his family, his fortune. "O my friends," he would reply, "Pamela, Clarissa, Grandison …!" It was in their world, not in the Rue Taranne, that he really lived when these brooding moods overtook him. And while he was writing *The Nun*, Sister Susan and Sister Theresa, the lady superior of Longchamp, and the libertine superior of Saint Eutropius, were as alive to him as Clarissa was alive to the score of correspondents who begged Richardson to spare her honour, not to let her die, to make Lovelace marry her, or by no means to allow Lovelace to marry her.

The Nun professes to be the story of a young lady whose family have thrust her into a convent, and her narrative, with an energy and reality that Diderot hardly ever surpassed, presents the odious sides of monastic life, and the various types of superstition, tyranny, and corruption that monastic life engenders. Yet Diderot had far too much genius to be tempted into the exaggerations of more vulgar assailants of monkeries and nunneries. He may have begun his work with the purpose of attacking a mischievous and superstitious system that mutilates human life, but he certainly continued it because he became interested in his creations. Diderot was a social destroyer by accident, but in intention he was a truly scientific moralist, penetrated by the spirit of observation and experiment; he shrunk from no excess in dissection, and found nothing in human pathology too repulsive for examination. Yet *The Nun* has none of the artificial violences of the modern French school, which loves moral disease for its own sake. The action is all very possible, and the types are all sufficiently human and probable. The close realistic touches which flowed from the intensity of the writer's illusion, naturally convey a certain degree of the same illusion to the mind of the reader.

Existence as it goes on in these strange hives is caught with what one knows to be true fidelity; its dulness, its littleness, its goings and comings, its spite, its reduction of the spiritual to the most purely mechanical.

"The first moments passed in mutual praises, in questions about the house that I had quitted, in experiments as to my character, my inclinations, my tastes, my understanding. They feel you all over; there is a number of little snares that they set for you, and from which they draw the most just conclusions. For example, they throw out some word of scandal, and then they look at you; they begin a story, and then wait to see whether you will ask for the end or will leave it there; if you make the most ordinary remark, they declare that it is charming, though they know well enough that it is nothing; they praise or they blame you with a purpose; they try to worm out your most hidden thoughts; they question you as to what you read; they offer you religious books and profane, and carefully notice your choice; they invite you to some slight infractions of the rule; they tell you little confidences, and throw out hints about the foibles of the Lady Superior. All is carefully gathered up and told over again. They leave you, they take you up again; they try to sound your sentiments about manners, about piety, about the world, about religion, about the monastic life, about everything. The result of all these repeated experiments is an epithet that stamps your character, and is always added by way of surname to the name that you already bear. I was called Sister Susan the Reserved."[12]

The portraits we feel to be to the life. The strongest of them all is undoubtedly the most disagreeable, the most atrocious; it is, if you will, the most infamous. We can only endure it as we endure to traverse the ward for epileptics in an hospital for the insane. It is appalling, it fills you with horror, it haunts you for days and nights, it leaves a kind of stain on the memory. It is a possibility of character of which the healthy, the pure, the unthinking have never dreamed. Such a portrait is not art, that is true; but it is science, and that delivers the critic from the necessity of searching his vocabulary for the cheap superlatives of moral censure. Whether it be art or science, however, men cannot but ask themselves how Diderot came to think it worth while to execute so painful a study. The only answer is that the irregularities of human nature—those more shameful parts of it, which in some characters survive the generations of social pressure that have crushed them down in civilised communities—had an irresistible attraction for the curiosity of his genius. The whole story is full of power; it abounds in phrases that have the stamp of genius; and suppressed vehemence lends to it strength. But it is fatally wanting in the elements of tenderness, beauty, and sympathy. If we chance to take it up for a second or for a tenth time, it infallibly holds us; but nobody seeks to return to it of his own will, and it holds us under protest.

If Richardson created one school in France, Sterne created another. The author of *Tristram Shandy* was himself only a follower of one of the greatest of French originals, and a follower at a long distance. Even those who have the keenest relish for our "good-humoured, civil, nonsensical, Shandean kind of a book," ought to admit how far it falls behind Rabelais in exuberance, force, richness of extravagance, breadth of colour, fulness of blood. They may claim, however, for Sterne what, in comparison with these great elements, are the minor qualities of simplicity, tenderness, precision, and finesse. These are the qualities that delighted the French taste. In 1762 Sterne visited Paris, and found *Tristram Shandy* almost as well known there as in London, and he instantly had dinners and suppers for a fortnight on his hands. Among them were dinners and suppers at Holbach's, where he made the acquaintance of Diderot, and where perhaps he made the discovery that "notwithstanding the French make such a pother about the word *sentiment*, they have no precise idea attached to it."[13] The *Sentimental Journey* appeared in 1768, and was instantly pronounced by the critics in both countries to be inimitable. It is no wonder that a performance of such delicacy of literary expression, united with so much good-nature, such easy, humane, amiable feeling, went to the hearts of the French of the eighteenth century. "My design in it," said Sterne, "was to teach us to love the world and our fellow-creatures better than we do, so it runs most upon those gentle passions and affections which aid so much to it."[14] This exactly fell in with the reigning Parisian modes, and with such sentiment as that of Diderot most of all. There were several French imitations of the *Sentimental Journey*,[15] but the only one that has survived in popular esteem, if indeed this can be said to have survived, is Diderot's *Jacques le Fataliste*.

It seems to have been composed about the time (1773) of Diderot's journey to Holland and St. Petersburg, of which we shall have more to say in a later chapter. Its history is almost as singular as the history of *Rameau's Nephew*. A contemporary speaks of a score of copies as existing in different parts of Germany, and we may conjecture that they found their way there from friends whom Diderot made in Holland, and some of them were no doubt sent by Grimm to his subscribers. The first fragment of it that saw the light in print was in a translation that Schiller made of its most striking episode, in the year 1785. This is another illustration of the eagerness of the best minds of Germany to possess and diffuse the most original products of French intelligence and hardihood. Diderot, as we have said, stands in the front rank along with Rousseau, along also with Richardson, Sterne, and Goldsmith, among those who in Germany kindled the glow of sentimentalism, both in its good and its bad forms. It was in Germany that the first complete version of the whole of *Jacques le Fataliste* appeared, in 1792. Not until four years later did the French obtain an original transcript. This they owed to the generosity of Prince Henri of Prussia, the brother of Frederick the Great; he presented it to the Institute.

"There is going about here," wrote Goethe in 1780, while Diderot was still alive, "a manuscript of Diderot's called *Jacques le Fataliste et son Maître*, and it is really first-rate—a very fine and exquisite meal, prepared and dished up with great skill, as if for the palate of some singular idol. I set myself in the place of this Bel, and in six uninterrupted hours swallowed all the courses in the order, and according to the intentions, of this excellentcook and *maître d'hôtel*."[16] He goes on to say that when other people came to read it, some preferred one story, and some another. On the whole, one is strongly inclined to judge that few modern readers will equal Goethe's unsparing appetite. The reader sighs in thinking of the brilliant and unflagging wit, the verve, the wicked graces of *Candide*, and we long for the ease and simplicity and light stroke of the *Sentimental Journey*. Diderot has the German heaviness. Perhaps this is because he had too much conscience, and laboured too deeply under the burdensome problems of the world. He could not emancipate himself sufficiently from the tumult of his own sympathies. At many a page both of *Jacques le Fataliste*, and of others of his pieces, we involuntarily recall the writer's own contention that excess of sensibility makes a mediocre actor. The same law is emphatically true of the artist. Diderot never writes as if his spirit were quite free—and perhaps it never was free. If we are to enjoy these reckless outbursts of all that is bizarre and grotesque, these defiances of all that is sane, coherent, and rational, we must never feel conscious of a limitation, or a possibility of stint or check. The draught must seem to come from an exhaustless fountain of boisterous laughter, irony, and caprice. Perfect fooling is so rare an art, that not half a dozen men in literature have really possessed it; perhaps only Aristophanes, Rabelais, Shakespeare. *Candide*, wonderful as it is, has many a stroke of malice, and *Tristram Shandy*, wonderful as that is too, is not without tinges of self-consciousness; and neither malice nor self-consciousness belongs to the greater gods of buffoonery. Cervantes and Molière, those great geniuses of finest temper, still have none of the reckless buffoonery of such scenes as that between Prince Henry and the drawer, or the mad extravagances of the *Merry Wives*; still less of the wild topsy-turvy of the *Birds* or the *Peace*. They have not the note of true Pantagruelism. Most critics, again, would find in Swift a truculence, sometimes latent and sometimes flagrant, that would deprive him, too, of his place among these great masters of free and exuberant farce. Diderot, at any rate, must rank in the second class among those who have attempted to tread a measure among the whimsical zigzags of unreason. The sincere sentimentalist makes a poor reveller.

We have spoken, as many others have done before us, of Diderot as imitating our two English celebrities, and in one sense that is a perfectly true description. In *Jacques le Fataliste* whole sentences are transcribed in letter and word from *Tristram Shandy*. Yet imitation is hardly the right word for the process by which Diderot showed that an author had seized and affected him. *La Religieuse* would not have been written if there had been no Richardson, nor *Jacques le Fataliste* if there had been no Sterne; yet Diderot's work is not really like the work of either of his celebrated contemporaries. They gave him the suggestion of a method and a sentiment to start from, and he mused and brooded over it until, from among the clouds of his imagination, there began to loom figures of his own, moving along a path which was also his own. This was the history of his adaptation of *The Natural Son* from Goldoni. We can only be sure that nothing became blithe in its passage through his mind. He was too much of a preacher to be an effective humorist.

There is in *Jacques le Fataliste* none of that gift of true creation which produced such figures as Trim, and my Uncle Toby, and Mr. Shandy. Jacques's master is a mere lay figure, and Jacques himself, with his monotonous catchword, *"Il était écrit là-haut,"* has no real personality; he has none of the naturalness that wins us to Corporal Trim, still less has he any touch of the profound humour of the immortal Sancho. The book is a series of stories, rather than Sterne's subtle amalgam of pathos, gentle irony, and frank buffoonery; and the stories themselves are for the most part either insipid or obscene. There is perhaps one exception. The longest and the most elaborate of them, that which Schiller translated, is more like one of the modern French novels of a certain kind, than any other production of the eighteenth century. The adventure of Madame de Pommeraye and the Marquis d'Arcis is a crude foreshadowing of a style that has been perfected by M. Feydeau and M. Flaubert. The Marquis has been the lover of Madame de Pommeraye; he grows weary of her, and in time the lady discovers the bitter truth. Resignation is not among her virtues, and in her rage and anguish she devises an elaborate plan of revenge, which she carries out with the utmost tenacity and resolution. It consists in leading him on, by skilful incitements, to marry a woman whom he supposes to be an angel of purity, but whom Madame de Pommeraye triumphantly reveals to him on the morning after his marriage as a creature whose past history has been one of notorious depravity. This disagreeable story, of which Balzac would have made a masterpiece, is told in an interesting way, and the humoristic machinery by which the narrative is managed is less tiresome than usual. It is at least a story with meaning, purpose, and character. It is neither a jumble without savour or point, nor is it rank and gross like half the pages in the book. "Your *Jacques*," Diderot supposes some one to say to him, "is only a tasteless rhapsody of facts, some real, others imaginary, written without grace, and distributed without order. How can a man of sense and conduct, who prides himself on his philosophy, find amusement in spinning out tales so obscene as these?"[17] And this is exactly what the modern critic is bound to ask. In Rabelais there is at least puissant laughter; in Montaigne, when he dwells on such matters, there is *naïveté*. In Diderot we do not even feel that he is having any enjoyment in his grossnesses; they have not even the bad excuse of seeming spontaneous and coming from the fulness of his heart. "Reader," he says, "I amuse myself in writing the follies that you commit; your follies make me laugh; and my book puts you out of humour. To speak frankly to you, I find that the more wicked of us two is not myself." Unhappily, he does not convey the impression of amusement to his readers; it has no infection in it, and if his book puts us out of humour, it is not by its satire on mankind, but by its essential want of point and want of meaning, either moral or æsthetic. The few masters of this style have known how to bind the heterogeneous elements together, if not by some deep-lying purpose, at least by some pervading mood of rich and mellow feeling. In *Jacques le Fataliste* is neither.

That men of the stamp of Goethe and Schiller should have found such a book of delicious feast, naturally makes the disparaging critic pause. In truth, we can easily see how it was. Like all the rest of Diderot's work, it breaks roughly in upon that starved formalism which had for long lain so heavily both on art and life. Its hardihood, its very license, its contempt of conventions, its presentation of common people and coarse passions and rough lives, all made it a dissolvent of the thin, dry, and frigid rules which tyrannised over the world, and interposed between the artist or the thinker and the real existence of man on the earth. When we think of what European literature was, it ceases to be wonderful that Goethe should have been unable for six whole hours to tear himself away from a book that so few men to-day, save under some compulsion, could persuade themselves to read through. On great wholesome minds the grossness left no stain, and the interest of Diderot's singularities worked as a stimulus to a happier originality in men of more disciplined endowments. And let us add, of more poetic endowments. It is the lack of poetry in *Jacques* that makes its irony so heavy to us. We only willingly suffer those to take us down into the depths who can also raise us on the wings of a beautiful fancy. Even Rabelais has his poetic moments, as in the picture of Cupid self-disarmed before the industrious serenity of the Muses. A single lovely image, like Sterne's figure of the recording angel, reconciles us to many a miry page. But in *Jacques le Fataliste*, Diderot never raises his eye for an instant to the blue æther, his ear catches no harmony of awe, of hope, nor even of a noble despair. With a kind of clumsy jubilancy he holds us fast in the ways and language of thick and clogged sense. The *fatrasie* of old France has its place in literature, but it can never be restored in ages when a host of moral anxieties have laid siege to men's souls. The uncommon is always welcome to the lover of art, but it must justify itself. *Jacques* has the quality of the uncommon; it is a curiously prepared dish, as Goethe said; but it lacks the pinch of salt and the handful of herbs with sharp diffusive flavour.

CHAPTER III.
ART.

In 1759 Diderot wrote for Grimm the first of his criticisms on the exhibition of paintings in the Salon. At the beginning of the reign of Lewis xv. these exhibitions took place every year, as they take place now. But from 1751 onwards, they were only held once in two years. Diderot has left his notes on every salon from 1759 to 1781, with the exception of that of 1773, when he was travelling in Holland and Russia.

We have already seen how Grimm made Diderot work for him. The nine *Salons* are one of the results of this willing bondage, and they are perhaps the only part of Diderot's works that has enjoyed a certain measure of general popularity. Mr. Carlyle describes them with emphatic enthusiasm: "What with their unrivalled clearness, painting the picture over again for us, so that we too *see* it, and can judge it; what with their sunny fervour, inventiveness, real artistic genius, which wants nothing but a *hand*, they are with some few exceptions in the German tongue, the only Pictorial Criticisms we know of worth reading."[18] I only love painting in poetry, Madame Necker said to Diderot, and it is into poetry that you have found out the secret of rendering the works of our modern painters, even the commonest of them. It would be a truly imperial luxury, wrote A. W. Schlegel, to get a collection of pictures described for oneself by Diderot.

There is a freshness, a vivacity, a zeal, a sincerity, a brightness of interest in his subject, which are perhaps unique in the whole history of criticism. He flings himself into the task with the perfection of natural abandonment to a joyous and delightful subject. His whole personality is engaged in a work that has all the air of being overflowing pleasure, and his pleasure is contagious. His criticism awakens the imagination of the reader. Not only do we see the picture; we hear Diderot's own voice in ecstasies of praise and storms of boisterous wrath. There is such mass in his criticism; so little of the mincing and niggling of the small virtuoso. In facility of expression, in animation, in fecundity of mood, in fine improvisation, these pieces are truly incomparable. There is such an *impetus animi et quædam artis libido*. Some of the charm and freedom may be due to the important circumstance that he was not writing for the public. He was not exposed to the reaction of a large unknown audience upon style; hence the absence of all the stiffness of literary pose. But the positive conditions of such success lay in the resources of Diderot's own character.

The sceptic, the dogmatist, the dialectician, and the other personages of a heterogeneous philosophy who existed in Diderot's head, all disappear or fall back into a secondary place, and he surrenders himself with a curious freedom to such imaginative beauty as contemporary art provided for him. Diderot was perhaps the one writer of the time who was capable on occasion of rising above the strong prevailing spirit of the time; capable of forgetting for a season the passion of the great philosophical and ecclesiastical battle. No one save Diderot could have been moved by sight of a picture to such an avowal as this:

> "Absurd rigorists do not know the effect of external ceremonies on the people; they can never have seen the enthusiasm of the multitude at the procession of the *Fête Dieu*, an enthusiasm that sometimes gains even me. I have never seen that long file of priests in their vestments; those young acolytes clad in their white robes, with broad blue sashes engirdling their waists, and casting flowers on the ground before the Holy Sacrament; the crowd as it goes before and follows after them hushed in religious silence, and so many with their faces bent reverently to the ground; I have never heard that grave and pathetic chant, as it is led by the priests and fervently responded to by an infinity of voices of men, of women, of girls, of little children, without my inmost heart being stirred, and tears coming into my eyes. There is in it something, I know not what, that is grand, solemn, sombre, and mournful."

Thus to find the material of religious reaction in the author of *Jacques le Fataliste* and the centre of the atheistic group, completes the circle of Diderot's immense and deep-lying versatility. And in his account of such a mood, we see how he came to be so great and poetical a critic; we see the sincerity, the alertness, the profound mobility, with which he was open to impressions of colour, of sound, of the pathos of human aspiration, of the solemn concourses of men.

France has long been sovereign in criticism in its literary sense. In that department she has simply never had, and has not now, any serious rival. In the profounder historic criticism, Germany exhibits her one great, peculiar, and original gift. In the criticism of art Germany has at least three memorable names; but save where history is concerned most modern German æsthetics are so clouded with metaphysical speculation as to leave the obscurity of a very difficult subject as thick as it was before. In France the beginnings of art-criticism were literary rather than philosophic, and with the exception of Cousin's worthless eloquence, and of the writers whose philosophy Cousin dictated, and of M. Taine's ingenious paradoxes, Diderot is the only writer who has deliberately brought a vivid spirit and a philosophic judgment to the discussion of the forms of Beauty, as things worthy of real elucidation. As far back as the time of the English Restoration, Dufresnoy had written in bad Latin a poem on the art of Painting, which had the signal honour of being translated into good English by no less illustrious a master of English than Dryden, and it was again translated by Mason, the friend of Reynolds and of

Gray. Imitations, applied to the pictorial art, of the immortal Epistle to the Pisos, came thick in France in the eighteenth century.[19] But these effusions are merely literary, and they are very bad literature indeed. The abbé Dubos published in 1719 a volume of Critical Reflections on Poetry and Painting, including observations also on the relations of those arts to Music. Lessing is known to have made use of this work in his *Laocöon*, and Diderot gave it a place among the books which he recommended in his Plan of a University.[20] This, as it is the earliest, seems to have been the best contribution to æsthetic thought before Lessing and Diderot. Daniel Webb, the English friend of Raphael Mengs, published an Enquiry into the Beauties of Painting (1760), and Diderot wrote a notice of it,[21] but it appears to have made no mark on his mind. André, a Jesuit father, wrote an Essay on the Beautiful (1741), which distributed the kinds of art with precision, but omitted to say in what the Beautiful consists. The abbé Batteux wrote a volume reducing the fine arts to a single principle, and another volume attempting a systematic classification of them. The first of these was the occasion of Diderot's Letter on Deaf Mutes, and Diderot described their author as a good man of letters, but without taste, without criticism, and without philosophy; *à ces bagatelles près, le plus joli garçon du monde.*[22]

Travellers to the land where criticism of art has been so slight, and where production has been so noble, so bounteous, so superb, published the story of what Italy had shown to them. Madame de Pompadour designed to make her brother the Superintendent of fine arts, and she despatched Cochin, the great engraver of the day, to accompany him in a studious tour through the holy land of the arts. Cochin was away nearly two years, and on his return produced three little volumes (1758), in which he deals such blows to some vaunted immortalities as made the idolators by convention not a little angry. The abbé Richard (1766) published six very stupid volumes on Italy, and such criticism on art as they contain is not worthy of serious remark. The President de Brosses spent a year in Italy (1739-40), and wrote letters to his friends at home, which may be read to-day with interest and pleasure for their graphic picture of Italian society; but the criticisms which they contain on the great works of art are those of a well-informed man of the world, taking many things for granted, rather than of a philosophical critic industriously using his own mind. His book recalls to us how true the eighteenth century was to itself in its hatred of Gothic architecture, that symbol and associate of mysticism, and of the age which the eighteenth century blindly abhorred as the source of all the tyrannical laws and cruel superstitions that still weighed so heavily on mankind. "You know the Palace of Saint Mark at Venice," says De Brosses: "*c'est un vilain monsieur, s'il eu fut jamais, massif, sombre, et gothique, du plus méchant goût!*"[23]

Dupaty, like De Brosses, an eminent lawyer, an acquaintance of Diderot and an early friend of a conspicuous figure of a later time, the ill-starred Vergniaud, travelled in Italy almost immediately before the Revolution (1785), and his letters, when read with those of De Brosses, are a curious illustration of the change that had come over the spirit of men in the interval. He leaves the pictures of the Pitti collection at Florence, and plunges into meditation in the famous gardens behind the palace, rejoicing with much expansion in the glories of light and air, in greenery and the notes of birds, and finally sums all up in one rapturous exclamation of the vast superiority of nature over art.[24]

It is impossible, in reading how deeply Diderot was affected by fifth-rate paintings and sculpture, not to count it among the great losses of literature that he saw few masterpieces. He never made the great pilgrimage. He was never at Venice, Florence, Parma, Rome. A journey to Italy was once planned, in which Grimm and Rousseau were to have been his travelling companions; [25] the project was not realised, and the strongest critic of art that his country produced never saw the greatest glories of art. If Diderot had visited Florence and Rome, even the mighty painter of the Last Judgment and the creator of those sublime figures in the New Sacristy at San Lorenzo, would have found an interpreter worthy of him. But it was not to be. "It is rare," he once wrote, "for an artist to excel without having seen Italy, just as a man seldom becomes a great writer or a man of great taste without having given severe study to the ancients."[26] Diderot at least knew what he lost.

French art was then, as art usually is, the mirror of its time, reproducing such imaginative feeling as society could muster. When the Republic and the Empire came, and twenty years of battle and siege, then the art of the previous generation fell into a degree of contempt for which there is hardly a parallel. Pictures that had been the delight of the town and had brought fortunes to their painters, rotted on the quays or were sold for a few pence at low auctions. Fragonard, who had been the darling of his age, died in neglect and beggary. David and his hideous art of the Empire utterly effaced what had thrown the contemporaries of Diderot into rapture.[27] Every one knows all that can be said against the French paintings of Diderot's time. They are executed hastily and at random; they abound in technical defects of colour, of drawing, of composition; their feeling is light and shallow. Watteau died in 1721—at the same premature age as Raphael,—but he remained as the dominating spirit of French art through the eighteenth century. Of course the artists went to Rome, but they changed sky and not spirit. The pupils of the academy came back with their portfolios filled with sketches in which we see nothing of the "lone mother of dead empires," nothing of the vast ruins and the great sombre desolate Campagna, but only Rome turned into a decoration for the scenes of a theatre or the panels of a boudoir. The Olympus of Homer and of Virgil, as has been well said, becomes the Olympus of Ovid. Strength, sublimity, even stateliness disappeared, unless we admit some of the first two qualities in the landscapes of Vernet. Not only is beauty replaced by prettiness, but by prettiness in season and out of season. The common incongruity of introducing a spirit of elegance and literature into the simplicities of the true pastoral, was condemned by Diderot as a mixture of Fontenelle with Theocritus. We do not know what name he would have given to that still more curious incongruity of taste, which made a publisher adorn a treatise on Differential and Integral Calculus with amusing plates by Cochin, and introduce dainty little vignettes into a Demonstration of the Properties of the Cycloid.

There is one true story that curiously illustrates the spirit of French art in those equivocal days. When Madame de Pompadour made up her mind to play pander to the jaded appetites of the king, she had a famous female model of the day introduced into a *Holy Family*, which was destined for the private chapel of the queen. The portrait answered its purpose; it provoked the curiosity and desire of the king, and the model was invited to the Parc-aux-Cerfs.[28] This was typical of the service that painting was expected to render to the society that adored it and paid for it. "All is daintiness, delicate caressing for delicate senses, even down to the external decoration of life, down to the sinuous lines, the wanton apparel, the refined commodity of rooms and furniture. In such a place and in such company, it is enough to be together to feel at ease. Their idleness does not weigh upon them; life is their plaything."[29]

Only let us not, while reserving our serious admiration for Titian, Rembrandt, Raphael, and the rest of the gods and demigods, refuse at least a measure of historic tolerance to these light and graceful creations. Boucher, whose dreams of rose and blue were the delight of his age, came away from Rome saying: "Raphael is a woman, Michael Angelo is a monster; one is paradise, the other is hell; they are painters of another world; it is a dead language that nobody speaks in our day. We others are the painters of our own age: we have not common sense, but we are charming." This account of them was not untrue. They filled up the space between the grandiose pomp of Le Brun and the sombre pseudo-antique of David, just as the incomparable grace and sparkle of Voltaire's lighter verse filled up the space in literature between Racine and Chénier. They have a poetry of their own; they are cheerful, sportive, full of fancy, and like everything else of that day, intensely sociable. They are, at any rate, even the most sportive of them, far less unwholesome and degrading than the acres of martyrdoms, emaciations, bad crucifixions, bad pietas, that make some galleries more disgusting than a lazar-house.[30]

For Watteau himself, the deity of the century, Diderot cared very little. "I would give ten Watteaus," he said, "for one Teniers." This was as much to be expected, as it was characteristic in Lewis XIV., when some of Teniers's pictures were submitted to him, imperiously to command "*ces magots là*" to be taken out of his sight.

Greuze (*b. 1725, d. 1805*) of all the painters of the time was Diderot's chief favourite. Diderot was not at all blind to Greuze's faults, to his repetitions, his frequent want of size and amplitude, the excess of gray and of violet in his colouring. But all these were forgotten in transports of sympathy for the sentiment. As we glance at a list of Greuze's subjects, we perceive that we are in the very heart of the region of the domestic, the moral, "*l'honnête*," the homely pathos of the common people. The Death of a father of a family, regretted by his children; The Death of an unnatural father, abandoned by his children; The beloved mother caressed by her little ones; A child weeping over its dead bird; A Paralytic tended by his family, or the Fruit of a Good Education:—Diderot was ravished by such themes. The last picture he describes as a proof that compositions of that kind are capable of doing honour to the gifts and the sentiments of the artist.[31] The *Girl bewailing her dead bird* throws him into raptures. "O, the pretty elegy!" he begins, "the charming poem! the lovely idyll!" and so forth, until at length he breaks into a burst of lyric condolence addressed to the weeping child, that would fill four or five of these pages.[32]

No picture of the eighteenth century was greeted with more enthusiasm than Greuze's *Accordée de Village*, which was exhibited in 1761. It seems to tell a story, and therefore even to-day, in spite of its dulled pink and lustreless blue, it arrests the visitor to one of the less frequented halls of the Louvre.[33] Paris, weary of mythology and sated with pretty indecencies, was fascinated by the simplicity of Greuze's village tale. "*On se sent gagner d'une émotion douce en le regardant*," said Diderot, and this gentle emotion was dear to the cultivated classes in France at that moment of the century. It was the year of the *New Heloïsa*.

The subject is of the simplest: a peasant paying the dower-money of his daughter. "The father"—it is prudent of us to borrow Diderot's description —"is seated in the great chair of the house. Before him his son-in-law standing, and holding in his left hand the bag that contains the money. The betrothed, standing also, with one arm gently passed under the arm of her lover, the other grasped by her mother, who is seated. Between the mother and the bride, a younger sister standing, leaning on the bride and with an arm thrown round her shoulders. Behind this group, a child standing on tiptoes to see what is going on. To the extreme left in the background, and at a distance from the scene, two women-servants who are looking on. To the right a cupboard with its usual contents—all scrupulously clean.... A wooden staircase leading to the upper floor. In the foreground near the feet of the mother, a hen leading her young ones, to whom a little girl throws crumbs of bread; a basin full of water, and on the edge of it, one of the small chickens with its beak up in the air so as to let the water go down." Diderot then proceeds to criticise the details, telling us the very words that he hears the father addressing to the bridegroom, and as a touch of observation of nature, that while one of the old man's hands, of which we see the back, is tanned and brown, the other, of which we see the palm, is white. "To the bride the painter has given a face full of charm, of seemliness, of reserve. She is dressed to perfection. That apron of white stuff could not be better; there is a trifle of luxury in her ornament; but then it is a wedding-day. You should note how true are the folds and creases in her dress, and in those of the rest. The charming girl is not quite straight; but there is a light and gentle inflexion in all her figure and her limbs that fills her with grace and truth. Indeed she is pretty and very pretty. If she had leaned more towards her lover, it would have been unbecoming; more to her mother and her father, and she would have been false. She has her arm half passed under that of her future husband, and the tips of her fingers rest softly on his hand; that is the only mark of tenderness that she gives him, and perhaps without knowing it herself: it is a delicate idea in the painter."[34]

"Courage, my good Greuze," he cries, "*fais de la morale en peinture*. What, has not the pencil been long enough and too long consecrated to debauchery and vice? Ought we not to be delighted at seeing it at last unite with dramatic poetry in instructing us, correcting us, inviting us to virtue?"[35] It has been sometimes said that Diderot would have exulted in the paintings of Hogarth, and we may admit that he would have sympathised with the spirit of such moralities as the Idle and the Industrious Apprentice, the Rake's Progress, and Mariage à la Mode. The intensity and power of that terrible genius would have had their attraction, but the minute ferocities of Hogarth's ruthless irony would certainly have revolted him. Such a scene as Lord Squanderfield's visit to the quack doctor, or as the Rake's debauch, would have filled him with inextinguishable horror. He could never have forgiven an artist who, in the ghastly pathos of a little child straining from the arms of its nurse towards the mother, as she lies in the very article of death, could still find in his heart to paint on it the dark patches of foul disease. He would have fled with shrieks from those appalling scenes of murder, torture, madness, bestial drunkenness, rapacity, fury—from that delirium of scrofula, palsy, entrails, the winding-sheet, and the grave-worm. Diderot's method was to improve men, not by making their blood curdle, but by warming and softening the domestic affections.

Diderot, as a critic, seems always to have remembered a pleasant remonstrance once addressed at the Salon by the worthy Chardin to himself and Grimm: "Gently, good sirs, gently! Out of all the pictures that are here seek the very worst; and know that two thousand unhappy wretches have bitten their brushes in two with their teeth, in despair of ever doing even as badly. Parrocel, whom you call a dauber, and who for that matter is a dauber, if you compare him to Vernet, is still a man of rare talent relatively to the multitude of those who have flung up the career in which they started with him." And then the artist recounts the immense labours, the exhausting years, the boundless patience, attention, tenacity, that are the conditions even of a mediocre degree of mastery. We are reminded of the scene in a famous work of art in our own day, where Herr Klesmer begs Miss Gwendolen Harleth to reflect, how merely to stand or to move on the stage is an art that requires long practice. "*O le triste et plat métier que celui de critique!*" Diderot cries on one occasion: "*Il est si difficile de produire une chose même médiocre; il est si facile de sentir la médiocrité.*"[36] No doubt, as experience and responsibility gather upon us, we learn how hard in every line is even moderate skill. The wise are perhaps content to find what a man can do, without making it a reproach to him that there is something else which he cannot do.

But Diderot knew well enough that Chardin's kindly principle might easily be carried too far. In general, he said, criticism displeases me; it supposes so little talent. "What a foolish occupation, that of incessantly hindering ourselves from taking pleasure, or else making ourselves blush for the pleasure that we have taken! And that is the occupation of criticism!"[37] Yet in one case he writes a score of pages of critical dialogue, in which the chief interlocutor is a painter who avenges his own failure by stringent attacks on the work of happier rivals of the year. And speaking in his own proper person, Diderot knows how to dismiss incompetence with the right word, sometimes of scorn, more often of good-natured remonstrance. Bad painters, a Parrocel, a Brenet, fare as ill at his hands as they deserved to do. He remarks incidentally that the condition of the bad painter and the bad actor is worse than that of the bad man of letters: the painter hears with his own ears the expressions of contempt for his talent, and the hisses of the audience go straight to the ears of the actor, whereas the author has the comfort of going to his grave without a suspicion that you have cried out at every page: "*The fool, the animal, the jackass!*" and have at length flung his book into a corner. There is nothing to prevent the worst author, as he sits alone in his library, and reads himself over and over again, from congratulating himself on being the originator of a host of rare and felicitous ideas.[38]

32

The one painter whom Diderot never spares is Boucher, who was an idol of the time, and made an income of fifty thousand livres a year out of his popularity. He laughs at him as a mere painter of fans, an artist with no colours on his palette save white and red. He admits the fecundity, the *fougue*, the ease of Boucher, just as Sir Joshua Reynolds admits his grace and beauty and good skill in composition.[39] Boucher, says Diderot, is in painting what Ariosto is in poetry, and he who admires the one is inconsistent if he is not mad for the other. What is wanting is disciplined taste, more variety, more severity. Yet he cannot refuse to concede about one of Boucher's pictures that after all he would be glad to possess it. Every time you saw it, he says, you would find fault with it, yet you would go on looking at it.[40] This is perhaps what the severest modern amateur, as he strolls carelessly through the French school at his leisure, would not in his heart care to deny.

Fragonard, whose picture of Coresus and Callirrhoë made a great sensation in its day, and still attracts some small share of attention in the French school, was not a favourite with Diderot. The Callirrhoë inspired an elaborate but not very felicitous criticism. Then the painter changed his style in the direction of Boucher, and as far away as possible from *l'honnête* and *le beau moral*, and Diderot turned away from him; at last describing an oval picture representing groups of children in heaven as "*une belle et grande omelette d'enfants*," heads, legs, thighs, arms, bodies, all interlaced together among yellowish clouds—"*bien omelette, bein douillette, bein jaune, et bien brûlée*."[41]

On the whole, we cannot wonder either that painters hold literary talk about their difficult and complex art so cheap, or that the lay public prizes it so much above its intrinsic worth. It helps the sluggish imagination and dull sight of the one, while it is apt to pass ignorantly over both the true difficulties and the true successes of the other. Diderot, unlike most of those who have come after him, had carefully studied the conditions prescribed to the painter by the material in which he works. Although he was a master of the literary criticism of art, he had artists among his intimate companions, and was too eager for knowledge not to wring from them the secrets of technique, just as he extorted from weavers and dyers the secrets of their processes and instruments. He makes no ostentatious display of this special knowledge, yet it is present, giving a firmness and accuracy to what would otherwise be too like mere arbitrary lyrics suggested by a painting, and not really dealing with it. His special gift was the transformation of scientific criticism into something with the charm of literature. Take, for instance, a picture by Vien:

"Psyche approaching with her lamp to surprise Love in his sleep.—The two figures are of flesh and blood, but they have neither the elegance, nor the grace, nor the delicacy that the subject required. Love seems to me to be making a grimace. Psyche is not like a woman who comes trembling on tiptoe. I do not see on her face that mixture of surprise, fear, love, desire, and admiration, which ought all to be there. It is not enough to show in Psyche a curiosity to see Love; I must also perceive in her the fear of awakening him. She ought to have her mouth half open, and to be afraid of drawing her breath. 'Tis her lover that she sees—that she sees for the first time, at the risk of losing him for ever. What joy to look upon him, and to find him so fair! Oh, what little intelligence in our painters, how little they understand nature! The head of Psyche ought to be inclined towards Love; the rest of her body drawn back, as it is when you advance towards a spot where you fear to enter, and from which you are ready to flee back; one foot planted on the ground and the other barely touching it. And the lamp; ought she to let the light fall on the eyes of Love? Ought she not to hold it apart, and to shield it with her hand to deaden its brightness? Moreover, that would have lighted the picture in a striking way. These good people do not know that the eyelids have a kind of transparency; they have never seen a mother coming in the night to look at her child in the cradle, with a lamp in her hand, and fearful of awakening it."[42]

There have been many attempts to imitate this manner since Diderot. No less a person than M. Thiers tried it, when it fell to him as a young writer for the newspapers to describe the Salon of 1822. One brilliant poet, novelist, traveller, critic, has succeeded, and Diderot's art-criticism is at least equalled in Théophile Gautier's pages on Titian's Assunta and Bellini's Madonna at Venice, or Murillo's Saint Anthony of Padua at Seville.[43]

Just as in his articles in the Encyclopædia, here too Diderot is always ready to turn from his subject for a moral aside. Even the modern reader will forgive the discursive apostrophe addressed to the judges of the unfortunate Calas, the almost lyric denunciation of an atrocity that struck such deep dismay into the hearts of all the brethren of the Encyclopædia.[44] But Diderot's asides are usually in less tragic matter. A picture of Michael Van Loo's reminds him that Van Loo had once a friend in Spain. This friend took it into his head to equip a vessel for a trading expedition, and Van Loo invested all his fortune in his friend's vessel. The vessel was wrecked, the fortune was lost, and the master was drowned. When Van Loo heard of the disaster, the first word that came to his mouth was—*I have lost a good friend.* And on this Diderot sails off into a digression on the grounds of praise and blame.

Here are one or two illustrations of the same moralising:

"The effect of our sadness on others is very singular. Have you not sometimes noticed in the country the sudden stillness of the birds, if it happens that on a fine day a cloud comes and lingers over the spot that was resounding with their music? A suit of deep mourning in company is the cloud that, as it passes, causes the momentary silence of the birds. It goes, and the song is resumed."

"We should divide a nation into three classes: the bulk of the nation, which forms the national taste and manners; those who rise above these are called madmen, originals, oddities; those who fall below are noodles. The progress of the human mind causes the level to shift, and a man often lives too long for his reputation.... He who is too far in front of his generation, who rises above the general level of the common manners, must expect few votes; he ought to be thankful for the oblivion that rescues him from persecution. Those who raise themselves to a great distance above the common level are not perceived; they die forgotten and tranquil, either like everybody else, or far away from everybody else. That is my motto."[45]

"But Vernet will never be more than Vernet, a mere man. No, and for that very reason all the more astonishing, and his work all the more worthy of admiration. It is, no doubt, a great thing, is this universe; but when I compare it with the energy of the productive cause, if I had to wonder at aught, it would be that its work is not still finer and still more perfect. It is just the reverse when I think of the weakness of man, of his poor means, of the embarrassments and of the short duration of his life, and then of certain things that he has undertaken and carried out."[46]

These digressions are one source of the charm of Diderot's criticism. They impart ease and naturalness to it, because they evidently reproduce the free movement of his mind as it really was, and not as the supposed dignity of authorship might require him to pretend. There is no stiffness nor sense, as we have said, of literary strain, and yet there is no disturbing excess of what is random, broken, *décousu*. The digression flows with lively continuity from the main stream and back again into it, leaving some cheerful impression or curious suggestion behind it. Something, we cannot tell what, draws him off to wonder whether there is not as much verve in the first scene of Terence and in the Antinoüs as in any scene of Molière or any work of Michael Angelo? "I once answered this question, but rather too lightly. Every moment I am apt to make a mistake, because language does not furnish me with the right expression for the truth at the moment. I abandon a thesis for lack of words that shall supply my reasons. I have one thing in the bottom of my heart, and I find myself saying another. There is the advantage of living in retirement and solitude. There a man speaks, asks himself questions, listens to himself, and listens in silence. His secret sensation develops itself little by little." Then when he is about to speak of one of Greuze's pictures, he bethinks himself of Greuze's vanity, and this leads him to a vein of reflection which it is good for all critics, whether public or private, to hold fast in their minds. "If you take away Greuze's vanity, you will take away his verve, you will extinguish his fire, his genius will undergo an eclipse. *Nos qualités tiennent de prés à nos défauts.*" And of this important truth, the base of wise tolerance, there follow a dozen graphic examples.[47]

Grétry, the composer, more than once consulted Diderot in moments of perplexity. It was not always safe, he says, to listen to the glowing man when he allowed his imagination to run away with him, but the first burst was of inspiration divine.[48] Painters found his suggestions as potent and as hopeful as the musician found them. He delighted in being able to tell an artist how he might change his bad picture into a good one.[49] "Chardin, La Grenée, Greuze, and others," says Diderot, "have assured me (and artists are not given to flattering men of letters) that I was about the only one whose images could pass at once to canvas, almost exactly as they came into my head." And he gives illustrations, how he instantly furnished to La Grenée a subject for a picture of Peace; to Greuze, a design introducing a nude figure without wounding the modesty of the spectator; to a third, a historical subject.[50] The first of the three is a curious example of the difficulty which even a strong genius like Diderot had in freeing himself from artificial traditions. For Peace, he cried to La Grenée, show me Mars with his breastplate, his sword girded on, his head noble and firm. Place standing by his side a Venus, full, divine, voluptuous, smiling on him with an enchanting smile; let her point to his casque, in which her doves have made their nest. Is it not singular that even Diderot sometimes failed to remember that Mars and Venus are dead, that they can never be the source of a fresh and natural inspiration, and that neither artist nor spectator can be moved by cold and vapid allegories in an extinct dialect? If Diderot could have seen such a treatment of La Grenée's subject as Landseer's *Peace*, with its children playing at the mouth of the slumbering gun, he would have been the first to cry out how much nearer this came to the spirit of his own æsthetic methods, than all the pride of Mars and all the beauty of Venus. He is truer to himself in the subject with which he met Greuze's perplexity in the second of his two illustrations. He bade Greuze paint the Honest Model; a girl sitting to an artist for the first time, her poor garments on the ground beside her; her head resting on one of her hands, and a tear rolling down each cheek. The mother, whose dress betrays the extremity of indigence, is by her side, and with her own hands and one of the hands of her daughter covers her face. The painter, witness of the scene, softened and touched, lets his palette or his brush fall from his hand. Greuze at once exclaimed that he saw his subject; and we may at least admit that this pretty bit of commonplace sentimentalism is more in Diderot's vein than pagan gods and goddesses.

Diderot is never more truly himself than when he takes the subject of a picture that is before him, and shows how it might have been more effectively handled. Thus:

> "The Flight into Egypt is treated in a fresh and piquant manner. But the painter has not known how to make the best of his idea. The Virgin passes in the background of the picture, bearing the infant Jesus in her arms. She is followed by Joseph and the ass carrying the baggage. In the foreground are the shepherds prostrating themselves, their hands upturned towards her, and wishing her a happy journey. Ah, what a fine painting, if the artist had known how to make mountains at the foot of which the Virgin had passed; if he had known how to make the mountains very steep, escarped, majestic; if he had covered them with moss and wild shrubs; if he had given to the Virgin simplicity, beauty, grandeur, nobleness; if

the road that she follows had led into the paths of some forest, lonely and remote; if he had taken his moment at the rise of day, or at its fall!"[51]

The picture of Saint Benedict by Deshays—whom at one moment Diderot pronounces to be the first painter in the nation—stirs the same spirit of emendation. Diderot thinks that in spite of the pallor of the dying saint's visage, one would be inclined to give him some years yet to live.

> "I ask whether it would not have been better that his legs should have sunk under him; that he should have been supported by two or three monks; that he should have had the arms extended, the head thrown back, with death on his lips and ecstasy on his brow. If the painter had given this strong expression to his Saint Benedict, consider, my friend, how it would have reflected itself on all the rest of the picture. That slight change in the principal figure would have influenced all the others. The celebrant, instead of being upright, would in his compassion have leaned more forward; distress and anguish would have been more strongly depicted in all the bystanders. There is a piece from which you could teach young students that, by altering one single circumstance, you alter all others, or else the truth disappears. You could make out of it an excellent chapter on the *force of unity*: you would have to preserve the same arrangement, the same figures, and to invite them to execute the picture according to the different changes that were made in the figure of the communicant."[52]

The admirable Salons were not Diderot's only contributions to æsthetic criticism. He could not content himself with reproductions, in eloquent language upon paper, of the combinations of colour and form upon canvas. No one was further removed from vague or indolent expansion. He returns again and again to examine with keenness and severity the principles, the methods, the distinctions of the fine arts, and though he is often a sentimentalist and a declaimer, he can also, when the time comes, transform himself into an accurate scrutiniser of ideas and phrases, a seeker after causes and differences, a discoverer of kinds and classes in art, and of the conditions proper to success in each of them. In short, the fact of being an eloquent and enthusiastic critic of pictures, did not prevent him from being a truly philosophical thinker about the abstract laws of art, with the thinker's genius for analysis, comparison, classification. Who that has read them can ever forget the dialogues that are set among the landscapes of Vernet in the Salons of 1767?[53] The critic supposes himself unable to visit the Salon of the year, and to be staying in a gay country-house amid some fine landscapes on the sea-coast. He describes his walks among these admirable scenes, and the strange and varying effects of light and colour, and all the movements of the sky and ocean; and into the descriptions he weaves a series of dialogues with an abbé, a tutor of the children of the house, upon art and landscape and the processes of the universe. Nothing can be more excellent and lifelike: it is not until the end that he lets the secret slip that the whole fabric has been a flight of fancy, inspired by no real landscape, but by the sea-pieces sent to the exhibition by Vernet.

This is an illustration of the variety of approach which makes Diderot so interesting, so refreshing a critic. He never sinks into what is mechanical, and the evidence of this is that his mind, while intent on the qualities of a given picture, yet moves freely to the outside of the picture, and is ever cordially open to the most general thoughts and moods, while attending with workmanlike fidelity to what is particular in the object before him.[54]

In the light of modern speculation upon the philosophy of the fine arts, Diderot makes no commanding figure, because he is so egregiously unsystematic. But as Goethe said, in a piece where he was withstanding Diderot to the face, *die höchste Wirkung des Geistes ist, den Geist hervorzurufen*—the highest influence of mind is to call out mind. This stimulating provocation of the intelligence was the master faculty in Diderot. For the sake of that men are ready to pardon all excesses, and to overlook many offences against the law of Measure. From such a point of view, Goethe's treatment of Diderot's Essay on Painting (written in 1765, but not given to the world until 1796) is an instructive lesson. "Diderot's essay," he wrote to Schiller, "is a magnificent work, and it speaks even more usefully to the poet than to the painter, though for the painter, too, it is a torch of powerful illumination." Yet Diderot's critical principle in the essay was exactly opposite to Goethe's; and when Goethe translated some portions of it, he was forced to add a commentary of stringent protest. Diderot, as usual, energetically extols nature, as the one source and fountain of true artistic inspiration. Even in what looks to us like defect and monstrosity, she is never incorrect. If she inflicts on the individual some unusual feature, she never fails to draw other parts of the system into co-ordination and a sort of harmony with the abnormal element. We say of a man who passes in the street that he is ill-shapen. Yes, according to our poor rules; but according to nature, it is another matter. We say of a statue that it is of fine proportions. Yes, according to our poor rules; but according to nature?[55]

In the same vein, he breaks out against the practice of drawing from the academic model. All these academic positions, affected, constrained, artificial, as they are; all these actions coldly and awkwardly expressed by some poor devil, and always the same poor devil, hired to come three times a week, to undress himself, and to play the puppet in the hands of the professor —what have these in common with the positions and actions of nature? What is there in common between the man who draws water from the well in your courtyard, and the man who pretends to imitate him on the platform of the drawing-school? If Diderot thought the seven years passed in drawing the model no better than wasted, he was not any more indulgent to the practice of studying the minutiæ of the anatomy of the human frame. He saw the risk of the artist becoming vain of his scientific acquirement, of his eye being corrupted, of his seeking to represent what is under the surface, of his forgetting that he has only the exterior to show. A practice that is intended to make the student look at nature most commonly tends to make him see nature other than she really is. To sum up, mannerism would disappear from drawing and from colour, if people would only scrupulously imitate nature. Mannerism comes from the masters, from the academy, from the school, and even from the antique.[56]

We may easily believe how many fallacies were discerned in such lessons as these by the author of *Iphigenie*, and the passionate admirer of the ancient marbles. Diderot's fundamental error, said Goethe, is to confound nature and art, completely to amalgamate nature with art. "Now Nature organises a living, an indifferent being, the Artist something dead, but full of significance; Nature something real, the Artist something apparent. In the works of Nature the spectator must import significance, thought, effect, reality; in a work of Art he will and must find this already there. A perfect imitation of Nature is in no sense possible; the Artist is only called to the representation of the surface of an appearance. The outside of the vessel, the living whole that speaks to all our faculties of mind and sense, that stirs our desire, elevates our intelligence —that whose possession makes us happy, the vivid, potent, finished Beautiful —for all this is the Artist appointed." In other words, art has its own laws, as it has its own aims, and these are not the laws and aims of nature. To mock at rules is to overthrow the conditions that make a painting or a statue possible. To send the pupil away from the model to the life of the street, the gaol, the church, is to send him forth without teaching him for what to look. To make light of the study of anatomy in art, is like allowing the composer to forget thorough bass in his enthusiasm, or the poet in his enthusiasm to forget the number of syllables in his verse. Again, though art may profit by a free and broad method, yet all artistic significance depends on the More and the Less. Beauty is a narrow circle in which one may only move in modest measure. And of this modest measure the academy, the school, the master, above all the antique, are the guardians and the teachers.[57]

It is unnecessary to labour the opposition between the two great masters of criticism. Goethe, as usual, must be pronounced to have the last word of reason and wisdom, the word which comprehends most of the truth of the matter. And it is delivered in that generous and loyal spirit which nobody would have appreciated more than the free-hearted Diderot himself. The drift of Goethe's contention is, in fact, the thesis of Diderot's Paradox on the Comedian. But the state of painting in France—and Goethe admits it—may have called for a line of criticism which was an exaggeration of what Diderot, if he had been in Goethe's neutral position, would have found in his better mind.[58]

There is a passage in one of the Salons which sheds a striking side-light on the difference between these two great types of genius. The difference between the mere virtuoso and the deep critic is that, in the latter, behind views on art we discern far-reaching thoughts on life. And in Diderot, no less than in Goethe, art is ever seen in its associations with character, aspiration, happiness, and conduct.

> "The sun, which was on the edge of the horizon, disappeared; over the sea there came all at once an aspect more sombre and solemn. Twilight, which is at first neither day nor night—an image of our feeble thoughts, and an image that warns the philosopher to stay in his speculations—warns the traveller too to turn his steps towards home. So I turned back, and as I continued the thread of my thoughts, I began to reflect that if there is a particular morality belonging to each species, so perhaps in the same species there is a different morality for different individuals, or at least for different kinds and collections of individuals. And in order not to scandalise you by too serious an example, it came into my head that there is perhaps a morality peculiar to artists or to art, and that this morality might well be the very reverse of the common morality. Yes, my friend, I am much afraid that man marches straight to misery by the very path that leads the imitator of nature to the sublime. To plunge into extremes—that is the rule for poets. To keep in all things the just mean—there is the rule for happiness. One must not make poetry in real life. The heroes, the romantic lovers, the great patriots, the inflexible magistrates, the apostles of religion, the philosophers *à toute outrance*—all these rare and divine insensates make poetry in their life, and that is their bane. It is they who after death provide material for great pictures. They are excellent to paint. Experience shows that nature condemns to misery the man to whom she has allotted genius, and whom she has endowed with beauty; it is they who are the figures of poetry. Then within myself I lauded the mediocrity that shelters one alike from praise and blame; and yet why, I asked myself, would no one choose to let his sensibility go, and to become mediocre? O vanity of man!"[59]

Goethe's *Tasso*, a work so full of finished poetry and of charm, is the idealised and pathetic version of the figure that Diderot has thus conceived for genius. The dialogues between the hapless poet and Antonio, the man of the world, are a skilful, lofty, and impressive statement of the problem that often vexed Diderot. Goethe sympathised with Antonio's point of view; he had in his nature so much of the spirit of conduct, of saneness, of the common reason of the world. And in art he was a lover of calm ideals. In Diderot, as our readers by this time know, these things were otherwise.

The essay on Beauty in the Encyclopædia is less fertile than most of Diderot's contributions to the subject.[60] It contains a careful account of two or three other theories, especially that of Hutcheson. The object is to explain the source of Beauty. Diderot's own conclusion is that this is to be found in "relations." Our words for the different shades of the beautiful are expressive of notions (acquired by experience through the senses) of order, proportion, symmetry, unity, and so forth. But, after all, the real question remains unanswered—what makes some relations beautiful, and others not so; and the same objects beautiful to me, and indifferent to you; and the same object beautiful to me to-day, and indifferent or disgusting to me to-morrow? Diderot does, it is true, enumerate twelve sources of such diversity of judgment, in different races, ages, individuals, moods, but their force depends upon the importation into the conception of beauty of some more definite element than the bare idea of relation. Some sentences show that he came very near to the famous theory of Alison, that beauty is only attributed to sounds and sights, where, and because, they recall what is pleasing, sublime, pathetic, and set our ideas and emotions flowing in one of these channels. But he does not get fairly on the track of either Alison's or any other decisive and marking adjective, with which to qualify his *rapports*. He wastes some time, moreover, in trying to bring within the four corners of his definition some uses of the terms of beauty, which are really only applied to objects by way of analogy, and are not meant to predicate the beautiful in any literal or scientific sense.

There is no more interesting department of æsthetic inquiry than the relations of the arts to one another, and the nature of the delimitations of the provinces of poetry, painting, sculpture, music. Diderot, from the very beginning of his career, had turned his thoughts to this intricate subject. In his letter on Deaf Mutes (1751) he had stated the problem—to collect the common beauties of poetry, painting, and music; to show their analogies; to explain how the poet, the painter, and the musician render the same image; to seize the fugitive emblems of their expression. Why should a situation that is admirable in a poem become ridiculous in a painting?[61] For instance, what is it that prevents a painter from reproducing the moment when Neptune raises his head above the tossing waters, as he is represented in Virgil:

> Interea magno misceri murmure pontum.
> Emissamque hiemem sensit Neptunus, et imis
> Stagna refusa vadis; graviter commotus, et alto
> Prospiciens, summâ placidum caput extulit undâ.

Diderot's answer to the question is an anticipation of the main position of the famous little book which appeared fifteen years afterwards, and which has been well described as the Organum of æsthetic cultivation. In *Laocoön* Lessing contends against Spence, the author of *Polymetis* against Caylus, and others of his contemporaries, that poetry and painting are divided from one another in aim, in effects, in reach, by the limits set upon each by the nature of its own material.[62] So Diderot says that the painter could not seize the Virgilian moment, because a body that is partially immersed in water is disfigured by an effect of refraction, which a faithful painter would be bound to reproduce; because the image of the body could not be seen transparently through the stormy waters, and therefore the god would have the appearance of being decapitated; because it is indispensable, if you would avoid the impression of a surgical amputation, that some visible portion of hidden limbs should be there to inform us of the existence of the rest.[63] He takes another instance, where a description that is admirable in poetry would be insupportable in painting. Who, he asks, could bear upon canvas the sight of Polyphemus grinding between his teeth the bones of one of the companions of Ulysses? Who could see without horror a giant holding a man in his enormous mouth, with blood dripping over his head and breast?

Among the many passages in which Diderot touches on the differences between poetry and painting, none is more just and true than that in which he implores the poet not to attempt description of details: "True taste fastens on one or two characteristics, and leaves the rest to imagination. 'Tis when Armida advances with noble mien in the midst of the ranks of the army of Godfrey, and when the generals begin to look at one another with jealous eyes, that Armida is beautiful to us. It is when Helen passes before the old men of Troy, and they all cry out—it is then that Helen is beautiful. And it is when Ariosto describes Alcina from the crown of her head to the soles of her feet, that notwithstanding the grace, the facility, the soft elegance of his verse, Alcina is not beautiful. He shows me everything; he leaves me nothing to do; he makes me wearied and impatient. If a figure walks, describe to me its carriage and its lightness; I will undertake the rest. If it is stooping, speak to me only of arms and shoulders; I will take all else on myself. If you do more, you confuse the kinds of work; you cease to be a poet, and become a painter or sculptor. One single trait, a great trait; leave the rest to my imagination. That is true taste, great taste."[64] And then he quotes with admiration Ovid's line of the goddess of the seas:

> Nec brachia longo
> Margine terrarum porrexerat Amphitrite.

Quel image! Quels bras! Quel prodigieux mouvement! Quelle figure! and so forth, after Diderot's manner.

Nobody will compare these detached and fragmentary deliverances with the full and easy mastery which Lessing, in *Laocöon* and its unfinished supplements, exhibits over the many ramifications of his central idea. We can only notice that Diderot had a foot on the track along which Lessing afterwards made such signal progress. The reader who cares to measure the advantage of Lessing's more serious and concentrated attention to his subject, may compare the twelfth chapter of *Laocöon* with Diderot's criticism on Doyen's painting of the Battle between Diomede and Aeneas.[65] As we see how near Diderot came to the real and decisive truths of all these matters, and yet how far he remains from the full perception of what a little consecutive study must have revealed to his superior genius, we can only think painfully of his avowal—"I have not the consciousness of having employed the half of my strength: *jusqu'à présent je n'ai que baguenaudé.*"

On the great art of music Diderot has said little that is worth attending to. Bemetzrieder, a German musician, who taught Diderot's daughter to play on the clavecin, wrote an elementary book called Lessons on the Clavecin and Principles of Harmony. This is pronounced by the modern teachers to be not less than contemptible. Diderot, however, with his usual boundless good nature, took the trouble to set the book in a series of dialogues, in which teacher, pupil, and a philosopher deal in all kinds of elaborate amenities, and pay one another many compliments. It reminds one of the old Hebrew grammar which is couched in the form of Conversations with a Duchess —"Your Grace having kindly condescended to approve of the plan that I have sketched. All this your Grace probably knows already, but your Grace has probably never attempted," and so forth.

The unwise things that men of letters have written from a good-natured wish to help their friends, are not so numerous that we need be afraid of extending to them a good-natured pardon. The beauty of Diderot's Salons is remarkable enough to cover a multitude of sins in other arts. There are few other compositions in European literature which show so well how criticism of art itself may become a fine art.

CHAPTER IV.
ST. PETERSBURG AND THE HAGUE.

"What would you say of the owner of an immense palace, who should spend all his life in going up from the cellars to the attics, and going down from attics to cellar, instead of sitting quietly in the midst of his family? That is the image of the traveller." Yet Diderot, whose words these are, resolved at the age of sixty to undertake no less formidable a journey than to the remote capital on the shores of the Neva. It had come into his head, or perhaps others had put it into his head, that he owed a visit to his imperial benefactress whose bounty had rendered life easier to him. He had recently made the acquaintance of two Russian personages of consideration. One of them was the Princess Dashkow, who was believed to have taken a prominent part in that confused conspiracy of 1762, which ended in the murder of Peter III. by Alexis Orloff, and the elevation of Catherine II. to the throne. Her services at that critical moment had not prevented her disgrace, if indeed they were not its cause, and in 1770 the Princess set out on her travels. Horace Walpole has described the curiosity of the London world to see the Muscovite Alecto, the accomplice of the northern Athaliah, the amazon who had taken part in a revolution when she was only nineteen. In England she made a pleasant impression, in spite of eyes of "a very Catiline fierceness." She was equally delighted with England, and when she went on from London to Paris, she took very little trouble to make friends in the capital of the rival nation. Diderot seems to have been her only intimate. The Princess (1770) called nearly every afternoon at his door, carried him off to dinner, and kept him talking and declaiming until the early hours of the next morning. The "hurricanes of his enthusiastic nature" delighted her, and she remembered for years afterwards how on one occasion she excited him to such a pitch that he sprang from his chair as if by machinery, strode rapidly up and down the room, and spat upon the floor with passion.[66]

The Prince Galitzin was a Russian friend of greater importance. Prince Galitzin was one of those foreigners, like Holbach, Grimm, Galiani, who found themselves more at home in Paris than anywhere else in the world. Living mostly among artists and men of letters, he became an established favourite. With Diderot's assistance (1767) he acquired for the Empress many of the pictures that adorn the great gallery at St. Petersburg, and Diderot praises his knowledge of the fine arts, the reason being that he has that great principle of true taste, the *belle âme*.[67] He wrote eclogues in French, and he attempted the more useful but more difficult task of writing in the half-formed tongue of his own country an account of the great painters of Italy and Holland.[68] Diderot makes the pointed remark about him, that he believed in equality of ranks by instinct, which is better than believing in it by reflection. [69] It was through the medium of this friendly and intelligent man that the Empress had acted in the purchase of Diderot's library. In 1769 he was appointed Russian minister at the Hague, and his chief ground for delight at the appointment was that it brought him within reach of his friends in Paris.

Diderot set out on his expedition some time in the summer of 1773—the date also of Johnson's memorable tour to the Hebrides—and his first halt was at the Dutch capital, then at the distance of a four days' journey from Paris. Here he remained for many weeks, in some doubt whether or not to persist in the project of a more immense journey. He passed most of his time with the Prince and Princess Galitzin, as between a good brother and a good sister. Their house, he notices, had once been the residence of Barneveldt. Men like Diderot are the last persons to think of their own historic position, else we might have expected to find him musing on the saving shelter which this land of freedom and tolerance had given to more than one of his great precursors in the literature of emancipation. Descartes had found twenty years of priceless freedom (1629-1649) among the Dutch burghers. The ruling ideas of the Encyclopædia came in direct line from Bayle (*d. 1706*) and Locke (*d. 1704*), and both Bayle and Locke, though in different measures, owed their security to the stout valour with which the Dutch defended their own land, and taught the English how to defend theirs, against the destructive pretensions of Catholic absolutism. Of these memories Diderot probably thought no more than Descartes thought about the learning of Grotius or the art of Rembrandt. It was not the age, nor was his the mind, for historic sentimentalism. "The more I see of this country," he wrote to his good friends in Paris, "the more I feel at home in it. The soles, fresh herrings, turbot, perch, are all the best people in the world. The walks are charming; I do not know whether the women are all very sage, but with their great straw hats, their eyes fixed on the ground, and the enormous fichus spread over their bosoms, they have the air of coming back from prayers or going to confession." Diderot did not fail to notice more serious things than this. His remarks on the means of travelling with most profit are full of sense, and the account which he wrote of Holland shows him to have been as widely reflective and observant as we should have expected him to be.[70] It will be more convenient to say something on this in connection with the stay which he again made at the Hague on his return from his pilgrimage to Russia.

After many hesitations the die was cast. Nariskin, a court chamberlain, took charge of the philosopher, and escorted him in an excellent carriage along the dreary road that ended in the capital reared by Peter the Great among the northern floods. It is worth while to digress for a few moments, to mark shortly the difference in social and intellectual conditions between the philosopher's own city and the city for which he was bound, and to touch on the significance of his journey. We can only in this way understand the position of the Encyclopædists in Europe, and see why it is interesting to the student of the history of Western civilisation to know something about them. It is impossible to have a clear idea of the scope of the revolutionary philosophy, as well as of the singular pre-eminence of Paris over the western world, until we have placed ourselves, not only at Ferney and Grandval, and in the parlours of Madame Geoffrin and Mademoiselle Lespinasse, but also in palaces at Florence, Berlin, Vienna, and St. Petersburg.

From Holland with its free institutions, its peaceful industry, its husbanded wealth, its rich and original art, its great political and literary tradition, to go to Russia was to measure an arc of Western progress, and to retrace the steps of the genius of civilisation. The political capital of Russia represented a forced and artificial union between old and new conditions. In St. Petersburg, says an onlooker, were united the age of barbarism and the age of civilisation, the tenth century and the eighteenth, the manners of Asia and the manners of Europe, the rudest Scythians and the most polished Europeans, a brilliant and proud aristocracy and a people sunk in servitude. On one side were elegant fashions, magnificent dresses, sumptuous repasts, splendid feasts, theatres like those which gave grace and animation to the select circles of London or Paris: on the other side, shopkeepers in Asiatic dress, coachmen, servants, and peasants clad in sheepskins, wearing long beards, fur caps, and long fingerless gloves of skin, with short axes hanging from their leathern girdles. The thick woollen bands round their feet and legs resembled a rude cothurnus, and the sight of these uncouth figures reminded one who had seen the bas-reliefs on Trajan's column at Rome, of the Scythians, the Dacians, the Goths, the Roxolani, who had been the terror of the Empire.[71] Literary cultivation was confined to almost the smallest possible area. Oriental as Russia was in many respects, it was the opposite of oriental in one: women were then, as they are still sometimes said to be in Russia, more cultivated and advanced than men. Many of them could speak half a dozen languages, could play on several instruments, and were familiar with the works of the famous poets of France, Italy, and England. Among the men, on the contrary, outside of a few exceptional families about the court, the vast majority were strangers to all that was passing beyond the limits of their own country. The few who had travelled and were on an intellectual level with their century, were as far removed from the rest of their countrymen as Englishmen are removed from Iroquois.

To paint the court of Catherine in its true colours it has been said that one ought to have the pen of Procopius. It was a hot-bed of corruption, intrigue, jealousy, violence, hatred. One day, surrounded by twenty-seven of her courtiers, Catherine said: "If I were to believe what you all say about one another, there is not one of you who does not richly deserve to have his head cut off." A certain princess was notorious for her inhuman barbarity. One day she discovered that one of her attendants was with child; in a frenzy she pursued the hapless Callisto from chamber to chamber, came up with her, dashed in her skull with a heavy weapon, and finally in a delirium of passion ripped up her body. When two nobles had a quarrel, they fell upon one another then and there like drunken navvies, and Potemkin had an eye gouged out in a court brawl. Such horrors give us a measure of the superior humanity of Versailles, and enable us also in passing to see how duelling could be a sign of a higher civilisation. The reigning passions were love of money and the gratification of a coarse vanity. Friendship, virtue, manners, delicacy, probity, said one witness, are here merely words, void of all meaning. The tone in public affairs was as low as in those of private conduct. I might as well, says Sir G. Macartney, quote Clarke and Tillotson at the divan of Constantinople, as invoke the authority of Puffendorf and Grotius here.

The character of the Empress herself has been more disputed than that of the society in which she was the one imposing personage. She stands in history with Elizabeth of England, with Catherine de' Medici, with Maria Theresa, among the women who have been like great men. Of her place in the record of the creation of that vast empire which begins with Prussia and ends with China, we have not here to speak. The materials for knowing her and judging her are only in our own time becoming accessible.[72] As usual, the mythic elements that surrounded her like a white fog from the northern seas out of which she loomed like a portent, are rapidly disappearing, and are replaced by the outlines of ordinary humanity, with more than the ordinary human measure of firmness, resolution, and energetic grasp of the facts of her position in the world.

We must go from the philosophers to the men of affairs for a true picture. These tell us that she offered an unprecedented mixture of courage and weakness, of knowledge and incompetence, of firmness and irresolution; passing in turn from the most opposite extremes, she presented a thousand diverse surfaces, until at last the observer had to content himself with putting her down as a consummate comedian. She had no ready apprehension. Too refined a pleasantry was thrown away upon her, and there was always a chance of her reversing its drift. No playful reference to the finances, or the military force, or even to the climate of her empire, was ever taken in good part.[73] The political part was the serious part of her nature. Catherine had the literary tastes, but not the literary skill, of Frederick. She is believed, on good evidence, to have written for the use of her grandsons not only an Abridgment of Russian History, but a volume of Moral Tales.[74] The composition of moral tales was entirely independent of morality. Just as Lewis XV. had a long series of Châteauroux, Pompadours, Dubarrys, so Catherine had her Orloffs and Potemkins, and a countless host of obscure and miscellaneous Wassiltchikows, Zavadowskys, Zoriczes, Korsaks. On the serious side, Lewis XIV. was her great pattern and idol. She resented criticism on that renowned memory, as something personal to herself. To her business as sovereign—*mon petit ménage*, as she called the control of her huge formless empire—she devoted as much indefatigable industry as Lewis himself had done in his best days. Notwithstanding all her efforts to improve her country, she was not popular, and never won the affection of her subjects; but she probably cared less for the opinion and sentiment of Russia than for the applause of Europe. Tragedy displeases her, writes the French Minister, and comedy wearies her; she does not like music; her table is without any sort of exquisiteness; in a garden she cares only for roses; her only taste is to build and to drill her court, for the taste that she has for reigning, and for making a great figure in the universe, is really not so much taste as a downright absorbing passion.

Gunning, the English chargé d'affaires, insists that the motive of all her patriotic labours was not benevolence, but an insatiable and unbounded thirst for fame. "If it were not so, we must charge her with an inconsistency amounting to madness, for undertaking so many immense works of public utility, such as the foundation of colleges and academies on a most extensive plan and at an enormous outlay, and then leaving them incomplete, not even finishing the buildings for them." They had served the purpose of making foreigners laud the glory of the Semiramis of the north, and that was enough. The arts and sciences, said the French Minister, have plenty of academies here, but the academies have few subjects and fewer pupils. How could there be pupils in a country where there is nobody who is not either a courtier, a soldier, or a slave? The Princess Sophie of Anhalt, long before she dreamed of becoming the Czarina Catherine II., had been brought up by a French governess, and the tastes that her governess had implanted grew into a passion for French literature, which can only be compared to the same passion in Frederick the Great. Catherine only continued a movement that had already in the reign of her predecessor gone to a considerable length. The social reaction against German political predominance had been accompanied by a leaning to France. French professors in art and literature had been tempted to Moscow, the nobles sent to Paris for their clothes and their furniture, and a French theatre was set up in St. Petersburg, where the nobles were forced to attend the performances under pain of a fine. Absentees and loiterers were hurried to their boxes by horse-patrols.

Catherine was more serious and intelligent than this in her pursuit of French culture. She had begun with the books in which most of the salt of old France was to be found, with Rabelais, Scarron, Montaigne; she cherished Molière and Corneille; and of the writers of the eighteenth century, apart from Voltaire, the author of Gil Blas was her favourite. Such a list tells its own tale of a mind turned to what is masculine, racy, pungent, and thoroughly sapid. "I am a Gauloise of the north," she said, "I only understand the old French; I do not understand the new. I made up my mind to get something out of your gentry, the learned men in *ist*: I have tried them; I made some of them come here; I occasionally wrote to them; they wearied me to death, and never understood me; there was only my good protector, Voltaire. Do you know it was Voltaire who made me the fashion?"[75] This was a confidential revelation, made long after most of the philosophers were dead. We might have penetrated the secret of her friendship for such a man as Diderot, even with less direct evidence than this. It was the vogue of the philosophers, and not their philosophy that made Catherine their friend. They were the great interest of Europe at this time, just as Greek scholars had been its interest in one century, painters in another, great masters of religious controversy in a third. "What makes the great merit of France," said Voltaire, "what makes its unique superiority, is a small number of sublime or delightful men of genius, who cause French to be spoken at Vienna, at Stockholm, and at Moscow. Your ministers, your intendants, your chief secretaries have no part in all this glory." This vogue of the philosophers brought the whole literature of their country into universal repute. In the depths of the Crimea a khan of the Tartars took a delight in having Tartufe and the Bourgeois Gentilhomme read aloud to him.[76]

As soon as Catherine came into power (1762), she at once applied herself to make friends in this powerful region. It was a matter of course that she should begin with the omnipotent pontiff at Ferney. Graceful verses from Voltaire were as indispensable an ornament to a crowned head as a diadem, and Catherine answered with compliments that were perhaps more sincere than his verses. She wonders how she can repay him for a bundle of books that he had sent to her, and at last bethinks herself that nothing will please the lover of mankind so much as the introduction of inoculation into the great empire; so she sends for Dr. Dimsdale from England, and submits to the unfamiliar rite in her own sacred person. Presents of furs are sent to the hermit of the Alps, and he is told how fortunate the imperial messenger counts himself in being despatched to Ferney. What flattered Voltaire more than furs was Catherine's promptitude and exactness in keeping him informed of her military and political movements against Turkey. It made him a centre of European intelligence in more senses than one, and helped him in his lifelong battle to pose, in his letters at least, as the equal of his friend, the King of Prussia. For D'Alembert the Empress professed an admiration only less than she felt for Voltaire. She was eager that he should come to Russia to superintend the instruction of the young Grand Duke. But D'Alembert was too prudent to go to St. Petersburg, as he was too prudent to go to Berlin. Montesquieu had died five years before her accession, but his influence remained. She habitually called the Spirit of Laws the breviary of kings, and when she drew up her Instruction for a new code, she acknowledged how much she had pillaged from Montesquieu. "I hope," she said, "that if from the other world he sees me at work, he will forgive my plagiarism for the sake of the twenty millions of men who will benefit by it." In truth the twenty millions of men got very little benefit indeed by the code. Montesquieu's own method might have taught her that not even absolute power can force the civil system of free labour into a society resting on serfdom. But it is not surprising that Catherine was no wiser than more democratic reformers who had drunk from the French springs. Or probably she had a lower estimate in her own heart of the value of her code for practical purposes than it suited her to disclose to a Parisian philosopher.

Catherine did not forget that, though the French at this time were pre-eminent in the literature of new ideas, yet there were meritorious and useful men in other countries. One of her correspondents was Zimmermann of Hanover, whose essay on Solitude the shelves of no second-hand bookseller's shop is ever without. She had tried hard to bribe Beccaria to leave Florence for St. Petersburg. She succeeded in persuading Euler to return to a capital whither he had been invited many years before by the first Catherine, and where he now remained.

Both Catherine's position and her temperament made the society of her own sex of little use or interest to her. "I don't know whether it is custom or inclination," she wrote, "but somehow I can never carry on conversation except with men. There are only two women in the world with whom I can talk for half an hour at once." Yet among her most intimate correspondents was one woman well known in the Encyclopædic circle. She kept up an active exchange of letters with Madame Geoffrin—that interesting personage, who though belonging to the bourgeoisie, and possessing not a trace of literary genius, yet was respectfully courted not only by Catherine, but by Stanislas, Gustavus, and Joseph II.[77]

On the whole then we must regard Catherine's European correspondence as at least in some measure the result of political calculation. Its purposes, as has been said, were partly those to which in our own times some governments devote a Reptile-fund. There is a letter from the Duchesse de Choiseul to

Madame du Deffand, her intimate friend, and the friend of so many of the literary circle, in which the secret of the relations between Catherine and the men of letters is very plainly told. "All that," she writes—protection of arts and sciences—"is mere luxury and a caprice of fashion in our age. All such pompous jargon is the product of vanity, not of principles or of reflection.... The Empress of Russia has another object in protecting literature; she has had sense enough to feel that she had need of the protection of the men of letters. She has flattered herself that their base praises would cover with an impenetrable veil in the eyes of her contemporaries and of posterity, the crimes with which she has astonished the universe and revolted humanity.... The men of letters, on the other hand, flattered, cajoled, caressed by her, are vain of the protection that they are able to throw over her, and dupes of the coquetries that she lavishes on them. These people who say and believe that they are the instructors of the masters of the world, sink so low as actually to take a pride in the protection that this monster seems in her turn to accord to them, simply because she sits on a throne."[78]

In short, the monarchs of the north understood and used the new forces of the men of letters, whom their own sovereign only recognised to oppress. The contrast between the liberalism of the northern sovereigns, and the obscurantism of the court of France, was never lost from sight. Marmontel's *Belisarius* was condemned by the Sorbonne, and burnt at the foot of the great staircase of the Palace of Justice; in Russia a group of courtiers hastened to translate it, and the Empress herself undertook one chapter of the work. Diderot, who was not allowed to enter the French Academy, was an honoured guest at the Russian palace. For all this Catherine was handsomely repaid. When Diderot visited St. Petersburg, Voltaire congratulated the Empress on seeing that unique man; but Diderot is not, he added, "the only Frenchman who is an enthusiast for your glory. We are lay missionaries who preach the religion of Saint Catherine, and we can boast that our church is tolerably universal."[79] We have already seen Catherine's generosity in buying Diderot's books, and paying him for guarding them as her librarian. "I should never have expected," she says, "that the purchase of a library would bring me so many fine compliments; all the world is bepraising me about M. Diderot's library. But now confess, you to whom humanity is indebted for the strong support that you have given to innocence and virtue in the person of Calas, that it would have been cruel and unjust to separate a student from his books."[80] "Ah, madam," replies the most graceful of all courtiers, "let your imperial majesty forgive me; no, you are not the aurora borealis; you are assuredly the most brilliant star of the north, and never was there one so beneficent as you. Andromeda, Perseus, Callisto are not your equals. All these stars would have left Diderot to die of starvation. He was persecuted in his own country, and your benefactions came thither to seek him! Lewis XIV. was less munificent than your majesty: he rewarded merit in foreign countries, but other people pointed it out to him, whereas you, madame, go in search of it and find it for yourself. Your generous pains to establish freedom of conscience in Poland are a piece of beneficence that the human race must ever celebrate."[81]

When the first Partition of Poland took place seven years later, Catherine found that she had not cultivated the friendship of the French philosophers to no purpose. The action of the dominant party in Poland enabled Catherine to take up a line which touched the French philosophers in their tenderest part. The Polish oligarchy was Catholic, and imposed crushing disabilities on the non-Catholic part of the population. "At the slightest attempt in favour of the non-Catholics," King Stanislas writes to Madame Geoffrin, of the Diet of 1764, "there arose such a cry of fanaticism! The difficulty as to the naturalisation of foreigners, the contempt for *roturiers* and the oppression of them, and Catholic intolerance, are the three strongest national prejudices that I have to fight against in my countrymen; they are at bottom good folk, but their education and ignorance render them excessively stubborn on these three heads."[82] Poland in short reproduced in an aggravated and more barbaric form those evils of Catholic feudalism, in which the philosophers saw the arch-curse of their own country. Catherine took the side of the Dissidents, and figured as the champion of religious toleration. Toleration was chief among the philosophic watchwords, and seeing that great device on her banners, the Encyclopædic party asked no further questions. So, with the significant exception of Rousseau, they all abstained from the cant about the Partition which has so often been heard from European liberals in later days. And so with reference to more questionable transactions of an earlier date, no one could guess from the writings of the philosophers that Catherine had ever been suspected of uniting with her husband in a plot to poison the Empress Elizabeth, and then uniting with her lover in a plot to strangle her husband. "I am quite aware," said Voltaire, "that she is reproached with some bagatelles in the matter of her husband, but these are family affairs with which I cannot possibly think of meddling."

One curious instance of Catherine's sensibility to European opinion is connected with her relations to Diderot. Rulhière, afterwards well known in literature as a historian, began life as secretary to Breteuil, in the French embassy at St. Petersburg. An eyewitness of the tragedy which seated Catherine on the throne, he wrote an account of the events of the revolution of 1762. This piquant narrative, composed by a young man who had read Tacitus and Sallust was circulated in manuscript among the salons of Paris (1768). Diderot had warned Rulhière that it was infinitely dangerous to speak about princes, that not everything that is true is fit to be told, that he could not be too careful of the feelings of a great sovereign who was the admiration and delight of her people. Catherine pretended that a mere secretary of an embassy could know very little about the real springs and motives of the conspiracy. Diderot had described the manuscript as painting her in a commanding and imperious attitude. "There was nothing of that sort," she said; "it was only a question of perishing with a madman, or saving oneself with the multitude who insisted on coming to the rescue." What she saw was that the manuscript must be bought, and she did her best first to buy the author and then, when this failed, to have him locked up in the Bastille. She succeeded in neither. The French government were not sorry to have a scourge to their hands. All that Diderot could procure from Rulhière was a promise that the work should not be published during the Empress's lifetime. It was actually given to the world in 1797. When Diderot was at St. Petersburg, the Empress was importunate to know the contents of the manuscript, which he had seen, but of which she was unable to procure a copy. "As far as you are concerned," he said, "if you attach great importance, Madame, to the decencies and virtues, the worn-out rags of your sex, this work is a satire against you; but if large views and masculine and patriotic designs concern you more, the author depicts you as a great princess." The Empress answered that this only increased her desire to read the book. Diderot himself truly enough described it as a historic romance, containing a mixed tissue of lies and truths that posterity would compare to a chapter of Tacitus.[83] Perhaps the only piece of it that posterity will really value is the page in which the writer describes Catherine's personal appearance; her broad and open brow, her large and slightly double chin, her hair of resplendent chestnut, her eyes of a brilliant brown into which the reflections of the light brought shades of blue. "Pride," he says, "is the true characteristic of her physiognomy. The amiability and grace which are there too only seem to penetrating eyes to be the effect of an extreme desire to please, and these seductive expressions somehow let the design of seducing be rather too clearly seen."

The first Frenchman whom Catherine welcomed in person to her court was Falconet, of whose controversy with the philosopher we shall have a few words to say in a later chapter. This introduction to her was due to Diderot. She had entreated him to find for her a sculptor who would undertake a colossal statue of Peter the Great. Falconet was at the height of his reputation in his own country; in leaving it he seems to have been actuated by no other motive than the desire of an opportunity of erecting an immense monument of his art, though Diderot's eloquence was not wanting. Falconet had the proverbial temperament of artistic genius. Diderot called him the Jean Jacques of sculpture. He had none of the rapacity for money which has distinguished so many artists in their dealings with foreign princes, but he was irritable, turbulent, restless, intractable. He was a chivalrous defender of poorer brethren in art, and he was never a respecter of persons. His feuds with Betzki, the Empress's faithful factotum, were as acrid as the feuds between Voltaire and Maupertuis. Betzki had his own ideas about the statue that was to do honour to the founder of the Empire, and he insisted that the famous equestrian figure of Marcus Aurelius should be the model. Falconet was a man of genius, and he retorted that what might be good for Marcus Aurelius would not be good for Peter the Great. The courtly battle does not concern us, though some of its episodes offer tempting illustrations of biting French malice. Falconet had his own way, and after the labour of many years, a colossus of bronze bestrode a charger rearing on a monstrous mass of unhewn granite. Catherine took the liveliest interest in her artist's work, frequently visiting his studio, and keeping up a busy correspondence. With him, as with the others, she insisted that he should stand on no ceremony, and should not spin out his lines with epithets on which she set not the smallest value. She may be said to have encouraged him to pester her with a host of his obscure countrymen in search of a living, and a little colony of Frenchmen whose names tell us nothing, hung about the Russian capital. Diderot's account of this group of his countrymen at St. Petersburg recalls the picture of a corresponding group at Berlin. "Most of the French who are here rend and hate one another, and bring contempt both on themselves and their nation: 'tis the most unworthy set of rascals that you can imagine."[84]

Diderot reached St. Petersburg towards the end of 1773, and he remained some five months, until the beginning of March, 1774. His impulsive nature was shocked by a chilly welcome from Falconet, but at the palace his reception was most cordial, as his arrival had been eagerly anticipated. The Empress always professed to detest ceremony and state. In a letter to Madame Geoffrin she insists, as we have already seen her doing with Falconet, on being treated to no oriental prostrations, as if she were at the court of Persia. "There is nothing in the world so ugly and detestable as greatness. When I go into a room, you would say that I am the head of Medusa: everybody turns to stone. I constantly scream like an eagle against such ways; yet the more I scream, the less are they at their ease…. If you came into my room, I should say to you,—Madame, be seated; let us chatter at our ease. You would have a chair in front of me; there would be a table between us. *Et puis des bâtons rompus, tant et plus, c'est mon fort.*"

This is an exact description of her real behaviour to Diderot. On most days he was in her society from three in the afternoon until five or six. Etiquette was banished. Diderot's simplicity and vehemence were as conspicuous and as unrestrained at Tsarskoe-selo as at Grandval or the Rue Taranne. If for a moment the torrent of his improvisation was checked by the thought that he was talking to a great lady, Catherine encouraged him to go on. *"Allons,"* she cried, *"entre hommes tout est permis."* The philosopher in the heat of exposition brought his hands down upon the imperial knees with such force and iteration, that Catherine complained that he made them black and blue. She was sometimes glad to seek shelter from such zealous enforcement of truth, behind a strong table. Watchful diplomatists could not doubt that such interviews must have reference to politics. Cathcart, the English ambassador, writes to his government that M. Diderot is still with the Empress at Tsarskoe-selo, "pursuing his political intrigues." And, amazing as it may seem, the French minister and the French ambassador both of them believed that they had found in this dreaming rhapsodical genius a useful diplomatic instrument. "The interviews between Catherine and Diderot follow one another incessantly, and go on from day to day. He told me, and I have reasons for believing that he is speaking the truth, that he has painted the danger of the alliance of Russia with the King of Prussia, and the advantage of an alliance with us. The Empress, far from blaming this freedom, encouraged him by word and gesture. 'You are not fond of that prince,' she said to Diderot. 'No,' he replied, 'he is a great man, but a bad king, and a dealer in counterfeit coin.' 'Oh,' said she laughing, 'I have had my share of his coin.'"

The first Partition of Poland had been finally consummated in the Polish Diet in the autumn of 1773, a few weeks before Diderot's arrival at St. Petersburg. Lewis xv., now drawing very near to his end, and D'Aiguillon, his minister, had some uneasiness at this opening of the great era of territorial revolution, and looked about in a shiftless way for an ally against Russia and Prussia. England sensibly refused to stir. Then France, as we see, was only anxious to detach Catherine from Frederick. All was shiftless and feeble, and the French government can have known little of the Empress, if they thought that Diderot was the man to affect her strong and positive mind. She told Ségur in later years what success Diderot had with her as apolitician.

"I talked much and frequently with him," said Catherine, "but with more curiosity than profit. If I had believed him, everything would have been turned upside down in my kingdom; legislation, administration, finances—all to be turned topsy-turvy to make room for impracticable theories. Yet as I listened more than I talked, any witness who happened to be present, would have taken him for a severe pedagogue, and me for his humble scholar. Probably he thought so himself, for after some time, seeing that none of these great innovations were made which he had recommended, he showed surprise and a haughty kind of dissatisfaction. Then speaking openly, I said to him:

Mr. Diderot, I have listened with the greatest pleasure to all that your brilliant intelligence has inspired; and with all your great principles, which I understand very well, one would make fine books, but very bad business. You forget in all your plans of reform the difference in our positions; you only work on paper, which endures all things; it opposes no obstacle either to your imagination or to your pen. But I, poor Empress as I am, work on the human skin, which is irritable and ticklish to a very different degree. I am persuaded that from this moment he pitied me as a narrow and vulgar spirit. For the future he only talked about literature, and politics vanished from our conversation."[85]

Catherine was mistaken, as we shall see, in supposing that Diderot ever thought her less than the greatest of men. Cathcart, the English ambassador, writes in a sour strain: "All his letters are filled with panegyrics of the Empress, whom he depicts as above humanity. His flatteries of the Grand Duke have been no less gross, but be it said to the young prince's honour, he has shown as much contempt for such flatteries as for the mischievous principles of this pretended philosopher."

Frederick tells D'Alembert that though the Empress overwhelms Diderot with favours, people at St. Petersburg find him tiresome and disputatious, and "talking the same rigmarole over and over again." In her letters to Voltaire, Catherine lets nothing of this be seen. She finds Diderot's imagination inexhaustible, and ranks him among the most extraordinary men that have ever lived; she delights in his conversation, and his visits have given her the most uncommon pleasure. All this was perhaps true enough. Catherine probably rated the philosopher at his true worth as a great talker and a singular and original genius, but this did not prevent her, any more than it need prevent us, from seeing the limits and measure. She was not one of the weaker heads who can never be content without either wholesale enthusiasm or wholesale disparagement.

Diderot had a companion who pleased her better than Diderot himself. Grimm came to St. Petersburg at this time to pay his first visit, and had a great success. "The Empress," wrote Madame Geoffrin to King Stanislas, "lavished all her graces on Grimm. And he has everything that is needed to make him worthy of them. Diderot has neither the fineness of perception, nor the delicate tact that Grimm has, and so he has not had the success of Grimm. Diderot is always in himself, and sees nothing in other people that has not some reference to himself. He is a man of a great deal of understanding, but his nature and turn of mind make him good for nothing, and, more than that, would make him a very dangerous person in any employment. Grimm is quite the contrary."[86]

In truth, as we have said before, Grimm was one of the shrewdest heads in the Encyclopædic party; he had much knowledge, a judgment both solid and acute, and a certain easy fashion of social commerce, free from raptures and full of good sense. Yet he was as devoted and ecstatic in his feelings about the Empress as his more impetuous friend. "Here," he says, "was no conversation of leaps and bounds, in which idleness traverses a whole gallery of ideas that have no connection with one another, and weariness draws you away from one object to skim a dozen others. They were talks in which all was bound together, often by imperceptible threads, but all the more naturally, as not a word of what was to be said had been led up to or prepared beforehand."

Grimm cannot find words to describe her verve, her stream of brilliant sallies, her dashing traits, her eagle's *coup d'œil*. No wonder that he used to quit her presence so electrified as to pass half the night in marching up and down his room, beset and pursued by all the fine and marvellous things that had been said. How much of all this is true, and how much of it is the voice of the bewildered courtier, it might be hard to decide. But the rays of the imperial sun did not so far blind his prudence, as to make him accept a pressing invitation to remain permanently in Catherine's service. When Diderot quitted St. Petersburg, Grimm went to Italy. After an interlude there, he returned to Russia and was at once restored to high favour. When the time came for him to leave her, the Empress gave him a yearly pension of two thousand roubles, or about ten thousand livres, and with a minute considerateness that is said not to be common among the great, she presently ordered that it should be paid in such a form that he should not lose on the exchange between France and Russia. Whether she had a special object in keeping Grimm in good humour, we hardly know. What is certain is that from 1776 until the fall of the French monarchy she kept up a voluminous correspondence with him, and that he acted as an unofficial intermediary between her and the ministers at Versailles. Every day she wrote down what she wished to say to Grimm, and at the end of every three months these daily sheets were made into a bulky packet and despatched to Paris by a special courier, who returned with a similar packet from Grimm. This intercourse went on until the very height of the Revolution, when Grimm at last, in February, 1792, fled from Paris. The Empress's helpful friendship continued to the end of her life (1796).[87]

Diderot arrived at the Hague on his return from Russia in the first week of April (1774), after making a rapid journey of seven hundred leagues in three weeks and a day. D'Alembert had been anxious that Frederick of Prussia should invite Diderot to visit him at Berlin. Frederick had told him that, intrepid reader as he was, he could not endure to read Diderot's books. "There reigns in them a tone of self-sufficiency and an arrogance which revolt the instinct of my freedom. It was not in such a style that Plato, Aristotle, Cicero, Locke, Gassendi, Bayle, and Newton wrote." D'Alembert replied that the king would judge more favourably of the philosopher's person than of his works; that he would find in Diderot, along with much fecundity, imagination, and knowledge, a gentle heat and a great deal of amenity.[88] Frederick, however, did not send the invitation, and Diderot willingly enough went homeward by the northern route by which he had come. He passed Königsberg, where, if he had known it, Kant was then meditating the Critic of Pure Reason. It is hardly probable that Diderot met the famous worthy who was destined to deal so heavy a blow to the Encyclopædic way of thinking, and to leave a name not less illustrious than Frederick or Catherine. A court official was sent in charge of the philosopher. The troubles of posting by the sea-road between Königsberg and Memel had moved him to the composition of some very bad verses on his first journey; and the horror of crossing the Dwina inspired others that were no better on his return. The weather was hard; four carriages were broken in the journey. He expected to be drowned as the ice creaked under his horses' feet at Riga, and he thought that he had broken an arm and a shoulder as he crossed the ferry at Mittau. But all ended well, and he found himself once more under the roof of Prince Galitzin at the Hague. Hence he wrote to his wife and his other friends in Paris, that it must be a great consolation to them to know that he was only separated from them by a journey of four days. That journey was not taken, however, for nearly four months. Diderot had promised the Empress that he would publish a set of the regulations for the various institutions which she had founded for the improvement of her realm. This could only be done, or could best be done, in Holland. His life there was spent as usual in the slavery of proof-sheets, tempered by daily bursts of conversation, rhapsody, discussion, and dreamy contemplation. He made the acquaintance of a certain Björnstähl, a professor of oriental languages at the university of Lund in Sweden, and a few pages in this obscure writer's obscure book contain the only glimpse that we have of the philosopher on his travels.[89] Diderot was as ecstatic in conversation, as we know him to have been in his correspondence, in praise of the august friend whom he had left. The least of his compliments was that she united the charms of Cleopatra to the soul of Cæsar, or sometimes it was, to the soul of Brutus.

"At the Hague," says Björnstähl, "we go about every day with M. Diderot. He has views extending over an incredibly wide field, possesses a vivacity that I cannot describe, is pleasant and friendly in intercourse, and has new and unusual observations to make on every subject.... Who could fail to prize him? He is so bright, so full of instruction, has so many new thoughts and suggestions, that nobody can help admiring him. But willingly as he talks when one goes to him, he shows to little advantage in large companies, and that is why he did not please everybody at St. Petersburg. You will easily see the reason why this incomparable man in such companies, where people talk of fashion, of clothes, of frippery, and all other sorts of triviality, neither gives pleasure to others nor finds pleasure himself." And the friendly Swede rises to the height of generalisation in the quaint maxim, Where an empty head shines, there a thoroughly cultivated man comes too short.

Björnstähl quotes a saying of Voltaire, that Diderot would have been a poet if he had not wished to be a philosopher—a remark that was rather due perhaps to Voltaire's habitual complaisance than to any serious consideration of Diderot's qualities. But if he could not be a poet himself, at least he knew

Pindar and Homer by heart, and at the Hague he never stirred out without a Horace in his pocket. And though no poet, he was full of poetic sentiment. Scheveningen, the little bathing-place a short distance from the Hague, was Diderot's favourite spot. "It was there," he writes, "that I used to see the horizon dark, the sea covered with white haze, the waves rolling and tumbling, and far out the poor fishermen in their great clumsy boats; on the shore a multitude of women frozen with cold or apprehension, trying to warm themselves in the sun. When the work was at an end and the boats had landed, the beach was covered with fish of every kind. These good people have the simplicity, the openness, the filial and fraternal piety of old time. As the men come down from their boats, their wives throw themselves into their arms, they embrace their fathers and their little ones; each loads himself with fish; the son tosses his father a codfish or a salmon, which the old man carries off in triumph to his cottage, thanking heaven that it has given him so industrious and worthy a son. When he has gone indoors, the sight of the fish rejoices the old man's mate; it is quickly cut in pieces, the less lucky neighbours invited, it is speedily eaten, and the room resounds with thanks to God, and cheerful songs."[90]

These scenes, with their sea-background, their animation, their broad strokes of the simple, tender, and real in life, may well have been after Diderot's own heart. He often told me, says Björnstähl, that he never found the hours pass slowly in the company of a peasant, or a cobbler, or any handicraftsman, but that he had many a time found them pass slowly enough in the society of a courtier. "For of the one," he said, "one can always ask about useful and necessary things, but the other is mostly, so far as anything useful is concerned, empty and void."

The characteristics of the European capitals a century ago were believed to be hit off in the saying, that each of them would furnish the proper cure for a given defect of character. The over-elegant were to go to London, savages to Paris, bigots to Berlin, rebels to St. Petersburg, people who were too sincere to Rome, the over-learned to Brussels, and people who were too lively to the Hague. Yet the dulness thus charged against the Hague was not universally admitted. Impartial travellers assigned to the talk of cultivated circles there a rank not below that of similar circles in France and England. Some went even farther, and declared Holland to have a distinct advantage, because people were never embarrassed either by the levity and sparkling wit of France on the one hand, nor by the depressing reserve and taciturnity of England on the other.[91] Yet Holland was fully within the sphere of the great intellectual commonwealth of the west, and was as directly accessible to the literary influences of the time as it had ever been. If Diderot had inquired into the vernacular productions of the country, he would have found that here also the wave of reaction against French conventions, the tide of English simplicity and domestic sentimentalism, had passed into literature. The *Spectator* and *Clarissa Harlowe* inspired the writers of Holland, as they had inspired Diderot himself.[92]

In erudition, it was still what, even after the death of Scaliger, it had remained through the seventeenth century, the most learned state of Europe; and the elder Hemsterhuys, with such pupils as Ruhnken and Valckenaer, kept up as well as he could the scholarly tradition of Gronovius and Grævius. But the eighteenth century was not the century of erudition. Scholarship had given way to speculation.

Among the interesting persons whom Diderot saw at the Hague, the most interesting is the amiable and learned son of the elder Hemsterhuys, himself by the way not Dutch, but the son of a Frenchman. Hemsterhuys had been greatly interested in what he had heard of Diderot's character,[93] though we have no record of the impression that was made by personal acquaintance. If Diderot was playfully styled the French Socrates, the younger Hemsterhuys won from his friends the name of the Dutch Plato. The Hollanders pointed to this meditative figure, to his great attainments in the knowledge of ancient literature and art, to his mellowed philosophising, to his gracious and well-bred style, as a proof that their country was capable of developing both the strength and the sensibility of human nature to their highest point.[94] And he has a place in the history of modern speculation. As we think of him and Diderot discussing, we feel ourselves to be placed at a point that seems to command the diverging streams and eddying currents of the time. In this pair two great tides of thought meet for a moment, and then flow on in their deep appointed courses. For Hemsterhuys, born a Platonist to the core, became a leader of the reaction against the French philosophy of illumination—of sensation, of experience, of the verifiable. He contributed a marked current to the mysticism and pietism which crept over Germany before the French revolution, and to that religious philosophy which became a point of patriotic honour both in Germany and at the Russian Court, after the revolutionary war had seemed to identify the rival philosophy of the Encyclopædists with the victorious fury of the national enemy. Jacobi, a chief of the mystic tribe, had begun the attack on the French with weapons avowedly borrowed from the sentimentalism of Rousseau, but by and by he found in Hemsterhuys more genuinely intellectual arguments for his vindication of feeling and the heart against the Encyclopædist claim for the supremacy of the understanding.

Diderot's hostess at the Hague is a conspicuous figure in the history of this movement. Prince Galitzin had married the daughter of Frederick's field-marshal, Schmettau. Goethe, who saw her (1797) many years after Diderot was dead, describes her as one of those whom one cannot understand without seeing; as a person not rightly judged unless considered not only in connection, but in conflict, with her time. If she was remarkable to Goethe when fifty years had set their mark upon her, she was even more so to the impetuous Diderot in all the flush and intellectual excitement of her youth. It was to the brilliance and versatility of the Princess Galitzin that her husband's house owed its consideration and its charm. "She is very lively," saidDiderot, "very gay, very intelligent; more than young enough, instructed and full of talents; she has read; she knows several languages, as Germans usually do; she plays on the clavecin, and sings like an angel; she is full of expressions that are at once ingenuous and piquant; she is exceedingly kind-hearted."[95] But he could not persuade her to take his philosophy on trust. Diderot is said, by the Princess's biographer, to have been a fervid proselytiser, eager tomake people believe "his poems about eternally revolving atoms, through whose accidental encounter the present ordering of the world was developed." The Princess met his brilliant eloquence with a demand for proof. Her ever-repeated *Why?* and *How?* are said to have shown "the hero of atheism his complete emptiness and weakness."[96] In the long run Diderot was completely routed in favour of the rival philosophy. Hemsterhuys became bound to the Princess by the closest friendship, and his letters to her are as striking an illustration as any in literature of the peculiar devotion and admiration which a clever and sympathetic woman may arouse in philosophic minds of a certain calibre—in a Condillac, a Joubert, a D'Alembert, a Mill. Though Hemsterhuys himself never advanced from a philosophy of religion to the active region of dogmatic professions, his disciple could not find contentment on his austere heights. In the very year of Diderot's death (1784) the Princess Galitzin became a catholic, and her son became not only a catholic but a zealous missionary of the faith in America.

This, however, was not yet. The patriotic Björnstähl was very anxious that Diderot should go to Stockholm, to see for himself that the Holstein blood was as noble in Sweden as it was in Russia. Diderot replied that he would greatly have liked to see on the throne the sovereign (Gustavus III.) who was so nearly coming to pay him a visit on his own fourth storey in Paris. But he confessed that he was growing homesick, and Stockholm must remain unvisited. In September (1774) Diderot set his face homewards. "I shall gain my fireside," he wrote on the eve of his journey, "never to quit it again for the rest of my life. The time that we count by the year has gone, and the time that we must count by the day comes in its stead. The less one's income, the more important to use it well. I have perhaps half a score of years at the bottom of my wallet. In these ten years, fluxions, rheumatisms, and the other members of that troublesome family will take two or three of them; let us try to economise the seven that are left, for the repose and the small happinesses that a man may promise himself on the wrong side of sixty." The guess was a good one. Diderot lived ten years more, and although his own work in the world was done, they were years of great moment both to France and the world. They witnessed the establishment of a republic in the American colonies, and they witnessed the final stage in the decay of the old monarchy in France. Turgot had been made controller-general in the months before Diderot's return, and Turgot's ministry was the last serious experiment in the direction of orderly reform. The crash that followed resounded almost as loudly at St. Petersburg and in Holland as in France itself, and Catherine, in 1792, ordered all the busts of Voltaire that had adorned the saloons and corridors of her palace to be thrust ignominiously down into the cellars.

CHAPTER V.
HELVÉTIUS.

Before proceeding to the closing chapter of Diderot's life, I propose to give a short account of three remarkable books, of all of which he was commonly regarded as the inspirer, which were all certainly the direct and natural work of the Encyclopædic school, and which all play a striking part in the intellectual commotions of the century.

The great attack on the Encyclopædia was made, as we have already seen, in 1758, after the publication of the seventh volume. The same prosecution levelled an angrier blow at Helvétius's famous treatise, *L'Esprit*. It is not too much to say, that of all the proscribed books of the century, that excited the keenest resentment. This arose partly because it came earliest in the literature of attack. It was an audacious surprise. The censor who had allowed it to pass the ordeal of official approval was cashiered, and the author was dismissed from an honorary post in the Queen's household.[97] The indictment described the book as "the code of the most hateful and infamous passions," as a collection into one cover of everything that impiety could imagine, calculated to engender hatred against Christianity and Catholicism. The court condemned the book to be burnt, and, as if to show that the motive was not mere discontent with Helvétius's paradoxes, the same fire consumed Voltaire's fine poem on Natural Religion. Less prejudiced authorities thought nearly as ill of the book, as the lawyers of the parliament and the doctors of the Sorbonne had thought. Rousseau pronounced it detestable, wrote notes in refutation of its principles, and was inspired by hatred of its doctrine to compose some of the most fervid pages in the Savoyard Vicar's glowing Profession of Faith.[98] Even Diderot, though his friendly feeling for the writer and his general leaning to speculative hardihood warped his judgment so far as to make him rank *L'Esprit* along with Montesquieu's *Spirit of Laws*, and Buffon's *Natural History*, among the great books of the century, still perceived and showed that the whole fabric rested on a foundation of paradox, and that, though there might be many truths of detail in the book, very many of its general principles are false.[99] Turgot described it as a book of philosophy without logic, literature without taste, and morality without goodness.[100]

In the same weighty piece of criticism, which contains in two or three pages so much permanently valuable truth, Turgot proceeds:—"When people wish to attack intolerance and injustice, it is essential in the first place to rest upon just ideas, for inquisitors have an interest in being intolerant, and viziers and subviziers have an interest in maintaining all the abuses of the government. As they are the strongest, you only give them a good excuse by sounding the tocsin against them right and left. I hate despotism as much as most people; but it is not by declamations that despotism ought to be attacked. And even in despotism there are degrees; there is a multitude of abuses in despotism, in which the princes themselves have no interest; there are others which they only allow themselves to practise, because public opinion is not yet fixed as to their injustice, and their mischievous consequences. People deserve far better from a nation for attacking these abuses with clearness, with courage, and above all by interesting the sentiment of humanity, than for any amount of eloquent reproach. Where there is no insult, there is seldom any offence.... There is no form of government without certain drawbacks, which the governments themselves would fain have it in their power to remedy, or without abuses which they nearly all intend to repress at least at some future day. We may therefore serve them all by treating questions of the public good in a calm and solid style; not coldly, still less with extravagance, but with that interesting warmth which springs from a profound feeling for justice and love of order."[101]

Of course it is a question whether, even in 1758, a generation before the convulsion, it was possible for the French monarchy spontaneously to work out the long list of indispensable improvements; still, at that date, Turgot might be excused for thinking that the progress which he desired might be attained without the violence to which Helvétius's diatribes so unmistakably pointed. His words, in any case, are worth quoting for their own grave and universal sense, and because they place us exactly at the point of view for regarding *L'Esprit* rightly. He seizes on its political aspect, its assault on government, and the social ordering of the time, as containing the book's real drift. In this, as in the rest of the destructive literature of the first sixty years of the century, the church was no doubt that part of the social foundations against which the assault was most direct and most vindictive, and it was the church, in the case of Helvétius's book, that first took alarm. Indeed, we may say that, from the very nature of things, in whatever direction the revolutionary host moved, they were sure to find themselves confronted by the church. It lay across the track of light at every point. Voltaire pierced its dogma. Rousseau shamed its irreligious temper. Diderot brought into relief the vicious absoluteness of its philosophy. Then came Helvétius and Holbach, not merely with criticism, but with substitutes. Holbach brought a new dogma of the universe, matter and motion, and fortuitous shapes. Helvétius brought a theory of human character, and a new analysis of morals—interest the basis of justice, pleasure the true interpretation of interest, and character the creature of education and laws.

To press such positions as these, was to recast the whole body of opinions on which society rested. As the church was the organ of the old opinions, Helvétius's book was instantly seized by the ecclesiastical authorities in accordance with a perfectly right instinct, and was made the occasion for the first violent raid upon a wholesale scale. When, however, we look beyond the smoke of the ecclesiastical battle, and weigh *L'Esprit* itself on its own merits, we see quite plainly that Helvétius was thinking less of the theological disputes of the day than of bringing the philosophy of sensation, the philosophy of Locke and Condillac, into the political field, and of deriving from it new standards and new forces for social reconstruction. And in spite of its shallowness and paradoxes, his book did contain the one principle on which, if it had been generally accepted, the inevitable transition might have taken place without a Reign of Terror.

It was commonly said, by his enemies and by his alarmed friends, that vanity and a restless overweening desire for notoriety was the inspiring motive of Helvétius. He came from a German stock. His great-grandfather settled in Holland, where he cured his patients by cunning elixirs, by the powder of ground stag's horn, and the subtle virtues of crocodiles' teeth. His grandfather went to push his fortunes in Paris, where he persuaded the public to accept the healing properties of ipecacuanha, and Lewis xiv. (1689) gave him a short patent for that drug.[102] The medical tradition of the family was maintained in a third generation, for Helvétius's father was one of the physicians of the Queen, and on one occasion performed the doubtful service to humanity of saving the life of Lewis xv. Helvétius, who was born in 1715, turned aside from the calling of his ancestors, and by means of the favour which his father enjoyed at court, obtained a position as farmer-general. This at once made him a wealthy man, but wealth was not enough to satisfy him without fame. He made attempts in various directions, in each case following the current of popularity for the hour. Maupertuis was the hero of a day, and Helvétius accordingly applied himself to become a geometer. Voltaire's brilliant success brought poetry into fashion, and so Helvétius wrote half a dozen long cantos on Happiness. Montesquieu caught and held the ear of the town by *The Spirit of Laws* (1748), and Helvétius was acute enough to perceive that speculation upon society would be the great durable interest of his time.[103] He at once set to work, and this time he set to work without hurry. In 1751 he threw up his place as farmer-general, and with it an income of between two or three thousand pounds a year,[104] and he then devoted himself for the next seven years to the concoction of a work that was designed to bring him immortal glory. "Helvétius sweated a long time to write a single chapter," if we may believe one of his intimates. He would compose and recompose a passage a score of times. More facile writers looked at him with amazement in his country-house, ruminating for whole mornings on a single page, and pacing his room for hours to kindle his ideas, or to strike out some curious form of expression.[105] The circle of his friends in Paris amused themselves in watching his attempts to force the conversation into the channel of the question that happened to occupy him for the moment. They gave him the satisfaction of discussion, and then they drew him to express his own views. "Then," says Marmontel, "he threw himself into the subject with warmth—as simple, as natural, as sincere as he is systematic and sophistic in his works. Nothing is less like the ingenuousness of his character and ordinary life, than the artificial and premeditated simplicity of his works. Helvétius was the very opposite in his character of what he professes to believe; he was liberal, generous, unostentatious, and benevolent."[106]

As it happens, there is a very different picture in one of Diderot's writings. While Diderot was on a journey he fell in with a lady who knew Helvétius's country. "She told us that the philosopher at his country seat was the unhappiest of men. He is surrounded by peasants and by neighbours who hate him. They break the windows of his mansion; they ravage his property at night; they cut his trees, and break down his fences. He dares not sally out to shoot a rabbit without an escort. You will ask me why all this? It comes of an unbridled jealousy about his game. His predecessors kept the estate in order with a couple of men and a couple of guns. Helvétius has four-and-twenty, and yet he cannot guard his property. The men have a small premium for every poacher that they catch, and they resort to every possible vexation in order to multiply their sorry profit. They are, for that matter, no better than so many poachers who draw wages. The border of his woods was peopled with the unfortunate wretches who had been driven from their homes into pitiful hovels. It is these repeated acts of tyranny that have raised up against him enemies of every kind, and all the more insolent, as Madame N. said, for having found out that the good philosopher is a trifle pusillanimous. I cannot see what he has gained by such a way of managing his property; he is alone on it, he is hated, he is in a constant state of fright. Ah, how much wiser our good Madame Geoffrin, when she said of a trial that tormented her: 'Finish my case. They want my money? I have some; give them money. And what can I do better with money than buy tranquillity with it?' In Helvétius's place, I should have said: 'They kill a few hares, or a few rabbits; let them kill. The poor creatures have no shelter save my woods, let them remain there.'"[107]

On the other hand, there are well-attested stories of Helvétius's munificence. There is one remarkable testimony to his wide renown for good-nature. After the younger Pretender had been driven out of France, he had special reasons on some occasion for visiting Paris. He wrote to Helvétius that he had heard of him as a man of the greatest probity and honour in France, and that to Helvétius, therefore, he would trust himself. Helvétius did not refuse the dangerous compliment, and he concealed the prince for two years in his house.[108] He was as benevolent where his vanity was less pleasantly flattered. More than one man of letters, including Marivaux, was indebted to him for a yearly pension, and his house was as open to the philosophic tribe as Holbach's. Morellet has told us that the conversation was not so good and so consecutive as it was at the Baron's. "The mistress of the house, drawing to her side the people who pleased her best, and not choosing the worst of the company, rather broke the party up. She was no fonder of philosophy than Madame Holbach was fond of it; but the latter, by remaining in a corner without saying a word, or else chatting in a low voice with her friends, was in nobody's way; whereas Madame Helvétius, with her beauty, her originality, and her piquant turn of nature, threw out anything like philosophic discussion. Helvétius had not the art of sustaining or animating it. He used to take one of us to a window, open some question that he had in hand, and try to draw out either some argument for his own view or some objection to it, for he was always composing his book in society. Or more frequently still, he would go out shortly after dinner to the opera or elsewhere, leaving his wife to do the honours of the house."[109] In spite of all this, Helvétius's social popularity became considerable. This, however, followed his attainment of celebrity, for when *L'Esprit* was published, Diderot scarcely met him twice in a year, and D'Alembert's acquaintance with him was of the slightest. And there must, we should suppose, have been some difficulty in cordially admitting even a penitent member of the abhorred class of farmers-general among the esoteric group of the philosophic opposition. There was much point in Turgot's contemptuous question, why he should be thankful to a declaimer like Helvétius, who showers vehement insults and biting sarcasms on governments in general, and then makes it his business to send to Frederick the Great a whole colony of revenue clerks. It was the stringent proceedings against his book that brought to Helvétius both vogue with the public and sympathy from the Encyclopædic circle.

To us it is interesting to know that Helvétius had a great admiration for England. Holbach, as we have already seen (above, vol. i. p. 270), did not share this, and he explained his friend's enthusiasm by the assumption that what Helvétius really saw in our free land was the persecution that his book had drawn upon him in France.[110] Horace Walpole, in one of his letters, announced to Sir Horace Mann that Helvétius was coming to England, bringing two Miss Helvétiuses with fifty thousand pounds a-piece, to bestow on two immaculate members of our most august and incorruptible senate, if he could find two in this virtuous age who would condescend to accept his money. "Well," he adds, in a spirit of sensible protest against these unprofitable international comparisons, "we may be dupes to French follies, but they are ten times greater fools to be the dupes of our virtues."[111] Gibbon met Helvétius (1763), and found him a sensible man, an agreeable companion, and the worthiest creature in the world, besides the merits of having a pretty wife and a hundred thousand livres a year. Warburton was invited to dine with him at Lord Mansfield's, but he could not bring himself to countenance a professed patron of atheism, a rascal, and a scoundrel.[112]

Let us turn to the book which had the honour of bringing all this censure upon its author. Whether vanity was or was not Helvétius's motive, the vanity of an author has never accounted for the interest of his public, and we may be sure that neither those who approved, nor those who abhorred, would have been so deeply and so universally stirred, unless they had felt that he touched great questions at the very quick. And, first, let a word be said as to the form of his book.

Grimm was certainly right in saying that a man must be without taste or sense to find either the morality or the colouring of Diderot in *L'Esprit*. It is tolerably clear that Helvétius had the example of Fontenelle before his eyes— Fontenelle, who had taught astronomical systems in the forms of elegant literature, and of whom it was said that *il nous enjôle à la vérité*, he coaxes us to the truth. *L'Esprit* is perhaps the most readable book upon morals that ever was written, for persons who do not care that what they read shall be scientifically true. Hume, who, by the way, had been invited by Helvétius to translate the book into English, wrote to Adam Smith that it was worth reading, not for its philosophy, which he did not highly value, but for its agreeable composition.[113] Helvétius intended that it should be this, and accordingly he stuffed it with stories and anecdotes. Many of them are very poor, many are inapposite, some are not very decent, others are spoiled in telling, but still stories and anecdotes they remain, and they carry a light-minded reader more or less easily from page to page and chapter to chapter. But an ingenuous student of ethics who should take Helvétius seriously, could hardly be reconciled by lively anecdotes to what, in his particular formula, seems a most depressing doctrine. Madame Roland read the celebrated book in her romantic girlhood, and her impression may be taken for that of most generous natures. "Helvétius made me wretched: he annihilated the most ravishing illusions; he showed me everywhere repulsive self-interest. Yet what sagacity!" she continues. "I persuaded myself that Helvétius painted men such as they had become in the corruption of society: I judged that it was good to feed one's self on such an author, in order to be able to frequent what is called the world, without being its dupe. But I took good care not to adopt his principles, merely in order to know man properly so-called. I felt myself capable of a generosity which he never recognises. With what delight I confronted his theories with the great traits in history, and the virtues of the heroes that history has immortalised."[114]

We have ventured to say that *L'Esprit* contained the one principle capable of supplying such a system of thinking about society as would have taught the French of that time in what direction to look for reforms. There is probably no instance in literature of a writer coming so close to a decisive body of salutary truth, and then losing himself in the by-ways of the most repulsive paradox that a perverse ingenuity could devise. We are able to measure how grievous was this miscarriage by reflecting that the same instrument which Helvétius actually held in his hand, but did not know how to use, was taken from him by a man of genius in another country, and made to produce reforms that saved England from a convulsion. Nobody pretends that Helvétius discovered Utilitarianism. Hume's name, for instance, occurs too often in his pages for even the author himself to have dreamed that his principle of utility was a new invention of his own. It would, as Mill has said, imply ignorance of the history of philosophy and of general literature not to be aware that in all ages of philosophy one of its schools has been utilitarian, not only from the time of Epicurus, but long before. But what is certain, and what would of itself be enough to entitle Helvétius to consideration, is that from Helvétius the idea of general utility as the foundation of morality was derived by that strong and powerful English thinker, who made utilitarianism the great reforming force of legislation and the foundation of jurisprudence. Bentham himself distinctly avowed the source of his inspiration.[115]

A fatal discredit fastened upon a book which yet had in it so much of the root of the matter, from the unfortunate circumstance that Helvétius tacked the principle of utility on to the very crudest farrago to be found in the literature of psychology. What happened, then, was that Rousseau swept into the field with a hollow version of a philosophy of reform, so eloquently, loftily, and powerfully enforced as to carry all before it. The democracy of sentimentalism took the place that ought to have been filled in the literature of revolutionary preparation by the democracy of utility. Rousseau's fiction of the Sovereignty of the People was an arbitrary and intrinsically sterile rendering of the real truth in Helvétius's ill-starred book.

To establish the proper dependence of laws upon one another, says Helvétius, "it is indispensable to be able to refer them all to a single principle, such as that of *the Utility of the Public, that is to say, of the greatest number of men submitted to the same form of government: a principle of which no one realises the whole extent and fertility; a principle that contains all Morality and Legislation.*"[116]

A man is just when all his actions tend to the public good. "To be virtuous, it is necessary to unite nobleness of soul with an enlightened understanding. Whoever combines these gifts conducts himself by *the compass of public utility*. This utility is the principle of all human virtues, and the foundation of all legislations. It ought to inspire the legislator, and to force the nations to submit to his laws."[117]

The principle of public utility is invariable, though it is pliable in its application to all the different positions in which, in their succession, a nation may find itself.[118]

The public interest is that of the greatest number, and this is the foundation on which the principles of sound morality ought invariably to rest. [119]

These extracts, and extracts in the same sense might easily be multiplied, show us the basis on which Helvétius believed himself to be building. Why did Bentham raise upon it a fabric of such value to mankind, while Helvétius covered it with useless paradox? The answer is that Bentham approached the subject from the side of a practical lawyer, and proceeded to map out the motives and the actions of men in a systematic and objective classification, to which the principle of utility gave him the key. Helvétius, on the other hand, instead of working out the principle, that actions are good or bad according as they do or do not serve the public interest of the greatest number, contented himself with reiterating in as many ways as possible the proposition that self-love fixes our measure of virtue. The next thing to do, after settling utility as the standard of virtue, and defining interest as a term applied to whatever can procure us pleasures and deliver us from pains,[120] was clearly to do what Bentham did,—to marshal pleasures and pains in logical array. Instead of this, Helvétius, starting from the proposition that "to judge is to feel," launched out into a complete theory of human character, which laboured under at least two fatal defects. First, it had no root in a contemplation of the march of collective humanity, and second, it considered only the purely egoistic impulses, to the exclusion of the opposite half of human tendencies. Apart from these radical deficiencies, Helvétius fell headlong into a fallacy which has been common enough among the assailants of the principle of utility; namely, of confounding the standard of conduct with its motive, and insisting that because utility is the test of virtue, therefore the prospect of self-gratification is the only inducement that makes men prefer virtue to vice.

This was what Madame du Deffand called telling everybody's secret. We approve conduct in proportion as it conduces to our interest. Friendship, *esprit-de-corps*, patriotism, humanity, are names for qualities that we prize more or less highly in proportion as they come more or less close to our own happiness; and the scale of our preferences is in the inverse ratio of the number of those who benefit by the given act. If it affects the whole of humanity or of our country, our approval is less warmly stirred than if it were an act specially devoted to our own exclusive advantage. If you want therefore to reach men, and to shape their conduct for the public good, you must affect them through their pleasures and pains.

To this position, which roused a universal indignation that amazed the author, there is no doubt a true side. It is worth remembering, for instance, that all penal legislation, in so far as deterrent and not merely vindictive, assumes in all who come whether actually or potentially within its sphere, the very doctrine that covered Helvétius with odium. And there is more to be said than this. As M. Charles Comte has expressed it: If the strength with which we resent injury were not in the ratio of the personal risk that we run, we should hardly have the means of self-preservation; and if the acts which injure the whole of humanity gave us pain equal to that of acts that injure us directly, we should be of all beings the most miserable, for we should be incessantly tormented by conduct that we should be powerless to turn aside. And again, if the benefits of which we are personally the object did not inspire in us a more lively gratitude than those which we spread over all mankind, we should probably experience few preferences, and extend few preferences to others, and in that case egoism would grow to its most overwhelming proportions. [121]

This aspect of Helvétius's doctrine, however, is one of those truths which is only valid when taken in connection with a whole group of different truths, and it was exactly that way of asserting a position, in itself neither indefensible nor unmeaning, which left the position open to irresistible attack. Helvétius's errors had various roots, and may be set forth in as many ways. The most general account of it is that even if he had insisted on making Self-love the strongest ingredient in our judgment of conduct, he ought at least to have given some place to Sympathy. For, though it is possible to contend that sympathy is only an indirect kind of self-love, or a shadow cast by self-love, still it is self-love so transformed as to imply a wholly different set of convictions, and to require a different name.

L'Esprit is one of the most striking instances in literature of the importance of care in choosing the right way of presenting a theory to the world. It seems as if Helvétius had taken pains to surround his doctrine with everything that was most likely to warn men away from it. For example, he begins a chapter of cardinal importance with the proposition that personal interest is the only motive that could impel a man to generous actions. "It is as impossible for him to love good for good's sake as evil for the sake of evil." The rest of the chapter consists of illustrations of this; and what does the reader suppose that they are? The first is Brutus, of all the people in the world. He sacrificed his son for the salvation of Rome, because his passion for his country was stronger than his passion as a father; and this passion for his country, "enlightening him as to the public interest," made him see what a service his rigorous example would be to the state. The other instances of the chapter point the same moral, that true virtue consists in suppressing inducements to gratify domestic or friendly feeling, when that gratification is hostile to the common weal.[122]

It may be true that the ultimate step in a strictly logical analysis reduces the devotion of the hero or the martyr to a deliberate preference for the course least painful to himself, because religion or patriotism or inborn magnanimity have made self-sacrifice the least painful course to him. But to call this heroic mood by the name of self-love, is to single out what is absolutely the most unimportant element in the transaction, and to insist on thrusting it under the onlooker's eye as the vital part of the matter. And it involves the most perverse kind of distortion. For the whole issue and difference between the virtuous man and the vicious man turns, not at all upon the fact that each behaves in the way that habit has made least painful to him, but upon the fact that habit has made selfishness painful to the first, and self-sacrifice painful to the second; that self-love has become in the first case transformed into an overwhelming interest in the good of others, and in the second not so. Was there ever a greater perversity than to talk of self-interest, when you mean beneficence, or than to insist that because beneficence has become bound up with a man's self-love, therefore beneficence *is* nothing but self-love in disguise? As if the fruit or the flower not only depends on a root as one of the conditions among others of its development, but is itself actually the root! Apart from the error in logic, what an error in rhetoric, to single out the formula best calculated to fill a doctrine with odious associations, and then to make that formula the most prominent feature in the exposition. Without any gain in clearness or definiteness or firmness, the reader is deliberately misled towards a form that is exactly the opposite of that which Helvétius desired him to accept.

In other ways Helvétius takes trouble to wound the generous sensibility and affront the sense of his public. Nothing can be at once more scandalously cynical and more crude than a passage intended to show that, if we examine the conduct of women of disorderly life from the political point of view, they are in some respects extremely useful to the public. That desire to please, which makes such a woman go to the draper, the milliner, and the dressmaker, draws an infinite number of workmen from indigence. The virtuous women, by giving alms to mendicants and criminals, are far less wisely advised by their religious directors than the other women by their desire to please; the latter nourish useful citizens, while the former, who at the best are useless, are often even downright enemies to the nation.[123] All this is only a wordy transcript of Mandeville's coarse sentences about "the sensual courtier that sets no limits to his luxury, and the fickle strumpet that invents new fashions every week." We cannot wonder that all people who were capable either of generous feeling or comprehensive thinking turned aside even from truth, when it was mixed in this amalgam of destructive sophistry and cynical illustration.

We can believe how the magnanimous youth of Madame Roland and others was discouraged by pages sown with mean anecdote. Helvétius tells us, with genuine zest, of Parmenio saying to Philotas at the court of Alexander the Great—"My son, make thyself small before Alexander; contrive for him now and again the pleasure of setting thee right; and remember that it is only to thy seeming inferiority that thou wilt owe his friendship." The King of Portugal charged a certain courtier to draw up a despatch on an affair with which he had himself dealt. Comparing the two despatches, the King found the courtier's much the better of the two: the courtier makes a profound reverence, and hastens to take leave of his friends: "*It is all over with me*," he said, "*the King has found out that I have more brains than he has.*"[124] Only mediocrity succeeds in the world. "Sir," said a father to his son, "you are getting on in the world, and you suppose you must be a person of great merit. To lower your pride, know to what qualities you owe this success: you were born without vices, without virtues, without character; your knowledge is scanty, your intelligence is narrow. Ah, what claims you have, my son, to the goodwill of the world."[125]

It lies beyond the limits of our task to enter into a discussion of Helvétius's transgressions in the region of speculative ethics, from any dogmatic point of view. Their nature is tolerably clear. Helvétius looked at man individually, as if each of us came into the world naked of all antecedent predispositions, and independent of the medium around us. Next, he did not see that virtue, justice, and the other great words of moral science denote qualities that are directly related to the fundamental constitution of human character. As Diderot said,[126] he never perceived it to be possible to find in our natural requirements, in our existence, in our organisation, in our sensibility, a fixed base for the idea of what is just and unjust, virtuous and vicious. He clung to the facts that showed the thousand different shapes in which justice and injustice clothed themselves; but he closed his eyes on the nature of man, in which he would have recognised their character and origin. Again, although his book was expressly written to show that only good laws can form virtuous men, and that all the art of the legislator consists in forcing men, through the sentiment of self-love, to be just to one another,[127] yet

Helvétius does not perceive the difficulty of assuming in the moralising legislator a suppression of self-love which he will not concede to the rest of mankind. The crucial problem of political constitutions is to counteract the selfishness of a governing class. Helvétius vaulted over this difficulty by imputing to a legislator that very quality of disinterestedness whose absence in the bulk of the human race he made the fulcrum of his whole moral system. [128]

Into this field of criticism it is not, I repeat, our present business minutely to enter. The only question for us, attempting to study the history of opinion, is what Helvétius meant by his paradoxes, and how they came into his mind. No serious writer, least of all a Frenchman in the eighteenth century, ever sets out with anything but such an intention for good, as is capable of respectable expression. And we ask ourselves what good end Helvétius proposed to himself. Of what was he thinking when he perpetrated so singular a misconstruction of his own meaning as that inversion of beneficence into self-love of which we have spoken? We can only explain it in one way. In saying that it is impossible to love good for good's sake, Helvétius was thinking of the theologians. Their doctrine that man is predisposed to love evil for evil's sake, removes conduct from the sphere of rational motive, as evinced in the ordinary course of human experience. Helvétius met this by contending that both in good and bad conduct men are influenced by their interest and not by mystic and innate predisposition either to good or to evil. He sought to bring morals and human conduct out of the region of arbitrary and superstitious assumption, into the sphere of observation. He thought he was pursuing a scientific, as opposed to a theological spirit, by placing interest at the foundation of conduct, both as matter of fact and of what ought to be the fact, instead of placing there the love of God, or the action of grace, or the authority of the Church.

We may even say that Helvétius shows a positive side, which is wanting in the more imposing names of the century. Here, for instance, is a passage which in spite of its inadequateness of expression, contains an unmistakable germ of true historical appreciation:—"However stupid we may suppose the Peoples to be, it is certain that, being enlightened by their interests, it was not without motives that they adopted the customs that we find established among some of them. The bizarre nature of these customs is connected, then, with the diversity of interests among these Peoples. In fact, if they have always understood, in a confused way, by the name of virtue the desire of public happiness; if they have in consequence given the name of good to actions that are useful to the country; and if the idea of utility has always been privately associated with the idea of virtue, then we may be sure that their most ridiculous, and even their most cruel, customs have always had for their foundation the real or seeming utility of the public good."[129]

If we contrast this with the universal fashion among Helvétius's friends, of denouncing the greater portion of the past history of the race, we cannot but see that, crude as is the language of such a passage, it contains the all-important doctrine which Voltaire, Rousseau, and Diderot alike ignored, that the phenomena of the conduct of mankind, even in its most barbarous phases, are capable of an intelligible explanation, in terms of motive that shall be related to their intellectual forms, exactly as the motives of the most polished society are related to the intellectual forms of such a society. There are not many passages in all the scores of volumes written in France in the eighteenth century on the origin of society where there is such an approach as this to the modern view.

Helvétius's position was that of a man searching for a new basis for morals. It was hardly possible for any one in that century to look to religion for such a base, and least of all was it possible to Helvétius. "It is fanaticism," he says in an elaborately wrought passage, "that puts arms into the hands of Christian princes; it orders Catholics to massacre heretics; it brings out upon the earth again those tortures that were invented by such monsters as Phalaris, as Busiris, as Nero; in Spain it piles and lights up the fires of the Inquisition, while the pious Spaniards leave their ports and sail across distant seas, to plant the Cross and spread desolation in America. Turn your eyes to north or south, to east or west; on every side you see the consecrated knife of Religion raised against the breasts of women, of children, of old men, and the earth all smoking with the blood of victims immolated to false gods or to the Supreme Being, and presenting one vast, sickening, horrible charnel-house of intolerance. Now what virtuous man, what Christian, if his tender soul is filled with the divine unction that exhales from the maxims of the Gospel, if he is sensible of the cries of the unhappy and the outcast, and has sometimes wiped away their tears—what man could fail at such a sight to be touched with compassion for humanity, and would not use all his endeavour to found probity, not on principles so worthy of respect as those of religion, but on principles less easily abused, such as those of personal interest would be?"[130]

This, then, is the point best worth seizing in a criticism of Helvétius. The direction of morality by religion had proved a failure. Helvétius, as the organ of reaction against asceticism and against mysticism, appealed to positive experience, and to men's innate tendency to seek what is pleasurable and to avoid what is painful. The scientific imperfection of his attempt is plain; but that, at any rate, is what the attempt signified in his own mind.

The same feeling for social reform inspired the second great paradox of

L'Esprit. This is to the effect that of all the sources of intellectual difference between one man and another, organisation is the least influential. Intellectual differences are due to diversity of circumstance and to variety in education. It is not felicity of organisation that makes a great man. There is nobody, in whom passion, interest, education, and favourable chance, could not have surmounted all the obstacles of an unpromising nature; and there is no great man who, in the absence of passion, interest, education, and certain chances, would not have been a blockhead, in spite of his happier organisation. It is only in the moral region that we ought to seek the true cause of inequality of intellect. Genius is no singular gift of nature. Genius is common; it is only the circumstances proper to develop it that are rare. The man of genius is simply the product of the circumstances in which he is placed. The inequality in intelligence (*esprit*) that we observe among men, depends on the government under which they live, on the times in which their destiny has fallen, on the education that they have received, on the strength of their desire to achieve distinction, and finally on the greatness and fecundity of the ideas which they happen to make the object of their meditations.[131]

Here again it would be easy to show how many qualifications are needed to rectify this egregious overstatement of propositions that in themselves contain the germ of a wholesome doctrine. Diderot pointed out some of the principal causes of Helvétius's errors, summing them up thus: "The whole of this third discourse seems to imply a false calculation, into which the author has failed to introduce all the elements that have a right to be there, and to estimate the elements that are there at their right value. He has not seen the insurmountable barrier that separates a man destined by nature for a given function, from a man who only brings to that function industry, interest, and attention."[132] In a work published after his death (1774), and entitled *De l'Homme*, Helvétius re-stated at greater length, and with a variety of new illustrations, this exaggerated position. Diderot wrote an elaborate series of minute notes in refutation of it, taking each chapter point by point, and his notes are full of acute and vigorous criticism.[133] Every reader will perceive the kind of answers to which the proposition that character is independent of organisation lies open. Yet here, as in his paradox about self-love, Helvétius was looking, and looking, moreover, in the right direction, for a rational principle of moral judgment, moral education, and moral improvement. Of the two propositions, though equally erroneous in theory, it was certainly less mischievous in practice to pronounce education and institutions to be stronger than original predisposition than to pronounce organisation to be stronger than education and institutions. It was all-important at that moment in France to draw people's attention to the influence of institutions on character; to do that was both to give one of the best reasons for a reform in French institutions, and also to point to the spirit in which such a reform should be undertaken. If Helvétius had contented himself with saying that, whatever may be the force of organisation in exceptional natures, yet in persons of average organisation these predispositions are capable of being indefinitely modified by education, by laws, and by institutions, then he would not only have said what could not be disproved, but he would have said as much as his own object required. William Godwin drew one of the most important chapters of his once famous treatise on *Political Justice* from Helvétius, but what Helvétius exaggerated into a paradox which nobody in his senses could seriously accept, Godwin expressed as a rational half-truth, without which no reformer in education or institutions could fairly think it worth while to set to work.[134]

The reader of Benjamin Constant's *Adolphe*, that sombre little study of a miserable passion, may sometimes be reminded of Helvétius. It begins with the dry surprise of youth at the opening world, for we need time, he says, to accustom ourselves to the human race, such as affectation, vanity, cowardice, interest have made it. Then we soon learn only to be surprised at our old surprise; we find ourselves very well off in our new conditions, just as we come to breathe freely in a crowded theatre, though on entering it we were almost stifled. Yet the author of this parching sketch of the distractions of an egoism that just fell short of being complete, suddenly flashes on us the unexpected but penetrating and radiant moral, *La grande question dans la vie, c'est la douleur que l'on cause*—the great question in life is the pain that we strike into the lives of others. We are not seldom refreshed, when in the midst of Helvétius's narrowest grooves, by some similar breath from the wider air. Among the host of sayings, true, false, trivial, profound, which are scattered over the pages of Helvétius, is one subtle and far-reaching sentence, which made a strong impression upon Bentham. "*In order to love mankind,*" he writes, "*we must expect little from them.*" This might, on the lips of a cynic, serve for a formula of that kind of misanthropy which is not more unamiable than it is unscientific. But in the mouth of Helvétius it was a plea for considerateness, for indulgence, and, above all, it was meant for an inducement to patience and sustained endeavour in all dealings with masses of men in society. "Every man," he says, "so long as his passions do not obscure his reason, will always be the more indulgent in proportion as he is enlightened." He knows that men are what they must be, that all hatred against them is unjust, that a fool produces follies just as a wild shrub produces sour berries, that to insult him is to reproach the oak for bearing acorns instead of olives.[135] All this is as wise and humane as words can be so, and it really represents the aim and temper of Helvétius's teaching. Unfortunately for him and for his generation, his grasp was feeble and unsteady. He had not the gift of accurate thinking, and his book is in consequence that which, of all the books of the eighteenth century, unites most of wholesome truth with most of repellent error.

CHAPTER VI.
HOLBACH'S SYSTEM OF NATURE.

The *System of Nature* was published in 1770, eight years before the death of Voltaire and of Rousseau, and it gathered up all the scattered explosives of the criticism of the century into one thundering engine of revolt and destruction. It professed to be the posthumous work of Mirabaud, who had been secretary to the Academy. This was one of the common literary frauds of the time. Its real author was Holbach. It is too systematic and coherently compacted to be the design of more than one man, and it is too systematic also for that one man to have been Diderot, as has been so often assumed. At the same time there are good reasons for believing that not only much of its thought, but some of the pages, were the direct work of Diderot. The latest editor of the heedless philosopher has certainly done right in placing among his miscellanea the declamatory apostrophe which sums up the teachings of this remorseless book. The rumour imputing the authorship to Diderot was so common, and Diderot himself was so disquieted by it, that he actually hastened away from Paris to his native Langres and to the Baths of Bourbonne, in order to be ready to cross the frontier at the first hint of a warrant being out against him.[136] Diderot has recorded his admiration of his friend's work. "I am disgusted," he said, "with the modern fashion of mixing up incredulity and superstition. What I like is a philosophy that is clear, definite, and frank, such as you have in the *System of Nature*. The author is not an atheist in one page, and a deist in another. His philosophy is all of one piece."[137]

No book has ever produced a more widespread shock. Everybody insisted on reading it, and almost everybody was terrified. It suddenly revealed to men, like the blaze of lightning to one faring through darkness, the formidable shapes, the unfamiliar sky, the sinister landscape, into which the wanderings of the last fifty years had brought them unsuspecting. They had had half a century of such sharp intellectual delight as had not been known throughout any great society in Europe since the death of Michael Angelo, and had perhaps north of the Alps never been known at all. And now it seemed to many of them, as they turned over the pages of Holbach's book, as if they stood face to face with the devil of the mediæval legend, come to claim their souls. Satire of Job and David, banter about Joshua's massacres and Solomon's concubines, invective against blind pastors of blinder flocks, zeal to place Newton on the throne of Descartes and Locke upon the pedestal of Malebranche, wishes that the last Jansenist might be strangled in the bowels of the last Jesuit—all this had given zest and savour to life. In the midst of their high feast, Holbach pointed to the finger of their own divinity, Reason, writing on the wall the appalling judgments that there is no God; that the universe is only matter in spontaneous movement; and, most grievous word of all, that what men call their souls die with the death of the body, as music dies when the strings are broken.

Galiani, the witty Neapolitan, who had so many good friends in the philosophic circle, anticipated the well-known phrase of a writer of our own day. "The author of the *System of Nature*," he said, "is the Abbé Terrai of metaphysics: he makes deductions, suspensions of payment, and causes the very Bankruptcy of knowledge, of pleasure, and of the human mind. But you will tell me that, after all, there were too many rotten securities; that the account was too heavily overdrawn; that there was too much worthless paper on the market. That is true, too, and that is why the crisis has come."[138] Goethe, then a student at Strasburg, has told us what horror and alarm the *System of Nature* brought into the circle there. "But we could not conceive," he says, "how such a book could be dangerous. It came to us so gray, so Cimmerian, so corpse-like, that we could hardly endure its presence; we shuddered before it as if it had been a spectre. It struck us as the very quintessence of musty age, savourless, repugnant."[139]

If this was the light in which the book appeared to the young man who was soon to be the centre of German literature, the brilliant veteran who had for two generations been the centre of the literature of France was both shocked by the audacity of the new treatise, and alarmed at the peril in which it involved the whole Encyclopædic brotherhood, with the Patriarch at their head. Voltaire had no sooner read the *System of Nature* than he at once snatched up his ever-ready pen and plunged into refutation.[140] At the same time he took care that the right persons should hear what he had done. He wrote to his old patron and friend Richelieu, that it would be a great kindness if he would let the King know that the abused Voltaire had written an answer to the book that all the world was talking about. I think, he says, that it is always a good thing to uphold the doctrine of the existence of a God who punishes and rewards; society has need of such an opinion. There is a curious disinterestedness in the notion of Lewis the Fifteenth and Richelieu, two of the wickedest men of their time, being anxious for the demonstration of a *Dieu vengeur*. Voltaire at least had a very keen sense of the meaning of a court that rewarded and punished. The author of the *System of Nature*, he wrote to Grimm, ought to have felt that he was undoing his friends, and making them hateful in the eyes of the king and the court.[141] This came true in the case of the great philosopher-king himself. Frederick of Prussia was offended by a book which spared political superstitions as little as theological dogma, and treated kings as boldly as it treated priests. Though keenly occupied in watching the war then waging between Russia and Turkey, and already revolving the partition of Poland, he found time to compose a defence of theism. 'Tis a good sign, Voltaire said to him, when a king and a plain man think alike: their interests are often so hostile, that when their ideas do agree, they must certainly be right.[142]

The philosophic meaning of Holbach's propositions was never really seized by Voltaire. He is, as has been justly said, the representative of ordinary common sense which, with all its declamations and its appeals to the feelings, is wholly without weight or significance as against a philosophic way of considering things, however humble the philosophy may be.[143] He hardly took more pains to understand Holbach than Johnson took to understand Berkeley. In truth it was a characteristic of Voltaire always to take the social, rather than the philosophic view of the great issues of the theistic controversy. One day, when present at a discussion as to the existence of a deity, in which the negative was being defended with much vivacity, he astonished the company by ordering the servants to leave the room, and then proceeding to lock the door. "Gentlemen," he explained, "I do not wish my valet to cut my throat to-morrow morning." It was not the truth of the theistic belief in itself that Voltaire prized, but its supposed utility as an assistant to the police. D'Alembert, on the other hand, viewed the dispute as a matter of disinterested speculation. "As for the existence of a supreme intelligence," he wrote to Frederick the Great, "I think that those who deny it advance far more than they can prove, and scepticism is the only reasonable course." He goes on to say, however, that experience invincibly proves both the materiality of the soul, and a material deity—like that which Mr. Mill did not repudiate—of limited powers, and dependent on fixed conditions.[144]

Let us now turn to the book itself. And first, as to its author. The reader of the *New Heloïsa* will remember that the heroine, after her repentance and her marriage, has only one chagrin in the world; that is the blank disbelief of her husband in the two great mysteries of a Supreme Being and another world. Wolmar, the husband, has always been supposed to stand for Rousseau's version of Holbach, and Holbach would hardly have complained of the portrait. The Wolmar of the novel is benevolent, active, patient, tranquil, friendly, and trustful. The nicely combined conjunction of the play of circumstance with the action of men pleases him, just as the fine symmetry of a statue or the skilful contrivance of dramatic effects would please him. If he has any dominant passion, it is a passion for observation; he delights in reading the hearts of men.[145]

All this seems to have been as true of the real Holbach as of the imaginary

Wolmar. We have already seen him as the intimate friend and constant host of Diderot. He was one of the best-informed men of his time (1723-89). He had an excellent library, a collection of pictures, and a valuable cabinet of natural history; and his poorer friends were as freely welcome to the use of all of them as the richest. His manners were cheerful, courteous, and easy; he was a model of simplicity, and kindliness was written on every feature. His hospitality won him the well-known nickname of the maître d'hôtel of philosophy, and his house was jestingly called the Café de l'Europe. On Sundays and Thursdays, without prejudice to other days, from ten to a score of men of letters and eminent foreign visitors, including Hume, Wilkes, Shelburne, Garrick, Franklin, Priestley, used to gather round his good dishes and excellent wine. It was noted, as a mark of the attractiveness of the company, that the guests, who came at two in the afternoon, constantly remained until as late as seven and eight in the evening. To one of those guests, who afterwards became the powerful enemy of the Encyclopædic group, the gaiety, the irreverence, the hardihood of speculation and audacity of discourse, were all as gall and wormwood. Rousseau found their atheistic sallies offensive beyond endurance. Their hard rationalism was odious to the great emotional dreamer, and after he had quarrelled with them all, he transformed his own impressions of the dreariness of atheism into the passionate complaint of Julie. "Conceive the torment of living in retirement with the man who shares our existence, and yet cannot share the hope that makes existence dear; of never being able with him either to bless the works of God, or to speak of the happy future that is promised us by the goodness of God; of seeing him, while doing good on every side, still insensible to everything that makes the delight of doing good; of watching him, by the most bizarre of contradictions, think with the impious, and yet live like a Christian. Think of Julie walking with her husband; the one admiring in the rich and splendid robe of the earth the handiwork and the bounteous gifts of the author of the universe; the other seeing nothing in it all save a fortuitous combination, the product of blind force! Alas! she cries, the great spectacle of nature, for us so glorious, so animated, is dead in the eyes of the unhappy Wolmar, and in that great harmony of being where all speaks of God in accents so mild and so persuasive, he only perceives eternal silence."[146]

Yet it is fair to the author of this most eloquent Ignoratio Elenchi, to notice that he honestly fulfilled the object with which he professed to set out —namely, to show to both the religious and philosophical parties that their adversaries were capable of leading upright, useful, and magnanimous lives. Whether he would have painted the imaginary Wolmar so favourably if he could have foreseen what kind of book the real Holbach had in his desk, is perhaps doubtful. For Holbach's opinions looked more formidable and sombre in the cold deliberateness of print than they had sounded amid the interruptions of lively discourse.

It is needless to say, to begin with, that the writer has the most marked of the philosophic defects of the school of the century. Perhaps we might put it more broadly, and call the disregard of historic opinion the natural defect of all materialistic speculation from Epicurus downwards.[147] Like all others of his school, Holbach has no perception nor sense of the necessity of an explanation how the mental world came to be what it is, nor how men came to think and believe what they do think and believe. He gives them what he deems unanswerable reasons for changing their convictions, but he never dreams of asking himself in what elements of human character the older convictions had their root, and from what fitness for the conduct of life they drew the current of their sap. Yet unless this aspect of things had been well considered, his unanswerable reasons were sure to fall wide of the mark. Opinions, as men began to remember, after social movement had thrown the logical century into discredit, have a history as well as a logic. They are bound up with a hundred transmitted prepossessions, and they have become identified with a hundred social customs that are the most dearly cherished parts of men's lives. Nature had as much to do with the darkness of yesterday as with the light of to-day; she is as much the accomplice of superstition as she is the oracle of reason. It was because they forgot all this that Holbach's school now seem so shallow and superficial. The whole past was one long working of the mystery of iniquity. "The sum of the woes of the human race was not diminished—on the contrary, it was increased by its religions, by its governments, by its opinions, in a word, by all the institutions that *it was led to adopt* on the plea of ameliorating its lot."[148] *On lui fit adopter!* But who were the *on*, and how did they work? With what instruments and what fulcrum? Never was the convenience of this famous abstract substantive more fatally abused. And if religion, government, and opinion had all aggravated the miseries of the human race, what had lessened them? For the Encyclopædic school never attempted, as Rousseau did, to deny that the world had, as a matter of fact, advanced towards happiness. It was because the Holbachians looked on mankind as slaves held in an unaccountable bondage, which they must necessarily be eager to throw off, that their movement, after doing at the Revolution a certain amount of good in a bad way, led at last to a mischievous reaction in favour of Catholicism.

Far more immediately significant than the philosophy of the *System of Nature* were the violence, directness, and pertinacity of its assault upon political government. Voltaire, as has so often been noticed, had always abstained from meddling with either the theory or the practical abuses of the national administration. All his shafts had been levelled at ecclesiastical superstition. Rousseau, indeed, had begun the most famous of his political speculations by crying that man, who was born free, is now everywhere in chains. But Rousseau was vague, abstract, and sentimental. In the *System of Nature* we have a clear presage of the trenchant and imperious invective which, twenty years after its publication, rang in all men's ears from the gardens of the Palais Royal and the benches of the Jacobins' Hall. The writer has plainly made up his mind that the time has at last come for dropping all the discreet machinery of apologue and parable, and giving to his words the edge of a sharpened sword. The vague disguises of political speculation, and the mannered reservations of a Utopia or New Atlantis, are exchanged for a passionate, biting, and loudly practical indictment. All over the world men are under the yoke of masters who neglect the instruction of their people, or only seek to cheat and deceive them. The sovereigns in every part of the globe are unjust, incapable, made effeminate by luxury, corrupted by flattery, depraved by license and impunity, destitute of talent, manners, or virtue. Indifferent to their duties, which they usually know nothing about, they are scarcely concerned for a single moment of the day with the well-being of their people; their whole attention is absorbed by useless wars, or by the desire to find at each instant new means of gratifying their insatiable rapacity. The state of society is a state of war between the sovereign and all the rest of its members. In every country alike the morality of the people is wholly neglected, and the one care of the government is to render them timorous and wretched. The common man desires no more than bread; he wins it by the sweat of his brow; joyfully would he eat it, if the injustice of the government did not make it bitter in his mouth. By the insanity of governments, those who are swimming in plenty, without being any the happier for it, yet wring from the tiller of the soil the very fruits that his arms have won from it. Injustice, by reducing indigence to despair, drives it to seek in crime resources against the woes of life. An iniquitous government breeds despair in men's souls; its vexations depopulate the land, the fields remain untilled, famine, contagion, and pestilence stalk over the earth. Then, embittered by misery, men's minds begin to ferment and effervesce, and what inevitably follows is the overthrow of a realm.[149]

If France had been prosperous, all this would have passed for the empty declamation of an excited man of letters. As it was, such declamation only described, in language as accurate as it was violent and stinging, the real position of the country. In the urgency of a present material distress, men were not over-careful that the basis of the indictment should be laid in the principles of a sound historical philosophy of society. We can hardly wonder at it. What is interesting, and what we do not notice earlier in the century, is that in the *System of Nature* the revolt against the impotence of society, and the revolt against the omnipotence of God, made a firm coalition. That coalition came to a bloody end for the time, four-and-twenty years after Holbach's book proclaimed it, when the Committee of Public Safety despatched Hébert, and better men than Hébert, to the guillotine for being atheists. Atheism, as Robespierre assured them, was aristocratic.

Holbach's work may be said to spring from the doctrine that the social deliverance of man depends on his intellectual deliverance, and that the key to his intellectual deliverance is only to be found in the substitution of Naturalism for Theism. What he means by Naturalism we shall proceed shortly to explain. The style, we may remark, notwithstanding the energy and coherence of the thought, is often diffuse and declamatory. Some one said of the *System of Nature*, that it contained at least four times too many words. Yet Voltaire, while professing extreme dislike of its doctrine, admitted that the writer had somehow caught the ear of the learned, of the ignorant, and of women. "He is often clear," said Voltaire, "and sometimes eloquent, yet he may justly be reproached with declamation, with repeating himself, and with contradicting himself, like all the rest of them."[150] Galiani made an over-subtle criticism on it, when he complained of the want of coolness and self-possession in the style, and then said that it looked as if the writer were pressed less to persuade other people than to persuade himself. This was a crude impression. Nobody can have any doubt of the writer's profound sincerity, or of his earnest desire to make proselytes. He knows his own mind, and hammers his doctrines out with a hard and iterative stroke that hits its mark. Yet his literary tone, in spite of its declamatory pitch, not seldom sinks into a drone. Holbach's contemporaries were in too fierce contact with the tusks and hooked claws of the Church, to have any mind for the rhythm of a champion's sentences or the turn of his periods. But now that the efforts of the heterodox have taught the Churches to be better Christians than they were a hundred years ago, we can afford to admit that Holbach is hardly more captivating in style, and not always more edifying in temper, than some of the Christian Fathers themselves.

What then is the system of Nature, and what is that Naturalism which is to replace the current faith in the deities outside of observable nature? The writer makes no pretence of feeling a tentative way towards an answer. From the very outset his spirit is that of dogmatic confidence. He is less a seeker than an expounder; less a philosopher than a preacher; and he boldly dismisses proof in favour of exhortation.

"Let man cease to search outside the world in which he dwells for beings who may procure him a happiness that nature refuses to grant; let him study that nature, let him learn her laws, and contemplate the energy and the unchanging fixity with which she acts; let him apply his discoveries to his own felicity, and submit in silence to laws from which nothing can withdraw him; let him consent to ignore the causes, surrounded as they are for him by an impenetrable veil; let him undergo without a murmur the decrees of universal force."

Science derived from experience is the source of all wise action. It is physical science (*la physique*), and experience, that man ought to consult in religion, morals, legislature, as well as in knowledge and the arts. It is by our senses that we are bound to universal nature; it is by our senses that we discover her secrets. The moment that we first experience them we fall into a void where our imagination leads us endlessly astray.

Movement is what establishes relations between our organs and external objects. Every object has laws of movement that are peculiar to itself. Everything in the universe is in movement; no part of nature is really at rest.
[151]

Whence does nature receive this movement? From herself, since she is the great whole, outside of which consequently nothing can exist. Motion is a fashion of being which flows necessarily from the essence of matter; matter moves by its own energy; its motion is due to forces inherent in it; the variety of its movements, and of the phenomena resulting from them, comes from variation of the properties, the qualities, the combinations, originally found in the different primitive matters of which nature is the assemblage.

Whence came matter? Matter has existed from all eternity, and a motion is one of the inherent and constitutive qualities of matter; motion also has existed from eternity.

The abstract idea of matter must be decomposed. Instead of regarding matter as a unique existence, rude, passive, incapable of moving itself, of combining itself, we ought to look upon it as a Kind of existence, of which the various individual members comprising the Kind, in spite of their having some common properties, such as extension, divisibility, figure, etc., still ought not to be ranged in a single class, nor comprised in a single denomination.

What is nature's process? Continual movement. From the stone which is formed in the bowels of the earth by the intimate combination, as they approach one another, of analogous and similar molecules, up to the sun, that vast reservoir of heated particles that gives light to the firmament; from the numb oyster up to man—we observe an uninterrupted progression, a perpetual chain of combination and movements, from which there result beings that only differ among one another by the variety of their elementary matters, and of the combination and proportion of these elements. From this variety springs an infinite diversity of ways of existing and acting. In generation, nutrition, preservation, we can see nothing but different sorts of matter differently combined, each of them endowed with its own movements, each of them regulated by fixed laws that cause them to undergo the necessary changes.

Let us notice here three of the author's definitions. (1.) *Motion is an effort, by which a body changes or tends to change its place.* (2.) Of the ultimate composition of Matter, Holbach says nothing definite, though he assumes molecular movement as its first law. He contents himself, properly enough perhaps in view of the destination of his treatise, with a definition "relatively to us." Relatively to us, then, *Matter in general is all that affects our senses in any fashion whatever; and the qualities that we attribute to different kinds of matter, are founded on the different impressions that they produce on us.* (3.) "When I say that Nature produces an effect, I do not mean to personify this Nature, which is an abstraction; I mean that the effect of which I am speaking is the necessary result of the properties of some one of those beings that compose the great whole under our eyes. Thus, when I say that Nature intends man to work for his own happiness, I mean by this that it is of the essence of a being who feels, thinks, wills, and acts, to work for his own happiness. By Essence I mean that which constitutes a being what it is, the sum of its properties, or the qualities according to which it exists and acts as it does."

All phenomena are necessary. No creature in the universe, in its circumstances and according to its given property, can act otherwise than as it does act. Fire necessarily burns whatever combustible matter comes within the sphere of its action. Man necessarily desires what either is, or seems to be, conducive to his comfort and wellbeing. There is no independent energy, no isolated cause, no detached activity, in a universe where all beings are incessantly acting on one another, and which is itself only one eternal round of movement, imparted and undergone, according to necessary laws. In a storm of dust raised by a whirlwind, in the most violent tempest that agitates the ocean, not a single molecule of dust or of water finds its place by *chance*; or is without an adequate cause for occupying the precise point where it is found. So, again, in the terrible convulsions that sometimes overthrow empires, there is not a single action, word, thought, volition, or passion in a single agent of such a revolution, whether he be a destroyer or a victim, which is not necessary, which does not act precisely as it must act, and which does not infallibly produce the effects that it is bound to produce, conformably to the place occupied by the given agent in the moral whirlwind.[152]

Order and disorder are abstract terms, and can have no existence in a Nature, where all is necessary and follows constant laws. Order is nothing more than necessity viewed relatively to the succession of actions. Disorder in the case of any being is nothing more than its passage to a new order; to a succession of movements and actions of a different sort from those of which the given being was previously susceptible. Hence there can never be either monsters or prodigies, either marvels or miracles, in nature. By the same reasoning, we have no right to divide the workings of nature into those of Intelligence and those of Chance. Where all is necessary, Chance can mean nothing save the limitation of man's knowledge.

The writer next has a group of chapters (vi.-x.) on Man, his composition, relations, and destiny. The chief propositions are in rigorous accord with the general conceptions that have already been set forth. All that man does, and all that passes in him, are effects of the energy that is common to him with the other beings known to us. But, before a true and comprehensive idea of the unity of nature was possible to him, he was so seized by the variety and complication of his organism and its movements that it never came into his mind to realise that they existed in a chain of material necessity, binding him fast to all other forces and modes of being. Men think that they remedy their ignorance of things by inventing words; so they explained the working of matter, in man's case, by associating with matter a hypothetical substance, which is in truth much less intelligible than matter itself. They regarded themselves as double; a compound of matter and something else miraculously united with it, to which they give the name of *mind* or *soul*, and then they proudly looked on themselves as beings apart from the rest of creation. In plain truth, Mind is only an *occult force*, invented to explain occult qualities and actions, and really explaining nothing. By Mind they mean no more than the unknown cause of phenomena that they cannot explain naturally, just as the Red Indians believed that it was spirits who produced the terrible effects of gunpowder, and just as the ignorant of our own day believe in angels and demons. How can we figure to ourselves a form of being, which, though not matter, still acts on matter, without having points of contact or analogy with it; and on the other hand itself receives the impulsions of matter, through the material organs that warn it of the presence of external objects? How can we conceive the union of body and soul, and how can this material body enclose, bind, constrain, determine a fugitive form of being, that escapes every sense? To resolve these difficulties by calling them mysteries, and to set them down as the effects of the omnipotence of a Being still more inconceivable than the human Soul itself, is merely a confession of absolute ignorance.

It is worth noticing that with the characteristic readiness of the French materialist school to turn metaphysical and psychological discussion to practical uses, Holbach discerned the immense new field which the materialist account of mind opened to the physician. "If people consulted experience instead of prejudice, medicine would furnish morality with the key of the human heart; and in curing the body, it would be often assured of curing the mind too…. The dogma of the spirituality of the soul has turned morality into a conjectural science, which does not in the least help us to understand the true way of acting on men's motives…. Man will always be a mystery for those who insist on regarding him with the prejudiced eyes of theology, and on attributing his actions to a principle of which they can never have any clear ideas" (ch. ix.). It is certainly true as a historical fact that the rational treatment of insane persons, and the rational view of certain kinds of crime, were due to men like Pinel, trained in the materialistic school of the eighteenth century. And it was clearly impossible that the great and humane reforms in this field could have taken place before the decisive decay of theology. Theology assumes perversity as the natural condition of the human heart, and could only regard insanity as an intolerable exaggeration of this perversity. Secondly, the absolute independence of mind and body which theology brought into such overwhelming relief naturally excluded the notion that, by dealing with the body, you might be doing something to heal the mind. Perhaps we are now in some danger of overlooking the potency of the converse illustration of what Holbach says: namely, the efficacy of mental remedies or preventives in the case of bodily disease.

If you complain—to resume our exposition—that the mechanism is not sufficient to explain the principle of the movements and faculties of the soul, the answer is, that it is in the same case with all the bodies in nature. In them the simplest movements, the most ordinary phenomena, the commonest actions, are inexplicable mysteries, whose first principles are for ever sealed to us. How shall we flatter ourselves that we know the first principle of gravity, by virtue of which a stone falls? What do we know of the mechanism that produces the attraction of some substances, and the repulsion of others? But surely the incomprehensibility of natural effects is no reason for assigning to them a cause that is still more incomprehensible than any of those within our cognisance.

It is not given to man to know everything; it is not given to him to know his own origin, nor to penetrate into the essence of things, nor to mount up to the first principle of things. What is given to him is to have reason, to have good faith, to concede frankly that he is ignorant of what he cannot know, and not to supplement his lack of certainty by words that are unintelligible, and suppositions that are absurd.

Suns go out and planets perish; new suns are kindled, and new planets revolve in new paths; and man—infinitely small portion of a globe that is itself only a small point in immensity—dreams that it is for him that the universe has been made, imagines that he must be the confidant of nature, and proudly flatters himself that he must be eternal! O man, wilt thou never conceive that thou art but an insect of a day? All changes in the universe; nature contains not a form that is constant; and yet thou wouldst claim that thy species can never disappear, and must be excepted from the great universal law of incessant change!

We may pause for a moment to notice how, in their deliberate humiliation of the alleged pride of man, the orthodox theologian and the atheistic Holbach use precisely the same language. But the rebuke of the latter was sincere; it was indispensable in order to prepare men's minds for the conception of the universe as a whole. With the theologian the rebuke has now become little more than a hollow shift, in order to insinuate the miracle of Grace. The preacher of Naturalism replaces a futile vanity in being the end and object of the creation, by a fruitful reverence for the supremacy of human reason, and a right sense of the value of its discreet and disciplined use. The theologian restores this absurd and misleading egoism of the race, by representing the Creator as above all else concerned to work miracles for the salvation of a creature whose understanding is at once pitifully weak and odiously perverse, and whose heart is from the beginning wicked, corrupt, and given over to reprobation. The difference is plainly enormous. The theologian discourages men; they are to wait for the miracle of conversion, inert or desperate. The naturalist arouses them; he supplies them with the most powerful of motives for the energetic use of the most powerful of their endowments. "Men would always have Grace," says Holbach, with excellent sense, "if they were well educated and well governed." And he exclaims on the strange morality of those who attribute all moral evil to Original Sin, and all the good that we do to Grace. "No wonder," he says, "that a morality founded on hypotheses so ridiculous should prove to be of no efficacy."[153]

This brings us to Holbach's treatment of Morals. The moment had come to France, which was reached at an earlier period in English speculation, when the negative course of thought in metaphysics drove men to consider the basis of ethics. How were right and wrong to hold their own against the new mechanical conception of the Universe? The same question is again urgent in men's minds, because the Darwinian hypothesis, and the mass of evidence for it, have again given a tremendous shake to theological conceptions, and startled men into a sense of the precariousness of the official foundations of virtue and duty.

Holbach begins by a most unflinching exposure of the inconsistency with all that we know of nature, of the mysterious theory of Free Will. This remains one of the most effective parts of the book, and perhaps the work has never been done with a firmer hand. The conclusion is expressed with a decisiveness that almost seems crude. There is declared to be no difference between a man who throws himself out of the window and the man whom I throw out, except this, that the impulse acting on the second comes from without, and that the impulse determining the fall of the first comes from within his own mechanism. You have only to get down to the motive, and you will invariably find that the motive is beyond the actor's own power or reach. The inexorable logic with which the author presses the Free-Willer from one retreat to another, and from shift to shift, leaves his adversary at last exactly as naked and defenceless before Holbach's vigorous and thoroughly realised Naturalism as the same adversary must always be before Jonathan Edwards's vigorous theism. "The system of man's liberty," Holbach says (II. ii.), with some pungency, "seems only to have been invented in order to put him in a position to offend his God, and so to justify God in all the evil that he inflicted on man, for having used the freedom which was so disastrously conferred upon him."

If man be not free, what right have we to punish those who cannot help committing bad actions, or to reward others who cannot help committing good actions? Holbach gives to this and the various other ways of describing fatalism as dangerous to society, the proper and perfectly adequate answer. He turns to the quality of the action, and connects with that the social attitude of praise and blame. Merit and demerit are associated with conduct, according as it is thought to affect the common welfare advantageously or the reverse. My indignation and my approval are as necessary as the acts that excite these sentiments. My feelings are neither more nor less spontaneous than the deciding motives of the actor. Whatever be the necessitating cause of our actions, I have a right to do my best by praise and blame, by reward and punishment, to strengthen or to weaken, to prolong or to divert, the motives that are the antecedents of the action; exactly as I have a right to dam up a stream, or to divert its course, or otherwise deal with it to suit my own convenience. Penal laws, for instance, are ways of offering to men strong motives, to weigh in the scale against the temptation of an immediate personal gratification. Holbach does not make it quite distinct that the object of penal legislation is in some cases to give the offender, as well as other people, a strong reason for thinking twice before he repeats the offence; yet in other cases, where the punishment is capital, the legislation does not aim at influencing the mind of the offender at all, but the minds of other people only. This is only a side illustration of a common weakness in most arguments on this subject. A thorough vindication of the penal laws, on the principles of a systematic fatalism, can only be successful, if we think less of the wrongdoer in any given case, than of affecting general motives, and building up a right habit of avoiding or accepting certain classes of action.

The writer then justly connects his scientific necessarianism in philosophy with humanity in punishment. He protests against excessive cruelty in the infliction of legal penalties, and especially against the use of torture, on two grounds; first, that experience demonstrates the uselessness of these superfluous rigours; and, second, that the habit of witnessing atrocious punishments familiarises both criminals and others with the idea of cruelty. The acquiescence of Paris for a few months in the cruelties of the Terror was no doubt due, on Holbach's perfectly sound principle, to the far worse cruelties with which the laws had daily made Paris familiar down to the last years of the monarchy. And Holbach was justified in expecting a greater degree of charitable and considerate judgment from the establishment in men's minds of a Necessarian theory. We are no longer vindictive against the individual doer; we wax energetic against the defective training and the institutions which allowed wrong motives to weigh more heavily with him than right ones. Punishment on the theory of necessity ought always to go with prevention, and is valued just because it is a force on prevention, and not merely an element in retribution.

Holbach answers effectively enough the common objection that his fatalism would plunge men's souls into apathy. If all is necessary, why shall I not let things go, and myself remain quiet? As if we *could* stay our hands from action, if our feelings were trained to proper sensibility and sympathy. As if it were possible for a man of tender disposition not to interest himself keenly in all that concerns the lot of his fellow-creatures. How does our knowledge that death is necessary prevent us from deploring the loss of a beloved one? How does my consciousness that it is the inevitable property of fire to burn, prevent me from using all my efforts to avert a conflagration?

Finally, when people urge that the doctrine of necessity degrades man by reducing him to a machine, and likening him to some growth of abject vegetation, they are merely using a kind of language that was invented in ignorance of what constitutes the true dignity of man. What is nature itself but a vast machine, in which our human species is no more than one weak spring? The good man is a machine whose springs are adapted so to fulfil their functions as to produce beneficent results for his fellows. How could such an instrument not be an object of respect and affection and gratitude?

In closing this part of Holbach's book, while not dissenting from his conclusions, we will only remark how little conscious he seems of the degree to which he empties the notions of praise and blame of the very essence of their old contents. It is not a modification, but the substitution of a new meaning under the old names. Praise in its new sense of admiration for useful and pleasure-giving conduct or motive, is as powerful a force and as adequate an incentive to good conduct and good motives, as praise in the old sense of admiration for a deliberate and voluntary exercise of a free-acting will. But the two senses are different. The old ethical association is transformed into something which usage and the requirements of social self-preservation must make equally potent, but which is not the same. If Holbach and others who hold necessarian opinions were to perceive this more frankly, and to work it out fully, they would prevent a confusion that is very unfavourable to them in the minds of most of those whom they wish to persuade. It is easy to see that the work next to be done in the region of morals, is the readjustment of the ethical phraseology of the volitional stage, to fit the ideas proper to the stage in which man has become as definitely the object of science as any of the other phenomena of the universe.

The chapter (xiii.) on the Immortality of the Soul examines this memorable growth of human belief with great vigour, and a most destructive penetration. As we have seen, the author repudiates the theory of a double energy in man, one material and the other spiritual, just as he afterwards repudiates the analogous hypothesis of a double energy in nature, one of the two being due to a spiritual mover outside of the external phenomena of the universe. Consistently with this renunciation of a separate spiritual energy in man, Holbach will listen to no talk of a spiritual energy surviving the destruction of the mechanical framework. To say that the soul will feel, think, enjoy, suffer, after the death of the body, is to pretend that a clock broken into a thousand pieces can continue to strike or to mark the hours. And having emphatically proclaimed his own refusal to share the common belief, he proceeds with good success to carry the war into the country of those who profess that belief, and defend it as the safeguard of society. We need not go through his positions. They are substantially those which are familiar to everybody who has read the Third Book of Lucretius's poem, and remembers those magnificent passages which are not more admirable in their philosophy than they are noble and moving in their poetic expression:—

Nam veluti pueri trepidant atque omnia caecis
In tenebris metuunt, sic nos in luce timemus
Interdum, nilo quae sunt metuenda magis quam
Quae pueri in tenebris pavitant finguntque futura.
Hunc igitur terrorem animi tenebrasque necessest
Non radii solis neque lucida tela diei
Discutiant, sed naturae species ratioque.

And so forth, down to the exquisite lines—

"Jam jam non domus accipiet te laeta, neque uxoi
Optima nec dulces occurrent oscula nati
Praeripere, et tacita pectus dulcedine tangent.
Non poteris factis florentibus esse, tuisque
Praesidium. Misero misere," aiunt, "omnia ademit
Una dies infesta tibi tot praemia vitae."
Illud in his rebus non addunt, "nec tibi earum
Jam desiderium rerum super insidet una."
Quod bene si videant animo dictisque sequantur,
Dissolvant animi magno se angore metuque.
"Tu quidem ut es leto sopitus, sic eris aevi
Quod superest cunctis privatu' doloribus aegris:
At nos horrifico cinefactum te prope busto
Insatiabiliter deflevimus, aeternumque
Nulla dies nobis maerorem e pectore demet."
Illud ab hoc igitur quaerendum est, quid sit amari
Tanto opere, ad somnum si res redit atque quietem,
Cur quisquam æterno possit tabescere luctu.

We may regret that Holbach, in dealing with these solemn and touching things, should have been so devoid of historic spirit as to buffet David, Mahomet, Chrysostom, and other holy personages, as superstitious brigands. And we may believe that he has certainly been too sweeping in denying any deterrent efficacy whatever to the fires of hell. But where Holbach found one person in 1770, he would find a thousand in 1880, to agree with him, that it is possible to think of commendations and inducements to virtue, that shall be at least as efficacious as the fiction of eternal torment, without being as cruel, as wicked, as infamous to the gods, and as degrading to men.

From his attack on Immortality, Holbach naturally turns with new energy, as do all who have passed beyond that belief, to the improvement of the education, the laws, the institutions, which are to strengthen and implant the true motives for turning men away from wrong and inspiring them to right. He draws a stern and prolonged indictment against the kings of the earth, in words that we have already quoted above, as unjust, incapable, depraved by license and impunity. One passage in this chapter is the scripture of a terrible prophecy, the very handwriting on the wall, which was to be so accurately fulfilled almost in the lifetime of the writer:—"The state of society is now a state of war of the Sovereign against all, and of each of its members against the other. Man is bad, not because he was born bad, but because he is made so; the great and the powerful crush with impunity the needy and the unfortunate, and these in turn seek to repay all the ill that has been done to them. They openly or privily attack a native land that is a cruel stepmother to them; she gives all to some of her children, while others she strips of all. Sorely they punish her for her partiality; they show her that the motives borrowed from another life are powerless against the passions and the bitter wrath engendered by a corrupt administration in the life here; and that all the terror of the punishments of this world is impotent against necessity, against criminal habits, against a dangerous organisation that no education has ever been applied to correct" (ch. xiv.). In another place: "A society enjoys all the happiness of which it is susceptible so soon as the greater number of its members are fed, clothed, housed; are able, in a word, without an excessive toil, to satisfy the wants that nature has made necessities to them. Their imagination is content so soon as they have the assurance that no force can ravish from them the fruits of their industry, and that they labour for themselves. By a sequence of human madness, whole nations are forced to labour, to sweat, to water the earth with their tears, merely to keep up the luxury, the fancies, the corruption of a handful of insensates, a few useless creatures. So have religious and political errors changed the universe into a valley of tears." This is an incessant refrain that sounds with hoarse ground-tone under all the ethics and the metaphysics of the book. There are scores of pages in which the same idea is worked out with a sombre vehemence, that makes us feel as if Robespierre were already haranguing in the National Assembly, Camille Desmoulins declaiming in the gardens of the Palais Royal, and Danton thundering at the Club of the Cordeliers. We already watch the smoke of the flaming châteaux, going up like a savoury and righteous sacrifice to the heavens.

From this point to the end of the first part of the book, it is not so much philosophy as the literature of a political revolution. There is a curious parenthesis in vindication not only of a contempt for death, but even of suicide; the writer pointing out with some malice that Samson, Eleazar, and other worthies caused their own death, and that Jesus Christ himself, if really the Son of God, dying of his own free grace, was a suicide, to say nothing of the various ascetic penitents who have killed themselves by inches.[154] "The fear of death, after all," he says, summing up his case, "will only make cowards; the fear of its alleged consequences will only make fanatics or melancholy pietists, as useless to themselves as to others. Death is a resource that we do ill to take away from oppressed virtue, reduced, as many a time it is, by the injustice of men to desperation." This was the doctrine in which the revolutionary generation were brought up, and the readiness with which men in those days inflicted death on themselves and on others showed how profoundly it had entered their souls.[155] We think, as we read, of Vergniaud and Condorcet carrying their doses of poison, of Barbaroux with his pistol, and Valazé with his knife, of Roland walking forth from Rouen among the trees on the Paris road, and there driving a cane-sword into his breast, as calmly as if he had been throwing off a useless vesture.

Holbach has been accused of reducing virtue to a far-sighted egoism,[156] and detached and crude propositions may be quoted, that perhaps give a literal warrant for the charge. Nominally he bases morality on happiness, but his real base is the happiness of the greatest number. To borrow Mr. Sidgwick's classification, Holbach is a universalistic and not an egoistic Hedonist. The spirit of what he says is, in fact, not individualist but social. "The good man is he to whom true ideas have shown his own interest or his own happiness to lie in such a way of acting, that others are forced to love and approve for their own interest…. It is man who is most necessary to the well-being of man…. Merit and virtue are founded on the nature of man, on his needs…. It is by virtue that we are able to earn the goodwill, the confidence, the esteem, of all those with whom we have relations; in a word, no man can be happy alone…. To be virtuous is to place one's interest in what accords with the interest of others; it is to enjoy the benefits and the delights that one is the means of diffusing among them…. The sentiments of self-love become a hundred times more delicious when we see them shared by all those with whom our destiny binds us. The habit of virtue excites wants within us that only virtue can satisfy; thus it is that virtue is ever its own recompense, and pays itself with the blessings that it procures for others" (ch. xv.)

Surely it is a childish or pedantic misinterpretation to represent this as egoism, whether armed or not with keen sight; and still worse to talk of it as over-throwing the barriers that keep in the throng of selfish appetites. "Every citizen should be made to feel that the section of which he is a member is a Whole, that cannot subsist and be happy without virtue; experience should teach him at every moment that the wellbeing of the members can only result from that of the whole body" (ch. xv.) To say of such a doctrine as this, that it is to invite every individual to make himself happy after his own will and fashion, and to pull down the barriers of the selfish appetites, is the very absurdity of philosophic prejudice. It is for us to look at Holbach's ethical doctrine in its widest practical application, and if we place ourselves at a social point of view, we cannot but perceive that the principle laid down in the words that we have just quoted, was the indispensable weapon against the anti-social selfishness of the oppressive privileged class. These words represent the ethical side of every popular and democratic movement. You may class Holbach's morality as the morality of self-interest, if you please; but its true base lay in social sympathy. To proclaim happiness as the test of virtue was to develop the doctrine of naturalism; for happiness is the outcome of a conformity to the natural condition of things. On the other hand, to insist that virtue lies in promoting the happiness of the body social as a whole, was to preach the most sovereign of all truths, in a state of things where the body social as a whole was kept distracted and miserable by the selfishness of a scanty few of its members. The Church, nominally built upon the morality of the Golden Rule, was perverted into being the great organ of sinister self-interest. The Atheists, apparently formulating the morality of the Epicureans, were in effect the teachers of public spirit and beneficence. And, taught in such circumstances, public spirit could only mean revolution. We may doubt whether Holbach had thought out the very different questions that may be fused under the easy phrase of a basis for morals. What are the sanctions of moral precepts? Why ought each to seek the happiness of all? What is the mark of the difference between right and wrong? What is the foundation of Conscience, or that habit of mind which makes right as such seem preferable to wrong? Clearly these are all entirely separate topics. Yet Holbach, it is obvious, had not divided them in his own mind, and he seems to think that one and the same answer will serve for what he mistook for one and the same question. He found it enough to say that every individual wishes to be happy, and that he cannot be happy unless he is on good terms with his neighbours; this reciprocity of needs and services he called the basis of morals. For a rough and common-sense view of the matter, such as Holbach sought to impress on his readers, this perhaps will do very well; but it is not the product of accurate and scientific thinking.

It is not necessary, again, to point out how Holbach, while expounding the System of Nature, left out of sight the great natural process by which the moral acquisition of one generation becomes the starting-point of further acquisitions in the next. He forgot the stages. He talks of Man as if all the races and eras of man were alike, and also as if each individual deliberately worked out sums in happiness on his own account. It would not only have been more true, according to modern opinions, but more in accordance with Holbach's own view of necessity, and of the irremovable chain that binds a man's conduct fast to a series of conditions that existed before he was born, if he had recognised conscience, moral preferences, interest in the public good, and all that he called the basis of morals, as coming to a man with the rest of the apparatus that the past imposes on the present, and not as due to any process of personal calculation.

Holbach had not clearly thought out the growth, the changes, varieties, and transformations among moral ideals. He was, of course, far too much in the full current of the eighteenth century not to feel that exultation in life and its most exuberant manifestations, which the conventional moralists of the theological schools had set down and proscribed as worldliness and fleshliness. "*Action*," he says in this very chapter; "*action is the true element of the human mind*; no sooner does man cease to act, than he falls into pain and weariness of spirit." No doubt this is too absolutely stated, if we are to take some millions of orientals into our account of the human mind, but it has been true of the nations of the west. Yet the recognition of this law did not prevent the writer from occasionally falling into some of the old canting commonplaces about people being happiest who have fewest wants. As if, on the contrary, that action which he describes as the true element of man, were not directly connected with the incessant multiplication of wants. We may take this, however, as a casual lapse into the common form of moralists of ascetic ages. In substance the *System of Nature* is essentially a protest against ascetic and quietist ideals.

The second half of the *System of Nature* treats of the Deity; the proofs of his existence; his attributes; the manner in which he influences the happiness of men. What is remarkable is that here we have an onslaught, not merely on the Church with its overgrowth of abuses, nor on Christianity with its overgrowth of superstitions, but on that great conception which is enthroned on unseen heights far above any Church and any form of Christianity. It is theism, in its purest as in its impurest shape, that the writer condemns. No more elaborate, trenchant, and unflinching attack on the very fundamental propositions of theology, natural or revealed, is to be found in literature. Pure rationalism has nothing to add to this destructive onslaught. The tone is not truly philosophic, because the writer habitually regards the notion of a God as an abnormal and morbid excrescence, and not as a natural growth in human development. He takes no trouble, and it would have been an incredible departure from the mental fashion of the time if he had taken any trouble, to explain theology, or to penetrate behind its forms to those needs, aspirations, and qualities of human constitution in which theology had its best justification, if not its earliest source. He regards it as an enemy to be mercilessly routed, not as a force with which he has to make his account. Still, as a piece of rough and remorseless polemic, the second part of the *System of Nature* remains full of remarkable energy and power. The most eager

Nescient or Denier to be found in the ranks of the assailants of theology in our own day is timorous and moderate compared with this direct and on-pressing swordsman. And the attack, on its own purely rationalistic ground, is thoroughly comprehensive. It is not made on an outwork here, or an outwork there; it encircles the whole compass of the defence. The conception of God is examined and resisted from every possible side—cosmological, ethical, metaphysical. To say that the argument is one-sided, is only to say that it is an attack. But the fact that the writer omits the contributions made under the temporal shelter of theology to morality and civilisation, does not alter the other fact that he states with unsurpassed vigour all that can be said against the intellectual absurdities and moral obliquities that theology has nourished and approved, and only too firmly planted.

Of the elaborate examination of the proofs of the existence of a God adduced by Descartes, Samuel Clarke, Malebranche, and Newton (ch. iv. and v.), we need only say that its whole force might have been summed up in the single proposition that the author once for all repudiates any *à priori* basis for any beliefs whatever. It would have been sufficient for philosophic purposes if he had contented himself with justifying and establishing that position. The fabric of orthodox demonstration would have fallen to the ground after the destruction of its foundations. Holbach rejected the whole *à priori* system; it was a matter of course therefore that he rejected each one of the twelve propositions which Clarke had invented by the *à priori* method. Holbach held that experience is the source and limit of knowledge, reasoning, and belief, and rejected as a fantastic impertinence of dreamy metaphysicians the assumption that our conceptions measure the necessities of objective existence. From that point of view, merely to state was to empty of all demonstrating quality such assertions as that something has existed from all eternity; an independent and immutable Being has existed from all eternity; this immutable and independent Being exists by himself, and is incomprehensible; the Being existing necessarily is necessarily single and unique—and so forth. Even if we accept this *à priori* method, and accept the first assumption that something must have existed from all eternity, it was open to Holbach to say, as Locke said on setting himself to examine Descartes' proof of a God: "I found that, by it, senseless matter might be the first eternal being and cause of all things, as well as an immaterial intelligent spirit." But what we feel is that the whole controversy is being conducted between two disputants on two different planes of thought, between two creatures dwelling in different elements. To apply to Clarke's propositions, or to the slightly different propositions of Malebranche, the test of experience, to measure them by the principle of relativity, must be fatal in the minds of such persons as already accept experience as the only right test in such a matter. It is exactly as if the action of an Italian opera should be criticised in the light of the conditions of real life: the whole performance must in an instant figure as an absurdity. No partisan of the lyric drama would consent to have it so judged, and the philosophic partisans of theology would perhaps have been wiser to keep clear of pretensions to *prove* their master thesis. They might have been content to keep it as an emotional creation, an imaginative hypothesis, a noble simplification of the chimeras of the primitive consciousness of the race.

As it was, neither side could be convinced by the other, for they had no common criterion. They had hardly even a common language. The only effect of Holbach's blows was to persuade the bystanders who thronged round the lists in that eager time, that the so-called proofs with which the high philosophic names were associated, were only proofs to those who accepted a way of thinking which it was the very characteristic of that age decisively to reject. The controversial force of this part of the attack simply lay in the piercing thoroughness with which the irreconcilable discrepancies between the seventeenth century notion of demonstration, and that notion in the eighteenth, were forced upon the reader's attention.

One other remark may be made. Whatever we may think of the success of the author's assault on the theistic hypothesis of the universe, it is impossible to deny that he at least succeeds in repelling the various assaults levelled on what is vulgarly termed atheism. He rightly urges the unreasonableness of taxing those who have formed to themselves intelligible notions of the moving power of the universe, with denying the existence of such a power; the absurdity of charging the very men who found everything that comes to pass in the world on fixed and constant laws, with attributing everything to chance. If by Atheist, he says, you mean a man who would deny the existence of a force inherent in matter, and without which you cannot conceive nature, and if to this moving force you give the name of God, then an Atheist would be a madman. Holbach then describes the sense in which Atheists both exist and, as he thinks, may well justify their existence. Their qualities are as follows: To be guided only by experience and the testimony of their senses, and to perceive nothing in nature except matter, essentially active and mobile and capable of producing all the beings that we see; to forego all search for a chimerical cause, and not to mistake for better knowledge of the moving force of the universe, merely a separate attribution of it to a Being placed outside of the great whole; to confess in good faith that their mind can neither conceive nor reconcile the negative attributes and theological abstractions with the human and moral qualities that are ascribed to the Divinity.

The chapter (ix.) on the superiority of Naturalism over Theism as a basis for the most wholesome kind of Morality, is still worth reading by men in search of weapons against the presumptuous commonplaces of the pulpit. In this sphere Holbach is as earnest and severe as the most rigorous moralist that ever wrote. People who talk of the moral levity of the destructive literature of the eighteenth century would be astonished, if they could bring themselves to read the books about which they talk, by the elevation of the *System of Nature*. The writer points out the necessarily evil influence upon morals of a Book popularly taken to be inspired, in which the Divinity is represented as now prescribing virtue, but now again prescribing crime and absurdity; who is sometimes the friend, and sometimes the enemy, of the human race; who is sometimes pictured as reasonable, just, and beneficent, and at other times as insensate: unjust, capricious, and despotic. Such divinities, and the priests of such divinities, are incapable of being the models, types, and arbiters of virtue and righteousness. No; we must seek a base for morality in the necessity of things. Whatever the Cause that placed man in the abode in which he dwells, and endowed him with his faculties—whether we regard the human species as the work of Nature, or of some intelligent Being distinct from Nature—the existence of man, such as we see him to be, is a fact. We see in him a being who feels, thinks, has intelligence, has self-love, who strives to make life agreeable to himself, and who lives in society with beings like himself; beings whom by his conduct he may make his friends or his enemies. It is on these universal sentiments that you ought to base morality, which is nothing more nor less than the science of the duties of man living in society. The moment you attempt to find a base for morals outside of human nature, you go wrong; no other is solid and sure. The aid of the so-called sanctions of theology is not only needless, but mischievous. The alliance of the realities of duty with theological phantoms exposes duty to the same ruin which daylight brings to the superstition that has been associated with duty. It sets up the arbitrary demands of a varying something, named Piety, in place of the plain requirements of Right. As for saying that without God man cannot have moral sentiments, or, in other words, cannot distinguish between vice and virtue, it is as if one said that, without the idea of God, man would not feel the necessity of eating and drinking.

The writer then breaks out into a long and sustained contrast, from which we may make a short extract to illustrate the heat to which the battle had now come:

"Nature invites man to love himself, incessantly to augment the sum of his happiness: Religion orders him to love only a formidable God who is worthy of hatred; to detest and despise himself, and to sacrifice to his terrible idol the sweetest and most lawful pleasures. Nature bids man consult his reason, and take it for his guide: Religion teaches him that this reason is corrupted, that it is a faithless, truthless guide, implanted by a treacherous God, to mislead his creatures. Nature tells man to seek light, to search for the truth: Religion enjoins upon him to examine nothing, to remain in ignorance. Nature says to man: 'Cherish glory, labour to win esteem, be active, courageous, industrious:' Religion says to him: 'Be humble, abject, pusillanimous, live in retreat, busy thyself in prayer, meditation, devout rites; be useless to thyself, and do nothing for others.' Nature proposes for her model, men endowed with noble, energetic, beneficent souls, who have usefully served their fellow-citizens: Religion makes a show and a boast of the abject spirits, the pious enthusiasts, the phrenetic penitents, the vile fanatics, who for their ridiculous opinions have troubled empires.... Nature tells children to honour, to love, to hearken to their parents, to be the stay and support of their old age: Religion bids them prefer the oracle of their God, and to trample father and mother under foot, when divine interests are concerned. Nature commands the perverse man to blush for his vices, for his shameless desires, his crimes: Religion says to the most corrupt: 'Fear to kindle the wrath of a God whom thou knowest not: but if against his laws thou hast committed crime, remember that he is easy to appease and of great mercy: go to his temple, humble thyself at the feet of his ministers, expiate thy misdeeds by sacrifices, offerings, prayers; these will wash away thy stain in the eyes of the Eternal.'"

Of course, philosophical criticism would have much to say about this glowing mass of furious propositions; for the first voice of Nature hardly whispers into the ear of the primitive man all these high and generous promptings. But if by Nature we here understand the Encyclopædists, and by Religion the Catholic Church in France at that moment, then Holbach's fiery antitheses are a tolerably fair account of the matter. And the political side of the indictment was hardly less just, though its hardihood appalled men like Voltaire.

"Nature says to man, 'Thou art free, and no power on earth can lawfully strip thee of thy rights:' Religion cries to him that he is a slave condemned by God to groan under the rod of God's representatives. Nature bids man to love the country that gave him birth, to serve it with all loyalty, to bind his interests to hers against every hand that might be raised upon her: Religion commands him to obey without a murmur the tyrants that oppress his country, to take their part against her, to chain his fellow-citizens under their lawless caprices. Yet if the Sovereign be not devoted enough to his priests, Religion instantly changes her tone; she incites the subjects to rebellion, she makes resistance a duty, she cries aloud that we must obey God rather than man.... If the nature of man were consulted on Politics, which supernatural ideas have so shamefully depraved, it would contribute far more than all the religion in the world to make communities happy, powerful, and prosperous under reasonable authority.... This nature would teach princes that they are men and not gods; that they are citizens charged by their fellow-citizens with watching over the safety of all.... Instead of attributing to the divine vengeance all the wars, the famines, the plagues that lay nations low, would it not have been more useful to show them that such calamities are due to the passions, the indolence, the tyranny of their princes, who sacrifice the nations to their hideous delirium? Natural evils demand natural remedies; ought not experience, therefore, long ago to have undeceived mortals as to those supernatural remedies, those expiations, prayers, sacrifices, fastings, processions, that all the peoples of the earth have so vainly opposed to the woes that overwhelmed them?... Let us recognise the plain truth, then, that it is these supernatural ideas that have obscured morality, corrupted politics, hindered the advance of the sciences, and extinguished happiness and peace even in the very heart of man."

Holbach was a vigorous propagandist. Two years after the appearance of his master-work he drew up its chief propositions in a short and popular volume, called *Good sense; or Natural Ideas opposed to Supernatural*. His zeal led him to write and circulate a vast number of other tractates and short volumes, the bare list of which would fill several of these pages, all inciting their readers to an intellectual revolt against the reigning system in Church and State. He lived to get a glimpse of the very edge and sharp bend of the great cataract. He died in the spring of 1789. If he had only lived five years longer, he would have seen the great church of Notre Dame solemnly consecrated by legislative decree to the worship of Reason, bishops publicly trampling on crosier and ring amid universal applause, and vast crowds exulting in processions whose hero was an ass crowned with a mitre.

CHAPTER VII.
RAYNAL'S HISTORY OF THE INDIES.

""Since Montesquieu's *Esprit des Lois*," says Grimm in his chronicle, "our literature has perhaps produced no monument that is worthier to pass to the remotest posterity, and to consecrate the progress of our enlightenment and diligence for ever, than Raynal's *Philosophical and Political History of European settlements and commerce in the two Indies*." Yet it is perhaps safe to say that not one hundred persons now living have ever read two chapters of the book for which this immortal future was predicted.

When the revolutionary floods gradually subsided, some of the monuments of the previous age began to show themselves above the surface of the falling waters. They had lost amid the stormy agitation of the deluge the shining splendour of their first days; still men found something to attract them after the revolution, as their grandfathers had done before it, in the pages of the *Spirit of Laws*, of the *New Heloïsa*, and the endless satires, romances, and poems of the great Voltaire. Raynal's book was not among these dead glories that came to life again. It disappeared utterly. Nor can it be said that it deserved a kinder fate. Its only interest now is for those who care to know the humour of men's minds in those præ-revolutionary days, when they could devour a long political and commercial history as if it had been a novel or a play, and when the turn of men's interests made of such a book "the Bible of two worlds for nearly twenty years."

Raynal is no commanding figure. Born in 1711, he came to Paris from southern France, and joined the troop of needy priests who swarmed in the great city, hopefully looking out for the prizes of the Church. Raynal is the hero of an anecdote which is told of more than one abbé of the time; whether literally true or not, it is probably a correct illustration of the evil pass to which ecclesiastical manners had come. He had, it was said, nothing to live upon save the product of a few masses. The Abbé Prévost received twenty sous for saying a mass; he paid the Abbé Laporte fifteen sous to be his deputy; the Abbé Laporte paid eight sous to Raynal to say it in his stead. But the adventurer was not destined to remain in this abject case, parasite humbly feeding on parasite. He turned bookmaker, and wrote a history of the Stadtholderate, a volume about the English Parliament, and, of all curious subjects for a man of letters of that date, an account of the divorce of King Henry the Eighth of England. He visited this country more than once, and had the honour in 1754 of being chosen a fellow of the Royal Society of London. [157] We have some difficulty in understanding how he came by such fame, just as we cannot tell how the man who had been glad to earn a few pence by saying masses, came shortly to be rich and independent. He is believed to have engaged in some colonial ventures, and to have had good luck. His enemies spread the dark report that he had made money in the slave trade, but in those days of incensed party spirit there was no limit to virulent invention. It is at least undeniable that Raynal put his money to generous uses. Among other things, he had the current fancy of the time, that the world could be made better by the copious writing of essays, and he delighted in founding prizes for them at the provincial academies. It was at Lyons that he proposed the famous thesis, not unworthy of consideration even at this day: *Has the discovery of America been useful or injurious to the human race?*

Raynal was one of the most assiduous of the guests at the philosophic meals of Baron Holbach and Helvétius; he was very good-humoured, easy to live with, and free from that irritable self-consciousness and self-love which is too commonly the curse of the successful writer, as of other successful persons. He did not go into company merely to make the hours fly. With him, as with Helvétius, society was a workshop. He pressed every one with questions as to all matters, great or small, with which the interlocutor was likely to be familiar.[158] Horace Walpole met him at "dull Holbach's," and the abbé at once began to tease him across the table as to the English colonies. Walpole knew as little about them as he knew about Coptic, so he made signs to his tormentor that he was deaf. On another occasion Raynal dined at Strawberry Hill, and mortified the vanity of his host by looking at none of its wonders himself, and keeping up such a fire of talk and cross-examination as to prevent anybody else from looking at them. "There never was such an impertinent and tiresome old gossip," cried our own gossip.[159]

Raynal failed to give better men than Horace Walpole the sense of power. When his greatest work took the public by storm, nobody would believe that he had written it. Just as in the case of the *System of Nature*, so people set down the *History of the Indies* to Diderot, and even the most moderate critics insisted that he had at any rate written not less than one-third of it. Many less conspicuous scribes were believed to have been Raynal's drudges. We can have no difficulty in supposing that so bulky a work engaged many hands. There is no unity of composition, no equal scale, no regularity of proportion; on the contrary, rhapsody and sober description, history and moral disquisition, commerce, law, physics, and metaphysics are all poured in, almost as if by hazard. We seem to watch half a dozen writers, each dealing with matters according to his own individual taste and his own peculiar kind of knowledge.

Indeed, it is a curious and most interesting feature in the literary activity of France in the eighteenth century, that the egoism and vanity of authorship were reduced by the conditions of the time to a lower degree than in any other generation since letters were invented. The suppression of self by the Jesuits was hardly more complete than the suppression of self by the most brilliant and effective of the insurgents against Jesuitry. Such intimate association as exists in our day between a given book and a given personality, was then thoroughly shaken by the constant necessity for secrecy. As we have seen, people hardly knew who set up that momentous landmark, the *System of Nature*. Voltaire habitually and vehemently denied every one of his most characteristic pieces, and though in the buzz of Parisian gossip the right name was surely hit upon for such unique performances as Voltaire's, yet the fame was far too broken and uncertain to reward his vanity, if the better part of himself had not been fully and sincerely engaged in public objects in which vanity had no part. Rousseau was an exception, but then Rousseau was in truth a reactionist, and not a loyal member of the great company of reformers. As for Diderot, he valued the author's laurel so cheaply, as we have seen, that with a gigantic heedlessness and Saturnian weariness of the plaudits or hisses of the audience, while supremely interested in the deeper movements of the tragi-comic drama of the world, he left some of his masterpieces lying unknown in forgotten chests. Again, in the case of the Encyclopædia, as we have also seen, Turgot as well as less eminent men bargained that their names should not be made public. Wherever a telling blow was to be dealt with the sword, or a new stone to be laid with the trowel, men were always found ready to spend themselves and be spent, without taking thought whether their share in the work should be nicely measured and publicly identified, or absorbed and lost in the whole of which it was a part.

Whatever may have been the secret of the authorship of Raynal's book, and whether or no even the general conception of such a performance was due to Raynal, it is at least certain that the original author, whoever he may have been, divined a remarkable literary opportunity. This divination is in authorship what felicity of experiment is to the scientific discoverer. The book came into immediate vogue. It was published in 1772; a second edition was demanded within a couple of years, and it is computed that more than twenty editions, as well as countless pirated versions, were exhausted before the universal curiosity and interest were satisfied. As the subject took the writer over the whole world, so he found readers in every part of the habitable globe. And among them were men for whom destiny had lofty parts in store. Zeal carried one young reader so far that he collected all the boldest passages into a single volume, and published it as *L'Esprit de Raynal*; an achievement for which, as he was a member of a religious congregation, he afterwards got into some trouble.[160] Franklin read and admired the book in London. Black

Toussaint Louverture in his slave-cabin at Hayti laboriously spelled his way through its pages, and found in their story of the wrongs of his race and their passionate appeal against slavery, the first definite expression of thoughts which had already been dimly stirred in his generous spirit by the brutalities that were every day enacted under his eyes. Gibbon solemnly immortalised Raynal by describing him, in one of the great chapters of the *Decline and Fall*, as a writer who "with a just confidence had prefixed to his own history the honourable epithets of political and philosophical."[161] Robertson, whose excellent *History of America*, covering part of Raynal's ground, was not published until 1777, complimented Raynal on his ingenuity and eloquence, and reproduced some of Raynal's historical speculations.[162]

Frederick the Great began to read it, and for some days spoke enthusiastically to his French satellites at dinner of its eloquence and reason. All at once he became silent, and he never spoke a word about the book again. He had suddenly come across half a dozen pages of vigorous rhapsodising, delivered for his own good:

"Oh Frederick, Frederick! thou wast gifted by nature with a bold and lively imagination, a curiosity that knew no bounds, a passion for industry. Humanity, everywhere in chains, everywhere cast down, wiped away her tears at the sight of thy earliest labours, and seemed to find a solace for all her woes in the hope of finding in thee her avenger. On the dread theatre of war thy swiftness, skill, and order amazed all nations. Thou wast regarded as the model of warrior-kings. There exists a still more glorious name: the name of citizen-king.... Once more open thy heart to the noble and virtuous sentiments that were the delight of thy young days." He then rebukes Frederick for keeping money locked up in his military chest, instead of throwing it into circulation, for his violent and arbitrary administration, and for the excessive imposts under which his people groaned. "Dare still more; give rest to the earth. Let the authority of thy mediation, and the power of thy arms, force peace on the restless nations. The universe is the only country of a great man, and the only theatre for thy genius; become then the benefactor of nations."[163]

In after days, when Raynal visited Berlin, overflowing with vanity and self-importance, he succeeded with some difficulty in procuring an interview with the King, and then Frederick took his revenge. He told Raynal that years ago he had read the history of the Stadtholderate, and of the English Parliament. Raynal modestly interposed that since those days he had written more important works. *"I don't know them,"* said the king, in a tone that closed the subject.[164]

More disinterested persons than Frederick set as low a value on Raynal's performance. One writer even compares the book to a quack mounted on a waggon, retailing to the gaping crowd a number of commonplaces against despotism and religion, without a single curious thing about them except their hardihood.[165] But the instinct of the gaping crowd was sound. Measured by the standard and requirements of modern science, Raynal's history is no high achievement. It may perhaps be successfully contended that the true conception of history has on the whole gone back, rather than advanced, within the last hundred years. There have been many signs in our own day of its becoming narrow, pedantic, and trivial. It threatens to degenerate from a broad survey of great periods and movements of human societies into vast and countless accumulations of insignificant facts, sterile knowledge, and frivolous antiquarianism, in which the spirit of epochs is lost, and the direction, meaning, and summary of the various courses of human history all disappear. Voltaire's *Essai sur les Mœurs* shows a perfectly true notion of what kind of history is worth either writing or reading. Robertson's *View of the Progress of Society in Europe from the Fall of the Roman Empire to the Sixteenth Century* is—with all its imperfections—admirably just, sensible, and historic in its whole scope and treatment. Raynal himself, though far below such writers as Voltaire and Robertson in judgment and temper, yet is not without a luminous breadth of outlook, and does not forget the superior importance of the effect of events on European development, over any possible number of minute particularities in the events themselves. He does not forget, for instance, in describing the Portuguese conquests in the East Indies, to point out that the most remarkable and momentous thing about them was the check that they inflicted on the growth of the Ottoman Power, at a moment in European history when the Christian states were least able to resist, and least likely to combine against the designs of Solyman.[166] This is really the observation best worth making about the Portuguese conquests, and it illustrates Raynal's habit, and the habit of the good minds of that century, of incessantly measuring events by their consequences to western enlightenment and freedom, and of dropping out of sight all irrelevancies of detail.

This signal merit need not blind us to Raynal's shortcomings in the other direction. There are very few dates. The total absence of references and authorities was condemned by Gibbon as "the unpardonable blemish of what is otherwise a most entertaining book." There is no criticism. As Raynal was a mere literary compiler, it was not to be expected that he should rise above the common deficiencies in the thought and methods of his time. It was not to be expected that he should deal with the various groups of phenomena among primitive races, in the scientific spirit of modern anthropology. It is true that he was contemporary with De Brosses, who ranks among the founders of the study of the origins of human culture. One sentence of De Brosses would have warned Raynal against a vicious method, which made nearly all that was written about primitive men by him and everybody else of the same school, utterly false, worthless, and deluding. "It is not in possibilities," said De Brosses, "it is in man himself that we must study man: it is not for us to imagine what man might have done, or ought to have done, but to observe what he did." Of the origin and growth of a myth, for example, Raynal had no rational idea. When he found a myth, what he did was to reduce it to the terms of human action, and then coolly to describe it as historical. The ancient Peruvian legend that laws and arts had been brought to their land by two divine children of the Sun, Manco-Capac and his sister-wife Manca-Oello, is transformed into a grave and prosaic narrative, in which Manco-Capac's achievements are minutely described with as much assurance as if that sage had been Frederick the Great, or Pombal, or any statesman living before the eyes of the writer. Endless illustrations, some of them amusing enough, might be given of this Euhemeristic fashion of dealing with the primitive legends of human infancy.

On the other hand, if Raynal turns myth into history, he constantly resorts to the opposite method, and turns the hard prose of real life into doubtful poetry. If he reduces the demi-gods to men, he delights also in surrounding savage men with the joyous conditions of the pastoral demi-gods. He can never resist an opportunity of introducing an idyll. It was the fashion of the time, begun by Rousseau and perfected by the author of *Paul and Virginia*. The taste for idylls of savage life had at least one merit; it was a way of teaching people that the life of savages is something normal, systematic, coherent, and not mere chaos, formless, and void, unrelated to the life of civilisation. A recent traveller had given an account of an annual ceremony in China, which Raynal borrowed without acknowledgment.[167] M. Poivré had described how the Emperor once every year went forth into the fields, and there with his own hand guided the plough as it traced the long furrows. Raynal elaborated this formality into a characteristic rhapsody on peace, simplicity, plenty, and the father of his people. As a caustic critic of M. Poivré remarked, if a Chinese traveller had arrived at Versailles on the morning of Holy Thursday, he would have found the King of France humbly washing the feet of twelve poor and aged men, yet, as Frenchmen knew, this would be no occasion for rapturous exultation over the lowliness and humanity of the French court.

In the same spirit Raynal made no scruple in filling his pages with the sentimental declamations in which the reaction of that day against the burden of a decaying system of social artifice found such invariable relief and satisfaction. None of these imaginary pieces of high sentiment was more popular than the episode of Polly Baker. It occurs in the chapters which describe the foundation of New England.[168] The fanaticism and intolerance of the Puritan Fathers of that famous land are set forth with the holy rage that always moved the reformers of the eighteenth century against the reformers of the seventeenth. Religion is boldly spoken of as a dreadful malady, whose severity extended even to the most indifferent objects. It may be admitted that the cruel persecution of the Quakers, and the grotesque horrors of witch-finding in New Salem, gave Raynal at least as good a text against Protestantism as he had found against Catholicism in the infernal doings in the West Indian Islands or in Peru. Even after this bloody fever had abated, says Raynal, the inhabitants still preserved a kind of rigorism that savours of the sombre days in which the Puritan colonies had their rise. He illustrates this by the case of a young woman who was brought before the authorities for the offence of having given birth to a child out of wedlock. It was her fifth transgression. Raynal, conceiving history after the manner of the author of the immortal speeches of Pericles, put into the mouth of the unfortunate sinner a long and eloquent apology. At the risk of her life, she cries, she has brought five children into existence. "I have devoted myself with all the courage of a mother's solicitude to the painful toil demanded by their weakness and their tender years. I have formed them to virtue, which is only another name for reason. Already they love their country, as I love it.... Is it a crime, then, to be fruitful, as the earth is fruitful, the common mother of us all?... And how am I not to cry out against the injustice of my lot, when I see that he who seduced and ruined me, after being the cause of my destruction, enjoys honour and power, and is actually seated in the tribunal where they punish my misfortune with rods and with infamy? Who was that barbarous lawgiver who, deciding between the two sexes, kept all his wrath for the weaker; for that luckless sex which pays for a single pleasure by a thousand dangers,"—and so forth. It need hardly be said that this is far too much in the vein, and almost in the words of Diderot, to have any authenticity. And as it happens, there is a piece of external evidence on the matter, which illustrates Raynal's curious lightheartedness as to historic veracity. Franklin and Silas Deane were one day talking together about the many blunders in Raynal's book, when the author himself happened to step in. They told him of what they had been speaking. "Nay," says Raynal, "I took the greatest care not to insert a single fact for which I had not the most unquestionable authority." Deane then fell on the story of Polly Baker, and declared of his own certain knowledge that there had never been a law against bastardy in Massachusetts. Raynal persisted that he must have had the whole case from some source of indisputable trustworthiness, until Franklin broke in upon him with a loud laugh, and explained that when he was a printer of a newspaper, they were sometimes short of news, and to amuse his customers he invented fictions that were as welcome to them as facts. One of these fictions was the legend of

Raynal's heroine. The abbé was not in the least disconcerted. "Very well, Doctor," he replied, "I would rather relate your stories than other men's truths."[169]

When all has been said that need be said about the glaring shortcomings of the *History of the Indies*, its popularity still remains to be accounted for. If we ask for the causes of this striking success, they are perhaps not very far to seek. For one thing, the book is remarkable both for its variety and its animation. Horace Walpole wrote about it to Lady Aylesbury in terms that do not at all overstate its liveliness: "It tells one everything in the world; how to make conquests, invasions, blunders, settlements, bankruptcies, fortunes, etc.; tells you the natural and historical history of all nations; talks commerce, navigation, tea, coffee, china, mines, salt, spices; of the Portuguese, English, French, Dutch, Danes, Spaniards, Arabs, caravans, Persians, Indians, of Louis XIV. and the King of Prussia, of La Bourdonnais, Dupleix, and Admiral Saunders; of rice, and women that dance naked; of camels, gingham, and muslin; of millions of millions of lires, pounds, rupees, and cowries; of iron cables and Circassian women; of Law and the Mississippi; and against all governments and religions."[170]

All this is really not too highly coloured. And Raynal's cosmorama exactly hit the tastes of the hour. The readers of that day were full of a new curiosity about the world outside of France, and the less known families of the human stock. It was no doubt more like the curiosity of keen-witted children than the curiosity of science. Montesquieu first stirred this interest in the unfamiliar forms of custom, institution, creed, motive, and daily manners. But while Montesquieu treated such matters fragmentarily, and in connection with a more or less abstract discussion on polity, Raynal made them the objects of a vivid and concrete picture, and presented them in the easier shape of a systematic history. Again, if the reading class in France were intelligently curious, it must be added, we fear, that they were not without a certain lubricity of imagination, which was pleasantly tickled by sensuous descriptions of the ways of life that were strange to the iron restraints of civilisation. Finally, the public of that day always chose to veil and confuse the furtive voluptuousness of the time by moral disquisition, and a light and busy meddling with the insoluble perplexities of philosophy. Here too the dexterous Raynal knew how to please the fancies of his patrons, and whether Diderot was or was not the writer of those pages of moral sophism and paradox, there is something in them which incessantly reminds us of his *Supplement to Bougainville's Voyages.*

Among the superficial causes of the popularity of Raynal's *History*, we cannot leave out the circumstance that it was composed after a very

112

interesting and critical moment in the colonial relations of France. The Seven Years' War ended in the expulsion of the French from Canada and from their possessions in the East Indies. When the peace of 1763 was made, this was counted the most disastrous part of that final record and sealing of misfortune. When we see with what attachment the ordinary Frenchman of to-day regards what is as yet the thankless possession of Algeria, we might easily have guessed, even if the correspondence of the time had set it forth less distinctly than it does, with what deep concern and mortification the French of that day saw the white flag and its lilies driven for ever from the banks of the St. Lawrence in the west, and the coast of Coromandel in the east. Raynal himself tells us with what zealous impatience the government attempted to make the nation forget its calamities, by stirring the hope of a better fortune in the region to which they gave the magnificent name of Equinoctial France. The establishment of a free and national population among the scented forests and teeming swamps of Guiana, was to bring rich compensation for the icy tracts of Canada. This utopia of a brilliant settlement in Guiana has steadily invested the minds of French statesmen from Choiseul down to Louis Napoleon, and its history is a striking monument of perversity and folly. But from 1763 to 1770, while Raynal was writing his book, men's minds were full of the heroic design, and this augmented their interest in the general themes which Raynal handled—colonisation, commerce, and the overthrow and settlement of new worlds by the old.

However much all these things may have quickened the popularity of Raynal's *History*, yet the true source of it lay deeper; lay in the fuel which the book supplied to the two master emotions of the hour—the hatred and contempt for religion, and the passion for justice and freedom. The subject easily lent itself to these two strong currents. Or we may say that hatred of religion, and passion for justice and freedom, were in fact the subjects, and that the commercial establishments and political relations of the new worlds in the east and west were only the setting and framework. Raynal was perhaps the first person to see that the surest way of discrediting Catholicism was to write some chapters of its history. Gibbon resorted to the same device shortly afterwards, and found in the contemptuous analysis of heresies, and the selfish and violent motives of councils and prelates, as good an occasion of piercing the Church as Raynal found in painting the abominable fraud and cruelty that made the presence of Christians so dire a curse to the helpless inhabitants of the new lands. And the same reproachful background which Gibbon so artistically introduced, in the humane, intelligent, and happy epoch of the pagan Antonines, Raynal invented for the same purpose of making Christianity seem uglier, in the imaginary simplicity and unbroken gladness of the native races whose blood was shed by Christian aggressors as if it had been water.

It would perhaps have been singular at a moment when men were looking round on every side for such weapons as might come to their hand, if they had missed the horrible action of Catholicism when brought into contact with the lower races of mankind. There is no more deplorable chapter in the annals of the race, and there is none which the historian of Christianity should be less willing to pass over lightly. The ruthless cruelty of the Spanish conquerors in the new world is a profoundly instructive illustration of the essential narrowness of the papal Christianity, its pitiful exclusiveness, its low and bad morality, and, above all, its incurable unfitness for dealing with the spirit and motives of men in face of the violent temptations with which the wealth of the new world now assailed and corrupted them. Catholicism had held triumphant possession of the conscience of Europe for a dozen centuries and more. The stories of the American Archipelago, of Mexico, of Peru, even if told by calmer historians than Raynal, show how little power, amid all this triumph of the ecclesiastical letter, had been won by the Christian spirit over the rapacity, the lust, the bloody violence of the natural man. They show what a superficial thing the professed religion of the ages of faith had been, how enormous a task remained, and how much the most arduous part of this task was to make Catholicism itself civilised and moral. For it is hardly denied that Christianity had done worse than merely fail to provide an effective curb on the cruel passions of men. The Spanish conquerors showed that it had nursed a still more cruel passion than the rude interests of material selfishness had ever engendered, by making the extermination or enslavement of these hapless people a duty to the Catholic Church, and a savoury sacrifice in the nostrils of the Most High.

It is true that a philosophic historian will have to take into account the important consideration that the reckless massacres perpetrated by the subjects of the Most Catholic King were less horrible and less permanently depraving than the daily offering of the bleeding hearts of human victims in the temples of Huitzilopochtli and Tezcatlipuk. He would have to remember, as even Raynal does, that if the slave-drivers and murderers were Catholics, so also was Las Casas, the apostle of justice and mercy. Still the fact remains, that the doctrine of moral obligations towards the lower races had not yet taken its place in Europe, any more than the doctrine of our obligation to the lower animals, our ministers and companions, has yet taken its place among Italians and Spaniards. The fact remains, that the old Christianity in the sixteenth century was unable to deal effectively with the new conditions in which the world found itself. As Catholicism now in France in the eighteenth century proved itself unable to harmonise the new moral aspirations and new social necessities of the time with the ancient tradition, Raynal was right in telling over again the afflicting story of her earlier failure, and in identifying the creed that murdered Calas and La Barre before their own eyes, with the creed that had blasted the future of the fairest portion of the new world two centuries before.

The mere circumstance, however, that the book was one long and powerful innuendo against the Church, would not have been enough to secure its vast popularity. Attacks on the Church had become cheap by this time. The eighteenth century, as it is one of the chief aims of these studies to show, had a positive side of at least equal importance and equal strength with its negative side. As we have so often said, its writers were inspired by zeal for political justice, for humanity, for better and more equal laws, for the amelioration of the common lot,—a zeal which in energy, sincerity, and disinterestedness, has never been surpassed. Raynal's work was perhaps, on the whole, the most vigorous and sustained of all the literary expressions that were given to the great social ideas of the century. It wholly lacked the strange and concentrated glow that burned in the pages of the Social Contract; on the other hand, it was more full of movement, of reality, of vivid and picturesque incident. It was popular, and it was concrete. Raynal's story went straight to the hearts of many people, to whom Rousseau's arguments were only half intelligible and wholly dreary. It was that book of the eighteenth century which brought the lower races finally within the pale of right and duty in the common opinion of France. The engravings that face the title-page in each of the seven volumes give the keynote to the effect that the seven volumes produced. In one we see a philosopher writing on a column those old words of dolorous pregnancy, *Auri sacra fames*, while in the distance Spanish and Portuguese ships ride at anchor, and on the shore white men massacre blacks. In another we see a fair woman, typifying bounteous Nature, giving her nourishment to a white infant at one breast, and to a black infant at the other, while she turns a pitiful eye to a scene in the background, where a gang of negro slaves work among the sugar-canes, under the scourge and the goad of ruthless masters. A third frontispiece gives us the story of Inkle and Yarico, which Raynal sets down to some English poet, but as no English poet is known to have touched that moving tale until the younger Colman dramatised it in 1787, we may suspect that Raynal had remembered it from Steele's paper in the *Spectator*. The last of these pieces represents a cultivated landscape, adorned with villages, and its ports thronged with shipping; in the foreground are two Quakers, one of them benignly embracing some young Indians, the other casting indignantly away from him a bow and its arrows, the symbols of division and war.

The most effective chapters in the book were, in truth, eloquent sermons on these simple and pathetic texts. They brought Negroes and Indians within the relations of human brotherhood. They preached a higher morality towards these poor children of bondage, they inspired a new pity, they moved more generous sympathies, and they did this in such a way as not merely to affect men's feelings about Indians and Negroes, slave-labour, and the yet more hateful slave-trade, but at the same time to develop and strengthen a general feeling for justice, equality, and beneficence in all the arrangements and relations of the social union all over the world. The same movement which brought the suffering blacks of the new world within the sphere of moral duty, and invested them with rights, intensified the same notion of rights and duties in association with the suffering people of France. This was the sentiment that reigned during the boyhood and youth of those who were destined, some twenty years after Raynal's book was first placed in their hands, to carry that sentiment out into a fiery and victorious reality.

Montesquieu had opened the various questions connected with slavery. We can have no better measure of the increased heat in France between 1750 and 1770 than the difference in tone between two authors so equal in popularity, if so unequal in merit, as Raynal and Montesquieu. The latter, without justifying the abuses or even the usage of slavery in any shape, had still sought to give a rational account of its growth as an institution.[171] Raynal could not read this with patience. He typifies all the passion of the revolt against the historic method. "Montesquieu," he says, "could not make up his mind to treat the question of slavery seriously. In fact, it is a degradation of reason to employ it, I will not say in defending, but even in combating an abuse so contrary to all reason. Whoever justifies so odious a system deserves from the philosopher the deepest contempt, and from the negro a dagger-stroke. 'If you put a finger on me, I will kill myself,' said Clarissa to Lovelace. And I would say to the man that should assail my freedom: If you come near me, I poniard you.... Will any one tell me that he who seeks to make me a slave, is only using his rights? Where are they, these rights? Who has stamped on them a mark sacred enough to silence mine? If thou thinkest thyself authorised to oppress me, because thou art stronger and craftier than I—then do not complain when my strong arms shall tear thy breast open to find thy heart; do not complain when in thy spasm-riven bowels thou feelest the deadly doom which I have passed into them with thy food. Be thou a victim in thy turn, and expiate the crime of the oppressor."[172]

Raynal then asks the political question, how we can hope to throw down an edifice that is propped up by universal passion, by established laws, by the rivalries of powerful nations, and by the force of prejudices more powerful still. To what tribunal, he cries, shall we carry the sacred appeal? He can find no better answer than that of Turgot and the Economists. It is to Kings that we must look for the redress of these monstrous abominations. It is for Kings to carry fire and sword among the oppressors. "Your armies," he cries, anticipating the famous expression of a writer of our own day, "will be filled with the holy enthusiasm of humanity." In a more practical vein, Raynal then warns his public of the terrible reckoning which awaits the whites, if the blacks ever rise to avenge their wrongs. The Negroes only need a chief courageous enough to lead them to vengeance and carnage. "Where is he, that great man, whom Nature owes to the honour of the human race? Where is he, that new Spartacus who will find no Crassus? Then the Black Code will vanish; how terrible will the White Code be!" We may easily realise the effect which vehement words like these had upon Toussaint, and upon those for whom Toussaint reproduced them.

Men have constantly been asking themselves what the great literary precursors of the Revolution would have thought, and how they would have acted, if they could have survived to the days of the Terror. What would Voltaire have said of Robespierre? How would Rousseau have borne himself at the Jacobin Club? Would Diderot have followed the procession of the Goddess of Reason? To ask whether these famous men would have sanctioned the Terror, is to insult great memories; but there is no reason to suppose that their strong spirits would have faltered. One or two of the younger generation of the famous philosophic party did actually see the break-up of the old order. Condorcet faced the storm with a heroism of spirit that has never been surpassed: disgust at the violent excesses of bad men could never make him unfaithful to the beneficence of the movement which their frenzy distorted.

Raynal was of weaker mould, and showed that there had been a stratum of cant and borrowed formulas in his eloquence. He lived into the very darkest days, and watched the succession of events with a keen eye. His heart began to quail very early. Long before the bloodier times of the internecine war between the factions, and on the eve of the attempted flight of the king, he addressed a letter to the National Assembly (May 31, 1791). The letter is not wanting in firm and courageous phrases. "I have long dared," he began, "to tell kings of their duties. Let me to-day tell the people of its errors, and the representatives of the people of the perils that menace us all." He then proceeded to inveigh in his old manner, but with a new purpose and a changed destination. This time it was not kings and priests whom he denounced, but a government enslaved by popular tyranny, soldiers without discipline, chiefs without authority, ministers without resources, the rudest and most ignorant of men daring to settle the most difficult political questions. How comes it, he asks, that after declaring the dogma of the liberty of religious opinions, you allow priests to be overwhelmed by persecution and outrage because they do not follow your religious opinions? In the same energetic vein he protests against the failure of the Constituent Assembly to found a stable and vigorous government, and to put an end to the vengeances, the seditions, the outbreaks, that filled the air with confusion and menace. It was in short a vigorous pamphlet, written in the interest of Malouet and the constitutional royalists. The Assembly listened, but not without some rude interruptions. Robespierre hastened to the tribune. After condemning the tone of Raynal's letter, he disclaimed any intention of calling down the severity either of the Assembly or of public opinion upon a man who still preserved a great name; he thought that a sufficient excuse for the writer's apostasy might be found in his advanced age. The Assembly agreed with Robespierre, and passed to the order of the day.[173]

Raynal lived to see his predictions fulfilled with a terrible bitterness of fulfilment. In spite of the anger which he had roused in the breasts of powerful personages, the aged man was not guillotined; he was not even imprisoned. All his property was taken from him, and he died in abject poverty in the spring of 1796. Let us hope that the misery of his end was assuaged by the recollection that he had once been a powerful pleader for noble causes.

CHAPTER VIII.
DIDEROT'S CLOSING YEARS.

At the end of a long series of notes and questions on points in anatomy and physiology, which he had been collecting for many years, Diderot wound up with a strange outburst:

"I shall not know until the end what I have lost or gained in this vast gaming-house, where I shall have passed some threescore years, dice-box in hand, *tesseras agitans.*

"What do I perceive? Forms. And what besides? Forms. Of the substance I know nothing. We walk among shadows, ourselves shadows to ourselves and to others.

"If I look at a rainbow traced on a cloud, I can perceive it; for him who looks at it from another angle, there is nothing.

"A fancy common enough among the living is to dream that they are dead, that they stand by the side of their own corpse, and follow their own funeral. It is like a swimmer watching his garments stretched out on the shore.

"Philosophy, that habitual and profound meditation which takes us away from all that surrounds us, which annihilates our own personality, is another apprenticeship for death."[174]

This was now to be seen. Diderot, as we have said, came back from his expedition to Russia in the autumn of 1744, tranquilly counting on half a score more years to make up the tale of his days. He remained in temper and habit through this long evening of his life what he had been in its morning and noontide—friendly, industrious, cheerful, exuberant in conversation, keenly interested in the march of liberal and progressive ideas. On his return his wife and daughter found him thin and altered. A few months of absence so often suffice to reveal that our friend has grown old, and that time is casting long shadows. Age seems to have come in a day, like sudden winter. He was as gay and as kindly as ever. Some of his friends had declared that he would never bethink himself of returning at all. "Time and space in his eyes," said Galiani, "are as in the eyes of the Almighty; he thinks that he is everywhere, and that he is eternal."[175] They had predicted for Diderot at St. Petersburg the fate of Descartes at the court of Queen Christina. But the philosopher triumphantly vindicated his character. "My good wife," said he, when he had reached the old familiar fourth floor, "prithee, count my things; thou wilt find no reason for scolding; I have not lost a single handkerchief."[176]

This cheerfulness, however, did not hide from his friends that he was subject to a languor which had been unknown before his journey to Russia. It was not the peevish fatigue that often brings life to an unworthy close. He remained true to the healthy temper of his prime, and found himself across the threshold of old age without repining. As the veteran Cephalus said to Socrates, regrets and complaints are not in a man's age, but in his temper; and he who is of a happy nature will scarcely feel the burden of the years.

In 1762 Diderot had written to Mdlle. Voland a page of affecting musings on the great pathetic theme:

> "You ask me why, the more our life is filled up and busy, the less are we attached to it? If that is true, it is because a busy life is for the most part an innocent life. We think less about Death, and so we fear it less. Without perceiving it, we resign ourselves to the common lot of all the beings that we watch around us, dying and being born again in an incessant, ever renewing circle. After having for a season fulfilled the tasks that nature year by year imposes on us, we grow weary of them, and release ourselves. Energies fade, we become feebler, we crave the close of life, as after working hard we crave the close of the day. Living in harmony with nature, we learn not to rebel against the orders that we see in necessary and universal execution.... There is nobody among us who, having worn himself out in toil, has not seen the hour of rest approach with supreme delight. Life for some of us is only one long day of weariness, and death a long slumber, and the coffin a bed of rest, and the earth only a pillow where it is sweet, when all is done, to lay one's head, never to raise it again. I confess to you that, when looked at in this way, and after the long endless crosses that I have had, death is the most agreeable of prospects. I am bent on teaching myself more and more to see it so."[177]

Again, we are reminded by Diderot's words on this last gentle epilogue to a harassing performance, of Plato's picture of aged Cephalus sitting in a cushioned chair, with the garland round his brows. "I was in the country almost alone, free from cares and disquiet, letting the hours flow on, with no other object than to find myself by the evening as sometimes one finds one's self in the morning, after a night that has been busy with a pleasant dream. The years had left me none of the passions that are our torment, none of the weariness that follows them; I had lost my taste for all the frivolities that are made so important by our hope that we shall enjoy them long. I said to myself: If the little that I have done, and the little that is left for me to do, should perish with me, what would the human race be the loser? What should I be the loser myself?"[178]

This was the mood in which Diderot wrote his singular apology for the life and character of Seneca. Rosenkranz makes the excellent reflection that though Diderot attained to a more free comprehension of Greek art, and especially of Homer, than most of his contemporaries, yet even with him the Roman element was dominant. It was Horace, Terence, Lucretius, Tacitus, Seneca, who to the very end came closer to him than any of the Greeks. The moralising reflection, the satirical tendency, the declamatory form of the

Romans, all had an irresistible attraction for him.[179] Both Roger Bacon and Francis Bacon had preceded him in admiration for Seneca, and Montaigne found Cicero tiresome and unprofitable compared with the author of the Epistles to Lucilius. "When there comes any misfortune to a European," says the imaginary oriental of Montesquieu's *Persian Letters*, "his only resource is the reading of a philosopher called Seneca."[180]

But Diderot was not a man to admire by halves, and to literary praise of Seneca's writings he added a thoroughgoing vindication of his career. In his early days he had referred disparagingly to Seneca,[181] but reflection or accident had made him change his mind. The cheap severity of abstract ethics has always abounded against Seneca, and this severity was what Diderot had all his life found insupportable. Holbach had induced Lagrange, a young man of letters whom he had rescued from want, to undertake the translation of Seneca, and when Lagrange died, Holbach prevailed on Naigeon, Diderot's fervid disciple, to complete and revise the work, which still remains the best of the French versions. That done, then both Holbach and Naigeon urged Diderot to write an account of the philosopher.

The Essay on the Reigns of Claudius and Nero[182] is marked by as much vehemence, as much sincerity of enthusiasm, as if Seneca had been Diderot's personal friend. There is a flame, a passion, about it, an ingenuous air of conviction, which are not common in historical apologies. It is inevitable, as the composition is Diderot's, that it should have many a rambling and declamatory page. His paraphrases of Tacitus are the most curious case in literature of the expansion of a style of sombre poetic concentration into the style of exuberant rhetoric. Both Grimm and a Russian princess of the blood urged him even to translate the whole of Tacitus's works, but it is certain that nobody in the world had ever less of Tacitean quality. Still the history is alive. "*I do not compose*," Diderot said in the dedication. "*I am no author; I read or I converse; I ask questions and I give answers.*" The writer throws himself into the historic situation with the vivid freshness of a contemporary, and if the criticism is sophistical, at least the picture is admirably dramatic. Seneca's position as the minister of Nero seemed exactly one of those cases which always excited Diderot's deepest interest—a case, we mean, in which the general rules of morality condemn, but common sense acquits.

Diderot, as we have already pointed out,[183] was always very near to the position that there is no such thing as an absolute rule of right and wrong, defining classes of acts unconditionally, but each act must be judged on its merits with reference to all the circumstances of the given case. Seneca's career tests this way of looking at things very severely. His connivance with the minor sensualities of Nero's youth, as a means of restraining him from downright crime, and of keeping a measure of order in the government, will perhaps be pardoned by most of those who realise the awful perils of the Empire. As Diderot says, nobody blames Fénelon or Bossuet for remaining at the court of Lewis XIV. in its days of license. But connivance with a king's amours, however degrading it may be from a certain point of view, is a very different thing from acquiescence in a king's murder of his mother. Even here Diderot's impetuosity carries him in two or three bounds over every obstacle. The various courses open to the minister, after the murder of Agrippina, are discussed and dismissed. What, after Nero had slain his mother, was there nothing left to be done by a firm, just, and enlightened man, with an immense burden of affairs on his back, and capable by his courage and benevolence, of bearing succour, repairing misfortunes, hindering depredations, removing the incompetent, and giving power to men of virtue, knowledge, and ability? If he had only saved the honour of a single good woman, or the life or fortune of a single good citizen; if he could bring a day of tranquillity to the provinces, or cross for a week the designs of the miscreants by whom the emperor was surrounded, then Seneca would have been blamed, and would have deserved blame, if he had either retired from court or put an end to his life.[184] This is all true enough, and if Seneca had been only a statesman, the world would probably have applauded him for clinging to the helm at all cost. Unhappily, he was not only a statesman, but a moralist. The two characters are always hard to reconcile, as perhaps any parliamentary candidate might tell us. The contrast between lofty writing and slippery policy has been too violent for Seneca's good fame, as it was for Francis Bacon's. It is ever at his own proper risk and peril that a man dares to present high ideals to the world.

One of the strangest of the many strange digressions in which the Essay on Claudius and Nero abounds, brings us within the glare of the great literary quarrel of the century. Soon after Rousseau settled in Paris for the last time, on his return from England and the subsequent vagabondage, it was known that he had written the *Confessions*, dealing at least as freely with the lives of others as with his own. He had even in 1770 and 1771 given readings of certain passages from them, until Madame d'Epinay, and perhaps also the Maréchale de Luxemburg, prevailed on the authorities to interfere. No one was angrier than Diderot, and in the first edition of the Essay, published in the year of Rousseau's death (1778), he incongruously placed in the midst of his disquisitions on the philosopher of the first century, a long and acrimonious note upon the perversities of the reactionary philosopher of the eighteenth. He was believed by those who talked to him to be in dread of the appearance of the *Confessions*, and we may accept this readily enough, without assuming that Diderot was conscious of hidden enormities which he was afraid of seeing publicly uncovered. Rousseau, as Diderot well knew, was so wayward, so strangely oblique both in vision and judgment, that innocence was no security against malice and misrepresentation.

Rousseau's name has never lacked fanatical partisans down to our own day, and Diderot was attacked by some of the earliest of them for his note of disparagement. The first part of the *Confessions*—all that Diderot ever saw—appeared in 1782, and in the same year Diderot published a second edition of the Essay on Claudius and Nero, so augmented by replies, inserted in season and out of season, to the diatribes of the party of Rousseau, that as it now stands the reader may well doubt whether the substance and foundation of the book is an apology for Seneca or a vindication of Denis Diderot. As Grimm said, we have to make up our minds to see the author suddenly pass from the palace of the Cæsars to the garret of MM. Royou, Grosier, and company; from Paris to Rome, and from Rome back again to Paris; from the reign of Claudius to the reign of Lewis xv.; from the college of the Sorbonne to the college of the augurs; to turn now to the masters of the world, and now to the yelping curs of literature; to see him in his dramatic enthusiasm making the one speak and the others answer; apostrophising himself and apostrophising his readers, and leaving them often enough in perplexity as to the personage who is speaking and the personage whom he addresses.[185] We may agree with Grimm that this gives an air of originality to the performance, but such originality is of a kind to displease the serious student, without really attracting the few readers who have a taste for rebelling against the pedantries of literary form. We become confused by the long strain of uncertainty whether we are reading about the Roman Emperor or the French King; about Seneca, Burrhus, and Thrasea, or Turgot, Malesherbes, and Necker.

Diderot's candour, simplicity, happy bonhommie, and sincerity in real interests raised him habitually above the pettiness, the bustling malice, the vain self-consciousness, the personalities that infest all literary and social cliques. It is surprising at first that Diderot, who had all his life borne the sting of the gnats of Grub Street with decent composure, should have been so moved by Rousseau, or by meaner assailants, whom Rousseau himself would have rudely disclaimed. The explanation seems to lie in this fact of human character, that a man of Diderot's temperament, while entirely heedless of criticism directed against his opinions or his public position, is specially sensitive to innuendoes against his private benevolence and loyalty. An insult to the force of his understanding was indifferent to him, but an affront to one's *belle âme* is beyond pardon. It was hard that a man who had prodigally thrown away the forces of his life for others should be charged with malignity of heart and an incapacity for friendship. This was the harder, because it was the moral fashion of that day to place friendliness, amiability, the desire to please and to serve, at the very head of all the virtues. The whole correspondence of the time is penetrated to an incomparable degree by a caressing spirit; it is sometimes too elaborate and far-fetched in expression, but it marks a vivid sociability, and even a true humanity, that softens and harmonises the sharpness of men's egotism.

Again, though Diderot himself is not ungenerously handled in the *Confessions*, there are passages about Madame d'Epinay and Madame d'Houdetot which not only stamp Rousseau with ingratitude towards two women who had treated him kindly, but which were calculated to make practical mischief among people still living. All this was atrocious in itself, and the atrocity seemed more black to Diderot than to others, because he had for some years known Madame d'Epinay as a friendly creature, and, above all, because Grimm was her lover. Perhaps we may add among the reasons that stirred him to pen these diatribes, a consciousness of the harm that Rousseau's sentimentalism had done to sound and positive thinking. But this, we may be sure, would be infinitely less potent than the motives that sprang from Diderot's own sentimentalism. The quarrel, for all save a few foolish partisans, is now dead, and we may leave the dust once more to settle thick upon it. Diderot's own way of reading history is not unworthy of imitation, and it is capable of application in spirit to private conduct no less than to the history of great public events. "Does the narrative present me with some fact that dishonours humanity? Then I examine it with the most rigorous severity; whatever sagacity I may be able to command, I employ in detecting contradictions that throw suspicion on the story. It is not so when an action is beautiful, lofty, noble. Then I never think of arguing against the pleasure that I feel in sharing the name of man with one who has done such an action. I will say more; it is to my heart, and perhaps too it is only conformable to justice, to hazard an opinion that tends to whiten an illustrious personage, in the face of authorities that seem to contradict the tenour of his life, of his doctrine, and of his general repute."[186]

The elaborate outbreak against Rousseau is perhaps Diderot's only breach of what ought thus to be a rule for all magnanimous men. Diderot, or his shade, paid the penalty. La Harpe retaliated for some slight wound to pitiful literary vanity, by a lecture on Seneca in which he raked up all the old accusations against Seneca's champion. La Harpe, for various reasons into which we need not now more particularly enter, got the ear of the European public in the years of reaction after he had himself deserted his old philosophic friends, and gone over to the conservative camp. He found the world eager to listen to all that could be said against men who were believed to have corrupted their age; and his bitter misrepresentations, not seldom invigorated by lies, were the origin of much of the vulgar prejudice that has only begun to melt away in our own generation.

Rousseau died in 1778. The more versatile literary genius of the century had died a couple of months earlier in the same year. It was not until the occasion of Voltaire's triumphant visit to Paris, after an absence of seven-and-twenty years, that he and Diderot at length met. Their correspondence had been less constant and less cordial than was common where Voltaire was concerned; but though their sympathy was imperfect, there was no lack of mutual goodwill and admiration. The poet is said to have done his best to push Diderot into the Academy, but the king was incurably hostile, and Diderot was not anxious for an empty distinction. He had none of that vanity nor eagerness for recognition—pardonable enough, for that matter—which such distinctions gratify. And he perhaps agreed with Voltaire himself, who said of academies and parliaments that, when men come together, their ears instantly become elongated. After Diderot's return from Russia Voltaire wrote to him: "I am eighty-three years of age, and I repeat that I am inconsolable at the thought of dying without ever having seen you. I have tried to collect around me as many of your children as possible, but I am a long way from having the whole family.... We are not so far apart, at bottom, and it only needs a conversation to bring us to an understanding."[187]

Of such conversations we have almost nothing to tell. No sacred bard has commemorated the salutation of the heroes. We only know that at the end of their first interview Diderot's facility of discourse had been so copious that, after he had taken his leave, Voltaire said: "The man is clever, assuredly; but he lacks one talent, and an essential talent—that of dialogue." Diderot's remark about Voltaire was more picturesque. "He is like one of those old haunted castles, which are falling into ruins in every part; but you easily perceive that it is inhabited by some ancient sorcerer."[188] They had a dispute as to the merits of Shakespeare, and Diderot displeased the patriarch by repeating the expression that we have already quoted (vol. i. p. 330) about Shakespeare being like the statue of St. Christopher at Notre Dame, unshapely and rude, but such a giant that ordinary men could pass between his legs without touching him.[189]

There was one man who might have told us a thousand interesting things both about Diderot's conversations with Voltaire, and his relations with other men. This man was Naigeon, to whom Diderot gave most of his papers, and who always professed, down to his death in 1814, to be Diderot's closest adherent and most authoritative expounder. Diderot was, as he always knew and said, less an author than a talker; not a talker like Johnson, but like Coleridge. If Naigeon could only have contented himself with playing reporter, and could have been blessed by nature with the rare art of Boswell. "We wanted," as Carlyle says, "to see and know how it stood with the bodily man, the working and warfaring Denis Diderot; how he looked and lived, what he did, what he said." Instead of which, nothing but "a dull, sulky, snuffling, droning, interminable lecture on Atheistic Philosophy," delivered with the vehemence of some pulpit-drumming Gowkthrapple, or "precious Mr. Jabesh Rentowel." Naigeon belonged to the too numerous class of men and women overabundantly endowed with unwise intellect. He was acute, diligent, and tenacious; fond of books, especially when they had handsome margins and fine bindings; above all things, he was the most fanatical atheist, and the most indefatigable propagandist and eager proselytiser which that form of religion can boast. We do not know the date of his first acquaintance with Diderot;[190] we only know that at the end of Diderot's days he had no busier or more fervent disciple than Naigeon. To us, at all events, whatever it may have been to Diderot, the acquaintance and discipleship have proved good for very little.

Our last authentic glimpse of Diderot is from the pen of a humane and enlightened Englishman, whose memory must be held in perpetual honour among us. Samuel Romilly, then a young man of four-and-twenty, visited Paris in 1781. He made the acquaintance of the namesake who had written the articles on watch-making in the Encyclopædia, and whose son had written the more famous articles on Toleration and Virtue. By this honest man Romilly was introduced to D'Alembert and Diderot. The former was in weak health and said very little. Diderot, on the contrary, was all warmth and eagerness, and talked to his visitor with as little reserve as if he had been long and intimately acquainted with him. He spoke on politics, religion, and philosophy. He praised the English for having led the way to sound philosophy, but the adventurous genius of the French, he said, had pushed them on before their guides. "You others," he continued, "mix up theology with your philosophy; that is to spoil everything, it is to mix up lies with truth; *il faut sabrer la théologie*—we must put theology to the sword." He was ostentatious, Romilly says, of a total disbelief in the existence of a God. He quoted Plato, "the author of all the good theology that ever existed in the world, as saying that there is a vast curtain drawn over the heavens, and that men must content themselves with what passes beneath that curtain, without ever attempting to raise it; and in order to complete my conversion from my unhappy errors, he read me all through a little work of his own"—of which we shall presently speak. On politics he talked very eagerly, "and inveighed with great warmth against the tyranny of the French government. He told me that he had long meditated a work upon the death of Charles the First; that he had studied the trial of that prince; and that his intention was to have tried him over again, and to have sent him to the scaffold if he had found him guilty, but that he had at last relinquished the design. In England he would have executed it, but he had not the courage to do so in France. D'Alembert, as I have observed was more cautious; he contented himself with observing what an effect philosophy had in his own time produced on the minds of the people. The birth of the Dauphin (known afterwards as Lewis XVII., the unhappy prisoner of the Temple) afforded him an example. He was old enough, he said, to remember when such an event had made the whole nation drunk with joy (1729), but now they regarded with great indifference the birth of another master."[191]

It was thus clear to the two veterans of the Encyclopædia that the change for which they had worked was at hand. The press literally teemed with pamphlets, treatises, poems, histories, all shouting from the house-tops open destruction to beliefs which fifty years before were actively protected against so much as a whisper in the closet. Every form of literary art was seized and turned into an instrument in the remorseless attack on *L'Infâme*. The conservative or religious opposition showed a weakness that is hardly paralleled in the long history of the mighty controversy. Ability, adroitness, vigour, and character were for once all on one side. Palissot was perhaps, after all, the best of the writers on the conservative side.[192] With all his faults, he had the literary sense. Some of what he said was true, and some of the third-rate people whom he assailed deserved the assault. His criticism on Diderot's drama, *The Natural Son*, was not a whit more severe than that bad play demanded.[193] Not seldom in the course of this work we have wished with Palissot that the excellent Diderot were less addicted to prophetic and apocalyptical turns of speech, that there were less of chaos round his points of burning and shining light, and that he had less title to the hostile name of the Lycophron of philosophy.[194] But the comedy of *The Philosophers* was a scandalous misrepresentation, introducing Diderot personally on the stage, and putting into his mouth a mixture of folly and knavery that was as foreign to Diderot as to any one else in the world. In 1782 the satirist again attacked his enemy, now grown old and weary. In *Le Satyrique*, Valère, a spiteful and hypocritical poetaster, is intended partially at least for Diderot. A colporteur, not ill-named as M. Pamphlet, comes to urge payment of his bill.

> Daignez avoir égard à mes vives instances.
> Je suis humilié d'y mettre tant de feu:
> Mais les temps sont si durs! le comptoir rend si peu!
> Imprimeur, Colporteur, Relieur, et Libraire,
> Avec tous ces métiers, je suis dans la misère:
> Mais j'ai toujours grand soin, malgré ma pauvreté,
> De ne peser mon gain qu'au poids de l'équité.
> Vous en allez juger par le susdit mémoire.
>   [*Il prend ses lunettes comme pour lire.*

VALÈRE. (*Avec humeur.*) Eh, monsieur, finissez.

M. PAMPHLET.   C'est trahir votre gloire
Que de vouloir caeher les immortels écrits

[*Il lit.*

Dont vous êtes l'auteur. *Les Boudoirs de Paris,*
On Journal des Abbés. L'Espion des Coulisses,
Ouvrage assez piquant sur les mœurs des actrices.

And the intention of the pleasantry is pointed by a malicious footnote, to the effect that people who might be surprised that a serious man like Valère should have written works of this licentious and frivolous kind, will conceive that in a moment of leisure a philosopher should write *Les Bijoux Indiscrèts*, for instance, and the next day follow it by a treatise on morality,[195]—as Diderot unhappily had done.

Palissot was not so good as Molière, Boileau, and Pope, as he was fatuous enough to suppose; but he was certainly better than the scribbler who asked—

Mais enfin de quoi se glorifie
Ce siècle de mollesse et de Philosophie?
Dites-moi: le Français a-t-il un cœur plus franc
Plus prodigue à l'état de son généreux sang,
Plus ardent à venger la plaintive innocence
Contre l'iniquité que soutient la puissance?
Le Français philosophe est-il plus respecté
Pour la foi, la candeur, l'exacte probité?
Où sont-ils ces Héros, ces vertueux modèles
Que l'Encyclopédie a couvé sous ses ailes?[196]

Tiresome doggrel of this kind was the strongest retort that the party of obscurantism could muster against the vigour, grace, and sparkle of Voltaire.

The great official champions of the old system were not much wiser than their hacks in the press. The churchmen were given over to a blind mind. The great edition of Voltaire's works which Beaumarchais was printing over the frontier at Kehl, excited their anger to a furious pitch. The infamous Cardinal de Rohan, archbishop of Strasburg (1781), denounced the publication as sacrilege. The archbishop of Paris (1785) thundered against the monument of scandal and the work of darkness. The archbishop of Vienne forbade the faithful of his diocese to subscribe to it under pain of mortal sin. In the general assembly of the clergy which opened in the summer of 1780, the bishops, in memorials to the king, deplored the homage paid to the famous writer who was "less known for the beauty of his genius and the superiority of his talents, than for the persevering and implacable war which for sixty years he had waged against the Lord and his Christ." They cursed in solemn phrase the "revolting blasphemies" of Raynal's *History of the Indies*, and declared that the publication of a new edition of that celebrated book with the name and the portrait of its author, showed that the most elementary notions of shame and decency lay in profound sleep.

In the midst of those prolonged cries of distress, we have no word of recognition that the only remedy for a moral disease is a moral remedy. The single resource that occurred to their debilitated souls was the familiar armoury of suppression, menace, violence, and tyranny. "Sire," they cried, "it is time to put a term to this deplorable lethargy." They reminded the king of the declaration of 1757, which inflicted on all persons who printed or circulated writings hostile to religion, the punishment of death. But "their paternal bowels shuddered at the sight of these severe enactments;" all that they sought was plenty of rigorous imprisonment, ruinous fining, and diligent espionage.[197] If the reader is revolted by the rashness of Diderot's expectation of the speedy decay of the belief in a God,[198] he may well be equally revolted by the obstinate infatuation of the men who expected to preserve the belief in a God by the spies of the department of police. Much had no doubt been done for the church in past times by cruelty and oppression, but the folly of the French bishops, after the reign of Voltaire and the apostolate of the Encyclopædia, lay exactly in their blindness to the fact that the old methods were henceforth impossible in France, and impossible for ever. How can we wonder at the hatred and contempt felt by men of the social intelligence of Diderot and D'Alembert for this desperate union of impotence and malignity?

The band of the precursors was rapidly disappearing. Grimm and Holbach, Catherine and Frederick, still survived.[199] D'Alembert, tended to the last hour by Condorcet with the lovable reverence of a son, died at the end of October 1783. Turgot, gazing with eyes of astonished sternness on a society hurrying incorrigibly with joyful speed along the path of destruction, had passed away two years before (1781). Voltaire, the great intellectual director of Europe for fifty years, and Rousseau, the great emotional reactionist, had both, as we know, died in 1778. The little companies in which, from Adrienne Lecouvreur, the Marquise de Lambert, and Madame de Tencin, in the first half of the century, groups of intelligent men and women had succeeded in founding informal schools of disinterested opinion, and in finally removing the centre of criticism and intellectual activity from Versailles to Paris, had now nearly all come to an end. Madame du Deffand died in 1780, Madame Geoffrin in 1779, and in 1776 Mdlle. Lespinasse, whose letters will long survive her, as giving a burning literary note to the vagueness of suffering and pain of soul. One of Diderot's favourite companions in older days, Galiani, the antiquary, the scholar, the politician, the incomparable mimic, the shrewdest, wittiest, and gayest of men after Voltaire, was feeling the dull grasp of approaching death under his native sky at Naples. Galiani's *Dialogues on the Trade in Grain* (1769-70) contained, under that most unpromising title, a piece of literature which for its verve, rapidity, wit, dialectical subtlety, and real strength of thought, has hardly been surpassed by masterpieces of a wider recognition. Voltaire vowed that Plato and Molière must have combined to produce a book that was as amusing as the best of romances, and as instructive as the best of serious books. Diderot, who had a hand in retouching the *Dialogues* for the press,[200] went so far as to pronounce them worthy of a place along with the *Provincial Letters* of Pascal, and declared that, like those immortal pieces, Galiani's dialogues would remain as a model of perfection in their own kind, long after both the subject and the personages concerned had lost their interest.[201] The prophecy has not come quite true, for the world is busy, and heedless, and much the prey of accident and capricious tradition in the books that it reads. Yet even now, although Galiani was probably wrong on the special issue between himself and the economists, it would be well if people would turn to his demolition, as wise as witty, of the doctrine of absolute truths in political economy. Galiani's constant correspondent was Madame d'Epinay, the kindly benefactress of Rousseau a quarter of a century earlier, the friend of Diderot, the more than friend of Grimm. In 1783 she died, and either in that year or the next, Mademoiselle Voland, who had filled so great a space in the life of Diderot. The ghosts and memories of his friends became the majority, and he consoled himself that he should not long survive.

The days of intellectual excitement and philanthropic hope seemed at their very height, but in fact they were over. "Nobody," said Talleyrand, "who has not lived before 1789, knows how sweet life can be." The old world had its last laugh over the *Marriage of Figaro* (April 1784), but in the laugh of Figaro there is a strange ring. Under all its gaiety, its liveliness, its admirable *naïveté*, was something sombre. It was pregnant with menace. Its fooling was the ironical enforcement of Raynal's trenchant declaration that "the law is nothing, if it be not a sword gliding indistinctly over the heads of all, and striking down whatever rises above the horizontal plane along which it moves."

Diderot himself is commonly accused of having fomented an atrocious spirit by the horrible couplet—

> Et ses mains ourdiraient les entrailles du prêtre,
> Au défaut d'un cordon pour étrangler les rois.[202]

That the verses could have actually excited the spirit of the Terrorists is impossible, for they were not given to the world until 1795. And in the second place, so far as Diderot's intention is concerned, any one who reads the piece from which the lines are taken, will perceive that the whole performance is in a vein of playful phantasy, and that the particular verses are placed dramatically in the mouth of a proclaimed Eleutheromane, or maniac for liberty.[203] Diderot was not likely to foresee that what he designed for an illustration of the frenzy of the Pindaric dithyramb, would so soon be mistaken for a short formula of practical politics.[204]

In 1780 his townsmen of Langres paid him a compliment, which showed that the sage was not without honour in his own country. They besought him to sit for his portrait, to be placed among the worthies in the town hall. Diderot replied by sending them Houdon's bronze bust, which was received with all distinction and honour. Naigeon hints that in the last years of his life Diderot paid more attention to money than he had ever done before;[205] not that he became a miser, but because, like many other persons, he had not found out until the close of a life's experience that care of money really means care of the instrument that procures some of the best ends in life. For a moment we may regret that he was too much occupied in attending to his affairs to take the unwise Naigeon's wise counsel, that he should devote himself to a careful revision of all that he had written. Perhaps Diderot's instinct was right. Among the distractions of old age, he had turned back to his Letter on the Blind, and read it over again without partiality. He found, as was natural, some defects in a piece that was written three-and-thirty years before, but he abstained from attempting to remove them, for fear that the page of the young man should be made the worse by the retouching of the old man. "There comes a time," he reflects, "when taste gives counsels whose justice you recognise, but which you have no longer strength to follow. It is the pusillanimity that springs from consciousness of weakness, or else it is the idleness that is one of the results of weakness and pusillanimity, which disgusts me with a task that would be more likely to hurt than to improve my work.

> Solve senescentem mature sanus equum, ne
> Peccet ad extremum ridendus et ilia ducat."

And so he contented himself with some rough notes of phenomena that were corroborative of the speculation of his youth.[206]

In the early spring of 1784 Diderot had an attack which he knew to be the presage of the end. Dropsy set in, and he lingered until the summer. The priest of Saint Sulpice, the centre of the philosophic quarter, came to visit him two or three times a week, hoping to achieve at least the semblance of a conversion. Diderot did not encourage conversation on theology, but when pressed he did not refuse it. One day when they found, as two men of sense will always find, that they had ample common ground in matters of morality and good works, the priest ventured to hint that an exposition of such excellent maxims, accompanied by a slight retractation of Diderot's previous works, would have a good effect on the world. "I daresay it would, monsieur le curé, but confess that I should be acting an impudent lie." And no word of retractation was ever made. As the end came suddenly, the priest escaped from the necessity of denying the funeral rites of the Church.

For thirty years Diderot had been steadfast to his quarters on an upper floor in the Rue Taranne, and even now, when the physicians told him that to climb such length of staircase was death to him, he still could not be induced to stir. It would have been easier, his daughter says, to effect a removal from Versailles itself. Grimm at length asked the Empress of Russia to provide a house for her librarian, and when the request was conceded, Diderot, who could never be ungracious, allowed himself to be taken from his garret to palatial rooms in the Rue de Richelieu. He enjoyed them less than a fortnight. Though visibly growing weaker every day, he did all that he could to cheer the people around him, and amused himself and them by arranging his pictures and his books. In the evening, to the last, he found strength to converse on science and philosophy to the friends who were eager as ever for the last gleanings of his prolific intellect. In the last conversation that his daughter heard him carry on, his last words were the pregnant aphorism that *the first step towards philosophy is incredulity.*

On the evening of the 30th of July 1784 he sat down to table, and at the end of the meal took an apricot. His wife, with kindly solicitude, remonstrated. *Mais quel diable de mal veux-tu que cela me fasse?* he said, and ate the apricot. Then he rested his elbow on the table, trifling with some sweetmeats. His wife asked him a question; on receiving no answer, she looked up and saw that he was dead. He had died as the Greek poet says that men died in the golden age—θνησκον δ' ὡς ὑπνω δεδμενοι, *they passed away as if mastered by sleep.* It had always been his opinion that an examination of the organs after death is a useful practice, and his wish that the operation should take place in his own case was respected. Nothing interesting or remarkable was revealed, and his remains were laid in the vaults of the church of Saint Roche.

So the curtain fell upon this strange tragi-comedy of a man of letters. There is no better epilogue than words of his own:—"We fix our gaze on the ruins of a triumphal arch, of a portico, a pyramid, a temple, a palace, and we return upon ourselves. All is annihilated, perishes, passes away. It is only the world that remains; only time that endures. I walk between two eternities. To whatever side I turn my eyes, the objects that surround me tell of an end, and teach me resignation to my own end. What is my ephemeral existence in comparison with that of the crumbling rock and the decaying forest? I see the marble of the tomb falling to dust, and yet I cannot bear to die! Am I to grudge a feeble tissue of fibres and flesh to a general law, that executes itself inexorably even on very bronze!"

CHAPTER IX.
CONCLUSION.

A few more pages must be given to one or two of Diderot's writings which have not hitherto been mentioned. An exhaustive survey of his works is out of the question, nor would any one be repaid for the labour of criticism. A mere list of the topics that he handled would fill a long chapter. A redaction of a long treatise on harmony, a vast sheaf of notes on the elements of physiology, a collection of miscellanea on the drama, a still more copious collection of miscellanea on a hundred points in literature and art, a fragment on the exercise of young Russians, an elaborate plan of studies for a proposed Russian University,—no less panurgic and less encyclopædic a critic than Diderot himself could undertake to sweep with ever so light a wing over this vast area. Everybody can find something to say about the collection of tales, in which Diderot thought that he was satirising the manners of his time, after the fashion of Rabelais, Montaigne, La Mothe-le-Vayer, and Swift. But not everybody is competent to deal, for instance, with the five memoirs on different subjects in mathematics (1748), with which Diderot hoped to efface the scandal of his previous performance.

I.

Decidedly the most important of the pieces of which we have not yet spoken must be counted the *Thoughts on the Interpretation of Nature* (1754). His study of Bacon and the composition of the introductory prospectus of the Encyclopædia had naturally filled Diderot's mind with ideas about the universe as a whole. The great problem of man's knowledge of this universe, —the limits, the instruments, the meaning of such knowledge, came before him with a force that he could not evade. Maupertuis had in 1751, under the assumed name of Baumann, an imaginary doctor of Erlangen, published a dissertation on the *Universal System of Nature*, in which he seems to have maintained that the mechanism of the universe is one and the same throughout, modifying itself, or being modified by some vital element within, in an infinity of diverse ways.[207] Leibnitz's famous idea, of making nature invariably work with the minimum of action, was seized by Maupertuis, expressed as the Law of Thrift, and made the starting-point of speculations that led directly to Holbach and the *System of Nature*.[208] The *Loi d'Epargne* evidently tended to make unity of all the forces of the universe the keynote or the goal of philosophical inquiry. At this time of his life, Diderot resisted Maupertuis's theory of the unity of vital force in the universe, or perhaps we should rather say that he saw how open it was to criticism. His resistance has none of his usual air of vehement conviction. However that may be, the theory excited his interest, and fitted in with the train of meditation which his thoughts about the Encyclopædia had already set in motion, and of which the *Pensées Philosophiques* of 1746 were the cruder prelude.

The *Thoughts on the Interpretation of Nature* are, in form as in title, imitated from those famous *Aphorismi de Interpretatione Naturæ et Regni Hominis*, which are more shortly known to all men as Bacon's *Novum Organum*.[209] The connection between the aphorisms is very loosely held. Diderot began by premising that he would let his thoughts follow one another under his pen, in the order in which the subjects came up in his mind; and he kept his word. Their general scope, so far as it is capable of condensed expression, may be described as a reconciliation between the two great classes into which Diderot found thinkers upon Nature to be divided; those who have many instruments and few ideas, and those who have few instruments and many ideas,—in other words, between men of science without philosophy, and philosophers without knowledge of experimental science.

In the region of science itself, again, Diderot foresees as great a change as in the relations between science and philosophy. "We touch the moment of a great revolution in the sciences. From the strong inclination of men's minds towards morals, literature, the history of nature and experimental physics, I would almost venture to assert that before the next hundred years are over, there will not be three great geometers to be counted in Europe. This science will stop short where the Bernouillis, the Eulers, the Maupertuis, the Clairauts, the Fontaines, the D'Alemberts, the Lagranges have left it. They will have fixed the Pillars of Hercules. People will go no further." Those who have read Comte's angry denunciations of the perversions of geometry by means of algebra, and of the waste of intellectual force in modern analysis, [210] will at least understand how such a view as Diderot's was possible. And no one will be likely to deny that, whether or not the pillars of the geometrical Hercules were finally set a hundred years ago, the great discoveries of the hundred years since Diderot have been, as he predicted, in the higher sciences. The great misfortune of France was that the supremacy of geometry coincided with the opening of the great era of political discussion. The definitions of Montesquieu's famous book, which opened the political movement in literature, have been shown to be less those of a jurisconsult than of a geometer.[211] Social truths, with all their profound complexity, were handled like propositions in Euclid, and logical deductions from arbitrary premises were treated as accurate representations of real circumstance. The repulse of geometry to its proper rank came too late.

Comte always liberally recognised Diderot's genius, and any reader of Comte's views on the necessities of subjective synthesis will discern the germ of that doctrine in the following remarkable section:

"When we compare the infinite multitude of the phenomena of nature with the limits of our understandings and the weakness of our organs, can we ever expect anything else from the slowness of our work, from the long and frequent interruptions, and from the rarity of creative genius than a few broken and separated pieces of the great chain that binds all things together? Experimental philosophy might work for centuries of centuries, and the materials that it had heaped up, finally reaching in their number beyond all combination, would still be far removed from an exact enumeration. How many volumes would it not need to contain the mere terms by which we should designate the distinct collections of phenomena, if the phenomena were known? When will the philosophic language be complete? If it were complete, who among men would be able to know it? If the Eternal, to manifest his power still more plainly than by the marvels of nature, had deigned to develop the universal mechanism on pages traced by his own hand, do you suppose that this great book would be more comprehensible to us than the universe itself? How many pages of it all would have been intelligible to the philosopher who, with all the force of head that had been conferred upon him, was not sure of having grasped all the conclusions by which an old geometer determined the relation of the sphere to the cylinder? We should have in such pages a fairly good measure of the reach of men's minds, and a still more pungent satire on our vanity. We should say, Fermat went to such a page, Archimedes went a few pages further.

"What then is our end? The execution of a work that can never be achieved, and which would be far beyond human intelligence if it were achieved. Are we not more insensate than the first inhabitants of the plain of Shinar? We know the immeasurable distance between the earth and the heavens, and still we insist on rearing our tower.

"But can we presume that there will not come a time when our pride will abandon the work in discouragement? What appearance is there that, narrowly lodged and ill at its ease here below, our pride should obstinately persist in constructing an uninhabitable palace beyond the earth's atmosphere? Even if it should so insist, would it not be arrested by the confusion of tongues, which is already only too perceptible and too inconvenient in natural history? Besides, it is utility that circumscribes all. It will be utility that in a few centuries will set bounds to experimental physics, as it is on the eve of setting bounds to geometry. I grant centuries to this study, because the sphere of its utility is infinitely more extensive than that of any abstract science, and it is without contradiction the base of our real knowledge."[212]

We cannot wonder that when Comte drew up his list of the hundred and fifty volumes that should form the good Positivist's library in the nineteenth century, he should have placed Diderot's *Interpretation of Nature* on one side of Descartes' *Discourse on Method*, with Bacon's *Novum Organum* on the other.

The same spirit finds even stronger and more distinct expression in a later aphorism:—"Since the reason cannot understand everything, imagination foresee everything, sense observe everything, nor memory retain everything; since great men are born at such remote intervals, and the progress of science is so interrupted by revolution, that whole ages of study are passed in recovering the knowledge of the centuries that are gone,—to observe everything in nature without distinction is to fail in duty to the human race.

Men who are beyond the common run in their talents ought to respect themselves and posterity in the employment of their time. What would posterity think of us if we had nothing to transmit to it save a complete insectology, an immense history of microscopic animals? No—to the great geniuses great objects, little objects to the little geniuses" (§ 54).

Diderot, while thus warning inquirers against danger on one side, was alive to the advantages of stubborn and unlimited experiment on the other. "When you have formed in your mind," he says, "one of those systems which require to be verified by experience, you ought neither to cling to it obstinately nor abandon it lightly. People sometimes think their conjectures false, when they have not taken the proper measures to find them true. Obstinacy, even, has fewer drawbacks than the opposite excess. By multiplying experiments, if you do not find what you want, it may happen that you will come on something better. *Never is time employed in interrogating nature entirely lost*" (§ 42). The reader will not fail to observe that this maxim is limited by the condition of verifiableness. Of any system that could not be verified by experience Diderot would have disdained to speak in connection with the interpretation of nature.

This, of course, did not prevent him from hypothesis and prophecy which he himself had not the means of justifying. For example, he said that just as in mathematics, by examining all properties of a curve we find that they are one and the same property presented under different faces, so in nature when experimental physics are more advanced, people will recognise that all the phenomena, whether of weight, or elasticity, or magnetism, or electricity, are only different sides of the same affection (§ 44). But he was content to leave it to posterity, and to build no fabric on unproved propositions.

In the same scientific spirit he penetrated the hollowness of every system dealing with Final Causes:

> "The physicist, whose profession is to instruct and not to edify, will abandon the *Why*, and will busy himself only with the *How....* How many absurd ideas, false suppositions, chimerical notions in those hymns which some rash defenders of final causes have dared to compose in honour of the Creator? Instead of sharing the transports of admiration of the prophet, and crying out at the sight of the unnumbered stars that light up the midnight sky, *The heavens declare the glory of God, and the firmament sheweth his handiwork*, they have given themselves up to the superstition of their conjectures. Instead of adoring the All-Powerful in the creation of nature, they have prostrated themselves before the phantoms of their imagination. If any one doubts the justice of my reproach, I invite him to compare Galen's treatise on the use of parts of the human body, with the physiology of Boerhaave, and the physiology of Boerhaave with that of Haller; I invite posterity to compare the systematic or passing views of Haller with what will be the

physiology of future times. Man praises the Eternal for his own poor views; and the Eternal who hears from the elevation of his throne, and who knows his own design, accepts the silly praise and smiles at man's vanity" (§ 56).

The world has advanced rapidly along this path since Diderot's day, and has opened out many new and unsuspected meanings by the way. Perhaps the advance has been less satisfactory in working out, in a scientific way, the philosophy that is implied in the following adaptation of the Leibnitzian and Maupertuisian suggestion of the law of economy in natural forces:
—"Astonishment often comes from our supposing several marvels, where in truth there is only one; from our imagining in nature as many particular acts as we can count phenomena, whilst *nature has perhaps in reality never produced more than one single act*. It seem even that, if nature had been under the necessity of producing several acts, the different results of such acts would be isolated; that there would be collections of phenomena independent of one another, and that the general chain of which philosophy assumes the continuity, would break in many places. *The absolute independence of a single fact is incompatible with the idea of an All; and without the idea of a Whole, there can be no Philosophy*" (§ 11).

At length Diderot concludes by a series of questions which he thinks that philosophers may perhaps count worthy of discussion. What is the difference, for example, between living matter and dead? Does the energy of a living molecule vary by itself, or according to the quantity, the quality, the forms of the dead or living matter with which it is united? We need not continue the enumeration, because Diderot himself suddenly brings them to an end with a truly admirable expression of his <u>sense of how</u> unworthy they are of the attention of serious men, who are able to measure the difference between a wise and beneficent use of intelligence, and a foolish and wasteful misuse of it. "When I turn my eyes," he says, "to the works of men, and see the cities that are built on every side, all the elements yoked to our service, languages fixed, nations civilised, harbours constructed, lands and skies measured—then the world seems to me very old. When I find man uncertain as to the first principles of medicine and agriculture, as to the properties of the commonest substances, as to knowledge of the maladies that afflict him, as to the pruning of trees, as to the best form for the plough, then it seems as if the earth had only been inhabited yesterday. And if men were wise, they would at last give themselves up to such inquiries as bear on their wellbeing, and would not take the trouble to answer my futile questions for a thousand years at the very soonest; or perhaps, even, considering the very scanty extent that they occupy in space and time, they would never deign to answer them at all."

II.

In 1769 Diderot composed three dialogues, of which he said that, with a certain mathematical memoir, they were the only writings of his own with which he was contented. The first is a dialogue between himself and D'Alembert; the second is D'Alembert's Dream, in which D'Alembert in his sleep continues the discussion, while Mdlle. Lespinasse, who is watching by his bedside, takes down the dreamer's words; in the third, Mdlle. Lespinasse and the famous physician, Bordeu, conclude the matter.[213] It is impossible, Diderot said to Mdlle. Voland, to be more profound and more mad: it is at once a supreme extravagance, and the most deep-reaching philosophy. He congratulated himself on the cleverness of placing his ideas in the mouth of a man who dreams, on the ground that we must often give to wisdom the air of madness, in order to secure admittance. Mdlle. Lespinasse was not so complacent. She made D'Alembert insist that the dialogue should be destroyed, and Diderot believed that he had burned the only existing copy. As a matter of fact, the manuscript was not published until 1830, when all the people concerned had long been reduced to dust. There are five or six pages, Diderot said to Mdlle. Voland, which would make your sister's hair stand on end. A man may be much less squeamish than Mdlle. Voland's sister, and still pronounce the imaginative invention of D'Alembert's Dream, and the sequel, to be as odious as anything since the freaks of filthy Diogenes in his tub. Two remarks may be made on this strange production. First, Diderot never intended the dialogues for the public eye. He would have been as shocked as the Archbishop of Paris himself, if he had supposed that they would become accessible to everybody who knows how to read. Second, though they are in form the most ugly and disgusting piece in the literature of philosophy, they testify in their own way to Diderot's sincerity of interest in his subject. Science is essentially unsparing and unblushing, and D'Alembert's Dream plunged exactly into those parts of physiology which are least fit to be handled in literature. The attempt to give an air of polite comedy to functions and secretions must be pronounced detestable, in spite of the dialectical acuteness and force with which Diderot pressed his point.

It would be impossible, in a book not exclusively designed for a public of professors, to give a full account of these three dialogues. It is indispensable to describe their drift, because it is here that Diderot figures definitely as a materialist. Diderot was in no sense the originator of the French materialism of the eighteenth century. He was preceded by Maupertuis, by Robinet, and by La Mettrie; and we have already seen that when he composed the Thoughts on the Interpretation of Nature (1754), he did not fully accept Maupertuis's materialistic thesis. Lange has shown that at a very early period in the movement the most consistent materialism was ready and developed, while such leaders of the movement as Voltaire and Diderot still leaned either on deism, or on a mixture of deism and scepticism.[214] The philosophy of D'Alembert's Dream is definite enough, and far enough removed alike from deism and scepticism.

"The thinking man is like a musical instrument. Suppose a clavecin to have sensibility and memory, and then say whether it would not repeat of itself the airs that you have played on its keys. We are instruments endowed with sensibility and memory. Our senses are so many keys, pressed by the nature that surrounds them, and they often press one another; and this, according to my judgment, is all that passes in a clavecin organised as you and I are organised.

"There is only one substance in the world. The marble of the statue makes the flesh of the man, and conversely. Reduce a block of marble to impalpable powder; mix this powder with humus, or vegetable earth; knead them well together; water the mixture; let it rot for a year, two years—time does not count. In this you sow the plant, the plant nourishes the man, and hence the passage from marble to tissue.

"Do you see this egg? With that you overturn all the schools of theology and all the temples of the earth. It is an insensible mass before the germ is introduced into it; and, after the germ is introduced, there is still an insensible mass, for the germ itself is only an inert fluid. How does this mass pass to another organisation, to life, to sensibility? By heat. What will produce heat? Movement. What will be the successive effects of movement? First, an oscillating point, a thread that extends, the flesh, the beak, and so forth."

Then follows the application of the same ideas to the reproduction of man —a region whither it is not convenient to follow the physiological inquirer. The result as to the formation of the organic substance in man is as unflinching as the materialism of Büchner.

> But doctor, cries Mdlle. Lespinasse, what becomes of vice and virtue? Virtue, that word so holy in all languages, that idea so sacred among all nations?
>
> BORDEU. We must transform it into beneficence, and its opposite into the idea of maleficence. A man is happily or unhappily born; people are irresistibly drawn on by the general torrent that conducts one to glory, the other to ignominy.
>
> MDLLE. LESPINASSE. And self-esteem, and shame, and remorse?
>
> BORDEU. Proclivities, founded on the ignorance or the vanity of a being who imputes to himself the merit or the demerit of a necessary instant.
>
> MDLLE. LESPINASSE. And rewards and punishments?
>
> BORDEU. Means of correcting the modifiable being that we call bad, and encouraging the other that we call good.[215]

The third dialogue we must leave. The fact that German books are written for a public of specialists allows Dr. Rosenkranz to criticise these dialogues with a freedom equal to Diderot's own, and his criticism is as full as usual of candour, patience, and weight. An English writer must be content to pass on, and his contentment may well be considerable, for the subject is perhaps that on which, above all others, it is most difficult to say any wise word.

III.

The Plan of a University for the Government of Russia was the work of Diderot's last years, but no copy of it was given to the public before 1813-14, when M. Guizot published extracts from an autograph manuscript confided to him by Suard. Diderot, with a characteristic respect for competence, with which no egotism can ever interfere in minds of such strength and veracity as his, began by urging the Empress to consult Ernesti of Leipsic, the famous editor of Cicero, and no less famous in his day (1707-1781) for the changes that he introduced into the system of teaching in the German universities. Of Oxford and Cambridge Diderot spoke more kindly than they then deserved.

The one strongly marked idea of the plan is what might have been expected from the editor of the Encyclopædia, namely, the elevation of what the Germans call real or technological instruction, and the banishment of pure literature as a subject of study from the first to the last place in the course. In the faculty of arts the earliest course begins with arithmetic, algebra, the calculation of probabilities, and geometry. Next follow physics and mechanics. Then astronomy. Fourthly, natural history and experimental physics. In the fifth class, chemistry and anatomy. In the sixth, logic and grammar. In the seventh, the language of the country. And it was not until the eighth, that Greek and Latin, eloquence and poetry, took their place among the objects or instruments of education. Parallel with this course, the student was to follow the first principles of metaphysics, of universal morality, and of natural and revealed religion. Here, too, history and geography had a place. In a third parallel, perspective and drawing accompanied the science of the first, and the philosophy and history of the second.

In the thorny field of religious instruction, Diderot expresses no opinion of his own, beyond saying that it is natural for the Empress's subjects to conform to her way of thinking. As her majesty thinks that the fear of pains to come has much influence on men's actions, and is persuaded that the total of small daily advantages produced by belief outweighs the total of evils wrought by sectarianism and intolerance, therefore students ought to be instructed in the mystery of the distinction of the two substances, in the immortality of the soul, and so forth.[216]

There is a story that one evening at St. Petersburg, Diderot was declaiming with stormy eloquence against the baseness of those who flatter kings; for such, he said, there ought to be a deeper and a fiercer hell. "Tell me, Diderot," said the Empress by and by, "what they say in Paris about the death of my husband." Instead of telling her the plain truth that everybody said that Peter had been murdered by her orders, the philosopher poured out a stream of the smoothest things. "Come now," said Catherine suddenly, "confess, if you are not walking along the path that leads to your deep hell, you are certainly coming very close to purgatory." Diderot's elaborate concessions to her majesty's political religion would, it is to be feared, have brought him still further in the same sulphureous track.

As we have often had to bewail Diderot's diffuseness, it is as well to remark that a long passage in the sketch of which we are speaking shows how close and concentrated he could be upon occasion. The two pages in which he demolishes the incorrigible superstition about Latin and Greek,[217] contain a thoroughly exhaustive summary of all the arguments and the answers. In the immense discussion about Latin and Greek that has taken place in the hundred years since Diderot's time, it is tolerably safe to say that not a single point has been brought forward which Diderot did not in these most pithy and conclusive pages attempt to deal with. He winds up with the position that, even for the man of letters, the present system of teaching Latin and Greek is essentially sterile. I am perfectly sure, he says, that Voltaire, who is not exactly a mediocrity as a man of letters, knows extremely little Greek, and that he is not twentieth nor even hundredth among the Latinists of the day.[218]

Following this sketch is printed a letter to the Countess of Forbach on the education of children. It is full of rich wisdom on its special subject. Nobody can read it without feeling that quality in Diderot which made his friends love him. And we see how, when he was called to practical counsel, he banished into their own sphere the explosive paradoxes with which he delighted to amuse his hours of speculative dreaming.

IV.

Romilly has told us that Diderot was bent on converting him from the error of his religious ways, and with that intention read to him a Conversation with the Maréchale de——.[219] It is believed to be an idealised version of a real conversation with Madame de Broglie, and was first printed, almost as soon as written (1777), in the correspondence in which Métra, in imitation of Grimm, informed a circle of foreign subscribers what was going on in Paris. The admirers of Diderot profess to look on this Conversation as one of the most precious pearls in his philosophic casket. It turns upon the conditions of belief and unbelief, represented by the two interlocutors respectively, and is a terse and graphic summary of the rationalistic objections to the creed of the church. The most conspicuous literary passage in it is a parable which has been attributed to Rousseau, but with which Rousseau had really nothing to do, beyond reproducing the spirit of its argument in the ever famous creed of the Savoyard Vicar.

A young Mexican, tired of his work, was sauntering one day on the seashore. He spied a plank, with one end resting on the land, and the other dipping into the water. He sat down on the plank, and there gazing over the vast space that lay spread out before him, he said to himself: "It is certain that my old grandmother is talking nonsense, with her history of I know not what inhabitants, who, at I know not what time, landed here from I know not where, from some country far beyond our seas. It is against common sense: do I not see the ocean touch the line of the sky? And can I believe, against the evidence of my senses, an old fable of which nobody knows the date, which everybody arranges according to his fancy, and which is only a tissue of absurdities, about which people are ready to tear out one another's eyes." As he was reasoning in this way, the waters rocked him gently on his plank, and he fell asleep. As he slept, the wind rose, the waves carried away the plank on which he was stretched out, and behold our youthful reasoner embarked on a voyage.

La Maréchale.—Alas, that is the image of all of us; we are each on our plank; the wind blows, and the flood carries us away.

C.—He was already far from the mainland when he awoke. No one was ever so surprised as our young Mexican, to find himself out on the open sea, and he was mightily surprised, too, when having lost from sight the shore on which he had been idly walking only an instant before, he saw the sea touching the line of the sky on every side. Then he began to suspect that he might have been mistaken, and that, if the wind remained in the same quarter, perhaps he would be borne to that very shore and among those dwellers on it, about whom his grandmother had so often told him.

La Maréchale.—And of his anxiety you say nothing.

C.—He had none. He said to himself: "What does it matter, provided that I find land? I have reasoned like a giddy-pate, granted; but I have been sincere with myself, and that is all that can be required of me. If it is no virtue to have understanding, at any rate it is no crime to be without it." Meanwhile the wind continued, the man and the plank floated on, and the unknown shore came into sight. He touched it, and behold him again on land.

La Maréchale.—Ah, we shall all of us see one another there, one of these days.

C.—I hope so, madam; wherever it may be, I shall always be very proud to pay you my homage. Hardly had he quitted his plank, and put his foot on the sand, when he perceived a venerable old man standing by his side. He asked him where he was, and to whom he had the honour of speaking. "I am the sovereign of the country," replied the old man; "you have denied my existence?"—"Yes, it is true."—"And that of my empire?"—"It is true!"—"I forgive you, because I am he who sees the bottom of all hearts, and I have read at the bottom of yours that you are of good faith; but the rest of your thoughts and your actions are not equally innocent." Then the old man, who held him by the ear, recalled to him all the errors of his life; and as each was mentioned, the young Mexican bowed himself upon the ground, beat his breast, and besought forgiveness.

V.

Of Falconet,[220] we have already spoken, as a sculptor of genius, and as one of Diderot's most intimate friends. Writing to Sophie Voland (Nov. 21, 1765), Diderot informs her that some pleasantries of Falconet's have induced him to undertake very seriously the defence of the sentiment of immortality and respect for posterity.[221] This apology was carried on in an energetic correspondence which lasted from the end of 1765 to 1767. Falconet's letters were burned by his grand-daughter for reasons unknown, and we have only such passages from them as are more specially referred to by Diderot himself. Falconet flattered himself that he had the best of the argument, and was eager that they should be published, but Diderot was sluggish or busy. The correspondence was imparted to Catherine of Russia, who took a lively interest in it, and to some others, but it was not given to the public—and then only partially—until 1830.

Diderot's position in these twelve letters may be described in general terms as being that the sentiment of immortality and respect for posterity move the heart and elevate the soul; they are two germs of great things, two promises as solid as any other, and two delights as real as most of the delights of life, but more noble, more profitable, and more virtuous. What Diderot means by immortality is not the religious dogma, that the individual personality will be objectively preserved and prolonged in some other mode of existence. On the contrary, it was his disbelief in this dogma of the churches that gave a certain keenness to his pleading for that other kind of immortality, which prolongs our personality only in the grateful and admiring memories of other people who come after us. He intended by the sentiment of immortality "the desire to surround one's name with lustre among posterity; to be the admiration and the talk of centuries to come; to obtain after death the same honours as we pay to those who have gone before us; to furnish a fine line to the historian; to inscribe one's own name by the side of those which we never pronounce without shedding a tear, heaving a sigh, or being touched by regret; to secure for ourselves the blessings that we have such a thrill in bestowing on Sully, Henry IV., and all the other benefactors of the human race."[222] The sphere that surrounds us, and in which the world admires us, the time in which we exist and listen to praise, the number of those who directly address to us the eulogy that we have deserved of them—all this is too small for the capacity of our ambitious souls. By the side of those whom we see prostrated before us, we place those who are not yet in the world. It is only this uncounted throng of adorers that can satisfy a mind whose impulses are ever towards the infinite. At night it is sweet to hear a distant concert, of which only snatches reach the ear, all to be bound into a melodious whole by the imagination, which is all the more charmed as the work is in the main its own. Even if all this were but the sweetness of a lovely dream, is then the sweetness of a dream as nothing? And am I to count for nothing a sweet dream that lasts as long as my life, and holds me in perpetual intoxication?

Falconet's answer was hard and positive. Contemporary glory suffices. What is fame, if I am not there to enjoy? The fear of contempt and disgrace is as strong a motive as you need, to incite men to great work. Glory after death is chimerical and uncertain. Think of all the great names that are clean forgotten, of all the great workers whose achievements are lost or effaced, of all the others whose works are attributed to those who did not execute them! Your posterity is no better than a lottery.

No, cries Diderot, with redoubled eloquence, rising to his noblest height, [223] "the present is an indivisible point that cuts in two the length of an infinite line. It is impossible to rest on this point and to glide gently along with it, never looking on in front, and never turning the head to gaze behind. The more man ascends through the past, and the more he launches into the future—the greater he will be.... And all these philosophers, and ministers, and truth-telling men, who have fallen victims to the stupidity of nations, the atrocities of priests, the fury of tyrants, what consolation was left for them in death? This, that prejudice would pass, and that posterity would pour out the vial of ignominy upon their enemies. O posterity, holy and sacred! Stay of the unhappy and the oppressed, thou who art just, thou who art incorruptible, who avengest the good man, who unmaskest the hypocrite, who draggest down the tyrant, may thy sure faith, thy consoling faith, never, never abandon me! Posterity is for the philosopher what the other world is for the devout!"

APPENDIX.
RAMEAU'S NEPHEW: A TRANSLATION.

[See vol. i. p. 348.]

[I have omitted such pages in the following translation as refer simply to personages who have lost all possibility of interest for our generation; nor did any object seem to be served by reproducing the technical points of the musical discussion. Enough is given, and given as faithfully as I know how, to show the reader what *Rameau's Nephew* is.]

In all weathers, wet or fine, it is my practice to go, towards five o'clock in the evening, to take a turn in the Palais Royal. I am he whom you may see any afternoon sitting by himself and musing in D'Argenson's seat. I keep up talk with myself about politics, love, taste, or philosophy; I leave my mind to play the libertine unchecked; and it is welcome to run after the first idea that offers, sage or gay, just as you see our young beaux in the Foy passage following the steps of some gay nymph, with her saucy mien, face all smiles, eyes all fire, and nose a trifle turned up; then quitting her for another, attacking them all, but attaching themselves to none. My thoughts,—these are the wantons for me. If the weather be too cold or too wet, I take shelter in the Regency coffee-house. There I amuse myself by looking on while they play chess. Nowhere in the world do they play chess so skilfully as in Paris, and nowhere in Paris as they do at this coffee-house; 'tis here you see Légal the profound, Philidor the subtle, Mayot the solid; here you see the most astounding moves, and listen to the sorriest talk, for if a man may be at once a wit and a great chess-player, like Légal, you may also be a great chess-player and a sad simpleton, like Joubert and Mayot.

One day I was there after dinner, watching intently, saying little, and hearing the very least possible, when there approached me one of the most eccentric figures in the country, where God has not made them lacking. He is a mixture of elevation and lowness, of good sense and madness; the notions of good and bad must be mixed up together in strange confusion in his head, for he shows the good qualities that nature has bestowed on him without any ostentation, and the bad ones without the smallest shame. For the rest, he is endowed with a vigorous frame, a particular warmth of imagination, and an astonishing strength of lungs. If you ever meet him, and if you are not arrested by his originality, you will either stuff your fingers into your ears, or else take to your heels. Heavens, what a monstrous pipe! Nothing is so little like him as himself. One time he is lean and wan, like a patient in the last stage of consumption; you could count his teeth through his cheeks; you would say he must have passed several days without tasting a morsel, or that he is fresh from La Trappe. A month after, he is stout and sleek, as if he had been sitting all the time at the board of a financier, or had been shut up in a Bernardine monastery. To-day in dirty linen, his clothes torn or patched, with barely a shoe to his foot, he steals along with a bent head; you are tempted to hail him and fling him a shilling. To-morrow all powdered, curled, in a fine coat, he marches past with head erect and open mien, and you would almost take him for a decent worthy creature. He lives from day to day, from hand to mouth, downcast or sad, just as things may go. His first care in a morning, when he gets up, is to know where he will dine; and after dinner, he begins to think where he may pick up a supper. Night brings disquiets of its own. Either he climbs to a shabby garret that he has, unless the landlady, weary of waiting for her rent, has taken the key away from him; or else he slinks to some tavern on the outskirts of the town, where he waits for daybreak over a piece of bread and a mug of beer. When he has not threepence in his pocket, as sometimes happens, he has recourse either to a hackney carriage belonging to a friend, or to the coachman of some man of quality, who gives him a bed on the straw beside the horses. In the morning, he still has bits of his mattress in his hair. If the weather is mild, he measures the Champs Elysées all night long. With the day he reappears in the town, dressed over night for the morrow, and from the morrow sometimes dressed for the rest of the week.

I do not rate these originals very highly. Other people make familiar acquaintances, and even friends, of them. They detain me perhaps once in a twelvemonth, if I happen to fall in with them. Their character stands out from the rest of the world, and breaks that wearisome uniformity which our bringing-up, our social conventions, and our arbitrary fashions have introduced. If one of them makes his appearance in a company, he is a piece of leaven which ferments and restores to each a portion of his natural individuality. He stirs people up, moves them, invites to praise or blame; he is the means of bringing out the truth, he gives honest people a chance of showing themselves, he unmasks the rogues; this is the time when a man of sense listens, and distinguishes his company.

I had known my present man long ago. He used to frequent a house to which his clever parts had opened the door. There was an only daughter. He swore to the father and mother that he would marry their daughter. They shrugged their shoulders, laughed in his face, told him he was out of his senses, and I saw in an instant that his business was done. He wanted to borrow a few crowns from me, which I gave him. He worked his way, I cannot tell how, into some houses where he had his plate laid for him, but on condition that he should never open his lips without leave. He held his tongue and ate away in a towering rage: it was excellent to watch him in this state of constraint. If he could not resist breaking the treaty, and ever began to open his mouth, at the first word all the guests called out *Rameau!* Then fury sparkled in his eyes, and he turned to his plate in a worse passion than ever. You were curious to know the man's name, and now you know it: 'tis Rameau, pupil of the famous man who delivered us from the plain-song that we had been used to chant for over a hundred years; who wrote so many unintelligible visions and apocalyptic truths on the theory of music, of which neither he nor anybody else understood a word; and from whom we have a certain number of operas that are not without harmony, refrains, random notions, uproar, triumphs, glories, murmurs, breathless victories, and dance-tunes that will last to all eternity; and who, after burying Lulli, the Florentine, will be himself buried by the Italian virtuosi,—a fate that he had a presentiment of, which made him gloomy and chagrined; for nobody is in such ill-humour, not even a pretty woman who awakes with a pimple on her nose, as an author threatened with loss of his reputation.

He comes up to me. Ah, ah! here you are, my philosopher! And what are you doing among this pack of idlers? Can it be possible that you too waste your time in pushing the wood?...

I.—No, but when I have nothing better to do, I amuse myself by watching people who push it well.

He.—In that case you are amusing yourself with a vengeance. Except Philidor and Légal, there is not one of them who knows anything about it.

I.—What of M. de Bussy?

He.—He is as a chess-player what Mademoiselle Clairon is as an actress; they know of their playing, one and the other, as much as anybody can learn.

I.—You are hard to please, and I see you can forgive nothing short of the sublimities.

He.—True, in chess, women, poetry, eloquence, music, and all such fiddle-faddle. What is the use of mediocrity in these matters?

I.—Little enough, I agree. But the thing is that there must be a great number of men at work, for us to make sure of the man of genius: he is one out of a multitude. But let that pass. 'Tis an age since I have seen you. Though I do not often think about you when you are out of sight, yet it is always a pleasure to me to meet you. What have you been about?

He.—What you, I, and everybody else are about—some good, some bad, and nothing at all. Then, I have been hungry, and I have eaten when opportunity offered; after eating, I have been thirsty, and now and then have had something to drink. Besides that, my beard grew, and as it grew I had it shaved.

I.—There you were wrong; it is the only thing wanting to make a sage of you.

He.—Ay, ay; I have a wide and furrowed brow, a glowing eye, a firm nose,

148

broad cheeks, a black and bushy eyebrow, a clean cut mouth, a square jaw. Cover this enormous chin with amplitude of beard, and I warrant you it would look vastly well in marble or in bronze.

I.—By the side of a Cæsar, a Marcus Aurelius, a Socrates.

He.—Nay, I should be better between Diogenes, Laïs, and Phryne. I am brazenfaced as the one, and I am happy to pay a visit to the others.

I.—Are you always well?

He.—Yes, commonly; but I am no great wonders to-day.

I.—Why, you have a paunch like Silenus, and a face like....

He.—A face you might take for I don't know what. The ill humour that dries up my dear master seems to fatten his dear pupil.

I.—And this dear master, do you ever see him now?

He.—Yes, passing along the street.

I.—Does he do nothing for you?

He.—If he has done anything for anybody, it is without knowing it. He is a philosopher after his fashion. He thinks of nobody but himself. His wife and his daughter may die as soon as they please; provided the church bells that toll for them continue to sound the *twelfth* and the *seventeenth*, all will be well. It is lucky for him, and that is what I especially prize in your men of genius. They are only good for one thing; outside of that, nothing. They do not know what it is to be citizens, fathers, mothers, kinsfolk, friends. Between ourselves, it is no bad thing to be like them at every point, but we should not wish the grain to become common. We must have men; but men of genius, no; no, on my word; of them we need none. 'Tis they who change the face of the globe; and in the smallest things folly is so common and so almighty, that you cannot mend it without an infinite disturbance. Part of what they have dreamt comes to pass, and part remains as it was; hence two gospels, the dress of a harlequin. The wisdom of Rabelais's moral is the true wisdom both for his own repose and that of other people: to do one's duty so so, always to speak well of the prior, and to let the world go as it lists. It must go well, for most people are content with it. If I knew history enough, I should prove to you that evil has always come about here below through a few men of genius, but I do not know history, no more than I know anything else. The deuce take me, if I have learnt anything, or if I find myself a pin the worse for not having learnt anything. I was one day at the table of the minister of the King of ——, who has brains enough for four, and he showed as plain as one and one make two, that nothing was more useful to people than falsehood, nothing more mischievous than truth. I don't remember his proofs very clearly, but it evidently followed from them that men of genius are detestable, and that if a child at its birth bore on its brow the mark of that dangerous gift of nature, it ought to be smothered or else thrown to the ducks.

I.—Yet such people, foes as they are to genius, all lay claim to it.

He.—I daresay they think so in their own minds, but I doubt if they would venture to admit it.

I.—Ah, that is their modesty. So you conceived from that a frightful antipathy to genius.

He.—One that I shall never get over.

I.—Yet I have seen the time when you were in despair at the thought of being only a common man. You will never be happy if the pro and the con distress you alike. You should take your side, and keep to it. Though people will agree with you that men of genius are usually singular, or as the proverb says, *there are no great wits without a grain of madness*, yet they will always look down on ages that have produced no men of genius. They will pay honour to the nations among whom they have existed; sooner or later, they rear statues to them, and regard them as the benefactors of the human race. With all deference to the sublime minister whom you have cited, I still believe that if falsehood may sometimes be useful for a moment, it is surely hurtful in the long-run; and so, on the other hand, truth is surely useful in the long-run, though it may sometimes chance to be inconvenient for the moment. Whence I should be tempted to conclude that the man of genius who cries down a general error, or wins credit for a great truth, is always a creature that deserves our veneration. It may happen that such an one falls a victim to prejudice and the laws; but there are two sorts of laws, the one of an equity and generality that is absolute, the other of an incongruous kind, which owe all their sanction to the blindness or exigency of circumstance. The latter only cover the culprit who infringes them with passing ignominy, an ignominy that time pours back on the judges and the nations, there to remain for ever. Whether is Socrates, or the authority that bade him drink the hemlock, in the worst dishonour in our day?

He.—Not so fast. Was he any the less for that condemned? Or any the less put to death? Or any the less a bad citizen? By his contempt for a bad law did he any the less encourage blockheads to despise good ones? Or was he any the less an audacious eccentric? You were close there upon an admission that would have done little for men of genius.

I.—But listen to me, my good man. A society ought not to have bad laws, and if it had only good ones, it would never find itself persecuting a man of genius. I never said to you that genius was inseparably bound up with wickedness, any more than wickedness is with genius. A fool is many a time far worse than a man of parts. Even supposing a man of genius to be usually of a harsh carriage, awkward, prickly, unbearable; even if he be thoroughly bad, what conclusion do you draw?

He.—That he ought to be drowned.

I.—Gently, good man. Now I will not take your uncle Rameau for an instance; he is harsh, he is brutal, he has no humanity, he is a miser, he is a bad father, bad husband, bad uncle; but it has never been settled that he is particularly clever, that he has advanced his art, or that there will be any talk of his works ten years hence. But Racine, now? He at any rate had genius, and did not pass for too good a man. And Voltaire?

He.—Beware of pressing me, for I am not one to shrink from conclusions.

I.—Which of the two would you prefer; that he should have been a worthy soul, identified with his till, like Briasson, or with his yard measure, like Barbier, each year producing a lawful babe, good husband, good father, good uncle, good neighbour, decent trader, but nothing more; or that he should have been treacherous, ambitious, envious, spiteful, but the author of *Andromaque, Britannicus, Iphigenie, Phèdre, Athalie*?

He.—For his own sake, on my word, perhaps of the two men it would have been a great deal better that he should have been the first.

I.—That is even infinitely more true than you think.

He.—Ah, there you are, you others! If we say anything good and to the purpose, 'tis like madmen or creatures inspired, by a hazard; it is only you wise people who know what you mean. Yes, my philosopher, I know what I mean as well as you do.

I.—Let us see. Now why did you say that of him?

He.—Because all the fine things he did never brought him twenty thousand francs, and if he had been a silk merchant in the Rue Saint Denis or Saint Honoré, a good wholesale grocer, an apothecary with plenty of customers, he would have amassed an immense fortune, and in amassing it, he could have enjoyed every pleasure in life; he would have thrown a pistole from time to time to a poor devil of a droll like me; we should have had good dinners at his house, played high play, drunk first-rate wines, first-rate liqueurs, first-rate coffee, had glorious excursions into the country. Now you see I know what I meant. You laugh? But let me go on. It would have been better for everybody about him.

I.—No doubt it would, provided that he had not put to unworthy use what gain he had made in lawful commerce, and had banished from his house all those gamesters, all those parasites, all those idle flatterers, all those depraved ne'er-do-wells, and had bidden his shop-boys give a sound beating to the officious creature who offers to play pander.

He.—A beating, sir, a beating! No one is beaten in any well-governed town. It is a decent enough trade; plenty of people with fine titles meddle with it. And what the deuce would you have him do with his money, if he is not to have a good table, good company, good wines, handsome women, pleasures of every colour, diversion of every sort? I would as lief be a beggar as possess a mighty fortune without any of these enjoyments. But go back to Racine. He was only good for people who did not know him, and for a time when he had ceased to exist.

I.—Granted, but weigh the good and bad. A thousand years from now he will draw tears, he will be the admiration of men in all the countries of the earth; he will inspire compassion, tenderness, pity. They will ask who he was, and to what land he belonged, and France will be envied. He brought suffering on one or two people who are dead, and in whom we take hardly any interest; we have nothing to fear from his vices or his foibles. It would have been better, no doubt, that he should have received from nature the virtues of a good man, instead of the talents of a great one. He is a tree which made a few other trees planted near him wither up, and which smothered the plants that grew at his feet; but he reared his height to the clouds, and his branches spread far; he lends his shadow to all who came, or come now, or ever shall come, to repose by his majestic trunk; he brought forth fruits of exquisite savour which are renewed again and again without ceasing.

We might wish that Voltaire had the mildness of Duclos, the ingenuousness of the Abbé Trublet, the rectitude of the Abbé d'Olivet. But as that cannot be, let us look at the thing on the side of it that is really interesting; let us forget for an instant the point we occupy in space and time, and let us extend our vision over centuries to come, and peoples yet unborn, and distant lands yet unvisited. Let us think of the good of our race: if we are not generous enough, at least let us forgive nature for being wiser than ourselves. If you throw cold water on Greuze's head, very likely you will extinguish his talent along with his vanity. If you make Voltaire less sensitive to criticism, he will lose the art that took him to the inmost depths of the soul of Merope, and will never stir a single emotion in you more.

He.—But if nature be as powerful as she is wise, why did she not make them as good as she made them great?

I.—Do you not see how such reasoning as that overturns the general order, and that if all were excellent here below, then there would be nothing excellent.

He.—You are right. The important point is that you and I should be here; provided only that you and I are you and I, then let all besides go as it can. The best order of things, in my notion, is that in which I was to have a place, and a plague on the most perfect of worlds, if I don't belong to it! I would rather exist, and even be a bad hand at reasoning, than not exist at all.

I.—There is nobody but thinks as you do, and whoever brings his indictment against the order of things, forgets that he is renouncing his own existence.

He.—That is true.

I.—So let us accept things as they are; let us see how much they cost us and how much they give us, and leave the whole as it is, for we do not know it well enough either to praise or blame it; and perhaps after all it is neither good nor ill, if it is necessary, as so many good folk suppose.

He.—Now you are going beyond me. What you say seems like philosophy, and I warn you that I never meddle with that. All that I know is that I should be very well pleased to be somebody else, on the chance of being a genius and a great man; yes, I must agree. I have something here that tells me so. I never in my life heard a man praised, that his eulogy did not fill me with secret fury. I am full of envy. If I hear something about their private life that is a discredit to them, I listen with pleasure: it brings us nearer to a level; I bear my mediocrity more comfortably. I say to myself: Ah, thou couldst never have done *Mahomet,* nor the eulogy on Maupeou. So I have always been, and I always shall be, mortified at my own mediocrity. Yes, I tell you I am mediocre, and it provokes me. I never heard the overture to the *Indes galantes* performed, nor the *Profonds abîmes de Ténare, Nuit, eternelle nuit,* sung without saying to myself: That is what thou wilt never do. So I was jealous of my uncle.

I.—If that is the only thing that chagrins you, it is hardly worth the trouble.

He.—'Tis nothing, only a passing humour. [Then he set himself to hum the overture and the air he had spoken of, and went on:]

The something which is here and speaks to me says: Rameau, thou wouldst fain have written those two pieces: if thou hadst done those two pieces, thou wouldst soon do two others; and after thou hadst done a certain number, they would play thee and sing thee everywhere. In walking, thou wouldst hold thy head erect, thy conscience would testify within thy bosom to thy own merit; the others would point thee out, There goes the man who wrote the pretty gavottes [and he hummed the gavottes. Then with the air of a man bathed in delight and his eyes shining with it, he went on, rubbing his hands:] Thou shalt have a fine house [he marked out its size with his arms], a famous bed [he stretched himself luxuriously upon it], capital wines [he sipped them in imagination, smacking his lips], a handsome equipage [he raised his foot as if to mount], a hundred varlets who will come to offer thee fresh incense every day [and he fancied he saw them all around him, Palissot, Poinsinet, the two Frérons, Laporte, he heard them, approved of them, smiled at them, contemptuously repulsed them, drove them away, called them back; then he continued:] And it is thus they would tell thee on getting up in a morning that thou art a great man; thou wouldst read in the *Histoire des Trois Siècles* that thou art a great man, thou wouldst be convinced of an evening that thou art a great man, and the great man Rameau would fall asleep to the soft murmur of the eulogy that would ring in his ears; even as he slept he would have a complacent air; his chest would expand, and rise, and fall with comfort; he would move like a great man ... [and as he talked he let himself sink softly on a bench, he closed his eyes, and imitated the blissful sleep that his mind was picturing. After relishing the sweetness of this repose for a few instants he awoke, stretched his arms, yawned, rubbed his eyes, and looked about him for his pack of vapid flatterers].

I.—You think, then, the happy mortal has his sleep?

He.—Think so! A sorry wretch like me! At night when I get back to my garret, and burrow in my truckle-bed, I shrink up under my blanket, my chest is all compressed, and I can hardly breathe; it seems like a moan that you can barely hear. Now a banker makes the room ring and astonishes a whole street. But what afflicts me to-day, is not that I snore and sleep meanly and shabbily, like a paltry outcast.

I.—Yet that is a sorry thing enough.

He.—What has befallen me is still more so.

I.—What is that?

He.—You have always taken some interest in me, because I am a *bon diable*, whom you rather despise at bottom, but who diverts you.

I.—Well, that is the plain truth.

He.—I will tell you. [Before beginning he heaved a profound sigh, and clasped his brow with his two hands. Then he recovers his tranquillity and says:]

You know that I am an ignoramus, a fool, a madman, an impertinent, a sluggard, a glutton....

I.—What a panegyric!

He.—'Tis true to the letter, there is not a word to take away; prithee, no debate on that. No one knows me better. I know myself and I do not tell the whole.

I.—I have no wish to cross you, and I will agree to anything.

He.—Well, I used to live with people, who took a liking for me, plainly because I was gifted with all these qualities to such a rare degree.

I.—That is curious. Until now I always thought that people hid these things even from themselves, or else that they granted themselves pardon, while they despised them in others.

He.—Hide them from themselves! Can men do that? You may be sure that when Palissot is all alone and returns upon himself, he tells a very different tale; you may be sure that when he talks quietly with his colleague, they candidly admit that they are only a pair of mighty rogues. Despise such things in others! My people were far more equitable, and they took my character for a perfect nonesuch; I was in clover; they feasted me, they did not lose me from their sight for a single instant without sighing for my return. I was their excellent Rameau, their dear Rameau, their Rameau the mad, the impertinent, the lazy, the greedy, the merryman, the lout. There was not one of these epithets which did not bring me a smile, a caress, a tap on the shoulder, a cuff, a kick; at table, a titbit tossed on to my plate; away from the table, a freedom that I took without consequences, for, do you see, I am a man without consequence. They do with me and before me and at me whatever they like, without my standing on any ceremony. And the little presents that showered on me! The great hound that I am, I have lost all! I have lost all for having had common sense once, one single time in my life. Ah! if that ever chances again!

I.—What was the matter, then?

He.—Rameau, Rameau, did they ever take you for that? The folly of having had a little taste, a trifle of wit, a spice of reason; Rameau, my friend, that will teach you the difference between what God made you, and what your protectors wanted you to be. So they took you by the shoulder, they led you to the door, and cried: "Be off, rascal; never appear more. He would fain have sense, reason, wit, I declare! Off with you; we have all these qualities and to spare!" You went away biting your thumb; it was your infernal tongue, that you ought to have bitten before all this. For not bethinking you of that, here you are in the gutter without a farthing, or a place to lay your head. You were well housed, and now you will be lucky if you get your garret again; you had a good bed, and now a truss of straw awaits you between M. de Soubise's coachman and friend Robbé. Instead of the gentle quiet slumber that you had, you will have the neighing and stamping of horses all night long—you wretch, idiot, possessed by a million devils!

I.—But is there no way of setting things straight? Is the fault you committed so unpardonable? If I were you, I should go find my people again. You are more indispensable to them than you suppose.

He.—Oh, as for that, I know that now they have me no longer to make fun for them, they are dull as ditch-water.

I.—Then I should go back: I would not give them time enough to learn how to get on without me, or to turn to some more decent amusement. For who knows what may happen?

He.—That is not what I am afraid of: that will never come to pass.

I.—But sublime as you may be, some one else may replace you.

He.—Hardly.

I.—Hardly, it is true. Still I would go with that lacklustre face, those haggard eyes, that open breast, that tumbled hair, in that downright tragic state in which you are now. I would throw myself at the feet of the divinity, and without rising I would say with a low and sobbing voice: "Forgive me, madam! Forgive me! I am the vilest of creatures. It was only one unfortunate moment, for you know I am not subject to common sense, and I promise you, I will never have it again so long as I live."

[The diverting part of it was that, while I discoursed to him in this way, he executed it pantomimically, and threw himself on the ground; with his eyes fixed on the earth, he seemed to hold between his two hands the tip of a slipper, he wept, he sobbed, he cried: "Yes, my queen, yes, I promise, I never will, so long as I live, so long as ever I live...." Then recovering himself abruptly, he went on in a serious and deliberate tone:]

He.—Yes, you are right; I see it is the best. Yet to go and humiliate one's self before a hussy, cry for mercy at the feet of a little actress with the hisses of the pit for ever in her ears! I, Rameau, son of Rameau, the apothecary of Dijon, who is a good man and never yet bent his knee to a creature in the world! I, Rameau, who have composed pieces for the piano that nobody plays, but which will perhaps be the only pieces ever to reach posterity, and posterity will play them—I, I, must go! Stay, sir, it cannot be [and striking his right hand on his breast, he went on:] I feel here something that rises and tells me: Never, Rameau, never. There must be a certain dignity attached to human nature that nothing can stifle; it awakes *à propos des bottes*; you cannot explain it; for there are other days when it would cost me not a pang to be as vile as you like, and for a halfpenny there is nothing too dirty for me to do.

I.—Then if the expedient I have suggested to you is not to your taste, have courage enough to remain a beggar.

He.—'Tis hard being a beggar, while there are so many rich fools at whose expense one can live. And the contempt for one's self, it is insupportable.

I.—Do you know that sentiment?

He.—Know it! How many times have I said to myself: What, Rameau, there are ten thousand good tables in Paris, with fifteen or twenty covers apiece, and of these covers not one for thee! There are purses full of gold which is poured out right and left, and not a crown of it falls to thee! A thousand witlings without parts and without worth, a thousand paltry creatures without a charm, a thousand scurvy intriguers, are all well clad, while thou must go bare! Canst thou be such a nincompoop as all this? Couldst thou not flatter as well as anybody else? Couldst thou not find out how to lie, swear, forswear, promise, keep or break, like anybody else? Couldst thou not favour the intrigue of my lady, and carry the love-letter of my lord, like anybody else? Couldst thou not find out the trick of making some shopkeeper's daughter understand how shabbily dressed she is, how two fine earrings, a touch of rouge, some lace, and a Polish gown would make her ravishing; that those little feet were not made for trudging through the mud; that there is a handsome gentleman, young, rich, in a coat covered with lace, with a

154

superb carriage and six fine lackeys, who once saw her as he passed, who thought her charming and wonderful, and that ever since that day he has taken neither bite nor sup, cannot sleep at nights, and will surely die of it?... He comes, he pleases, the little maid vanishes, and I pocket my two thousand crowns. What, thou hast a talent like this, and yet in want of bread? Shame on thee, wretch! I recalled a crowd of scoundrels who were not a patch upon me, and yet were rolling in money. There was I in serge, and they in velvet; they leaned on gold-headed canes, and had fine rings on their fingers. And what were they? Wretched bungling strummers, and now they are a kind of fine gentlemen. At such times I felt full of courage, my soul inflamed and elevated, my wits alert and subtle, and capable of anything in the world. But this happy turn did not last, it would seem, for so far I have not been able to make much way. However that may be, there is the text of my frequent soliloquies, which you may paraphrase as you choose, provided you are sure that I know what self-contempt is, and that torture of conscience which comes of the usefulness of the gifts that heaven has bestowed on us; that is the cruellest stroke of all. A man might almost as well never have been born.

[I had listened to him all the time, and as he enacted the scene with the poor girl, with my heart moved by two conflicting emotions, I did not know whether to give myself up to the longing I had to laugh, or to a transport of indignation. I was distressingly perplexed between two humours; twenty times an uncontrollable burst of laughter kept my anger back, and twenty times the anger that was rising from the bottom of my soul suddenly ended in a burst of laughter. I was confounded by so much shrewdness and so much vileness, by ideas now so just and then so false, by such general perversity of sentiments, such complete turpitude, and such marvellously uncommon frankness. He perceived the struggle going on within me:] What ails you? said he.

I.—Nothing.

He.—You seem to be disturbed.

I.—And I am.

He.—But now, after all, what do you advise me to do?

I.—To change your way of talking. You unfortunate soul, to what abject state have you fallen!

He.—I admit it. And yet, do not let my state touch you too deeply; I had no intention, in opening my mind to you, to give you pain. I managed to scrape up a few savings when I was with the people. Remember that I wanted nothing, not a thing, and they made me a certain allowance for pocket-money.

[He again began to tap his brow with one of his fists, to bite his lips, and to roll his eyes towards the ceiling, going on to say:]

But 'tis all over; I have put something aside; time has passed, and that is always so much gained.

I.—So much lost, you mean.

He.—No, no; gained. People grow rich every moment; a day less to live, or a crown to the good, 'tis all one. When the last moment comes, one is as rich as another; Samuel Bernard, who by pillaging and stealing and playing bankrupt, leaves seven and twenty million francs in gold, is just like Rameau, who leaves not a penny, and will be indebted to charity for a shroud to wrap round him. The dead man hears not the tolling of the bell; 'tis in vain that a hundred priests bawl dirges for him, and that a long file of blazing torches go before: his soul walks not by the side of the master of the ceremonies. To moulder under marble, or to moulder under clay, 'tis still to moulder. To have around one's bier children in red and children in blue, or to have not a creature, what matters it? And then, look at this wrist, it was stiff as the devil; the ten fingers, they were so many sticks fastened into a metacarpus made of wood; and these muscles were like old strings of catgut, drier, stiffer, harder to bend than if that they had been used for a turner's wheel; but I have so twisted and broken and bent them. What, thou wilt not go? And I say that thou shalt....

[And at this, with his right hand he seized the fingers and wrist of his left hand, and turned them first up and then down. The extremity of the fingers touched the arm, till the joints cracked again. I was afraid every instant that the bones would remain dislocated.]

I.—Take care, you will do yourself a mischief.

He.—Don't be afraid, they are used to it. For ten years I have given it them in a very different style. They had to accustom themselves to it, however they liked it, and to learn to find their place on the keys and to leap over the strings. So now they go where they must.

[At the same moment he threw himself into the attitude of a violin-player; he hummed an allegro of Locatelli's; his right arm imitated the movement of the bow; his left hand and his fingers seemed to be feeling along the handle. If he makes a false note, he stops, tightens or slackens his string, and strikes it with his nail, to make sure of its being in tune, and then takes up the piece where he left off. He beats time with his foot, moves his head, his feet, his hands, his arms, his body, as you may have seen Ferrari or Chiabran, or some other virtuoso in the same convulsions, presenting the image of the same torture, and giving me nearly as much pain; for is it not a painful thing to watch the torture of a man who is busy painting pleasure for my benefit? Draw a curtain to hide the man from me, if he must show me the spectacle of a victim on the rack. In the midst of all these agitations and cries, if there occurred one of those harmonious passages where the bow moves slowly over several of the strings at once, his face put on an air of ecstasy, his voice softened, he listened to himself with perfect ravishment; it is undoubted that the chorus sounded both in his ears and mine. Then replacing his imaginary instrument under his left arm with the same hand by which he held it, and letting his right hand drop with the bow in it, said:]

Well, what do you think of it?

I.—Wonderful!

He.—Not bad, I fancy; it sounds pretty much like the others.... [And then he stooped down, like a musician placing himself at the piano.]

I.—Nay, I beg you to be merciful both to me and to yourself.

He.—No, no; now that I have got you, you shall hear me. I will have no vote that is given without your knowing why. You will say a good word for me with more confidence, and that will be worth a new pupil to me.

I.—But I am so little in the world, and you will tire yourself all to no purpose.

He.—I am never tired.

[As I saw that it was useless to have pity on my man, for the sonata on the violin had bathed him in perspiration, I resolved to let him do as he would. So behold him seated at the piano, his legs bent, his head thrown back towards the ceiling, where you would have thought he saw a score written up, humming, preluding, dashing off a piece of Alberti's or Galuppi's, I forget which. His voice went like the wind, and his fingers leapt over the imaginary keys. The various passions succeeded one another on his face; you observed on it tenderness, anger, pleasure, sorrow; you felt the piano notes, the forte notes, and I am sure that a more skilful musician than myself would have recognised the piece by the movement and the character, by his gestures, and by a few notes of airs which escaped from him now and again. But the absurd thing was to see him from time to time hesitate and take himself up as if he had gone wrong.]

Now, you perceive, said he, rising and wiping away the drops of sweat which rolled down his cheeks, that we know how to place our third, our superfluous fifth, and that we know all about our dominants. Those enharmonic passages, about which the dear uncle makes such fuss, they are not like having the sea to swallow; we can manage them well enough.

I.—You have given yourself a great deal of trouble to show me that you are uncommonly clever; but I would have taken your word for it.

He.—Uncommonly clever; oh no! For my trade, I know it decently, and that is more than one wants; for in this country is one obliged to know all that one shows?

I.—No more than to know all that one teaches.

He.—That is true, most thoroughly true. Now, sir philosopher, your hand on your conscience, speak the truth; there was a time when you were not a man of such substance as you are to-day.

I.—I am not so very substantial even now.

He.—But you would not go now to the Luxembourg in summer-time.... You remember?

I.—No more of that. Yes, I do remember.

He.—In an overcoat of gray shag?

I.—Ay, ay.

He.—Terribly worn at one side, with one of the sleeves torn; and black woollen stockings mended at the back with white thread.

I.—Yes, anything you like.

He.—What were you doing in the alley of Sighs?

I.—Cutting a shabby figure enough, I daresay.

He.—You used to give lessons in mathematics?

I.—Without knowing a word about them. Is not that what you want to come to?

He.—Exactly so.

I.—I learnt by teaching others, and I turned out some good pupils.

He—That may be; but music is not like algebra or geometry. Now that you are a substantial personage....

I.—Not so substantial, I tell you.

He.—And have a good lining to your purse....

I.—Not so good.

He.—Let your daughter have masters.

I.—Not yet; it is her mother who looks to her education, for one must have peace in one's house.

He.—Peace in one's house? You have only that, when you are either master or servant, and it should be master. I had a wife—may heaven bless her soul—but when it happened sometimes that she played malapert, I used to mount the high horse, and bring out my thunder. I used to say like the Creator: Let there be light, and there was light. So for four years we had not ten times in all one word higher than another. How old is your child?

I.—That has nothing to do with the matter.

He.—How old is your child, I say?

I.—The devil take you, leave my child and her age alone, and return to the master she is to have.

He.—I know nothing so pig-headed as a philosopher. In all humility and supplication, might one not know from his highness the philosopher, about what age her ladyship, his daughter, may be?

I.—I suppose she is eight.

He.—Eight! Then four years ago she ought to have had her fingers on the keys.

I.—But perhaps I have no fancy for including in the scheme of her education a study that takes so much time and is good for so little.

He.—And what will you teach her, if you please?

I.—To reason justly, if I can; a thing so uncommon among men, and more uncommon still among women.

He.—Oh, let her reason as ill as she chooses, if she is only pretty, amusing, and coquettish.

I.—As nature has been unkind enough to give her a delicate organisation with a very sensitive soul, and to expose her to the same troubles in life as if she had a strong organisation and a heart of bronze, I will teach her, if I can, to bear them courageously.

He.—Let her weep and give herself airs, and have nerves all on edge like the rest, if only she is pretty, amusing, and coquettish. What, is she to learn no dancing nor deportment?

I.—Yes, just enough to make a curtsey, to have a good carriage, to enter a room gracefully, and to know how to walk.

He.—No singing?

I.—Just enough to pronounce her words well.

He.—No music?

I.—If there were a good teacher of harmony, I would gladly entrust her to him two hours a day for two or three years, not any more.

He.—And instead of the essential things that you are going to suppress?...

I.—I place grammar, fables, history, geography, a little drawing, and a great deal of morality.

He.—How easy it would be for me to prove to you the uselessness of all such knowledge in a world like ours? Uselessness, do I say? Perhaps even the danger! But I will for the moment ask you a single question, will she not require one or two masters?

I.—No doubt.

He.—And you hope that these masters will know the grammar, the fables, the history, the geography, the morality, in which they will give her lessons? Moonshine, my dear mentor, sheer moonshine! If they knew these things well enough to teach them to other people, they never would teach them?

I.—And why?

He.—Because they would have spent all their lives in studying them. It is necessary to be profound in art and science, to know its elements thoroughly. Classical books can only be well done by those who have grown gray in harness; it is the middle and the end which light up the darkness of the beginning. Ask your friend D'Alembert, the coryphæus of mathematics, if he thinks himself too good to write about the elements. It was not till after thirty or forty years of practice that

158

my uncle got a glimpse of the profundities and the first rays of light in musical theory.

I.—O madman, arch-madman, I cried, how comes it that in thine evil head such just ideas go pell-mell with such a mass of extravagances?

He.—Who on earth can find that out? 'Tis chance that flings them to you, and they remain. If you do not know the whole of a thing, you know none of it well; you do not know whither one thing leads, nor whence another has come, where this and that should be placed, which ought to pass the first, and where the second would be best. Can you teach well without method? And method, whence comes that? I vow to you, my dear philosopher, I have a notion that physics will always be a poor science, a drop of water raised by a needle-point from the vast ocean, a grain loosened from an Alpine chain. And then, seeking the reasons of phenomena! In truth, one might every whit as well be ignorant, as know so little and know it so ill; and that was exactly my doctrine when I gave myself out for a music-master. What are you musing over?

I.—I am thinking that all you have told me is more specious than solid. But that is no matter. You taught, you say, accompaniment and composition.

He.—Yes.

I.—And you knew nothing about either.

He.—No, i' faith; and that is why there were worse than I was, namely those who fancied they knew something. At any rate, I did not spoil either the child's taste or its hands. When they passed from me to a good master, if they had learnt nothing, at all events they had nothing to unlearn, and that was always so much time and so much money saved.

I.—What did you do?

He.—What they all do! I got there, I threw myself into a chair. "What shocking weather! How tiring the streets are!" Then some gossip: "Mademoiselle Lemierre was to have taken the part of Vestal in the new opera, but she is in an interesting condition for the second time, and they do not know who will take her place. Mademoiselle Arnould has just left her little Count: they say she is negotiating with Bertin.... That poor Dumesnil no longer knows either what he is saying or what he is doing.... Now, Miss, take your book." While Miss, who is in no hurry, is looking for her book, which is lost, while they call the housemaid and scold and make a great stir, I continue—"The Clairon is really incomprehensible. They talk of a marriage which is outrageously absurd: 'tis that of Miss ... what is her name? a little creature that used to live with so and so, etcetera, etcetera:—Come, Rameau, you are talking nonsense; it is impossible.—I don't talk nonsense at all; they even say it is done. There is a rumour that Voltaire is dead, and so much the better.—And pray, why so much the better?—Because he must be going to give us something more laughable than usual; it is always his custom to die a fortnight before." What more shall I tell you? I used to tell certain naughtinesses that I brought from houses where I had been, for we are all of us great fetchers and carriers. I played the madman, they listened to me, they laughed, they called out: How charming he is! Meanwhile Missy's book had been found under the sofa, where it had been pulled about, gnawed, torn by a puppy or a kitten. She sat down to the piano. At first she made a noise on it by herself; then I went towards her, after giving her mother a sign of approbation. The mother: "That is not bad; people have only to be in earnest, but they are not in earnest; they would rather waste their time in chattering, in disarranging things, in gadding hither and thither, and I know not what besides. Your back is no sooner turned, M. Rameau, than the book is shut up, not to be opened until your next visit; still you never scold her." Then, as something had to be done, I took hold of her hands and placed them differently; I got out of temper, I called out "*Sol, Sol, Sol*, Miss, it is a *Sol*." The mother: "Have you no ear? I am not at the piano, and I can't see your book, yet I know it ought to be a *Sol*. You are most troublesome to your teacher; I can't tell how he is so patient; you do not remember a word of what he says to you; you make no progress...." Then I would lower my tone rather, and throwing my head on one side, would say: "Pardon me, madam, all would go very well if the young lady liked, if she only studied a little more; but it is not bad." The mother: "If I were you, I should keep her at one piece for a whole year." "Oh, as for that, she shall not leave it before she has mastered every difficulty, and that will not be as long as you may think." "Monsieur Rameau, you flatter her, you are too good. That is the only part of the lesson which she will keep in mind, and she will take care to repeat it to me upon occasion...." And so the time got over; my pupil presented me my little fee, with the curtsey she had learnt from the dancing master. I put it into my pocket while the mother said: "Very well done, mademoiselle; if Favillier were here, he would applaud you." I chattered a moment or two for politeness' sake, and behold, that was what they call a music lesson.

I.—Well, and now it is quite another thing?

He.—Another thing! I should think so, indeed. I get there. I am deadly grave; I take off my cuffs hastily, I open the piano, I run my fingers over the keys, I am always in a desperate hurry. If they keep me waiting a moment, I cry out as if they were robbing me of a crown piece: in an hour from now I must be so and so; in two hours, with the duchess of so and so; I am expected to dine with a handsome marchioness, and then, on leaving her, there is a concert at the baron's....

I.—And all the time nobody is expecting you anywhere at all?

He.—No.

I.—What vile arts!

He.—Vile, forsooth! Why vile? They are customary among people like me; I don't lower myself in doing like everybody else. I was not the inventor of them, and it would be most absurd and stupid in me not to conform to them. Of course, I know very well that if you go to certain principles of some morality or other, which all the world have in their mouths, and which none of them practise, you will find black is white, and white will become black. But, my philosopher, there is a general conscience, just as there is a general grammar; and then the exceptions in each language that you learned people call—what is it you call them?

I.—Idioms.

He.—Ah, exactly; well, each condition of life has its exceptions to the general conscience, to which I should like to give the title of idioms of vocation.

I.—I understand. Fontenelle speaks well, writes well, though his style swarms with French *idioms*.

He.—And the sovereign, the minister, the banker, the magistrate, the soldier, the man of letters, the lawyer, the merchant, the artisan, the singing master, the dancing master, are all most worthy folk, though their practice strays in some points from the general conscience, and abounds in moral idioms. The older the institution, the more the idioms; the worse the times, the more do idioms multiply. The man is worth so much, his trade is worth the same; and reciprocally. At last, the trade counts for so much, the man for the same. So people take care to make the trade go for as much as they can.

I.—All that I gather clearly from this twisted stuff is, that there are very few callings honestly carried on, and very few honest men in their callings.

He.—Good, there are none at all; but in revenge, there are few rogues out of their own shops; and all would go excellently but for a certain number of persons who are called assiduous, exact, fulfilling their strict duty most rigorously, or, what comes to the same thing, for ever in their shops, and carrying on their trade from morning until night, and doing nothing else in the world. So they are the only people who grow rich and are esteemed.

I.—By force of idioms.

He.—That is it; I see you understand me. Now, an idiom that belongs to nearly all conditions—for there are some that are common to all countries and all times, just as there are follies that are universal—a common idiom, is to procure for one's self as many customers as one possibly can; a common folly is to believe that he is cleverest who has most of them. There are two exceptions to the general conscience, with which you must comply. There is a kind of credit; it is nothing in itself, but it is made worth something by opinion. They say, *good character is better than golden girdle*: yet the man who has a good character has not a golden girdle, and I see nowadays that the golden girdle hardly stands in much need of character. One ought, if possible, to have both girdle and character, and that is my object when I give myself importance by what you describe as vile arts, and poor unworthy tricks. I give my lesson and I give it well; behold the general rule. I make them think I have more lessons to give than the day has hours; behold the idiom.

I.—And the lesson; you do give it well?

He.—Yes, not ill; passably. The thorough bass of the dear master has simplified all that. In old days I used to steal my pupil's money. Yes, I stole it, that is certain; now I earn it, at least like my neighbours.

I.—And did you steal it without remorse?

He.—Oh, without remorse. They say that if one thief pilfers from another, the devil laughs. The parents were bursting with a fortune, which had been got the Lord knows how. They were people about the court, financiers, great merchants, bankers. I helped to make them disgorge, I and the rest of the people they employed. In nature, all species devour one another; so all ranks devour one another in society. We do justice on one another, without any meddling from the law. The other day it was Deschamps, now it is Guimard, who avenges the prince of the financier; and it is the milliner, the jeweller, the upholsterer, the hosier, the draper, the lady's-maid, the cook, the saddler, who avenge the financier of Deschamps. In the midst of it all, there is only the imbecile or the sloth who suffers injury without inflicting it. Whence you see that these exceptions to the general conscience, or these moral idioms about which they make such a stir, are nothing, after all, and that you only need to take a clear survey of the whole.

I.—I admire yours.

He.—And then misery! The voice of conscience and of honour is terribly weak, when the stomach calls out. Enough to say that if ever I grow rich I shall be bound to restore, and I have made up my mind to restore in every possible fashion, by eating, drinking, gambling, and whatever else you please.

I.—I have some fears about your ever growing rich.

He.—I have suspicions myself.

I.—But if things should fall so, what then?

He.—I would do like all other beggars set on horseback: I would be the most insolent ruffler that has ever been seen. Then I should recall all that they have made me go through, and should pay them back with good interest all the advances that they have been good enough to make me. I am fond of command, and I will command. I am fond of praise, and I will make them praise me. I will have in my pay the whole troop of flatterers, parasites, and buffoons, and I'll say to them, as has been said to me: "Come, knaves, let me be amused," and amused I shall be; "Pull me some honest folk to pieces," and so they will be, if honest folk can be found. We will be jolly over our cups, we will have all sorts of vices and whimsies; it will be delicious. We will prove that Voltaire has no genius; that Buffon, everlastingly perched upon his stilts, is only a turgid declaimer; that Montesquieu is nothing more than a man with a touch of ingenuity; we will send D'Alembert packing to his fusty mathematics. We will welcome before and behind all the pigmy Catos like you, whose modesty is the prop of pride, and whose sobriety is a fine name for not being able to help yourselves.

I.—From the worthy use to which you would put your riches, I perceive what a pity it is that you are a beggar. You would live thus in a manner that would be eminently honourable to the human race, eminently useful to your countrymen, and eminently glorious for yourself.

He.—You are mocking me, sir philosopher. But you do not know whom you are laughing at. You do not suspect that at this moment I represent the most important part of the town and the court. Our millionaires in all ranks have, or have not, said to themselves exactly the same things as I have just confided to you; but the fact is, the life that I should lead is precisely their life. What a notion you people have; you think that the same sort of happiness is made for all the world. What a strange vision! Yours supposes a certain romantic spirit that we know nothing of, a singular character, a peculiar taste. You adorn this incongruous mixture with the name of philosophy; but now, are virtue and philosophy made for all the world? He has them who can get them, and he keeps them who can. Imagine the universe sage and philosophical; agree that it would be a most diabolically gloomy spot. Come, long live philosophy! The wisdom of Solomon for ever! To drink good wines, to cram one's self with dainty dishes, to rest in beds of down: except that, all, all is vanity and vexation of spirit.

I.—What, to defend one's native land?

He.—Vanity; there is native land no more; I see nought from pole to pole but tyrants and slaves.

I.—To help one's friends?

He.—Vanity; has one any friends? If one had, ought we to turn them into ingrates? Look well, and you will see that this is all you get by doing services. Gratitude is a burden, and every burden is made to be shaken off.

I.—To have a position in society and fulfil its duties?

He.—Vanity; what matters it whether you have a position or not, provided you are rich, since you only seek a position to become rich? To fulfil one's duties, what does that lead to? To jealousy, trouble, persecution. Is that the way to get on? Nay, indeed: to see the great, to court them, study their taste, bow to their fancies, serve their vices, praise their injustice—there is the secret.

I.—To watch the education of one's children?

He.—Vanity; that is a tutor's business.

I.—But if this tutor, having picked up his principles from you, happens to neglect his duties, who will pay the penalty?

He.—Not I, at any rate, but most likely the husband of my daughter, or the wife of my son.

I.—But suppose that they both plunge into vice and debauchery?

He.—That belongs to their position.

I.—Suppose they bring themselves into dishonour?

He.—You never come into dishonour, if you are rich, whatever you do.

I.—Suppose they ruin themselves?

He.—So much the worse for them.

I.—You will not pay much heed to your wife?

He.—None whatever, if you please. The best compliment, I think, that a man can pay his dearer half, is to do what pleases himself. In your opinion, would not society be mightily amusing if everybody in it was always attending to his duties?

I.—Why not? The evening is never so fair to me as when I am satisfied with my morning.

He.—And to me also.

I.—What makes the men of the world so dainty in their amusements, is their profound idleness.

He.—Pray do not think that; they are full of trouble.

I.—As they never tire themselves, they are never refreshed.

He.—Don't suppose that either. They are incessantly worn out.

I.—Pleasure is always a business for them, never the satisfaction of a necessity.

He.—So much the better; necessity is always a trouble.

I.—They wear everything out. Their soul gets blunted, weariness seizes them. A man who should take their life in the midst of all their crushing abundance would do them a kindness. The only part of happiness that they know is the part that loses its edge. I do not despise the pleasures of the senses: I have a palate, too, and it is tickled by a well-seasoned dish or a fine wine; I have a heart and eyes, and I like to see a handsome woman. Sometimes with my friends, a gay party, even if it waxes somewhat tumultuous, does not displease me. But I will not dissemble from you that it is infinitely pleasanter to me to have succoured the unfortunate, to have ended some thorny business, to have given wholesome counsel, done some pleasant reading, taken a walk with some man or woman dear to me, passed instructive hours with my children, written a good page, fulfilled the duties of my position, said to the woman that I love a few soft things that bring her arm round my neck. I know actions which I would give all that I possess to have done. *Mahomet* is a sublime work; I would a hundred times rather have got justice for the memory of the Calas. A person of my acquaintance fled to Carthagena; he was the younger son in a country where custom transfers all the property to the eldest. There he learns that his eldest brother, a petted son, after having despoiled his father and mother of all that they possessed, had driven them out of the castle, and that the poor old souls were languishing in indigence in some small country town. What does he do—this younger son who in consequence of the harsh treatment he had received at the hand of his parents had gone to seek his fortune far away? He sends them help; he makes haste to set his affairs in order, he returns with his riches, he restores his father and mother to their home, and finds husbands for his sisters. Ah, my dear Rameau, that man looked upon this period as the happiest in his life; he had tears in his eyes when he spoke to me of it, and even as I tell you the story, I feel my heart beat faster, and my tongue falter for sympathy.

He.—Singular beings, you are!

I.—'Tis you who are beings much to be pitied, if you cannot imagine that one rises above one's lot, and that it is impossible to be unhappy under the shelter of good actions.

He.—That is a kind of felicity with which I should find it hard to familiarise myself, for we do not often come across it. But, then, according to you, we should be good.

I.—To be happy, assuredly.

He.—Yet I see an infinity of honest people who are not happy, and an infinity of people who are happy without being honest.

I.—You think so.

He.—And is it not for having had common sense and frankness for a moment, that I don't know where to go for a supper to-night?

I.—Nay, it is for not having had it always; it is because you did not perceive in good time that one ought first and foremost to provide a resource independent of servitude.

He.—Independent or not, the resource I had provided is at any rate the most comfortable.

I.—And the least sure and least decent.

He.—But the most conformable to my character of sloth, madman, and good-for-nought.

I.—Just so.

He.—And since I can secure my happiness by vices which are natural to me, which I have acquired without labour, which I preserve without effort, which go well with the manners of my nation, which are to the taste of those who protect me, and are more in harmony with their small private necessities than virtues which would weary them by being a standing accusation against them from morning to night, why, it would be very singular for me to go and torment myself like a lost spirit, for the sake of making myself into somebody other than I am, to put on a character foreign to my own, and qualities which I will admit to be highly estimable, in order to avoid discussion, but which it would cost me a great deal to acquire, and a great deal to practise, and would lead to nothing, or possibly to worse than nothing, through the continual satire of the rich among whom beggars like me have to seek their subsistence. We praise virtue, but we hate it, and shun it, and know very well that it freezes the marrow of our bones—and in this world one must have one's feet warm. And then all that would infallibly fill me with ill-humour; for why do we so constantly see religious people so harsh, so querulous, so unsociable? 'Tis because they have imposed a task upon themselves which is not natural to them. They suffer, and when people suffer, they make others suffer too. That is not my game, nor that of my protectors either; I have to be gay, supple, amusing, comical. Virtue makes itself respected, and respect is inconvenient; virtue insists on being admired, and admiration is not amusing. I have to do with people who are bored, and I must make them laugh. Now it is absurdity and madness which make people laugh, so mad and absurd I must be; and even if nature had not made me so, the simplest plan would still be to feign it. Happily, I have no need to play hypocrite; there are so many already of all colours, without reckoning those who play hypocrite with themselves.... If your friend Rameau were to apply himself to show his contempt for fortune, and women, and good cheer, and idleness, and to begin to Catonise, what would he be but a hypocrite? Rameau must be what he is—a lucky rascal among rascals swollen with riches, and not a mighty paragon of virtue, or even a virtuous man, eating his dry crust of bread, either alone, or by the side of a pack of beggars. And, to cut it short, I do not get on with your felicity, or with the happiness of a few visionaries like yourself.

I.—I see, my friend, that you do not even know what it is, and that you are not even made to understand it.

He.—So much the better, I declare; so much the better. It would make me burst with hunger and weariness, and may be, with remorse.

I.—Very well, then, the only advice I have to give you, is to find your way back as quickly as you can into the house from which your impudence drove you out.

He.—And to do what you do not disapprove absolutely and yet is a little

164

repugnant to me relatively?

I.—What a singularity!

He.—Nothing singular in it at all; I wish to be abject, but I wish to be so without constraint. I do not object to descend from my dignity…. You laugh?

I.—Yes, your dignity makes me laugh.

He.—Everybody has his own dignity. I do not object to come down from mine, but it must be in my own way, and not at the bidding of others. Must they be able to say to me, Crawl—and behold me, forced to crawl? That is the worm's way, and it is mine; we both of us follow it—the worm and I—when they leave us alone, but we turn when they tread on our tails. They have trodden on my tail, and I mean to turn. And then you have no idea of the creature we are talking about. Imagine a sour and melancholy person, eaten up by vapours, wrapped twice or thrice round in his dressing-gown, discontented with himself, and discontented with every one else; out of whom you hardly wring a smile, if you put your body and soul out of joint in a hundred different ways; who examines with a cold considering eye the droll grimaces of my face, and those of my mind, which are droller still. I may torment myself to attain the highest sublime of the lunatic asylum, nothing comes of it. Will he laugh, or will he not? That is what I am obliged to keep saying to myself in the midst of my contortions; and you may judge how damaging this uncertainty is to one's talent. My hypochondriac, with his head buried in a night-cap that covers his eyes, has the air of an immovable pagod, with a string tied to its chin, and going down under his chair. You wait for the string to be pulled, and it is not pulled; or if by chance the jaws open, it is only to articulate some word that shows he has not seen you, and that all your drolleries have been thrown away. This word is the answer to some question which you put to him four days before; the word spoken, the mastoid muscle contracts, and the jaw sticks.

[Then he set himself to imitate his man. He placed himself on a chair, his head fixed, his hat coming over his eyebrows, his eyes half-shut, his arms hanging down, moving his jaw up and down like an automaton:] Gloomy, obscure, oracular as destiny itself—such is our patron.

At the other side of the room is a prude who plays at importance, to whom one could bring one's self to say that she is pretty, because she is pretty, though she has a blemish or two upon her face. *Item*, she is more spiteful, more conceited, and more silly than a goose. *Item*, she insists on having wit. *Item*, you have to persuade her that you believe she has more of it than anybody else in the world. *Item*, she knows nothing, and she has a turn for settling everything out of hand. *Item*, you must applaud her decisions with feet and hands, jump for joy, and scream with admiration:—"How fine that is, how delicate, well said, subtly seen, singularly felt! Where do women get that? Without study, by mere force of instinct, and pure light of nature! That is really like a miracle! And then they want us to believe that experience, study, reflection, education, have anything to do with the matter!..." And other fooleries to match, and tears and tears of joy; ten times a day to kneel down, one knee bent in front of the other, the other leg drawn back, the arms extended towards the goddess, to seek one's desire in her eyes, to hang on her lips, to wait for her command, and then start off like a flash of lightning. Where is the man who would subject himself to play such a part, if it is not the wretch, who finds there two or three times a week the wherewithal to still the tribulation of his inner parts?

I.—I should never have thought you were so fastidious.

He.—I am not. In the beginning I watched the others, and I did as they did, even rather better, because I am more frankly impudent, a better comedian, hungrier, and better off for lungs. I descend apparently in a direct line from the famous Stentor....

[And to give me a just idea of the force of his organ, he set off laughing, with violence enough to break the windows of the coffee-house, and to interrupt the chess-players.]

I.—But what is the good of this talent?

He.—You cannot guess?

I.—No; I am rather slow.

He.—Suppose the debate opened, and victory uncertain; I get up, and, displaying my thunder, I say: "That is as mademoiselle asserts.... That is worth calling a judgment. There is genius in the expression." But one must not always approve in the same manner; one would be monotonous, and seem insincere, and become insipid. You only escape that by judgment and resource; you must know how to prepare and place your major and most peremptory tones, to seize the occasion and the moment. When, for instance, there is a difference in feeling, and the debate has risen to its last degree of violence, and you have ceased to listen to one another, and all speak at the same time, you ought to have your place at the corner of the room which is farthest removed from the field of battle, to have prepared the way for your explosion by a long silence, and then suddenly to fall like a thunder-clap over the very midst of the combatants. Nobody possesses this art as I do. But where I am truly surprising is in the opposite way—I have low tones that I accompany with a smile, and an infinite variety of approving tricks of face; nose, lips, brow, eyes, all make play; I have a suppleness of reins, a manner of twisting the spine, of shrugging the shoulders, extending the fingers, inclining the head, closing the eyes, and throwing myself into a state of stupefaction, as if I had heard a divine angelic voice come down from heaven; that is what flatters. I do not know whether you seize rightly all the energy of that last attitude. I did not invent it, but nobody has ever surpassed me in its execution. Behold, behold!

I.—Truly, it is unique.

He.—Think you there is a woman's brain that could stand that?

I.—It must be admitted that you have carried the talent of playing the madman, and of self-debasement, as far as it can possibly be carried.

He.—Try as hard as they will, they will never touch me—not the best of them. Palissot, for instance, will never be more than a good learner. But if this part is amusing at first, and if you have some relish in inwardly mocking at the folly of the people whom you are intoxicating, in the long run that ceases to be exciting, and then after a certain number of discoveries one is obliged to repeat one's self. Wit and art have their limits. 'Tis only God Almighty and some rare geniuses, for whom the career widens as they advance.

I.—With this precious enthusiasm for fine things, and this facility of genius of yours, is it possible that you have invented nothing?

He.—Pardon me; for instance, that admiring attitude of the back, of which I spoke to you; I regard it as my own, though envy may contest my claim. I daresay it has been employed before: but who has felt how convenient it was for laughing in one's sleeve at the ass for whom one was dying of admiration! I have more than a hundred ways of opening fire on a girl under the very eyes of her mother, without the latter suspecting a jot of it; yes, and even of making her an accomplice. I had hardly begun my career before I disdained all the vulgar fashions of slipping a *billet-doux*; I have ten ways of having them taken from me, and out of the number I venture to flatter myself there are some that are new. I possess in an especial degree the gift of encouraging a timid young man; I have secured success for some who had neither wit nor good looks. If all that was written down, I fancy people would concede me some genius.

I.—And would do you singular honour.

He.—I don't doubt it.

I.—In your place, I would put those famous methods on paper. It would be a pity for them to be lost.

He.—It is true; but you could never suppose how little I think of method and precepts. He who needs a protocol will never go far. Your genius reads little, experiments much, and teaches himself. Look at Cæsar, Turenne, Vauban, the Marquise de Tencin, her brother the cardinal, and the cardinal's secretary, the Abbé Trublet, and Bouret! Who is it that has given lessons to Bouret? Nobody; 'tis nature that forms these rare men.

I.—Well, but you might do this in your lost hours, when the anguish of your empty stomach, or the weariness of your stomach overloaded, banishes slumber.

He.—I'll think of it. It is better to write great things than to execute small ones. Then the soul rises on wings, the imagination is kindled; whereas it shrivels in amazement at the applause which the absurd public lavishes so perversely on that mincing creature of a Dangeville, who plays so flatly, who walks the stage nearly bent double, who stares affectedly and incessantly into the eyes of every one she talks to, and who takes her grimaces for finesse, and her little strut for grace; or on that emphatic Clairon, who becomes more studied, more pretentious, more elaborately heavy, than I can tell you. That imbecile of a pit claps hands to the echo, and never sees that we are a mere worsted ball of daintinesses ('Tis true the ball grows a trifle big, but what does it matter?), that we have the finest skin, the finest eyes, the prettiest bill; little feeling inside, in truth; a step that is not exactly light, but which for all that is not as awkward as they say. As for sentiment, on the other hand, there is not one of these stage dames whom we cannot cap.

I.—What do you mean by all that? Is it irony or truth?

He.—The worst of it is that this deuced sentiment is all internal, and not a glimpse of it appears outside; but I who am now talking to you, I know, and know well, that she has it. If it is not that, you should see, if a fit of ill-humour comes on, how we treat the valets, how the waiting-maids are cuffed and trounced, what kicks await our good friend, if he fails in an atom of that respect which is our due. 'Tis a little demon, I tell you, full of sentiment and dignity. Ah, you don't quite know where you are, eh?

I.—I confess I can hardly make out whether you are speaking in good faith or in malice. I am a plain man. Be kind enough to be a little more outspoken, and to leave your art behind for once....

He.—What is it? why it is what we retail before our little patroness about the Dangeville or the Clairon, mixed up here and there with a word or two to put you on the scent. I will allow you to take me for a good-for-nothing, but not for a fool; and 'tis only a fool, or a man eaten up with conceit, who could say such a parcel of impertinences seriously.

I.—But how do people ever bring themselves to say them?

He.—It is not done all at once, but little by little you come to it. *Ingenii largitor venter.*

I.—Then hunger must press you very hard.

He.—That may be; yet strong as you may think them, be sure that those to whom they are addressed are much more accustomed to listen to them than we are to hazard them.

I.—Is there anybody who has courage to be of your opinion?

He.—What do you mean by anybody? It is the sentiment and language of the whole of society.

I.—Those of you who are not great rascals must be great fools.

He.—Fools! I assure you there is only one, and that is he who feasts us to cheat him.

I.—But how can people allow themselves to be cheated in such gross fashion? For surely the superiority of the Dangeville and the Clairon is a settled thing.

He.—We swallow until we are full to the throat any lie that flatters us, and take drop by drop a truth that is bitter to us. And then we have the air of being so profoundly penetrated, so true.

I.—Yet you must once, at any rate, have sinned against the principles of art, and let slip, by an oversight, some of those bitter truths that wound; for, in spite of the wretched, abject, vile, abominable part you play, I believe you have at bottom some delicacy of soul.

He.—I! not the least in the world. Deuce take me if I know what I am! In a general way, I have a mind as round as a ball, and a character fresh as a water-willow. Never false, little interest as I have in being true; never true, little interest as I have in being false. I say things just as they come into my head; sensible things, then so much the better; impertinent things, then people take no notice. I let my natural frankness have full play. I never in all my life gave a thought, either beforehand, what to say, or while I was saying it, or after I had said it. And so I offend nobody.

I.—Still that did happen with the worthy people among whom you used to live, and who were so kind to you.

He.—What would you have? It is a mishap, an unlucky moment, such as there always are in life; there is no such thing as unbroken bliss: I was too well off, it could not last. We have, as you know, the most numerous and the best chosen company. It is a school of humanity, the renewal of hospitality after the antique. All the poets who fall, we pick them up; all decried musicians, all the authors who are never read, all the actresses who are hissed, a parcel of beggarly, disgraced, stupid, parasitical souls, and at the head of them all I have the honour of being the brave chief of a timorous flock. It is I who exhort them to eat the first time they come, and I who ask for drink for them—they are so shy. A few young men in rags who do not know where to lay their heads, but who have good looks; a few scoundrels who bamboozle the master of the house, and put him to sleep, for the sake of gleaning after him in the fields of the mistress of the house. We seem gay, but at bottom we are devoured by spleen and a raging appetite. Wolves are not more famishing, nor tigers more cruel. Like wolves when the ground has been long covered with snow, we raven over our food, and whatever succeeds we rend like tigers. Never was seen such a collection of soured, malignant, venomous beasts. You hear nothing but the names of Buffon, Duclos, Montesquieu, Rousseau, Voltaire, D'Alembert, Diderot; and God knows the epithets that bear them company! Nobody can have any parts if he is not as stupid as ourselves. That is the plan on which Palissot's play of *The Philosophers* has been conceived. And you are not spared in it, any more than your neighbours.

I.—So much the better. Perhaps they do me more honour than I deserve. I should be humiliated if those who speak ill of so many clever and worthy people took it into their heads to speak well of me.

He.—Everybody must pay his scot. After sacrificing the greater animals, then we immolate the others.

I.—Insulting science and virtue for a living, that is dearly-earned bread!

He.—I have already told you, we are without any consistency; we insult all the world, and afflict nobody. We have sometimes the heavy Abbé d'Olivet, the big Abbé Le Blanc, the hypocrite Batteux. The big abbé is only spiteful before he has had his dinner; his coffee taken, he throws himself into an arm-chair, his feet against the ledge of the fireplace, and sleeps like an old parrot on its perch. If the noise becomes violent he yawns, stretches his arms, rubs his eyes, and says: "Well, well, what is it?" "It is whether Piron has more wit than Voltaire." "Let us understand; is it wit that you are talking about, or is it taste? For as to taste, your Piron has not a suspicion of it." "Not a suspicion of it?" "No." And there we are, embarked in a dissertation upon taste. Then the patron makes a sign with his hand for people to listen to him, for if he piques himself upon one thing more than another, it is taste. "Taste," he says, "taste is a thing...." But, on my soul, I don't know what thing he said that it was, nor does he.

Then sometimes we have friend Robbé. He regales us with his equivocal stories, with the miracles of the convulsionnaires which he has seen with his own eyes, and with some cantos of a poem on a subject that he knows thoroughly. His verses I detest, but I love to hear him recite them—he has the air of an energumen. They all cry out around him: "There is a poet worth calling a poet!..."

Then there comes to us also a certain noodle with a dull and stupid air, but who has the keenness of a demon, and is more mischievous than an old monkey. He is one of those figures that provoke pleasantries and sarcasms, and that God made for the chastisement of those who judge by appearances, and who ought to have learnt from the mirror that it is as easy to be a wit with the air of a fool as to hide a fool under the air of a wit. 'Tis a very common piece of cowardice to immolate a good man to the amusement of the others; people never fail to turn to this man; he is a snare that we set for the new-comers, and I have scarcely known one of them who was not caught ...

[I was sometimes amazed at the justice of my madman's observations on men and characters, and I showed him my surprise.] That is, he answered, because one derives good out of bad company, as one does out of libertinism. You are recompensed for the loss of your innocence by that of your prejudices; in the society of the bad, where vice shows itself without a mask, you learn to understand them. And then I have read a little.

I.—What have you read?

He.—I have read, and I read, and I read over and over again Theophrastus and La Bruyère and Molière.

I.—Excellent works, all of them.

He.—They are far better than people suppose; but who is there who knows how to read them?

I.—Everybody does, according to the measure of his intelligence. *He.*—

No; hardly anybody. Could you tell me what people look for in them? *I.*—

Amusement and instruction.

He.—But what instruction, for that is the point?

I.—The knowledge of one's duties, the love of virtue, the hatred of vice.

He.—For my part, I gather from them all that one ought to do, and all that one ought not to say. Thus, when I read the *Avare*, I say to myself: "Be a miser if thou wilt, but beware of talking like the miser." When I read *Tartufe*, I say: "Be a hypocrite if thou wilt, but do not talk like a hypocrite. Keep the vices that are useful to thee, but avoid their tone and the appearances that would make thee laughable." To preserve thyself from such a tone and such appearances, it is necessary to know what they are. Now these authors have drawn excellent pictures of them. I am myself, and I remain what I am, but I act and I speak as becomes the character. I am not one of those who despise moralists; there is a great deal of profit to be got from them, especially with those who have applied morality to action. Vice only hurts men from time to time; the characteristics of vice hurt them from morning to night. Perhaps it would be better to be insolent than to have an insolent expression. One who is insolent in character only insults people now and again; one who is insolent in expression insults them incessantly. And do not imagine that I am the only reader of my kind. I have no other merit in this respect than having done on system, from a natural integrity of understanding, and with true and reasonable vision, what most others do by instinct. And so their readings make them no better than I am, and they remain ridiculous in spite of themselves, while I am only so when I choose, and always leave them a vast distance behind me; for the same art which teaches me how to escape ridicule on certain occasions teaches me also on certain others how to incur it happily. Then I recall to myself all that the others said, and all that I read, and I add all that issues from my own originality, which is in this kind wondrous fertile.

I.—You have done well to reveal these mysteries to me, for otherwise I should have thought you self-contradictory.

He.—I am not so in the least, for against a single time when one has to avoid ridicule, happily there are a hundred when one has to provoke it. There is no better part among the great people than that of fool. For a long time there was the king's fool; at no time was there ever the king's sage, officially so styled. Now I am the fool of Bertin and many others, perhaps yours at the present moment, or perhaps you are mine. A man who meant to be a sage would have no fool, so he who has a fool is no sage; if he is not a sage he is a fool, and perhaps, even were he the king himself, the fool of his fool. For the rest, remember that in a matter so variable as manners, there is nothing absolutely, essentially, and universally true or false; if not that one must be what interest would have us be, good or bad, wise or mad, decent or ridiculous, honest or vicious. If virtue had happened to be the way to fortune, then I should either have been virtuous, or I should have pretended virtue, like other persons. As it was, they wanted me to be ridiculous, and I made myself so; as for being vicious, nature alone had taken all the trouble that was needed in that. When I use the term vicious, it is for the sake of talking your language; for, if we came to explanations, it might happen that you called vice what I call virtue, and virtue what I call vice.

Then we have the authors of the Opéra Comique, their actors and their actresses, and oftener still their managers, all people of resource and superior merit. And I forget the whole clique of scribblers in the gazettes, the *Avant Coureur*, the *Petites Affiches*, the *Année littéraire*, the *Observateur littéraire*.

I.—The *Année littéraire*, the *Observateur littéraire*! But they detest one another.

He.—Quite true, but all beggars are reconciled at the porringer. That cursed *Observateur littéraire*, I wish the devil had had both him and his sheet! It was that dog of a miserly priest who caused my disaster. He appeared on our horizon for the first time; he arrived at the hour that drives us all out of our dens, the hour for dinner. When it is bad weather, lucky the man among us who has a shilling in his pocket to pay for a hackney-coach! He is free to laugh at a comrade for coming besplashed up to his eyes and wet to the skin, though at night he goes to his own home in just the same plight. There was one of them some months ago who had a violent brawl with the Savoyard at the door. They had a running account; the creditor insisted on being paid, and the debtor was not in funds, and yet he could not go upstairs without passing through the hands of the other.

Dinner is served; they do the honours of the table to the abbé—they place him at the upper end. I come in and see this. "What, abbé, you preside? That is all very well for to-day, but to-morrow you will come down, if you please, by one plate; the day after by another plate, and so on from plate to plate, now to right and now to left, until from the place that I occupied one time before you, Fréron once after me, Dorat once after Fréron, Palissot once after Dorat, you become stationary beside me, poor rascal as you are—*che siedo sempre come*"—[an Italian proverb not to be decently reproduced].

The abbé, who is a good fellow, and takes everything in good part, bursts out laughing; Mademoiselle, struck by my observation and by the aptness of my comparison, bursts out laughing; everybody to right and left burst out laughing, except the master of the house, who flies into a huff, and uses language that would have meant nothing if we had been by ourselves—

"Rameau, you are an impertinent."

"I know I am, and it is on that condition that I was received here."

"You are a scoundrel."

"Like anybody else."

"A beggar."

"Should I be here, if I were not?"

"I will have you turned out of doors."

"After dinner I will go of my own will."

"I recommend you to go."

We dined: I did not lose a single toothful. After eating well and drinking amply, for after all Messer Gaster is a person with whom I have never sulked, I made up my mind what to do, and I prepared to go; I had pledged my word in presence of so many people that I was bound to keep it. For a considerable time I hunted up and down the room for my hat and cane in every corner where they were not likely to be, reckoning all the time that the master of the house would break out into a new torrent of injuries, that somebody would interpose, and that we should at last make friends by sheer dint of altercation. I turned on this side and that, for I had nothing on my heart; but the master, more sombre and dark-browed than Homer's Apollo as he lets his arrows fly among the Greeks, with his cap plucked farther over his head than usual, marched backwards and forwards up and down the room. Mademoiselle approaches me: "But, mademoiselle," say I, "what has happened beyond what happens every day? Have I been different from what I am on other days?"

"I insist on his leaving the house."—"I am leaving.... But I have given no ground of offence."—"Pardon me; we invite the abbé and...." It was he who was wrong to invite the abbé, while at the same time he was receiving me, and with me so many other creatures of my sort.—"Come, friend Rameau, you must beg the abbé's pardon."—"I shall not know what to do with his pardon."—"Come, come, all will be right."—They take me by the hand, and drag me towards the abbé's chair; I look at him with a kind of admiring wonder, for who before ever asked pardon of the abbé? "All this is very absurd, abbé; confess, is it not?" And then I laugh, and the abbé laughs too. So that is my forgiveness on that side; but I had next to approach the other, and that was a very different thing. I forget exactly how it was that I framed my apology.—"Sir, here is the madman...."—"He has made me suffer too long; I wish to hear no more about him."—"He is sorry."—"Yes, I am very sorry."—"It shall not happen again."—"Until the first rascal...."—I do not know whether he was in one of those days of ill-humour when mademoiselle herself dreads to go near him, or whether he misunderstood what I said, or whether I said something wrong: things were worse than before. Good heavens, does he not know me? Does he not know that I am like children, and that there are some circumstances in which I let anything and everything escape me? And then, God help me, am I not to have a moment of relief? Why, it would wear out a puppet made of steel, to keep pulling the string from night to morning, and from morning to night! I must amuse them, of course, that is the condition; but I must now and then amuse myself. In the midst of these distractions there came into my head a fatal idea, an idea that gave me confidence, that inspired me with pride and insolence: it was that they could not do without me, and that I was indispensable.

I.—Yes, I daresay that you are very useful to them, but that they are still more useful to you. You will not find as good a house every day; but they, for one madman who falls short, will find a hundred to take his place.

He.—A hundred madmen like me, sir philosopher; they are not so common, I can tell you! Flat fools—yes. People are harder to please in folly than in talent or virtue. I am a rarity in my own kind, a great rarity. Now that they have me no longer, what are they doing? They find time as heavy as if they were dogs. I am an inexhaustible bagful of impertinences. Every minute I had some fantastic notion that made them laugh till they cried; I was a whole Bedlam in myself.

I.—Well, at any rate you had bed and board, coat and breeches, shoes, and a pistole a month.

He.—That is the profit side of the account; you say not a word of the cost of it all. First, if there was a whisper of a new piece (no matter how bad the weather), one had to ransack all the garrets in Paris, until one had found the author; then to get a reading of the play, and adroitly to insinuate that there was a part in it which would be rendered in a superior manner by a certain person of my acquaintance. —"And by whom, if you please?"—"By whom? a pretty question! There are graces, finesse, elegance."—"Ah, you mean Mademoiselle Dangeville? Perhaps you know her?"—"Yes, a little; but 'tis not she."—"Who is it, then?"—I whispered the name very low. "She?"—"Yes, she," I repeated with some shame, for sometimes I do feel a touch of shame; and at this name you should have seen how long the poet's face grew, if indeed he did not burst out laughing in my face. Still, whether he would or not, I was bound to take my man to dine; and he, being naturally afraid of pledging himself, drew back, and tried to say "No, thank you." You should have seen how I was treated, if I did not succeed in my negotiation! I was a blockhead, a fool, a rascal; I was not good for a single thing; I was not worth the glass of water which they gave me to drink. It was still worse at their performance, when I had to go intrepidly amid the cries of a public that has a good judgment of its own, whatever may be said about it, and make my solitary clap of the hand audible, draw every eye to me, and sometimes save the actress from hisses, and hear people murmur around me—"He is one of the valets in disguise belonging to the man who.... Will that knave be quiet?" They do not know what brings a man to that; they think it is stupidity, but there is one motive that excuses anything.

I.—Even the infraction of the civil laws.

He.—At length, however, I became known, and people used to say: "Oh, it is Rameau!" My resource was to throw out some words of irony to save my solitary applause from ridicule, by making them interpret it in an opposite sense.

Now agree that one must have a mighty interest to make one thus brave the assembled public, and that each of these pieces of hard labour was worth more than a paltry crown? And then at home there was a pack of dogs to tend, and cats for which I was responsible. I was only too happy if Micou favoured me with a stroke of his claw that tore my cuff or my wrist. Criquette is liable to colic; 'tis I who have to rub her. In old days mademoiselle used to have the vapours; to-day, it is her nerves. She is beginning to grow a little stout; you should hear the fine tales they make out of this.

I.—You do not belong to people of this sort, at any rate?

He.—Why not?

I.—Because it is indecent to throw ridicule on one's benefactors.

He.—But is it not worse still to take advantage of one's benefits to degrade the receiver of them?

I.—But if the receiver of them were not vile in himself, nothing would give the benefactor the chance.

He.—But if the personages were not ridiculous in themselves they would not make subjects for good tales. And then, is it my fault if they mix with rascaldom? Is it my fault if, after mixing themselves up with rascaldom, they are betrayed and made fools of? When people resolve to live with people like us, if they have common sense, there is an infinite quantity of blackness for which they must make up their minds. When they take us, do they not know us for what we are, for the most interested, vile, and perfidious of souls. Then if they know us, all is well. There is a tacit compact that they shall treat us well, and that sooner or later we shall treat them ill in return for the good that they have done us. Does not such an agreement subsist between a man and his monkey or his parrot?... If you take a young provincial to the menagerie at Versailles, and he takes it into his head for a freak to push his hands between the bars of the cage of the tiger or the panther, whose fault is it? It is all written in the silent compact, and so much the worse for the man who forgets or ignores it. How I could justify by this universal and sacred compact the people whom you accuse of wickedness, whereas it is in truth yourselves whom you ought to accuse of folly.... But while we execute the just decrees of Providence on folly, you who paint us as we are, you execute its just decrees on us. What would you think of us, if we claimed, with our shameless manners, to enjoy public consideration? That we are out of our senses. And those who look for decent behaviour from people who are born vicious and with vile and bad characters—are they in their senses? Everything has its true wages in this world. There are two Public Prosecutors, one at your door, chastising offences against society; nature is the other. Nature knows all the vices that escape the laws. Give yourself up to debauchery, and you will end with dropsy; if you are crapulous, your lungs will find you out; if you open your door to ragamuffins, and live in their company, you will be betrayed, laughed at, despised. The shortest way is to resign, one's self to the equity of these judgments, and to say to one's self: That is as it should be; to shake one's ears and turn over a new leaf, or else to remain what one is, but on the conditions aforesaid....

I.—You cannot doubt what judgment I pass on such a character as yours?

He.—Not at all; I am in your eyes an abject and most despicable creature; and I am sometimes the same in my own eyes, though not often: I more frequently congratulate myself on my vices than blame myself for them; you are more constant in your contempt.

I.—True; but why show me all your turpitude?

He.—First, because you already know a good deal of it, and I saw that there was more to gain than to lose, by confessing the rest.

I.—How so, if you please?

He.—It is important in some lines of business to reach sublimity; it is especially so in evil. People spit upon a small rogue, but they cannot refuse a kind of consideration to a great criminal; his courage amazes you, his atrocity makes you shudder. In all things, what people prize is unity of character.

I.—But this estimable unity of character you have not quite got: I find you from time to time vacillating in your principles; it is uncertain whether you get your wickedness from nature or study, and whether study has brought you as far as possible.

He.—I agree with you, but I have done my best. Have I not had the modesty to recognise persons more perfect in my own line than myself. Have I not spoken to you of Bouret with the deepest admiration? Bouret is the first person in the world for me.

I.—But after Bouret you come.

He.—No.

I.—Palissot, then?

He.—Palissot, but not Palissot alone.

I.—And who is worthy to share the second rank with him?

He.—The Renegade of Avignon.

I.—I never heard of the Renegade of Avignon, but he must be an astonishing man.

He.—He is so, indeed.

I.—The history of great personages has always interested me.

He.—I can well believe it. This hero lived in the house of a good and worthy descendant of Abraham, promised to the father of the faithful in number equal to the stars in the heavens.

I.—In the house of a Jew?

He.—In the house of a Jew. He had at first surprised pity, then goodwill, then entire confidence, for that is how it always happens: we count so strongly on our kindness, that we seldom hide our secrets from anybody on whom we have heaped benefits. How should there not be ingrates in the world, when we expose this man to the temptation of being ungrateful with impunity? That is a just reflection which our Jew failed to make. He confided to the renegade that he could not conscientiously eat pork. You will see the advantage that a fertile wit knew how to get from such a confession. Some months passed, during which our renegade redoubled his attentions; when he believed his Jew thoroughly touched, thoroughly captivated, thoroughly convinced that he had no better friend among all the tribes of Israel ... now admire the circumspection of the man! He is in no hurry; he lets the pear ripen before he shakes the branch; too much haste might have ruined his design. It is because greatness of character usually results from the natural balance between several opposite qualities.

I.—Pray leave your reflections, and go straight on with your story.

He.—That is impossible. There are days when I cannot help reflecting; 'tis a malady that must be allowed to run its course. Where was I?

I.—At the intimacy that had been established between the Jew and the renegade.

He.—Then the pear was ripe.... But you are not listening; what are you dreaming about?

I.—I am thinking of the curious inequality in your tone, now so high, now so low.

He.—How can a man made of vices be one and the same?... He reaches his friend's house one night, with an air of violent perturbation, with broken accents, a face as pale as death, and trembling in every limb. "What is the matter with you?"—"We are ruined." "Ruined, how?"—"Ruined, I tell you, beyond all help."—"Explain."—"One moment, until I have recovered from my fright."— "Come, then, recover yourself," says the Jew.... "A traitor has informed against us before the Holy Inquisition, you as a Jew, me as a renegade, an infamous renegade...." Mark how the traitor does not blush to use the most odious expressions. It needs more courage than you may suppose to call one's self by one's right name; you do not know what an effort it costs to come to that.

I.—No, I daresay not. But "the infamous renegade——"

He.—He is false, but his falsity is adroit enough. The Jew takes fright, tears his beard, rolls on the ground, sees the officers at his door, sees himself clad in the *Sanbenito*, sees his *auto-da-fè* all made ready. "My friend," he cries, "my good,

175

tender friend, my only friend, what is to be done?"

"What is to be done? Why show ourselves, affect the greatest security, go about our business just as we usually do. The procedure of the tribunal is secret but slow; we must take advantage of its delays to sell all you have. I will hire a boat, or I will have it hired by a third person—that will be best; in it we will deposit your fortune, for it is your fortune that they are most anxious to get at; and then we will go, you and I, and seek under another sky the freedom of serving our God, and following in security the law of Abraham and our own consciences. The important point in our present dangerous situation is to do nothing imprudent."

No sooner said than done. The vessel is hired, victualled, and manned, the Jew's fortune put on board; on the morrow, at dawn, they are to sail, they are free to sup gaily and to sleep in all security; on the morrow they escape their prosecutors. In the night, the renegade gets up, despoils the Jew of his portfolio, his purse, his jewels, goes on board, and sails away. And you think that this is all? Good: you are not awake to it. Now when they told me the story, I divined at once what I have not told you, in order to try your sagacity. You were quite right to be an honest man; you would never have made more than a fifth-rate scoundrel. Up to this point the renegade is only that; he is a contemptible rascal whom nobody would consent to resemble. The sublimity of his wickedness is this, that he was himself the informer against his good friend the Israelite, of whom the Inquisition took hold when he awoke the next morning, and of whom a few days later they made a famous bonfire. And it was in this way that the renegade became the tranquil possessor of the fortune of the accursed descendant of those who crucified our Lord.

I.—I do not know which of the two is most horrible to me—the vileness of your renegade, or the tone in which you speak of it.

He.—And that is what I said: the atrocity of the action carries you beyond contempt, and hence my sincerity. I wished you to know to what a degree I excelled in my art, to extort from you the admission that I was at least original in my abasement, to rank me in your mind on the line of the great good-for-noughts, and to hail me henceforth—*Vivat Mascarillus, fourbum imperator*!

[Here the discussion is turned aside, by Rameau's pantomimic performance of a fugue, to various topics in music.[224]]

I.—How does it happen that with such fine tact, such great sensibility for the beauties of the musical art, you are so blind to the fine things of morality, so insensible to the charms of virtue?

He.—It must be because there is for the one a sense that I have not got, a fibre that has not been given to me, a slack string that you may play upon as much as you please, but it never vibrates. Or it may be because I have always lived with those who were good musicians but bad men, whence it has come to pass that my ear has grown very fine, and my heart has grown very deaf. And then there is something in race. The blood of my father and the blood of my uncle is the same blood; my blood is the same as that of my father; the paternal molecule was hard and obtuse, and that accursed first molecule has assimilated to itself all the rest.

I.—Do you love your child?

He.—Do I love it, the little savage! I dote on it.

I.—Will you not then seriously set to work to arrest in it the consequences of the accursed paternal molecule?

He.—I shall labour in vain, I fancy. If he is destined to grow into a good man, I shall not hurt him; but if the molecule meant him for a ne'er-do-well like his father, then all the pains that I might have taken to make a decent man of him would only be very hurtful to him, Education incessantly crossing the inclination of the molecule, he would be drawn as it were by two contrary forces, and would walk in zigzags along the path of life, as I see an infinity of other people doing, equally awkward in good and evil. These are what we call *espèces*, of all epithets the most to be dreaded, because it marks mediocrity and the very lowest degree of contempt. A great scoundrel is a great scoundrel, but he is not an *espèce*. Before the paternal molecule had got the upper hand, and had brought him to the perfect abjection at which I have arrived, it would take endless time, and he would lose his best years. I do not meddle at present; I let him come on. I examine him; he is already greedy, cunning, idle, lying, and a cheat; I'm much afraid that he is a chip of the old block.

I.—And you will make him a musician, so that the likeness may be exact?

He.—A musician! Sometimes I look at him and grind my teeth, saying: If thou wert ever to know a note of music, I believe I would wring thy neck.

I.—And why so, if you please?

He.—Music leads to nothing.

I.—It leads to everything.

He.—Yes, when people are first-rate. But who can promise himself that his child shall be first-rate. The odds are ten thousand to one that he will never be anything but a wretched scraper of catgut. Are you aware that it would perhaps be easier to find a child fit to govern a realm, fit to be a great king, than one fit for a great violin player.

I.—It seems to me that agreeable talents, even if they are mediocre, among a people who are without morals, and are lost in debauchery and luxury, get a man rapidly on in the path of fortune.

He.—No doubt, gold and gold; gold is everything, and all the rest without gold is nothing. So instead of cramming his head with fine maxims which he would have to forget, on pain of remaining a beggar all the days of his life, what I do is this: when I have a louis, which does not happen to me often, I plant myself in front of him, I pull the louis out of my pocket, I show it to him with signs of admiration, I raise my eyes to heaven, I kiss the louis before him, and to make him understand still better the importance of the sacred coin, I point to him with my finger all that he can get with it, a fine frock, a pretty cap, a rich cake; then I thrust the louis into my pocket, I walk proudly up and down, I raise the lappet of my waistcoat, I strike my fob; and in that way I make him see that it is the louis in it that gives me all this assurance.

I.—Nothing could be better. But suppose it were to come to pass that, being so profoundly penetrated by the value of the louis, he were one day....

He.—I understand you. One must close one's eyes to that; there is no moral principle without its own inconvenience. At the worst 'tis a bad quarter of an hour, and then all is over.

I.—Even after hearing views so wise and so bold, I persist in thinking that it would be good to make a musician of him. I know no other means of getting so rapidly near great people, of serving their vices better, or turning your own to more advantage.

He.—That is true; but I have plans for a speedier and surer success. Ah, if it were only a girl! But as we cannot do all that we should like, we must take what comes, and make the best of it, and not be such idiots as most fathers, who could literally do nothing worse, supposing them to have deliberately planned the misery of their children—namely, give the education of Lacedæmon to a child who is destined to live in Paris. If the education is bad, the morals of my country are to blame for that, not I. Answer for it who may; I wish my son to be happy, or what is the same thing, rich, honoured, and powerful. I know something about the easiest ways of reaching this end, and I will teach them to him betimes. If you blame me, you sages, the multitude and success will acquit me. He will put money in his purse, I can tell you. If he has plenty of that, he will lack nothing else, not even your esteem and respect.

I.—You may be mistaken.

He.—Then perhaps he will do very well without it, like many other people.

[There was in all this a good deal of what passes through many people's minds, and much of the principle according to which they shape their own conduct; but they never talk about it. There, in short, is the most marked difference between my man and most of those about us. He avowed the vices that he had, and that others have; but he was no hypocrite. He was neither more nor less abominable than they; he was only more frank, and more consistent, and sometimes he was profound in the midst of his depravity. I trembled to think what his child might become under such a master. It is certain that after ideas of bringing-up, so strictly traced on the pattern of our manners, he must go far, unless prematurely stopped on the road.]

He.—Oh, fear nothing. The important point, the difficult point, to which a good father ought to attend before everything else, is not to give to his child vices that enrich, or comical tricks such as make him valuable to people of quality—all the world does that, if not on system as I do, at least by example and precept. The important thing is to impress on him the just proportion, the art of keeping out of disgrace and the arm of the law. There are certain discords in the social harmony that you must know exactly how to place, to prepare, and to hold. Nothing so tame as a succession of perfect chords; there needs something that stimulates, that resolves the beam, and scatters its rays.

I.—Quite so; by your image you bring me back from morals to music, and I am very glad, for, to be quite frank with, you, I like you better as musician than as moralist.

He.—Yet, I am a mere subaltern in music, and a really superior figure in morals.

I.—I doubt that; but even if it were so, I am an honest man, and your principles are not mine.

He.—So much the worse for you. Ah, if I only had your talents!

I.—Never mind my talents; let us return to yours.

He.—If I could only express myself like you! But I have an infernally absurd jargon—half the language of men of the world and of letters, half of Billingsgate.

I.—Nay, I am a poor talker enough. I only know how to speak the truth, and that does not always answer, as you know.

He.—But it is not for speaking the truth—on the contrary, it is for skilful lying that I covet your gift. If I knew how to write, to cook up a book, to turn a dedicatory epistle, to intoxicate a fool as to his own merits, to insinuate myself into the good graces of women!

I.—And you do know all that a thousand times better than I. I should not be worthy to be so much as your pupil.

He.—How many great qualities lost, of which you do not know the price.

I.—I get the price that I ask.

He.—If that were true, you would not be wearing that common suit, that rough waistcoat, those worsted stockings, those thick shoes, that ancient wig.

I.—I grant that; a man must be very maladroit not to be rich, if he sticks at nothing in order to become rich. But the odd thing is that there are people like me who do not look on riches as the most precious thing in the world; bizarre people, you know.

He.—Bizarre enough. A man is not born with such a twist as that. He takes the trouble to give it to himself, for it is not in nature.

I.—In the nature of man?

He.—No; for everything that lives, without exception, seeks its own wellbeing at the expense of any prey that is proper to its purpose; and I am perfectly sure that if I let my little savage grow up without saying a word to him on the matter, he would wish to be richly clad, sumptuously fed, cherished by men, loved by women, and to heap upon himself all the happiness of life.

I.—If your little savage were left to himself, let him only preserve all his imbecility, and add to the scanty reason of the child in the cradle the violent passions of a man of thirty—why he would strangle his father and dishonour his own mother.

He.—That proves the necessity of a good education, and who denies it? And what is a good education but one that leads to all sorts of enjoyments without danger and without inconvenience?

I.—I am not so far from your opinion, only let us keep clear of explanations.

He.—Why?

I.—Because I am afraid that we only agree in appearance, and that if we once begin to discuss what are the dangers and the inconveniences to avoid, we should cease to understand one another.

He.—What of that?

I.—Let us leave all this, I tell you; what I know about it I shall never get you to learn, and you will more easily teach me what I do not know, and you do know, in music. Let us talk about music, dear Rameau, and tell me how it has come about that with the faculty for feeling, retaining, and rendering the finest passages in the great masters, with the enthusiasm that they inspire in you, and that you transmit to others, you have done nothing that is worth....

Instead of answering me, he shrugged his shoulders, and pointing to the sky with his finger, he cried: The star! the star! When Nature made Leo, Vinci, Pergolese, Duni, she smiled. She put on a grave and imposing air in shaping my dear uncle Rameau, who for half a score years they will have called the great Rameau, and of whom very soon nobody will say a word. When she tricked up his nephew, she made a grimace, and a grimace, and again a grimace. [And as he said this, he put on all sorts of odd expressions: contempt, disdain, irony; and he seemed to be kneading between his fingers a piece of paste, and to be smiling at the ridiculous shapes that he gave it; that done, he flung the incongruous pagod[225] away from him, and said:] It was thus she made me, and flung me by the side of the other pagods, some with huge wrinkled paunches, and short necks, and great eyes projecting out of their heads, stamped with apoplexy; others with wry necks; some again with wizened faces, keen eyes, hooked noses. All were ready to split with laughing when they espied me, and I put my hands to my sides and split with laughter when I espied them, for fools and madmen tickle one another; they seek and attract one another. If when I got among them, I had not found ready-made the proverb about *the money of fools being the patrimony of people with wits*, they would have been indebted to me for it. I felt that nature had put my lawful inheritance into the purses of the pagods, and I devised a thousand means of recovering my rights.

I.—Yes, I know all about your thousand means; you have told me of them, and I have admired them vastly. But with so many resources, why not have tried that of a fine work?...

He.—When I am alone I take up my pen and intend to write; I bite my nails and rub my brow; your humble servant, good-bye, the god is absent. I had convinced myself that I had genius; at the end of the time I discover that I am a fool, a fool, and nothing but a fool. But how is one to feel, to think, to rise to heights, to paint in strong colours, while haunting with such creatures as those whom one must see if one is to live; in the midst of such talk as one has to make and to hear, and such idle gossip: "How charming the boulevard was to-day!" "Have you heard the little Marmotte? Her playing is ravishing." "Mr. So-and-so had the handsomest pair of grays in his carriage that you can possibly imagine." "The beautiful Mrs. So-and-so is beginning to fade; who at the age of five-and-forty would wear a headdress like that?" "Young Such-and-such is covered with diamonds, and she gets them cheap."

"You mean she gets them dear."

"No, I do not."

"Where did you see her?"

"At the play."

"The scene of despair was played as it had never been played before." "The Polichinelle of the Fair has a voice, but no delicacy, no soul." "Madame So-and-so has produced two at a birth; each father will have his own child...." And yet you suppose that this kind of thing, said and said again, and listened to every day of the week, sets the soul aglow and leads to mighty things.

I.—Nay, it were better to turn the key of one's garret, drink cold water, eat dry bread, and seek one's true self.

He.—Maybe, but I have not the courage. And then the idea of sacrificing one's happiness for the sake of a success that is doubtful! And the name that I bear? Rameau! It is not with talents as it is with nobility; nobility transmits itself, and increases in lustre by passing from grandfather to father, and from father to son, and from son to grandson, without the ancestor impressing a spark of merit on his descendant; the old stock ramifies into an enormous crop of fools; but what matter? It is not so with talents. Merely to obtain the renown of your father, you must be cleverer than he was; you must have inherited his fibre. The fibre has failed me, but the wrist is nimble, the fiddle-bow scrapes away, and the pot boils; if there is not glory, there is broth.

I.—If I were in your place, I would not take it for granted; I would try.... Whatever it be that a man applies himself to, nature meant him for it.

He.—She makes mighty blunders. For my part, I do not look down from heights, whence all seems confused and blurred,—the man who prunes a tree with his knife, all one with the caterpillar who devours its leaf; a couple of insects, each at his proper task. Do you, if you choose, perch yourself on the epicycle of the planet Mercury, and thence distribute creation, in imitation, of Réaumur; he, the classes of flies into seamstresses, surveyors, reapers; you, the human species into joiners, dancers, singers, tilers. That is your affair, and I will not meddle with it. I am in this world, and in this world I rest. But if it is in nature to have an appetite—for it is always to appetite that I come back, and to the sensation that is ever present to me—then I find that it is by no means consistent with good order not to have always something to eat. What a precious economy of things! Men who are over-crammed with everything under the sun, while others, who have a stomach just as importunate as they, a hunger that recurs as regularly as theirs, have not a bite. The worst is the constrained posture to which want pins us down. The needy man does not walk like anybody else; he jumps, he crawls, he wriggles, he limps, he passes his whole life in taking and executing artificial postures.

I.—What are postures?

He.—Ask Noverre.[226] The world offers far more of them than his art can imitate.

I.—Ah, there are you too—to use your expression or Montaigne's—*perched on the epicycle of Mercury*, and eyeing the various pantomimes of the human race.

He.—No, no, I tell you; I'm too heavy to raise myself so high. No sojourn in the fogs for me. I look about me, and I assume my postures, or I amuse myself with the postures that I see others taking. I am an excellent pantomime as you shall judge.

[Then he set himself to smile, to imitate the admirer, the suppliant, the fawning complaisant; he expects a command, receives it, starts off like an arrow, returns, the order is executed, he reports what he has done; he is attentive to everything; he picks up something that has fallen; he places a pillow or a footstool; he holds a saucer; he brings a chair, opens a door, closes a window, draws the curtains, gazes on the master and mistress; he stands immovable, his arms hanging by his side, his legs exactly straight; he listens, he seeks to read their faces, and then he adds:— That is my pantomime, very much the same as that of all flatterers, courtiers, valets, and beggars.

The buffooneries of this man, the stories of the abbé Galiani, the extravagances of Rabelais, have sometimes thrown me into profound reveries. They are three stores whence I have provided myself with ridiculous masks that I place on the faces of the gravest personages, and I see Pantaloon in a prelate, a satyr in a president, a pig in a monk, an ostrich in a minister, a goose in his first clerk.]

I.—But according to your account, I said to my man, there are plenty of beggars in the world, and yet I know nobody who is not acquainted with some of the steps of your dance.

He.—You are right. In a whole kingdom there is only one man who walks, and that is the sovereign.

I.—The sovereign? There is something to be said on that. For do you suppose that one may not from time to time find even by the side of him, a dainty foot, a pretty neck, a bewitching nose, that makes him execute his pantomime. Whoever has need of another is indigent, and assumes a posture. The king postures before his mistress, and before God he treads his pantomimic measure. The minister dances the step of courtier, flatterer, valet, and beggar before his king. The crowd of the ambitious cut a hundred capers, each viler than the rest, before the minister. The abbé, with his bands and long cloak, postures at least once a week before the patron of livings. On my word, what you call the pantomime of beggars is only the whole huge bustle of the earth....

He.—But let us bethink ourselves what o'clock it is, for I must go to the opera.

I.—What is going on?

He.—Dauvergne's *Trocqueurs*. There are some tolerable things in the music; the only pity is that he has not been the first to say them. Among those dead, there are always some to dismay the living. What would you have? *Quisque suos patimur manes.* But it is half-past five, I hear the bell ringing my vespers. Good day, my philosopher; always the same, am I not?

I.—Alas, you are; worse luck.

He.—Only let me have that bad luck for forty years to come! Who laughs last has the best of the laugh.

THE END.

Lightning Source UK Ltd.
Milton Keynes UK
UKHW010635240820
368739UK00001B/218